THE LOST SONG
OF GOLIATH

Ronald A. Lindsay

ISBN 13: 978-1-7337338-0-9
Nineteenth Street Publishers

For Carter and Alan
May they live in a world that knows nothing of war

So David arose and went over, he and the six hundred men who were with him, to Achish the son of Maoch, king of Gath. And David dwelt with Achish at Gath … And the number of days that David dwelt in the country of the Philistines was a year and four months.

Samuel 27: 2–7

PROLOGUE

*L*atvian author stirs controversy with alternative take on Goliath
NEW YORK — From ten stories up, the demonstrators' chanting is muffled but still audible. A sudden increase in volume draws lanky Latvian writer Anda Hofmanis to the window in her hotel room.

"Looks like some Muslims have joined the Jewish protestors. I'm glad I have been able to bring people together," she says with a weak smile.

Hofmanis is in New York to promote her book *The Lost Song of Goliath*, and her book is the reason several dozen protestors are marching outside her Manhattan hotel.

Some Jewish groups have accused Hofmanis of anti-Semitism. Her book depicts the ancient Israelites in less than flattering terms. In particular, Hofmanis portrays the Israelites as land-hungry aggressors and David as more of a schemer than an underdog hero.

Hofmanis dismisses these complaints as failing to grasp the difference between fact and fiction, noting that her book is a novel which provides the Philistine perspective on events. "It would be ridiculous to have the Philistines praise their enemies or recognize the Israelites as the chosen people."

But why write a novel giving the Philistine perspective?

"The struggle between the Philistines and Israelites, the duel between David and Goliath—this story is one of the most famous in the world; it's been told and retold countless times, but, essentially, the story remains the same. It's told from one side only."

Hofmanis's decision to present the Philistine side of the story has caused some to view her book as veiled advocacy for contemporary Palestinians.

"My book has no political agenda," Hofmanis counters. "It's a story, a story about human beings and their hopes, prejudices, loves, failings ..." She throws her long arms in the air. "It's a novel. I think the fact that some Muslims, as well as some Jews, have objected to it shows it's not a political pamphlet."

Hofmanis's novel has provoked protest by some Muslims on the ground that it contradicts verses in the Qur'an which reference David and Goliath. The Qur'an states that David defeated Goliath with God's assistance.

In prior interviews, Hofmanis has alluded to her Latvian nationality as part of the motivation for her novel. How so?

"Latvia is a small country. It's a country that has been overrun and occupied many times, and even today its continued existence is threatened. The Philistines effectively disappeared from history. We know little about their culture, and much of what we know is filtered through the eyes of their opponents. Might the same fate befall Latvia? I hope not, but if so, I hope that some future writer or historian will tell our story."

After taking a sip from her coffee, Hofmanis continues, "The traditional story of David and Goliath, of the Israelites and Philistines, is one of war and bloody conflict, of strife, of hatred of one people against another, all done in God's name. I don't find this very inspiring. The notion that there is a God who blesses territorial conquest is absurd. Yes, my story is not the traditional story, but my changes are for the better, I think. It's the story of David and Goliath retold for our time."

PART I

INTO THE VALLEY OF ELAH

Achish turned abruptly to one of his guards and said, "Bring my horse around." Another guard brought him his helmet and once Achish had secured this on his head, he strode toward the tent's entrance. Nearly outside, he paused and looked back at me over his shoulder, but our eyes did not meet. He opened his mouth to say something, but apparently thought better of it. He left.

I looked down at my hands. They were still stained with my companion's blood; the priest's tunic had not removed all of it.

Ephat, my assigned shield bearer, asked me if I wanted a cloth. I shook my head. "But do help me strap on my javelin. I'll carry the short spear."

Emerging from Achish's tent, I glanced upward at the early morning sun. Still low in the sky, its slanting rays nonetheless warmed my face. I paused, listening for a moment to the birdsongs of the dawn.

The moments before combat usually excited me, overpowered me, shutting out all thoughts, all sensation, other than my narrow focus on the impending challenge. This time was different though. Death awaited me in the valley and that certainty made me more, not less, aware of all that surrounded me. I saw the air, touched the murmurs of the soldiers, smelled the embrace of my encasing armor, and tasted the shit of hundreds of men and animals. I didn't move.

But a glimpse of a beckoning hand of an officer reminded me. I had a role to play. Although the performance of that role was now designed to be my deathtrap, I decided to carry myself in accordance with expectations—or at least try to. Whether this was from an obscure sense of duty or just the comfort a familiar routine provided me, I don't know. Whatever the cause, I set off, striding forward confidently through our ranks, with a fierce, snarling look. I lifted my spear above my head, and yelled, "Damn, I'm hungry. I guess I need to eat Hebe for breakfast." My shout elicited a roar from our forces. Those with swords beat them rhythmically against their shields, the sound echoing across the hills.

Things continued in this fashion for a few more moments, but then something happened. Thinking about my plan as I walked toward my death, I couldn't help laughing. It was absurd to think that all my striving, all that I loved and hated, all that I fought for and against was now being eclipsed by one very narrow, humble ambition: to fall forward at the right moment. I then laughed even heartier at the realization that I was laughing.

Those soldiers I passed as I burst into laughter interpreted my amusement as an irrepressible show of confidence.

"Look at Goliath; he's laughing! This is like a festival for him."

"Ten victories in single combat with only a few scratches to show for it. This *is* fucking entertainment for him."

The ranks began laughing themselves and let out loud cheers and shouts of encouragement. I nodded in their direction and again reflexively lifted my spear, and tried to shout, "On to victory!" But this time my arm trembled a bit and my words emerged mangled—"On … ta … viky!" The drug Achish had given me was taking effect.

"What did he say?"

"He said he's going to fuck the Hebe's ass with his spear, then bite off his head. He's chewing on it already."

More laughter. More shouts.

I approached the limits of our lines, which by standard agreement were 200 paces from the field of combat, or 400 paces from the Hebrews' front lines—still close enough to view the action but far enough away from the enemy to provide reaction time in the event of a surprise attack. Even a good archer would have difficulty getting his arrow to travel accurately much more than 300 paces, and a sudden cavalry charge could not cover that ground before an adequate defensive formation could take shape.

Achish and his retinue were about five rows back from the crest of the hill. He was mounted, and he moved his horse toward me as I drew near.

His face showed a mixture of glee, anticipation, and concern—the face of a gambler who has wagered a large sum thinking the roll of the die will fall his way, but who recognizes the outcome is not certain.

"May Dagon smile upon you today, Goliath, and may he through you deliver victory and peace for our people." This was addressed more to our forces than to me, as Achish rose up on his horse and turned his head to face the soldiers.

I fixed my gaze on him as best I could and replied coldly, "Majesty, Dagon, as always, will work his will through us."

This was not the accepted formulaic response and a look of anxiety flickered across Achish's face. He chewed his lip for a moment, then looked down at the boy he had forced upon me as my shield bearer. "Ephat, do you know your duty?"

"Yes, Majesty."

"Then fulfill it." Looking at me, Achish said, "Go, Goliath. On to victory." These last words were delivered stingily as Achish turned his horse away.

On to something. I resumed my march, past the remaining soldiers on top of the hill, and then over the crest and down the hillside past the last few rows of our forces, a contingent of mixed arms positioned on the slope who, if necessary, could serve as a sacrificial rear guard or the vanguard of our attack, depending on the circumstances. While passing these last ranks and changing my step to match the incline, an unfamiliar sensation, a combination of numbness and tingling, crept from my toes to my ankles. My legs seemed a bit unsteady. Falling would not be a problem, but I needed to make sure it was forward.

Further down the slope, into the valley, our lines receding behind us. The shouts of the soldiers grew less distinct. The thin, crusty, dull-colored earth on top of the ridge gave way to greenery and scattered flowers gripping the hillside. Deceptive dewy freshness. Across the valley, I could see the Hebrew champion begin his descent as well. My shield bearer had a sharp intake of breath. Was he scared? By the rules of engagement he was not to be harmed—intentionally. But on one occasion my own errant missile had cut short the life of a shield bearer.

What did I know about this boy, Ephat, anyway? Nothing, apart from the smell of his sweat. I would think Achish had told him he had nothing to be afraid of. Or had he simply ordered the boy to make sure to keep my shield out of reach?

I looked over to the boy and in turning my head I brought on yet another new sensation. It was as though I had a cold but instead of my nose being blocked, my thoughts were blocked, trapped in some viscous liquid. I stopped. Instinctively I sniffled and my mind did clear. Or it seemed to.

Ephat was about twelve or thirteen. His hands were shaking, but I didn't know whether this was from fear or the weight of the shield. His eggshell colored tunic was spotless, and his sandals were so new they seemed to shine. The sleeves of his tunic had alternating black and red stripes above the elbow. The son of a nobleman.

Thinking about the boy caused me to think of my own boyhood. I then began to recall other scattered bits and pieces of my life. My first combat. The taste, fragrance, and feel of Altara … our embraces. Among this flow of memories, one memory in particular kept pressing itself on me, one immovable anchor among the torrent of other thoughts: what Ahirom had said about life. How we delude ourselves into thinking we are something substantial, something enduring, when we are but a series of thoughts and feelings, not inhering in one soul, but simply connected through intentions and desires. These intentions and desires propel our bodies through a tunnel of time—until that tunnel ends.

A sudden turn of my left leg snapped me from my reverie. A jet of rocks flew down the slope as my foot slipped. My head was swimming, but I was alert enough to know I was stumbling. I caught my balance, planting my left foot in some star flowers that were growing on the hillside, crushing their white blossoms. I heard Ephat say, "Sir, the path forward is over here. To your right."

The path forward? There remained no path forward. I was at Elah and here is where all paths, taken and untaken, converged and stopped.

PART II

TASTE OF BLOOD

1

Altara grabbed the top of her thin robe of white linen, pinching it between her thumb and fingers, and pulled it up over her. Reclining on her bed, face still flushed, looking at the ceiling, she said nothing.

I have never been good at conversation, and I certainly didn't know what to say in this situation, given my limited experience. That, and the fact that I was still savoring the taste of her in my mouth, kept me mute as well. At first, I enjoyed the quiet comfort, but then I began to grow anxious. Was Altara waiting for me to say something? If so, what? For the first time, I cared about what a woman thought of me, and I didn't want to say something that would make her no longer tolerant of my company, but I also didn't want to give her the impression that I was a wordless idiot.

The silence lengthened until it became unbearable. Tongue-tied, I got up from the mat where I had been sitting next to her bed, grabbed my tunic, and pulled it on. I felt I should leave, if only to walk off my increasing sense of panic.

"Where do you think you're going?"

I turned and faced Altara, who was now sitting up in her bed.

"I … I …"

"Not even a good-bye kiss?" she said laughing. "After your lips have been so kind to me this evening? Come, sit down."

I returned to the mat, sat down and looked up at her. She had rolled over to face me, her head propped on up one hand, the other hand idly

5

playing in her copper-colored hair. There was silence again for another long moment and then she said, "Tell me about yourself."

"Well, you know who I am."

"Oh, yes, Goliath, the mighty champion of Gath!" she said teasingly. "But … I still don't know much else about you."

"Not much to say."

"Oh, come on. I don't even know if your parents are alive or are here …"

"My father's dead. Mother still alive."

"And?"

"And what?

"Do I have to drag things out of you? How did he die? Were you young? Did you always want to be a soldier? Who are your friends? You know, tell me about yourself."

I gave a half-smile and a shrug. "I don't know …"

She leaned over, extending her left hand until it touched my face. "Please," she said. Her eyes pleaded but it was her touch that persuaded. Her touch was a charm that made me yield, and as it had made me a slave of passion earlier that evening, it now forced me to submit to her request.

2

It was about a year after I had joined the army, so I was around seventeen. The peace that had prevailed between the Hebrews and us had lasted for a few years, but the Hebrews had again decided to try to expand their territory. Why they did this, I do not know. I do know that they claimed to have the right to all our land based on what their false gods had said—which obviously caused us Palestim grave concern—but I don't know why they decided to renew their efforts at this juncture. I'd heard they had a new king, so perhaps that was the explanation. The Hebrews were also more numerous than we were, as evidenced by the larger armies they had fielded in the past. Perhaps their greater numbers increased their boldness. They thought they could push aside, so why not do so? Thieves may need no greater motivation than the likelihood of success.

We in Gath felt the Hebrew threat especially keenly. Gath was the easternmost major city of the Palestim. Hebrew territory was little more than a day's walk away; men on horses could cover the distance in a few hours. We needed to maintain this thin separation from the Hebrews. At all costs, we needed to prevent them from establishing settlements that could endanger our lines of communication with the few Palestim villages east of us or with the city of Ekron to the north.

But this is precisely what they had done. One day, after the midday meal, our whole company was ordered to gather in the barracks courtyard. Commander Bellon informed us that the Hebrews were in the process of establishing a settlement about a day's march away, halfway between Gath and Ekron. The settlement was slightly northwest of us, and this placed it unmistakably within Palestim territory. The settlement had gone unnoticed for some time, perhaps over a month, because it was not close to any trail or Palestim farms. The secluded location strongly suggested the Hebrews were very much aware that we would not tolerate their presence if known— that and their efforts to create defensive structures, which was unusual for a small village. As Bellon explained, "The Hebrew village itself appears to have no more than fifteen houses and other buildings. However, they have dug a trench around the entire site with stakes arrayed along the top of the trench's far slope. They've also started to build a wall close by the trench so it would be very difficult to obtain a foothold to climb the wall even if one were able to get past the ditch. Fortunately, they've only started the wall. In most places, two rows of stone have been laid down, and along much of the eastern side, only one row has been laid down. We will be attacking from the eastern side at dawn. We hope to catch them sleeping, and anyway the sun will be in their eyes."

"Do they have soldiers on site or just armed villagers?" one sub-officer asked.

"Soldiers have been spotted. Perhaps as many as twenty. In addition, you can expect in a settlement such as this the villagers will have taken some effort to acquaint themselves with weapons of some sort. We will be attacking with a force of thirty-six, along with three horsemen, not counting me. We will also have about ten volunteer archers from the city. They won't take part in the attack, but they will help provide cover if we need to withdraw. But we won't be withdrawing. Our force should be sufficient provided we have the element of surprise."

"What are our orders regarding the village and villagers?"

"No quarter. We want to make an example of this settlement to serve as a warning to the Hebrews. Take special care to make sure no one escapes. It would not take them long to reach Hebrew territory and we don't want to be faced with an attack on the way home. Bear in mind that we will need to stay on site for a day to destroy the village. We will burn what can be burned, take down their wall, and fill in the ditch."

Bellon then turned his attention to procedure. "The sub-officers will choose who will go and who will stay. They will discuss with you your different assignments. Tomorrow will be used to practice for the assault. This will take place outside the city walls. Then those who are going on the expedition will leave at daybreak the following morning. Whether you go or stay, there's absolutely to be no contact with family members or anyone else until our mission is completed."

After Bellon finished his address, the sub-officers went through the ranks. Patibal stopped before me. "Goliath, I think you're ready. You'll be in my squad. I want you to arm yourself with a javelin, short spear, sword, and dagger. Bring a shield. They may have archers. Also, bring a rope. Look for me in the courtyard in the morning. Understood? Questions?"

"No questions, sir."

The next morning the squads assembled in the courtyard. I went up to Patibal. There were eight of us in the squad, including Patibal. I was pleased to see that my close friend, Antenon, was in our group. "I have good news for you," Patibal said. "We have the honor of being in the vanguard. Outside the barracks, you'll see that we have some donkeys serving as pack animals. Among the other items they're carrying are a couple of wooden platforms. One platform will be for us; the other platform is for Agenor's squad. The Hebrews, of course, have their own entryways into their village and we plan to seize those intact. But … maybe we won't. Also, it would be good to have multiple points of entry so we can quickly overwhelm whatever defenses they put up. The platforms are to go over their trench. You need to work together on this and work quickly. As you place the platform over the trench, you'll need to secure the end of the platform on our side of the trench. Otherwise, the platform will be too unstable and sway too much. Remember they have stakes on the other side of the trench, so on the far side of the trench the platform will likely be resting on those stakes and not the ground, and it will be tilted upward at an angle."

"What about securing the other end of the platform?"

"Well, that's a problem isn't it—because you're not at the other end. Once you're across you can secure the other end but you need to get across. So, the first ones on the platform need to crawl, getting as low as you can. That also has the benefit of making you less of a target. If you stand upright, then the platform is going to tip up like this," he gestured with his left hand, bringing it up suddenly. "You may fall in the ditch, which wouldn't be good, would it?"

Our faces must have betrayed our perplexity at how all this was all going to work because Patibal said, "Look, it's not really that complicated, and anyway that's why we're taking today to practice. You'll get the hang of it soon enough."

After all the squads received their instructions, we left the barracks. We marched some distance into the countryside, into a stony, barren area, not near any farms. We stopped near a dry creek bed. Bellon then spoke.

"The two squads with the platforms are going to go over their maneuvers in this area. This creek bed will serve as the Hebrews' ditch. Patibal, Agenor, take over."

The two squad leaders then instructed us to back away from the creek bed until we were several hundred paces distant.

"Fine, stop right here," Patibal ordered. "Here's what's going to happen tomorrow. We'll probably stop about this distance from the Hebrew settlement. You're then going to unfasten the platforms from the donkeys' backs. You may have noticed already the platforms are in two pieces. Our carpenters have skillfully crafted a way to join the two pieces together quickly. See here. You have a male end and a female end. The male end slides into the female end. Should be a nice tight fit, just like a good fuck. After the happy couple are joined together, four of you, two on each side, will run with the platform to the ditch. There are leather straps on each side of the platform so holding the platform should be easy, even for you fuckups. Once you reach the ditch, two of you are to hammer pegs into the ground as the others position the platform. Then tie the platform to the pegs using rope. You have to move fast. Today, only the flies will be buzzing by your head; tomorrow it could be arrows. Let's start. We're going to stay here today until we get it right."

The drills lasted past midday. We all took turns running with the platform and hammering the posts. There weren't too many mishaps, not after the first few attempts. Patibal decided I would be one of those carrying the platform; I would also be one of the two soldiers hammering the pegs into the ground. He did select back-ups as well. In case something "unfortunate" happened, he said. After resting for a short time, we marched back to the city. Once all were back, Bellon addressed the company again.

"The drills went well today. I'm more confident than ever that we'll prevail. For those going on the expedition, gather your weapons and pack your mantles and gear this evening. Fresh bread will be given to you in the morning. Fill your goatskins with water before you leave. There's only one well between here and the Hebrew village."

I was excited that evening. Too excited to eat much of my evening meal or to sleep well. Plus, as one might expect, there was a lot of whispering among the soldiers that night, despite repeated commands from the subofficers to shut up and go to sleep.

I was up before dawn, as were many others. The aroma of baking bread pervaded the courtyard. We relieved ourselves, washed our hands and faces quickly, and had a small, hurried breakfast. We then put on our armor and gathered our gear and weapons. In addition to our helmets, each soldier had a bronze corselet. We had combat tunics on underneath. These were thicker than regular tunics and they also had a leather apron extending from the abdomen to the thighs. They were terribly hot. We also had bronze greaves lined with cloth but we would put these on only when we were ready to assault the settlement; wearing them while marching would only impede our progress.

We left the barracks, gathering in the street outside. The commanders and sub-officers then positioned us for the march. Those of us on foot were in a long column, two abreast. I was placed near the rear, right before the pack animals. When I asked Patibal why, he said, "You have a large stride. If we put you and some of the other fast walkers in front, separation will be created in the column. We want to stay together, boy."

Before we departed the city, there was one more thing to do. We needed to assemble before the palace to obtain the blessings of the king and high priest. King Maoch was already seated on the ceremonial platform in front of the palace as we approached. Maoch was formally attired, with a richly embroidered purple robe with a white border with black and red stripes. On the body of the robe itself, in golden thread, there was a pattern of sun and swan characteristic of our people. The traditional fluted crown adorned his head.

The high priest was at Maoch's side. Offering tables to Dagon and Bel, god of war, were on the platform. Incense was burning and its sweet, spicy smell filled the air. The high priest poured a libation of wine and then water in the basins on the offering tables; following this, he placed fresh bread on each of the tables. Wine, water, and bread: the stuff of life to preserve us as we challenged death.

The priest then intoned a prayer:

I know that Dagon and Bel
Bless their chosen king and people;
They answer our prayers
And by their power give great victories.
We trust in our soldiers
We trust in our iron
But we trust most in the power of our gods.
Our enemies will stumble and fall
But we will rise and stand firm.
Then we shall shout for joy
And celebrate our triumph by praising you, O Dagon and Bel.

The ritual was short. The gods were aware of the passage of the sun, which they controlled. The sun was just rising when Maoch ended the ceremony with a booming, "On to victory!"

We set out.

We marched at a steady, but reasonably brisk pace, as brisk as the slower soldiers could maintain. Bellon wanted to get close to the Hebrew settlement by nightfall. The goal would be to set up camp about one hour away from the settlement, which would be close enough to strike them at the beginning of the day tomorrow, but not so close that we would be detected before the attack.

We were in high spirits when we started and intermittently we would spontaneously break into song. At this stage, there was no one around, so there was no fear of giving ourselves away. Plus, we had scouts. Two horsemen accompanying us would ride ahead for a bit, splitting off in different directions, and then ride back to us, reporting to Bellon on what, if anything, they observed. For most of the day, there was nothing to report.

Progress was good up until the midday break. But after the break—even though we took but a few minutes to piss, cram down some bread, gulp water, and rest our legs—we seemed to be more sluggish. There was an audible groan as we sat up and moved back into formation, and as we began our march again grumbling replaced our earlier singing. Our pace slackened.

Matters grew worse as we drew closer to the village because to avoid detection, Bellon had us veer east, through the beginnings of hill country. These weren't mountains by any means, but some of the hills had steep inclines and we had to scramble up, at times on all fours, grasping at handholds so we wouldn't slip. The donkeys showed great reluctance to make these climbs, perhaps displaying greater intelligence than we possessed. However, our purpose and the persuasive power of some rough prodding got them going again.

For us human beasts, Bellon's words served as goads. As the afternoon waned, his frustration became palpable. He was obviously concerned we would not be in position before nightfall. He dismounted and urged us forward with curses and insults, saying if an old man like him could keep a quick pace, we should be able to do the same. He didn't mention he had been riding most of the day.

As the sun was setting, the scouts came back from another reconnaissance. We took a break and sat and refreshed ourselves with water. Bellon and the junior commander, Sardon, conferred with the two scouts. Bellon then called for us to assemble. He ordered quiet as he said he didn't want to scream his orders. No Hebrews had been spotted, but we were now perhaps a little less than two hours walk away from the settlement and it was possible that someone walking to or from the settlement might hear us.

"I know it's getting dark now," he said. "But there's enough of a moon tonight to give us sufficient light to move forward a bit further, provided we move carefully. The scouts know in which direction we should head and we will follow their lead. Remember this: keep together! It's important we don't lose track of each other in the dark. We will march for another hour so and then make camp. Now back into formation!"

We regrouped and by the time we did so the sun had disappeared completely. The moon was a bit more than half-full, but the sky was not cloudless, so some of its light was obscured. We lurched forward, stopped, moved ahead again tentatively, picked up speed, then slowed down. At times, the rear of the column found itself walking to the side of those in front. Our movement was like that of an indecisive and confused snake, whose tail had lost contact with its head.

Then the donkeys balked again. Why? They're donkeys. No other explanation needed. The six soldiers who were guiding the donkeys pulled and tugged at them to no avail. They asked for the four of us in the rear of the column to give them a hand. Antenon, who was immediately ahead of me, asked those soldiers in front of him to stop and to tell the others to stop, but they either didn't hear him or they ignored him because they continued on their way—which we didn't realize until we finally had coaxed the donkeys into action again. We looked around. No sign of the others. Moment of panic. Curses.

"Gods, what are we going to do?" Antenon said.

"Shh, Shh … everyone, just be quiet," I said. "If we listen, we should be able to pick up the sounds of the column's movement. They can't be too far ahead."

Sure enough, we soon picked up the muffled sounds of the column's footsteps over to our left. I grabbed my rope, let it unravel, and told the others, "Everyone take hold of this rope so we won't lose track of each other as we try to catch up." They did so and in a few moments we were reunited with our comrades.

Presently, Bellon instructed the column to halt and to camp for the night. We were behind a low ridge which provided us some protection. Other than posting sentries we would not be taking any other defensive precautions, such as digging a ditch. No time to do that and we would not have been able to do that effectively in the dark anyway. For obvious reasons, we were not going to light any torches.

We set ourselves down, remaining in a tight circle so no one would get separated during the night and we would be able to assemble quickly in the morning. I removed my armor, threw one mantle on the ground, and drew another one over me as I lay down. Even though it was late spring, a stiff breeze had begun to blow and it was chilly. I looked up to the moon and the clouds had grown thicker. It probably would be overcast tomorrow—so much for having the sun in the Hebrews' eyes!

Thoughts were racing through my head as I lay there and I feared I would not get any rest, but I actually fell asleep quickly, with exhaustion overcoming excitement.

Antenon nudged me awake.

"It's time, Goliath."

I looked up and the whole company was stirring. It was still dark, which was good. We still had about an hour's worth of marching to do before we reached the settlement. It was also misting, which was not especially desirable.

Stepping carefully in the dark, we set out again slowly. Bellon had cautioned us against talking, so each man had only his own thoughts to keep him company, which was like being chained to a jumpy and anxious companion.

We made good time, all things considered, but it was already turning light as we neared the settlement, so our timing was off. There was now some chance we would be spotted before we could launch our attack.

Our last cover was a small hill about 400 paces from the settlement. Our column halted there. The donkeys were to stay behind with a couple of soldiers. The commanders and sub-officers went over the plan of attack again with the rest of us. We were to cross the open area in front of the settlement as fast as possible, staying low to the ground. Dagon willing, we might be able to reach the bottom of the rise on which the settlement was situated before we were seen.

Three squads were to lead the attack. One squad would go to the Hebrew entryway that was positioned at the southeast end of the settlement. The entryway—which was a simple wooden platform not dissimilar to the platforms we had with us, except wider and sturdier—would be raised, of course, but our soldiers would try to lower it with ropes and grappling hooks. The sentry that was positioned there would be dispatched quickly with a volley of arrows and javelins, with any luck being silenced before he could raise the alarm. Simultaneous with the assault on the entryway, the two squads with platforms would race up the hill, place their platforms over the ditch, securing the near end through ropes tied to posts, as we had been instructed to do. We would then crawl across the platforms into the settlement. Our hope was that we would get the bulk of our forces into the settlement before most of the Hebrew soldiers were even awake.

It didn't quite work out that way.

⊫╪╬═►

3

The beginning of the assault went smoothly. We dashed to the bottom of the hill. We paused, waiting to hear any sound from the settlement which would indicate we had been seen. Nothing. So far so good. Our objective was now just above us.

We then ran up the hill as quietly as possible, but a couple of dozen soldiers running uphill at top speed carrying wooden platforms are bound to make some noise. The Hebrew sentry turned in the direction of the sound and as we had lost the benefit of the cover of darkness, I'm sure he didn't mistake us for a merchant's caravan. He did hesitate for a moment before yelling his lungs out—perhaps the sudden terror momentarily robbed him of his voice—but he did manage several shouts before being cut down by a shower of arrows. Within a moment or two, maybe a dozen Hebrew soldiers streamed out of a building in the village like angry bees from a hive.

Meanwhile, the squad at the entryway had problems forcing the Hebrew platform down. We knew from advance scouting that it was secured by rope to the fragmentary wall on both sides. Our thought had been that by use of hooks and brute force we could loosen the grip of these fastenings and lower the platform, but the platform budged only slightly. We didn't realize until later that the entryway was also secured by a rope connecting a ring at the center of the platform with a post on the other side of the wall.

Our lack of success at the entryway made it imperative that we get our own platforms down quickly. In my squad, Antenon and I rapidly hammered the pegs into the ground while the others laid the platform across the ditch. We then tied the platform to the pegs. I was the first one on the platform. I'd left my javelin behind, to be brought into the village later (I hoped), and I crawled forward with my spear in my right hand, my sword and shield strapped to my back, and my knife in my belt. I nearly slid off the platform, it was so wet from the persistent mist, but I scurried quickly and was near the

15

end when I saw a Hebrew running toward me with a spear. He launched it just as I made my awkward leap onto the low wall. The spear hit the platform with a thud, exactly where I'd been a moment before.

I was now on the ground, having tumbled off the wall, in the process letting go of my spear so I would not impale myself as I fell. I struggled to my feet to find the Hebrew vaulting on top of me, knife in hand. I caught the wrist of his knife hand with my left hand, grabbed hold of his tunic with my right hand, and used his momentum to throw us both onto the ground. This knocked the knife out of his hand. We grappled and rolled like wild dogs, screaming all the while. Each of us tried to break free of the other's grip with little success. The Hebrew then tore at my ear with his teeth and I returned the favor by biting his nose. A terrible crunch of bone and cartilage. We broke apart, he got to his feet first and, while I was still on my knees, he delivered a kick to my chin. I reeled back a bit, but didn't collapse, and as he ventured a kick again, I grabbed his foot and twisted him over. He was tipped on his side. I felt for my knife, pulled it from its sheath, and plunged it into his neck, eliciting a yelp and a gush of wine-red blood.

I looked up. I saw that most of my squad had made it across the ditch and were either engaged in hand-to-hand combat with the Hebrews or were dodging arrows from a couple of Hebrews who had set themselves up about fifty paces in back of the others. I also saw that the other squad with a platform was still on the other side of the ditch. It looked like their platform had slid to the side, with one end in the ditch. I got up as quickly as I could, and as I did my shield reminded me that it was still on my back. Sharp pain. The edge of the shield had cut into me as I had rolled around. No time to brood on that. I freed my shield from its straps, held it in my right hand facing the arrows, picked up my spear, and rushed to join my comrades, who were trying to make it to the entryway to cut the rope that still held the Hebrew platform in place.

I first encountered a Hebrew who seemed to be getting the better of a comrade, Batnoam. Indeed, the arrival of the tip of my spear in the Hebrew's side could not have been more timely as he had just knocked Batnoam's sword out of his hands. I forced my spear in as far as it could go, in the process also sliding it up and under the Hebrew's rib cage. I tried to pull it back out, but the tip must have been caught on his ribs because all I succeeded in recovering was the shaft itself, slick with blood and viscera. I threw it aside.

The entryway was now but ten paces away. Batnoam and I joined Patibal and Antenon who were already there, hoping to find an interval of time between fending off attacks to be able to cut the entryway rope. Patibal, Antenon, and I formed a defensive perimeter as Batnoam cut the rope. The platform came down. Our soldiers now rushed across. Any chance the Hebrews had to hold off our attack was now gone. A few of them beat a hasty retreat to the shelter their buildings provided, even though this only meant postponing the inevitable. Beast and man will both struggle to stay alive even as they face death.

I stopped at the entryway for a moment, thinking about crossing back over to the other side to retrieve my javelin. I just started back over, when I ran into Sardon, the deputy commander.

"Where do you think you're going, Goliath? I don't think now's the time to retreat."

"Sir, I want to retrieve my javelin."

"No, don't bother. Look, just get that one that's over there." He pointed to a comrade who was on the ground, having been unlucky enough to receive arrows in his shoulder and thigh. Blood was flowing freely from his thigh wound. I stooped next to him; he was still alive. His name was Melqath.

I tried to think how I could stop his bleeding, but I didn't have anything with me that would serve. I had a cloth I used for washing, and I did place it on the wound, applying some pressure. Melqath recoiled from my touch. I realized I was probably pushing the arrowhead in deeper. I stretched the cloth as far as it could go, but I could not wrap it around the thigh.

Sardon came up. "Leave him. There are some Hebrews trying to escape by their other gate. Grab his javelin and let's go."

I looked at Melqath. He didn't beg or protest. He merely said, "Water, please." I left him my goatskin.

Some Hebrews were trying to flee the village by their northwest entryway. Two men, two women, and a few young children, two of whom were in the arms of their mothers. One of our soldiers was already upon them, but one of the Hebrew men was desperately fending him off as the other man lowered the entryway platform. The platform fell and the party made their way across the ditch—minus their one valiant defender who had now absorbed a fatal sword thrust into his abdomen. He dropped his own sword to grab his belly, vainly trying to hold in his spilling guts.

I had run up to the entryway, javelin in hand. The Hebrew man was just to the other side of the ditch, but he'd soon be below the lip of the hill and out of view. I positioned myself as I was trained to do, took a couple steps forward, and launched my javelin. It struck him in the upper right leg, just below his buttocks. His body jerked up for an instant then fell. He wasn't dead yet, but he would be. Still, he struggled to crawl forward, grabbing the ground in front of him and dragging himself ahead with his hands while his life drained away.

The women and children might have been able to make it down the hill had they continued to run, but they stopped, looking bewildered, perhaps unsure what to do now that they had lost their two defenders.

A couple of our soldiers seized the women. One had her throat cut immediately. The other was thrown on the ground and the two soldiers climbed on top of her. The infants they had been holding were tossed aside. All the children were wailing.

"Goliath, finish the children," I heard Sardon yell, as I turned to trot toward the buildings in the settlement. I pretended not to hear. Not that I thought the Hebrew children should be allowed to live, but being a butcher didn't fit the image I had of myself as a soldier.

Several of my comrades were going in and out of buildings looking for hiding Hebrews. Others were trying to set fire to the few buildings that presumably had already been cleared of any loot worth taking. They were having some trouble with this latter task as the mist had now developed into a steady rain. As I approached the cluster of buildings, I saw two Hebrew archers climb on the roof of a house. They began shooting. Gods! I switched from a leisurely pace to an all-out run to the side of the house. I yelled out to those near me that we had a couple of live ones still. Patibal was nearby. He found some of our own archers, positioned them so they could pin down, if not kill, the Hebrews on the roof, and then directed some of us to break down the door and enter the house, holding our shields in front of us as protection. We kicked the door several times and it gave way. Our eyes darted about, searching the courtyard for any sign of movement. Nothing. Several goats were bleating in the stable, more frightened than even we were.

An arrow hit my shield. Our noisy entry had not gone unnoticed, and one of the roof archers had turned his attention and projectiles to us. We split our party into two, three of us going to one side of the courtyard, four to the other. An arrow zipped by my head, plunging into the throat of the soldier behind me, who collapsed with a hideous bloody gargle.

"When are our archers going to hit home?" I asked the soldier next to me when we had reached the relative safety of a side room off the courtyard. No sooner had I asked this, then an arrow pierced the one Hebrew archer who had been aiming for us. The arrow hit him chest high. He fell to his knees, dropping his bow. He then tried to get up, but toppled over into the courtyard. That left one archer to deal with.

Realizing his plight, the remaining Hebrew abandoned the roof and ducked into the second-story living area of the house. His ultimate doom was unavoidable but he was hoping to sell his life at a high price. Hidden in the dark recesses of one of the rooms, he could see us out of the windows, but we could not see him.

Patibal gave the proper order for such a situation. "Get some torches and set fire to the place. Try to start with the wooden supports in the back. After you have the fire going, two of you stay behind to take the fucker down if he tries to escape. Oh … and save the goats, if possible."

Once the place was alight, I left the house with most of the others. By the time we emerged, it appeared the settlement was firmly in our hands. Most buildings were smoking. I didn't notice any resistance, only corpses littering the street. I tried to avoid walking on these, not out of any respect, but to avoid slipping on their wet, lumpy surfaces and having a loose blade find its way into my ass.

Not sure what to do next, I and several others began to mill around. Among the soldiers in this loose grouping was the veteran who had been my tormentor since I joined the army, Scourge. Or so we called him. When Scourge noticed me, he cackled and said, "Big boy, have you pissed yourself yet?"

A sub-officer came up to our group. He told us, "Check out that house over there. No one's been there yet. Could be hiding some holdouts."

About eight of us went to the building. The front door was already ajar. We proceeded cautiously. Suddenly, a mother cat ran out in front of us, out of the stable, holding a kitten by the neck. She had probably been hiding in the stable, and now that she was frightened by us, she was hoping to make it to a safer place, perhaps the hearth at the back of the courtyard. An archer drew back his bow and let fly an arrow that hit the cat in the neck.

She dropped instantly. The kitten was thrown from her mouth. It scampered away.

"Great shot," Scourge said.

My reaction was, "Why'd you do that?"

The archer looked at me as though I was speaking in an unknown tongue.

"What you mean why'd I do that? Target practice. Don't have many chances to try to hit a moving target, especially a small one moving fast." He walked past me with a look of scorn, in the process pushing his elbow into my chest.

Having dispatched any feline foes, we searched the rooms downstairs, in the process grabbing bits of food and stuffing them into our mouths. We looked for anything of value, but came up empty. We did find a pot with some honey which detained us as we gorged on it, dipping some bread into it.

"Goliath, move back from the pot, damn it," Scourge said. "You're dripping blood into it."

"What?"

"Your ear, damn it, your ear. You're bleeding. You probably cut it when you fell on your own sword," Scourge said with a mocking laugh.

I felt my left ear where the first Hebrew had bitten me. Sticky with blood, and the normal smooth rim of my ear had been replaced by jagged pieces of flesh. I ran my fingers around the edge until I got to the lobe, which seemed mostly intact.

"Stop playing with your fucking ear. As long as you can still hear, you're fine."

Having gone through the downstairs, we proceeded to the second level, using a ladder that had been propped up against the left side courtyard rooms. This led to a roof that covered the left side rooms, and this roof led directly to the second level rooms at the back of the house, which typically served as living quarters.

As we approached the door to the quarters, we were startled by a frenzied yell as a woman bolted out the door with a large knife in her hands. She plowed into the lead soldier, trying to run the blade into his neck, but her aim was off by a bit and she hit the side of his helmet and the blade broke off. Still, she had knocked him off his feet and together they rolled off the roof onto the courtyard below.

"My back, my fucking back," the soldier yelled.

The woman tried to get up, but the soldier had his sword out and he managed to reach over and slice her legs, cutting the left one to the bone. He then propped himself up on his left hand and with his right plunged the sword into her back. She let out a cry and then a moan.

"Let's fuck the bitch before she dies," one of our party said as he started back down the ladder.

The rest of us looked at each other for a moment. We were still startled by what had just occurred. Finally, someone said, "We should clear the house first." There was no dissent, so we continued into the living quarters. I sneaked a look back at the courtyard before we entered the rooms. The soldier who had climbed down the ladder had removed his corselet and helmet. He had also pulled up the robe of the woman, up to where the sword had entered. It appeared he was having difficulty separating her legs.

The residential area at the back was actually one large room separated into different chambers by curtains, similar to the arrangement of many houses. The first chamber had enough light from the door that we could see there was no person there and little else. Some mats, some pots. There was not as much light in the second chamber as it had only a small window facing the outside, but again it was obvious that no person was present. Nothing more than a table and a couple of chairs. The third chamber was the darkest, with no opening, so we were understandably wary and on edge. It was a couple of moments before any of us ventured away from the curtain into the chamber itself, but our eyes slowly adjusted. It appeared to be a storage area. A number of amphorae, pots, and jugs. There was also a pile of mantles in the corner. Each one of us looked in the various containers, hoping they might hold something valuable—silver ideally, but if not, some jewelry or copper pieces. While we were so engaged, one of us cried out, "Wait, there's something moving under the mantles."

We looked. A moment or two passed and then the mantles did move slightly, as if a person underneath was shifting his body. But it couldn't have been a big body. Swords drawn, we approached the pile. Two soldiers grabbed the mantles on top and tossed them aside, and a sword was thrust into the remaining layer. A scream. The last few mantles were removed to reveal a girl, perhaps twelve. She stood up, terrified, and then she started to weep and babble, her eyes overflowing with tears. We couldn't understand a word she was saying, but it would not have made any difference if we had.

The other soldiers fell on her like a pack of wolves, tearing at her clothes, biting her, pushing her down. Scourge yelled, "Pin her to the floor so we can have a go at her." Scourge ripped off what little remained of her clothing and got on top of her. The others squatted around her laughing, poking their fingers into her knobby breasts or squeezing them.

I drew back. I stood there for a moment, then, fleeing from my thoughts, I retreated into the other chambers and walked around, breaking apart the spare furniture and smashing any pottery that was ready to hand. The sound of the shattering pottery helped mask the weeping and screaming from the other chamber.

As I reached for one last pot, I felt a knife against my throat. "Look, you big sissy," Scourge growled. "You're going to share in this Hebe's cunt with the rest of us or I'll cut your throat for being a fag or a Hebe lover, or both."

I pointed to the smashed pottery. "I was just trying to clean up," I responded with a weak laugh.

Why I didn't strike Scourge as he withdrew his knife, I don't know. Instead, I followed him back into the third chamber.

"Look hear," Scourge announced. "I want to give my boy Goliath a turn."

"But I ..." one soldier protested.

"Don't worry. You'll get your chance."

I looked at the girl. She reeked of the filth and sweat that had been the gift of the soldiers that preceded me. Their spittle and snot adorned her face. Still, when I saw her young cunt, bloody though it was, I grew hard. I entered her and in a few moments it was over.

I then made the mistake of looking at her face. I had seen horror and terror in her eyes before, but now her eyes had a vacant look, glazed by an emptiness that unsettled me. It gave me the chilling feeling that I had been fucking a specter or a shadow.

Repulsed but also compelled, I forced myself to look more closely at her eyes and instead of seeing myself reflected I stared into an abyss of blackness. I pulled out with a suppressed shriek which caused some laughter in those around me. "By the gods, Goliath, was it that good ... or that bad?"

I had laid my sword to the side while I was fucking. Now I picked it up and swiftly cut the girl's throat. As blood spurted from the gash, I looked at her again. For an instant her face seemed transformed; she looked like Dedra, my younger sister.

The reaction from my comrades was swift and fierce.

"What the fuck did you do that for, you idiot?"

"Fuck you, Goliath. Couldn't you wait until everyone had their turn? You're a monster."

"I say we turn Goliath over and fuck him."

Much pushing and shoving, which grew progressively more intense. Someone drew a sword. I still had mine in my hand, dripping blood.

"In Dagon's name, what the fuck is going on here?" This was the booming voice of Patibal, who had entered the chamber with another sub-officer. "I came here to find out why you idiots were taking so long, to see if you'd run into any resistance, and I find you're fighting each other. I'll have all of you flogged."

"Goliath here has killed this girl," Scourge said.

"Yes, and …?"

"Well, you see, we were all taking turns. He had his turn, but he didn't let some others have theirs."

Patibal looked down at the girl; he moved his feet to avoid the blood still seeping from her wound. He then looked at me warily, contemplating what to say, measuring me, wondering what my reaction would be. Finally, he said, "Goliath, go check the roof over the right side of the courtyard. I don't think anyone's been there yet."

"Patibal," someone protested, "there's no one there. Aren't you going to …?"

"*You*," Patibal poked his finger in the soldier's chest, "*you* are going to shut up. Along with the rest of you. All of you come with me. We'll start a fire in the hearth. Goliath, when you're finished your search come down to the courtyard. We will then set fire to this place."

As he pushed the others out of the chamber, Patibal leaned back to me and whispered, "Take your time. Let tempers fade."

I waited until the others left the chamber, and then followed. The roof over the right side of the courtyard didn't connect to the living quarters. One had to access it by climbing onto the roof over the living quarters and then down a ladder, so I first had to retrace our path through the back quarters.

Once on the roof over the right side of the courtyard, I made a desultory search. There really wasn't much there, certainly no one hiding. This was good because I was numb and distracted; my mind kept taking me back to the Hebrew girl. If someone had leaped out from behind one of the couple of large amphorae, I would have been an easy kill, as I was completely inattentive.

But it turned out there was someone hiding. I thought I heard the merest hint of a squeak and I looked into a basket. There was the kitten whose mother had been slain in the courtyard. Apparently, he had made his way up here, hoping to get away from all that loud noise and frightening smells. I picked him up. He was black, with a delicate patch of white under his jaw. He didn't resist. Instead he clung to me, and he soon revealed why. He worked his way over my arm, his claws pricking my skin as he did so, over the shoulder of my corselet, and he then started sucking away at my neck, slurping at some imaginary milk. He was hungry.

I sat down. I looked out over the burning settlement. Smoke was starting to sting my eyes. Here I sat, a victor in my first battle, my eyes watering and my sole booty a Hebrew kitten avidly pursuing a desire that couldn't be fulfilled.

4

After I finished telling Altara about my first combat, silence—an uneasy silence for me—hung over us for a few moments. I realized that once I had begun telling my story to Altara, I let the flow of my words carry me along, without giving any thought to how my words might affect her. Before my rambling, I was worried she might think me a mute idiot; now I worried she might consider me a brutal braggart.

"I hope that did not upset you," I said weakly. "I mean … you asked … but I probably shouldn't have told you about my first combat." Then I added stupidly, "I'm not a rapist, you know. Killing is killing, but …"

She looked directly at me. "Don't explain. War is horrible. I know that." She shook her head. "Or maybe I should not say that. I've been fortunate enough not to have personal experience of war, but my mother told me about what she witnessed." Altara's words trailed off.

"Do you want to tell me about that?"

A pause. "Not really, no."

She must have sensed that I felt rebuffed, because she placed her hand on my cheek again. "I'd still rather hear more about you. Maybe something less … less violent. Tell me of your family. You have a sister, yes? You mentioned her when … Well, you mentioned her."

"I'm not used to talking so much about myself."

"New experiences can be pleasant, as we proved this evening," she said with a knowing laugh. Then she leaned closer, the space between us narrowing to an eyelash. She kissed my forehead, then my eyes. "What did your eyes see as a child? Make me see your memories."

⚔

5

"Goliath, Goliath!" my mother yelled. "Don't go so far away. And don't go so deep in the stream. You might fall."

But what five-year-old listens to their mother when adventure beckons?

I was with my mother by the stream outside Gath where she washed laundry. Along with my aunt, she did laundry for those who could afford to have someone else do the task. Not that it cost much. Her labors earned us some grain, cheese, and, less frequently, some scraps of pork or mutton. Clothes, usually worn. An occasional copper piece or two from one of the nobles if she had an especially demanding task.

However, although the rewards for this work were not great, and the work itself was tiring and tiresome, it made sense because my father and uncle were smiths. Their tunics required frequent washing and since my mother and aunt had to do laundry more often than most women, why not earn some additional benefit while they were at it?

At five, I was old enough to help my mother, but still young enough to be mostly a nuisance. After my mother rinsed the clothes in the stream, removing some of the surface dirt and grime, they would be placed in a tub half-filled with a mixture of water and urine. My job was to step up and down on the clothes, in the process swirling them around in the solution. Treading the clothes in this fashion was fun for me, so it didn't really seem like a chore. The fact that I was moving my feet around in piss didn't bother me either. Like many young children, I found piss and shit not only sources of repugnance but also of interest and amusement, and I derived some sort of perverse pleasure from the process. The smell …well, it wasn't jasmine but it was tolerable.

I would do my clothes dance off-and-on for a while and then I could stop. The clothes had to soak. Eventually, there would be two additional tubs to fill, but while my mother was rinsing the next batch, I was free to occupy myself with what kids do: run around, inspect bugs, throw rocks at birds.

One day, I was especially interested in targeting a bird whose sharp call— a *kee-wick* repeated three or four times—for some reason I found annoying. Later I would learn this was a sparrowhawk, but at the time all I knew was that its repetitious, grating call was demanding my attention. Granted, it was a fairly attractive bird, blue-gray in plumage on top, with pale coloring under-neath, but in my mind this simply made it all the more tempting a target.

There were some nicely sized rocks, maybe twenty paces away, in the middle of the stream. They were well-rounded and large enough to have an impact but small enough to fit in my hand. I scampered off as soon as my footwork for the first tub was finished. My mother yelled for me to come back, but I ignored her. I thought I wouldn't have any problem with my foot-ing, and I didn't really. But my avian adversary got the better of me. The bird called out as I was weaving my way between some large rocks. I looked up, lost my balance, then fell forward. I felt a sharp pain in my right leg. I whim-pered of course, but my primary emotion at the time was embarrassment. I pushed myself up; I noticed that a warm liquid was running down my leg along with the cool waters from the stream. I was bleeding. Badly. Big gash right below my knee.

I had seen animals cut open, of course. I had seen people take ill and die, including my baby sister, who died from a fever of some sort and a con-tinual coughing and gagging that stole away her breath. And I had seen and experienced small cuts. But until that time, I had not seen any human bleed like this. I was too bewildered to cry. I walked back toward my mother in a daze finally calling out to her.

She looked up. She emitted a soft cry and then sprang into action. She pulled me onto the bank, turned me over on my back, wrapped a garment around my legs, and then took me up in her arms. At that moment, though, my aunt, who had come over hurriedly, bumped into my mother, and my mother and I both fell down.

"Let me help you carry him."

"No," my mother protested, "just help me up and then run to the guard for help."

There was a guard posted near the top of the slope that ran down to the stream. His job, in which he seemed to take only an occasional interest, was to watch over those outside the city gates: women washing laundry, women gathering water, and so forth. My aunt scurried up the incline to get his attention, as my mother carried me as best and as fast as she could.

My aunt and the soldier were still in frantic discussion—my aunt gesturing more than talking—as my mother drew near to them. She held me out to the soldier who looked bewildered. He put his spear on the ground, made a move to grab me, turned back to his spear, picked it up, repeated this cycle, and then rushed off, yelling over his shoulder, "I'll get help." It was my first introduction to military confusion.

My mother let out an exasperated moan, and then began to run with me to the city. At least she was on even ground now.

As we drew closer to the city, I could feel my mother's pace slow. She was growing tired, and her breath was coming in shallow pants. Still, she managed to call out to various people to go run and tell my father I had cut my leg open. The bloomery where my father worked was a good distance away, at the far north-east of the city. We were approaching from the west side.

We neared the city gate. The garment in which I was being carried was drenched in blood. My mother's robe was also heavily stained. Exhausted, she knelt about twenty paces from the gate and began to call out for assistance, but before she could finish, my aunt and several men rushed out from the gate. The men gathered me in their arms, and the second part of the relay was underway. My mother trailed behind.

I felt my body melt away, and I was losing track of some of my surroundings, but as we were perhaps halfway through the city I saw my father approach at a trot, accompanied by his brother. My father was carrying a thin iron rod in his right hand, which was covered with a heavy glove. The rod was glowing at its tip. His brother was holding some rags and a bowl.

At my father's direction, I was placed on the ground, with my arms and legs spread and pinned down. My uncle took diluted olive oil from the bowl and wiped my wound with the cloths so my father could have a good view of the wound. I would like to say I was brave boy, but in truth I squirmed, wriggled, and cried out when I saw that hot iron approach my leg. But the arms that held me were strong and my father moved swiftly and deftly, cauterizing the wound with the heated rod. I fainted from the pain, but the bleeding stopped.

Stopping the blood flow from a deep wound was one thing, but many a person who has managed to stanch the flow of blood dies later from illness. A foul-smelling wound festers, the person becomes feverish, and then he dies, perhaps after lingering a week or two. My later experience on the battlefield would confirm that many deaths occur after the combat is finished.

So, my mother proved to be my savior twice over. She had to tend to me for days, applying honey, animal fat, and clean cloths to the wound, changing this dressing often, and then spoon feeding me and cooling me off with water when I developed a low fever. I survived my own folly, but only because of her care. My mother and I had disagreements later …

⊰⊱

6

I didn't finish my thought. I looked at Altara. "I don't think you want to hear about family disputes," I said.

She gave a half shrug. 'I would be interested, but it seems like you may not be comfortable talking about it. You stopped mid-sentence."

I looked away. "Oh, I don't know. I suppose I was going to say something about how I don't appreciate my mother enough." I picked at the mat with my fingers.

"That doesn't make you different from most men. We women are seldom appreciated enough."

"Is that right?" I asked as I turned back to her.

"I may not know much, but I know that," she said with a twinkle in her eyes. "Here's something I don't know. How does cauterization work? I mean, I know it does. I've seen it used." When she said this her hand went to her right cheek, which bore a scar. "But how does the heat stop the flow of blood?"

"I'm not entirely sure myself. But I know from having worked with my father that heat changes the shape of things, even iron. Perhaps heat changes the shape of the blood, making it solid. Don't know."

"So, you worked with your father making iron?"

"Oh, yes. Although he and my uncle made the iron. I was just a helper. But I almost became a smith. Gods, I also almost became a scribe." I caught myself after saying this, realizing it was an exaggeration. "Well, perhaps …"

"A scribe? I didn't know you could write."

"I can't really, but …"

"Now you have to tell me that story."

⊨╪═

7

I was big, even as a child, and at least my father thought me capable of learning important skills, so a few months after I turned ten, I joined my father and uncle in the bloomery, the iron-making shop for our city.

Their craft provided only a modest income, but it placed them in a position of importance within the city and their skills were widely respected. It was a respect that came with some burdens, however. Iron weapons were vital for our defense. They gave us an advantage over the more numerous Hebrews who had not yet mastered the skill of iron-making. Their edged weapons were of bronze only. Obviously, we wanted to maintain that advantage so we Palestim guarded the knowledge of our craft jealously. My father needed permission to travel outside Gath. He also needed to account for all customers and visitors who came to the bloomery by providing their names to one of the city magistrates every week. Moreover, no one could purchase a blade or sharp instrument of any sort absent permission of a magistrate, as evidenced by his seal over the picture of a sword.

My father was scrupulous in following these rules. The penalty for any violation was death.

In truth, I doubt that my father could have explained the process for making iron in any way that would have been helpful to our enemies. He never told me. He showed me. Like many skills, the ability to produce good quality iron and to shape it for a specific purpose, whether for a sword, a spear point, a hammer, or fittings for a chariot, was something acquired only by practice, learning alongside an experienced craftsman.

The initial product of the furnace was a bloom, a lumpy black mixture of metal and slag. This bloom then had to reheated and hammered to yield any sort of usable substance. Most iron artifacts, of course, required several cycles of heating and hammering; moreover, the various pieces of the artifact had to be welded by heating them until they burned bright orange and then promptly hammering them together until they formed a bond.

The final shaping of the artifact required a prodigious amount of hammering with varying degrees of force and at a variety of angles.

Not infrequently, even for someone with skills like my father and uncle, the process ended in failure. Even when it seemed like the desired result had been obtained, the tool or weapon turned out to be too soft to be durable. Worse was a weapon that was too brittle and that shattered or split after a few impacts. This usually resulted in the death of its unlucky owner, so my father and uncle did not receive too many direct complaints about this particular type of flaw, but on one occasion a comrade of a fallen warrior expressed his dissatisfaction with the work of our bloomery, and not in very polite terms.

Fortunately, though, my father and uncle turned out a reliable product on a regular enough basis that their positions were secure and our city and, importantly, the king, nobility, and military commanders were pleased with their work.

My own tasks in the few years I worked in the bloomery required nothing like the level of skill demanded of a smith. I carried out some of the needed auxiliary tasks. I helped bring in the wood we used to produce charcoal. I helped load the furnace, after having been taught the appropriate level of charcoal and ore to utilize. I emptied the furnace and shoveled the slag into a pile behind the bloomery. But my most important task was to work the bellows. These forced air into the furnace and caused the fire to burn hotter. How this worked I didn't fully understand. I knew fire needed air to burn (we quenched fire by throwing sand or water on the flames) so perhaps adding more air to the fire provided it with some combustible element in the air. But whether this was the true explanation or not, I never learned. I did quickly learn how tiring it was to work the bellows. The first few times I was given this task only the desire not to disappoint my father gave me the strength to continue.

The work in the bloomery was exhausting. Also, the bloomery was oppressively hot. In the summer, combined with the sun's sweltering heat, it was almost unbearable. Many summer days we did shut down mid-day, resuming again in the evening. And the work made us filthy. But these were happy times for me. My father treated me as a colleague, not a child, and I considered the demands he placed on me as proof of his trust and not a burden.

I was also permitted to share the afternoon meal with my father and uncle. They talked. I listened. I learned. Learned about many things, but especially the situation of our people, the Palestim. There was one conversation I recall in particular. It was the day after the closing of the fall festival of Hishara. As part of the formal closing of the festival, a poet told the tale of the Palestim.

I was as attentive to the poet's recitation as someone my age could be, but I understood only snippets of what I heard: we Palestim obeyed Dagon, who told us to cross the sea to a new land; this land would be our new home; the Egyptians tried to kill us but Dagon caused a storm that scattered their forces; we would live forever in our new homeland as long as we honored the gods, and especially Dagon. I do remember being moved by the words at the end of the story:

> *There is no one like Dagon*
> *Who storms through the heavens to help us;*
> *He defeats all our foes*
> *So we Palestim can live in peace, untroubled.*
> *Our enemies come fawning to us*
> *And our domains will endure forever.*

Anyway, that day I brought the bread and cheese from home as usual. When I arrived at the bloomery, my uncle and father were already seated on their mats, so I poured the diluted olive oil over my hands quickly, rubbed them together once or twice, told myself they were clean enough, and sat down to eat with them. There was silence at first as we attacked our food. The bloomery never failed to work up an appetite. But after a few chews, my uncle spoke up.

"Megath may be getting too old for his recitation," my uncle opined. "He stumbled over his words even more than last year and repeated himself about three or four times."

"Maybe he wanted to emphasize certain points," my father responded.

My uncle snorted. "What, it was important for us to be told twice how many mummified cats the Egyptians brought with them?"

My father shrugged. "Megath deserves some respect. I couldn't remember our people's story and tell it—and neither could you."

"What's that have to do with it? Other people can't do what we do, but if we turned out soft iron every day, we'd find ourselves out of work pretty soon."

"I don't think stumbling over a few lines is the same as turning out shoddy iron."

"But that's his calling! He's a poet! He's supposed to get it right."

My father just waved this last declaration away with his left hand.

There was a pause for a couple of moments, and then my uncle spoke up again.

"And what is the point of talking about all those damn cats? Yes, I know it shows the power of Dagon that he brought the cats back to life and that they then tore through their wrappings and ran away, but... but... it just seems so silly to me."

"Dagon has great power, and don't disrespect him."

My uncle turned his eyes skyward, "Dear Dagon, please know that I recognize your power, indeed I just mentioned your unsurpassed power to my hard of hearing brother, and that I am deeply grateful for all your blessings, but," and here he turned to my father, "it seems to me that this part of the story doesn't show you proper respect. I don't think Dragon would be concerned about a bunch of dead cats."

"The Egyptians worship their cats. They treat them as gods. So, this part of the story shows that Dagon is mightier than their gods."

My uncle made no verbal response, but he shook his head to indicate he wasn't persuaded.

Emboldened by this exchange, I decided to ask a question.

"The sea. How big is it? The poet says it took seven days for our people to cross, but he did not say how fast they traveled."

My father and uncle looked at each other. "It's big," my father said. "Bigger than you can imagine. I've been to Ashkelon and stood on the shore. As far as you can see, it's water."

My uncle broke off a small piece of bread and rubbed it several times between his fingers until only a tiny crumb remained. "See this crumb. If you put it next to the krater"—he pointed to the krater we used for storing our water— "it's like a city next to the sea."

I reflected on this and recalled some of what the poet had said about the dangers and hardships of the voyage. "So, we made this long journey because Dagon promised us this land, like the poet said."

"Uh-huh."

"If Dragon promised us this land, why then do the Hebrews attack us?"

My father raised his eyebrows and looked at me intently for a moment. "The Hebrews don't respect Dagon or any of our gods."

"Why not?"

"They're stupid," my uncle said. "A bunch of stupid thieves who can't work their own land properly so they want to take ours."

"Does that mean they'll keep attacking us?"

"Maybe," my father said. "Only Dagon knows what will happen. But if we show the proper respect to Dagon and the other gods, and we make use of the gifts they have given us, including our iron, we will triumph."

We finished our meal, but my childish curiosity would not allow me to let the subject drop.

"But if we told the Hebrews about Dagon's promise to us, wouldn't they stop fighting? Because then they would know they couldn't win."

My uncle stood up, brushing some crumbs away from his mouth. "Didn't I tell you the Hebrews are stupid? They know about Dagon. They know this land is ours. It makes no difference."

"They have their own gods," my father interjected. "Just like the Egyptians have their gods. This is why they don't respect Dagon."

"Ha! They keep their main god in a chest. Can you imagine? Their god must think he can hide from Dagon."

My father stood up. "Ready to return to work?"

I remained seated. "So, the fighting will go on?'

My father looked at me for a long moment. "Maybe not. We seem to be at peace now. Perhaps that will continue."

My uncle spat on the ground, mumbling his disapproval, disagreement, or both.

"But one thing is certain, if we don't get back to work, we won't be prepared if we are attacked again. Let's go. Enough questions."

⟱⟰

8

I paused, thinking about how or if I should continue my story.

"You going to stop there?" Altara asked.

"I'm thinking."

"If you're wondering whether I want you to continue, I do."

33

I didn't respond.

"But only if you want to." She sighed and lay back on her bed, stretched out, face turned toward the ceiling.

What is it about this woman, I asked myself, that makes me want to talk about things I haven't spoken about with anyone else? I met her just over a day ago.

Haltingly, I said, "It's … to go further … to tell you how I learned a few letters … I'd have to tell you about Phodan."

Altara propped herself back up, turning toward me again. "If you're worried I'm going to judge you because you did—what? Steal from somebody? None of us are without fault. Certainly, not the people I know. And earlier you told me about the girl …What I mean to say …"

I knew what she was thinking: what could be worse than that rape. I didn't want her lingering on that thought, so I interrupted her. "With Phodan, it's not so much what I did, but what I did not do."

She extended her left hand and moved it gently over my right cheek. "You do have a way of making things intriguing. Now you must go on."

⚔

9

As I was saying, we had some years of peace then. At times of peace, boys had more freedom to roam outside the city. Of course, most days we were working, but on the monthly festival days we had some leisure time. On those days, after the procession of Dagon and his wife Hishara to the main temple, the offerings and sacrifice, and the ritual hymns, the rest of the day was ours. Dagon, forgive me, but I must confess that I eagerly awaited the concluding words of the closing hymn, "Hail to Thee, Dagon, Lord of all the Gods, Maker of Life, Sustainer, to Thou, Most Gracious and Merciful, we rededicate ourselves." At that moment, with a great shout, the whole populace expressed their rejoicing, and my joy was most sincerely and deeply felt— because now I could play.

Sometimes we remained within the city, but especially during the late spring and summer, when the variegated stink of the city clung to us, we escaped through the city gates as quickly as we could. "We" at that time were five or six in number: myself, Astynath, my cousin, Amenon, Agarath,

Phodan, and occasionally, Abdas. Finding ourselves at liberty, we ran like wild horses, although probably with less purpose. The feeling of being on our own, unimpeded by work or adult supervision, was an intense pleasure which excited us and compelled us to dart about, lest by standing still the sensation consume us. Some 500 paces from the city walls there was a grove of wild, uncultivated olive trees. Unpruned, these trees could grow fairly tall, maybe twenty-five cubits, and developed a wide girth, making them appropriate silent companions for our games. We would run around and around these trees, climb up some of them, climb back down, climb back up again, and so on, all the while laughing like madmen.

Once enough of our initial energy had dissipated so we could actually think about doing something, we settled into games of our own devising. Naturally, many of these games involved competition. There was a hillock not far from the grove, and one game we played frequently involved defending the top of this mound. The hillock was richer in vegetation than most, with grasses and wildflowers, especially hyssop and white mustard, so when rolling down the slope, there was little danger of cutting ourselves on stony ground.

The game had several different variations, with occasionally one boy being called upon to defend against all others, but more often there were two defenders on top and three or four attackers. Sometimes sticks could be used as weapons, but typically our hands and feet served as shields and swords. And then there were times when the defenders of the mound were blindfolded so they would not know the direction or the exact moment of the attack—although the giggling of Amenon often gave him away.

I was bigger than the others so if one of us was selected to be the sole defender, that honor usually fell to me. I protested when this happened, but secretly I was pleased. It gave me an opportunity to test my strength and, over time, to see how it was increasing. It was impossible to defend the hill forever against four, let alone five, others. The pulls, pushes, and punches would inevitably force me to the ground, and then, after an interval of wrestling, I would be shoved down the hill. But the time during which I was able to remain on top gradually lengthened.

Although being sole defender was a welcome challenge, it was wearying. So as the afternoon wore on, I would become an attacker or, if I resumed the defender role, I would insist on having allies. When this happened, oftentimes some of the others would conspire and would vote Phodan to be my co-defender. Phodan, although older than the rest of us, was physically delicate and slight. His weak arms did not add much power to our defense. These, of course, were the reasons he was selected, and these reasons, although unstated, were known to all of us, including Phodan. But although Phodan did not supply muscle, he was tenacious and spirited. If all he could do was block an assault from the side by interposing his body between me and the attacker, he would do so. I admired him for this, and our frequent positioning as allies caused a bond to form between us.

Phodan was also smart. His superior intelligence was shown in a number of different ways. First, he could read and write. His father was a scribe who worked for one of the lords, which explains how he learned this skill. He often offered to teach me how to write a few words, but with the impatience and imprudence typical of youth, I usually declined. Over time, I did learn the signs for maybe twenty or thirty words, my name and the names of my sisters and the words for mother, father, water, bread, cheese, and iron, and other such things, but that was about it. One time he did press me, saying I should try to learn a few more words to which I responded, "Shit."

"Don't be so dismissive. I think it's a good thing to learn to write …"

"Yes, I want to learn a new word."

"But you said …"

"Shit. I want to learn the word for shit."

We both laughed, and I greatly expanded my capacity for writing by learning how to write the word for excrement.

Phodan also displayed his mental power in board games. There were various versions of mancala that we children played, but Phodan preferred a demanding version of the game, called Siege, that even adults found difficult. The object was to place one's pieces in a way that prevented the other player from being able to make a move. He taught me the game and I became fascinated with it. He beat me soundly almost every time we played, especially at the beginning, but this lack of success only redoubled my determination to improve my skill in the game. We played whenever both of us had a break from our daily work. That summer when he taught me how to play, we would rendezvous at midday, when less obsessed city inhabitants were resting, at the portico near the temple. Here in the shade we would spend an hour or so gaming, moving the black and white pebbles across the board, with Phodan making his moves quickly and me plodding along. On the rare occasions when I would beat him, I think he may have become inattentive due to the long time he had to wait for me to move. But Phodan never gave excuses for his losses, nor did he boast of his frequent triumphs. He would simply ask me to play again the next day or whenever I might have some free time. He was, I guess, my closest friend.

But our relationship changed the following year. As the spring festival for Qetesh approached, Phodan told me he would not be able to see me for some time. Naturally, I asked why. He seemed embarrassed. He muttered something about business matters. I was curious, but since he evidently did not want to talk about it, I did not question him further.

At the spring festival, I learned the reason for his absence. The five priests for the city were arrayed on the temple steps to receive and bless the offerings and to perform the ritual sacrifices. They were attended by two acolytes. One of the acolytes was Phodan. Yes, it was him. His head was shaved so initially I did not recognize him, but it was definitely him.

I was surprised, although I probably should not have been. The priests, along with the scribes and a few merchants and nobles, were, with rare exceptions, the only literate people in the city. Phodan had clearly demonstrated his ability in this area so this was not an unsuitable vocation for him … but still.

Priests are respected. They are intermediaries between us and the divine. But perhaps because of this, they are considered … well, different. Set apart. Not quite one of us. Also, there are some who feel resentment toward the priests, although this resentment is not expressed except in whispered asides and mumbled grumbling. Put simply, the priests live off the toil of others. (Dagon, I report; I do not complain!) The haunches and other fine cuts of meat that are piled high on the offering tables do not just disappear nor are they allowed to rot. After the gods have their fill, the priests remove the offerings for their own use. They consume more meat than anyone other than the king, yet they labor not to produce this food. Even with respect to ordinary fare such as bread and cheese, the priests are not involved in production. A temple stable is managed for them and bread is supplied from the king's ovens.

Moreover, except for communal processions and temple rites, the priests' only significant interaction with the mass of people is to provide care to the seriously ill or injured. Most of the priests are trained in the healing arts. One might think that this would inspire gratitude, and it has in some, but perhaps because their success in healing is out of proportion to the offerings expected, appreciation of their work as healers is not widespread. This distance, this remove from the daily routines of others makes them seem remote.

In any case, on this day when Phodan first appeared as an acolyte, my companions and I gathered at the west gate after the end of the ceremonies in preparation for our running launch into the countryside. When we had all arrived except for Phodan, Astynath spoke up.

"Good. We're all here. Let's go."

"Shouldn't we wait for Phodan?" I asked.

"Phodan? You saw him. He's not coming."

"I don't know. Maybe you're right. I think we should wait for him just the same."

"He's too good for us now. That precious thing. Priests don't dirty their hands. Don't you know that, lunkhead?"

"He's not a priest yet. I don't know what the rules are for acolytes, nor do you."

"I don't want him anyway. He's slow and a poor fighter."

"He gives the best he can."

"Oh, I see, Goliath has a boyfriend," Astynath said mockingly, as he began a mincing walk. "Kissy-kissy."

I shoved him roughly to the ground. At the time, I had scant understanding of sexual relations, but I knew that men were not supposed to be lovers.

Agarath grabbed my arm. "Hey, hey. Take it easy. Let's wait a few more moments, and then we'll go. Agreed?"

I nodded.

We used two tipsy men sitting outside their house to measure the time. We agreed to depart as soon as they finished their cups. They finished. Phodan did not appear.

Once in the fields, we followed our usual routine and we quickly forgot the momentary unpleasantness by the gate. On the hilltop, we played as roughly as usual, but without any animosity. The afternoon was waning and we were all resting on the mound when I noticed a figure approaching in the distance.

"Who's that?" I wondered aloud.

It was Phodan.

When he was perhaps thirty paces away, he yelled out a greeting. I was the only one who returned it.

He was out of breath as he came up the hill.

"Why are you here?" Astynath asked. "We're getting ready to leave."

"Sorry, I thought I could still catch you here." Phodan looked around. "There's still some daylight left. Why don't we have a few more rounds?"

"No, not with you."

"But why . . ."

"We said *no.*"

Then the insults began. Like all boys, we often engaged in banter. In fact, I was dubbed "the carob," because of my dark skin. When Astynath was in an especially nasty mood, which was not uncommon, he would even call me "the Nubian." I sloughed these off with a grunt or playful shove and returned the favor, calling Astynath "the dwarf"—he was short and compact— Agarath "toothy"—an ironic nickname bestowed precisely because of the prominent gaps in his smile—and so forth.

But this afternoon the jesting turned into jeering and the ribbing became ridicule. The taunts became as cruel and sharp as a dagger.

"Take your bald head back where it came from. Grab hold of your priests' legs if you want to wrestle. That's all you're good for."

"Baldy, baldy. Damn, look at that egg. An eagle must have had twins!"

"Here," Agarath said, as he grabbed some dirt and spat on it. "Let me draw a line down the middle of your skull so you'll look just like the ass you are."

Phodan pushed Agarath away, but then Amenon grabbed Phodan's arm and spun him around. "Oh, look, you're doing a dance. Dance, woman, dance."

"Dance like the fag you are," Astynath echoed, with undisguised malice.

This merciless mockery continued for another moment or two. I said nothing. *I said nothing.* I did not join in with the others, but I did nothing to stop them either. Like a tongue-tied fool, I simply stood to one side as my best friend was being humiliated.

Verbally assailed on all sides, Phodan eventually turned and walked away, his shoulders slumped, with yet more taunts trailing behind him. He turned to look at me before he was too far away. Our eyes met. His look was not one of anger or even reproach, but rather revealed a bottomless disappointment. I broke off our gaze before he did.

Why had I done nothing? I have asked myself that many times. One moment's decision or indecision can yield years of regret. It wasn't fear. I could have knocked Astynath's and Agarath's heads together and that would have been the end of that. Was I too dull and slow to react?

The thing is I don't have an answer, and perhaps that's what troubles me most. It wasn't like I betrayed Phodan for a reason; I betrayed him for no reason.

⊨╬╪⊨

10

Altara and I were both silent for a while after I finished telling her about Phodan. Then she said, "This event seems to trouble you still. Have you not tried to reconcile with your friend?"

"Former friend. No, the thing is I was too ashamed to try to speak with him for years, and then maybe about three or four years later, he moved to Ekron."

"So, you lost the possibility of becoming a scribe because you no longer had someone to teach you how to write?"

"Not exactly," I said to Altara. "I'm not even sure that I had thought about becoming a scribe at this time. It's a bit more complicated."

⊨╬╪⊨

11

With my friendship broken, I threw myself into work, and there was plenty of it. We even acquired a new and unexpected set of customers.

Peace continued to prevail. It now had been over four years since any conflict with the Hebrews. This lull in hostilities may have been the principal cause for a change in policy that for some appeared ill-advised. We began to sell iron implements to the Hebrews.

As I learned later, there had always been trade and other contact between our two peoples. This was especially true for the villages that straddled the borderlands between us and the Hebrews. Here, except for time of conflict, the exchange of goods was frequent. Various goods were traded in the villages, with the type of goods being dependent principally on who had a surplus of what at the time: wool, bread, cheese, olive oil, and wine being the usual items of exchange. Occasionally, a luxury item was offered for trade, such as jewelry or an embroidered robe—more likely than not the legacy of someone's plundering.

There was less frequent trade with our five major cities—Gath, Gaza, Ashkelon, Ekron, and Ashdod. A trading expedition to a city was a major effort requiring a significant number of goods to be traded to be profitable, which, in turn, necessitated a significant investment in mules and men. Such expeditions were undertaken only in time of a solemn truce between our peoples, which the kings of our five cities all pledged to respect. Nonetheless, Gath, being the Palestim city closest to the Hebrews, engaged in a not insignificant amount of commerce with them. The two items we most often acquired from the Hebrews were their wine and wood. The Hebrews, whose land was hillier than the coastal plain on which we lived, produced good varieties of wine from the stony soil found in those hills. They also had access to timber, especially in the north of their country. Our forges required charcoal, and the production of charcoal consumed a prodigious amount of wood. This, combined with a less plentiful supply of forested land to begin with, resulted in much of our land being stripped of trees. Oak trees, our preferred source of wood for charcoal, were especially scarce.

Possibly it was the Hebrews' realization how important their wood was for our iron production that prompted them to negotiate for the right to acquire iron tools: hammers, chisels, scythes, plowshares, and the like. Whatever the background, our king granted them a license to obtain these goods.

This was to be a highly regulated exchange. On the three or four occasions when our bloomery was the site for the trade, the Hebrews arrived under armed escort. Furthermore, my father and uncle did not engage in any bartering. The terms for the trade were already established by the authorities, and, not unexpectedly, the authorities took possession of all the silver, cloth, and wine brought by the Hebrews. We were allocated the wood along with some copper pieces worth maybe a few shekels.

I still remember the first occasion when this exchange took place. My uncle was seething at the very idea of engaging in commerce with the Hebrews, and he spent the better part of the morning pacing and cursing.

"Fucking Hebes! I can't believe we have to give over to them the product of our labors. It sickens me to think of it."

"The king deems it best," my father responded placidly. "And we both know we could use the wood."

"Wood to make charcoal to make iron to make tools which we then give to the Hebes. What part of that makes any sense to you?"

A shrug served as my father's initial answer. A few moments later he added, "Well, we're not giving them our best pieces. I think they'll find some of those scythe blades pretty soft."

"What ... when they try to sink them into some of our soldiers?"

It was one of our soldiers, a junior commander to be precise, with a squad of four, who called out to us to signal the approach of the Hebrew merchants. My father and uncle both instinctively straightened. The commander entered our outer room, where we were gathered, along with the tools to be exchanged, which were laid out on top of or propped against a table. The commander inspected the tools quickly, to ensure they were no more nor no less than had been authorized, glanced at us, gave us a nod, and then ordered one of his men to bring two of the merchants into the room, along with one of Gath's merchants, who would serve as an interpreter.

I'm not sure what I expected— Giants? Midgets? Men with horns?— but what struck me most was just the ordinariness of these two men. They looked just like us, although their beards were heavier and fuller than those worn by most of our men. Also, they wore long shifts instead of standard tunics, a garment I later learned was favored by their merchants to emphasize the fact that they did not have to get on their knees to do any work. The first real sign that they were foreigners was when they spoke. Their tongue was incomprehensible to me. I giggled quietly as they spoke. Some of their sounds were guttural, as if they had trouble clearing their throat.

The dialogue began as soon as the blindfolds were removed from the two Hebrew merchants. As they had been taken into the city, past our defensive walls, their eyes had been covered. Unveiled, their eyes blinked for a moment. The older merchant appeared tired, some of the glow gone from his eyes and the flesh of his face hanging heavy.

The interpreter, on the other hand, was alert to the point of being on edge. His eyes darted quickly from the Hebrews to the commander to my uncle and father and back again.

"They said they come in peace and they are grateful for this opportunity to engage in trade that will bring benefit to everyone."

"Go tell them to go fuck themselves," my uncle said.

The interpreter looked over to the commander who shook his head. The interpreter then said something to Hebrews that, based on the faint smiles that came to the merchants' faces, was not an accurate translation of my uncle's statement.

There followed some discussion of the terms of the trade, confirming the items to be exchanged. The merchants then walked over to the table where the tools were displayed.

More guttural sounds. The interpreter said, "They're going to inspect the tools and in doing so wish to lift them up and hold them."

"Fine," the commander said.

They went down the line of tools, with the younger one lifting the tools, holding them up so both merchants could look at them. Several whispered conversations between them.

"What are they saying?" my father asked.

The interpreter seemed unsure. "They ... They're just talking about the tools."

One of the hammers seemed to occupy their attention for more than a moment. They turned it over this way and that, and the older merchant gestured to something on the underside of the hammer's head.

Sounds were directed to the interpreter.

"They want to take this hammer outside so they can look at it in a better light."

"What's the problem?" my father asked.

"They think there may be a crack," the interpreter said with some hesitation.

My uncle's face reddened, and I noticed his hands trembling. He seemed to be on the point of saying something when my father put a firm hand on his shoulder and applied some pressure.

The commander turned to my father and uncle and said flatly, "I don't see a problem with that. It's what anyone would do." The commander then turned to the interpreter, "We're going to the doorway and no further. There's sufficient light there for them to inspect the hammer. And tell them they are to concentrate on the hammer. I don't want them looking around."

The commander led the way to the doorway followed by the merchants and interpreter, with my father and uncle trailing behind. I was curious so I also moved toward the entrance. Just outside, the commander turned around and raised his hands to indicate that the merchants were not to go any further. They then looked at the hammer in the light, again turning it this way and that to get a better view of what they thought was some defect. They then handed the hammer to the interpreter and said something to him.

"They definitely think there's a crack … here," the interpreter pointed and handed the hammer to my father.

My father walked past the merchants into the sunlight. He held the hammer up and ran his finger across the underside. He then stepped back to the merchants, held out the hammer to them and said forcefully, "That's a scratch, not a crack."

Following the translation, the merchants talked and then said something to the interpreter.

"They do not wish to dispute. They say they respect the smith but there's a difference of opinion. They'll take the hammer but they will hold back one bundle of wood."

My uncle turned back inside, seeming to sway as his emotion made him unsteady. He looked at me and said, "I knew these bastards would try to cheat us in some way."

My father looked at the commander. "The city sets the price, but if I give up my hammer, I want to receive full value for it. It's not defective."

"I agree. I don't have the authority to bargain in this manner anyway. If they decide not to take some pieces, then they can withhold some wood. But they can't take the pieces and then refuse to pay." The commander then told the interpreter, "Tell them that."

This was explained to the merchants. They spent a few moments talking quietly to each other. The older one then gave a long message to the interpreter to relay.

"They will take the hammer and pay as agreed. They want to establish good relations and hope for the opportunity to trade in the future. 'May the hammer prove as strong as the bonds of peace that should be forged between our peoples,' is what he said. They also ask for the blessings of their gods upon us."

"Fine, then, let's get on with it."

The various tools were tied together in appropriate groupings and wrapped in cloth. The merchants produced their sacks, the tools were placed inside, and the exchange was made. The trade over, the merchants departed.

That evening my mother had a splendid meal for us: a lentil stew with more than a few pieces of pork, large portions of bread, and yogurt with raisins. I was surprised. I knew today was a grain grinding day. On grain grinding days, my mother, sisters, aunt, and cousins would together spend hours working the heavy, basalt grinding stones, laboriously eliciting from the kernels flour for our bread. This process was both tedious and tiring, and combined with the other tasks my mother carried out, she was usually too exhausted to do much cooking on such days. Grain grinding days meant plenty of fresh bread for the evening meal, but little else.

My older sister, Avram, detected my puzzlement without me saying a word and decided to clarify matters for me. "One of the nobles gave us fresh pork today. I took over mother's load of grain so she could cook." She uttered this as if to rebuke me, simultaneously holding out for my inspection her rough, red, nicked hands. "So, don't take all the stew for yourself."

"We have this meat because it's a gift from the king and lords, in gratitude for the iron we produced for trade today," my father said matter-of-factly. "Goliath helped us make that iron. Show some respect for your brother." He then gave her a hug to indicate he wasn't cross with her. "We will share this meal like all other meals. All have contributed to it."

A good meal puts one in a good mood. With our bellies full, we stayed up longer than usual, even though we were all tired. My parents joined me and my sisters on the mats in our bedroom—separated by a curtain from their room—and we sang and told stories for some time. Dedra, my younger sister, loved to hear the story of the fox and the grapes, even though she had heard it many times before. Avram preferred stories about Hishara.

As I listened, I also thought about the events of the day. I was anxious while the exchange was taking place, but as I reflected on it, I became curious about some aspects of the trade, in particular, the role of the interpreter. Perhaps because it was the first time I'd heard people speaking in a foreign tongue.

After my mother had finished another story, and there were a few moments of contented quiet, I ventured a question.

"Papa, how is it that our merchant was able to understand what the Hebrews were saying?"

My father raised his eyebrows, thought for a moment, and said, "He is a merchant. He has dealt with the Hebrews before, so he knows how they speak."

"But then the first time he met them … how were they able to understand each other?"

A pause. "I don't know … maybe he had a fellow merchant who was already acquainted with the language who helped him to understand."

I let this sink in for a moment; I wasn't entirely satisfied with the answer. "But then who helped the first merchant to understand?"

My father drew himself up into a sitting position. "Look, we all learn to speak, right? And we do that by seeing how other people use words. So, these merchants … they spend time doing their trades, and they see how the Hebrews use their words. You know, someone will point to something, maybe some wine, and they'll say 'yaeen' or whatever word it is that the Hebrews use for wine. Then the merchants will know that's the word that the Hebrews use for wine. And they learn other words that way. Just like you kids did when you learned to speak. Your mother and I would point things out and repeat the words for them."

I considered this for a moment. It seemed like a good explanation. But I wasn't sure it was a complete explanation.

"Papa, do you remember when the Hebrews left, the interpreter said that they said they wanted their gods to bless us."

"Yes, I remember that."

"So how did our merchant understand they were talking about their gods? Is he acquainted with their gods?"

My father looked at me intently for a moment, but not with any anger. He appeared interested in the question.

"He … he is able to understand the names they use because … because he could hear them use these names, I guess, when he visits their cities, maybe seeing their sacrifices. Or perhaps they talked to him about their gods."

"So, the interpreter can understand them because they just have different names for the gods? Like they use different words for iron or wine?"

"Stop pestering your father with so many questions," my mother interrupted. "You can ask our priests."

Dedra kicked me under the mantle that was covering us both. "You ask silly questions."

"No, no, it's alright," my father said. "Son, it's fine to ask questions, but some questions are not easy to answer. Look …" My father seemed to struggle to find the right words. "It's not just that the Hebrews use different names. They believe different things. We've talked about this before. They don't respect our gods."

"But why is it not bad to trade with them?"

"Our king has made this decision. He would not do this unless the priests at the temple approved."

Silence. Then my father continued, "Anyway, I'm really tired now. It's time for all of us to go to sleep."

I had trouble sleeping that night. I was still curious about how translation worked. Later, I discovered it's not too difficult to pick up at least some words used by people who speak different tongues. What one learned depended mostly on one's activities and type of contact—which explains why many of the Hebrew words I eventually learned were curses and insults. And, of course, I also learned to ask where the silver was hidden. But that was in the future. As I lay awake that evening, it still seemed mysterious to me.

Because I was awake for a while, I could make out some of my parents' murmurings behind their curtain.

"Goliath is smart, maybe too smart to be working as a smith."

"But you need him. And what else would he do?"

"Astynath will be old enough soon to work in the bloomery."

"Do you want him?"

My father said something here, but I could not make out what he said. But I did hear what followed.

"He might learn to read and write. He could be a scribe. He has command of some words already."

"It's too late for that. And how would we pay for the instruction?"

"I don't know … Perhaps if he were willing to serve as an acolyte."

My parents' voices trailed off at this point, or maybe I didn't want to hear any more. I was repulsed by the thought of having my head shaved and serving as an assistant to the priests. And would I have to work with Phodan, possibly having him as my tutor? If I still remembered and was feeling remorseful for my betrayal of him, I'm sure he had not forgotten either. It's not that I feared him really, but …

Interesting how when we wrong someone, we don't want to be reminded of it.

And then there were the priests themselves. I liked the familiarity of the bloomery. I knew my father and uncle. The priests? They were of us and yet not of us. They seemed like strangers to me.

But then the thought of penetrating the mystery of writing did intrigue me. I was envious of the skill that Phodan had—perhaps even resented it? It gave him power, perhaps a power greater than the strength conferred by muscles. The more I thought about it, the more I began to think I'd like to have that power as well. I had already learned to write a few words. Sure, not many, but I hadn't really tried. I could memorize the rest of the signs, no? After all, I had memorized the various seals used by the different nobles, officials, and merchants who patronized the bloomery. I knew the lord who lived near the king had a galloping horse with a wind-whipped mane on his seal whereas Commander Bellon had a horse with a bridle. If I could recognize these marks, could deciphering writing be much more difficult?

These conflicting thoughts dueled in my head until sleep overcame me.

But the possibility of my becoming a scribe was not foreclosed by my parents' doubts or my own ambivalence, but by other circumstances.

12

Some months after my parents' nighttime discussion of my future, an alarm went through the city. It was in the evening, after my father and I had returned home but before we had started our supper. The crier for our neighborhood went through the streets yelling for the men to assemble, while banging together a couple of pieces of metal to get their attention.

My father started to go out the door, turned to look at me, and then motioned for me to go with him.

There was an open area about 100 paces from our house where the men gathered. When the crier was satisfied that he had a sufficient crowd, he gave us the news.

"Ayun has been attacked by brigands. The king is sending a detachment there to destroy the enemy. All able-bodied men are to report to their assigned positions."

At the time, I only half understood the significance of this news and of the king's orders. I realized this meant that a number of our soldiers would be going to Ayun and my father would have to take his position on the wall near the east gate—but little else. Later I learned the reasoning behind some of these actions.

Ayun was a settlement about two to three hours walk to the northwest. There were a number of such settlements around Gath, just as there were a number of such settlements around other Palestim cities. The obvious disadvantage to living in such settlements was vulnerability to attack. Typically, they had little in the way of defenses, perhaps a low wall or a ditch. The advantage was availability of land to cultivate and, therefore, access to a more reliable supply of food than a city dweller might have. Not that much thought was given to these advantages and disadvantages. People usually lived and died where they were born.

Like the other four Palestim cities, Gath had some more or less full-time soldiers. The king supported twenty-four soldiers; the nobles another twelve; and then each of our four neighborhoods was responsible for supporting twelve soldiers. These were foot soldiers. The nobles and the king had horses; the king's household also had a few chariots.

If an outlying settlement was attacked, and the attackers appeared to be brigands or some other small force, then a detachment would be sent in the hope of saving some of the villagers—often a vain hope—or of encountering the enemy and killing them.

On this occasion, about half of our standing force left the city, along with five or six nobles on horseback. With much of our soldiery gone, it was left to the men of the city to mount the walls or take up other defensive positions. This was a prudent precaution, but the reality was that brigands or other irregular forces rarely attacked the city. Such an attack would be futile give the protection provided by our walls.

Anyway, after the meeting broke up, my father returned with me to the house. We went up the stairs to the second level where our sleeping quarters were. He met my mother on the stairs. She was visibly excited, and she and my father exchanged words hurriedly. I was excited myself so I did not pay close attention to their conversation, but I did hear my mother say, "He's too young."

My father walked on into their bedroom. I stayed on the stairs with my mother. We did not talk. Her head was tilted to one side and her face wore an expression of sorrow and concern. She was wringing her hands.

My father emerged a moment later with a bronze and leather shield, a bronze helmet on his head, and an iron sword that he was in the process of buckling on. He had forged the sword himself, so I'm sure he had trust in it.

"Goliath, come here."

I hastened up the stairs.

"I want you to come with me this evening. There's no need to be frightened ..."

"I'm *not* frightened."

"No, of course not. But I was going to say that we're safe inside the walls of our city. Our soldiers will probably kill these bandits and any way I don't think these bandits will be attacking Gath. This will, though, be a good experience for you. You're fifteen. About time you learned to take part in our city's defense. Now, I'm going to give you a sword. Keep it sheathed. I don't want you taking it out and swinging it around— you'd probably hurt someone, most likely yourself. Understand?"

"Yes, papa."

"Fine, then, I'll get your sword." He laid the shield against the wall, returned to the bedroom, and came back with another sword in a leather sheath. He strapped it on me, across my lower back.

"Let's go. Let me know if you have trouble walking with that."

"I won't have any trouble." Naturally, as soon as I said this I almost stumbled down the stairs. The sword wasn't that heavy, but I was not accustomed to it and it was heavy enough to throw my balance off. Fortunately, I reached the bottom of the stairs without impaling myself.

We walked briskly to the city walls.

The wall near the east gate was a casemate wall. There was a storehouse built into the inner wall which we walked through. Among other items in the storehouse were some javelins. My father picked up one. As we exited the storehouse, to our right was the stairway that took us to the walkway behind the parapet. We ascended.

There were two other men on this section of the parapet. My father and they exchanged wordless greetings. My father offered no explanation for my presence and none was requested. It was understood I was learning about my duties as a citizen.

The role of my father and the other two citizen-defenders was to help keep a watch out for any movement and, if necessary, to repel any attack. In truth, it was unlikely they would be the first to spot anything untoward, as there were guard towers on each side of the gate and the towers were about six cubits higher than the parapet. As for anyone scaling the walls, this would not be possible without a ladder or a rope fastened to the parapet, which were both unlikely. The walls were twelve cubits high. We were safe.

We settled in. Along with my father, I let my eyes sweep the area in front of our walls, back and forth. We would do this for a couple of moments, stop, step back, give our eyes an instant's rest, and then resume our watchful stance again. The sky grew dark as evening gave way to night, but there was a gibbous moon out and few clouds, so visibility wasn't bad.

Maybe an hour passed. Maybe more.

Then we heard the horses. Two, three—no, four horses. They seemed to be going past our walls, heading further east away from the city, but then they made a sudden turn, toward our section of the wall.

A guard in the tower closest to us called out, demanding that they identify themselves. But before a reply came, the guard yelled, "Brigands!"

The horses' hooves announced they had arrived beneath us. My father told me to duck, and as soon as he uttered this instruction, an object came flying over the parapet. It landed on my left shoulder and rolled away. It was a human head. It had been atop the neck of one of our soldiers. The face—or what remained of it—had been mutilated. The eyes and nose were gone.

"Fucking pigs," my father yelled. He grabbed his javelin and leaned over the parapet to hurl it at whatever target he could find, but before the javelin left his hand an arrow plowed through his head, entering beneath his chin. The force of the arrow spun him around so that he faced me—but his face was now no more than a grotesque mask. He fell forward onto me and I might have been pushed back off the parapet had not one of the other men grabbed him from behind at the same time. As it was, my open mouth brushed against his open wounds and, gasping, I swallowed his blood. I could not cry out as my mouth was covered, so nothing prevented me from hearing the laughter of the brigand as he galloped away. The brigands had no intent of attacking the city. The shot had been taken for amusement only, and it had fulfilled its purpose.

⚔

13

"So ended my childhood," I said, looking at Altara. Her eyes had changed. Some of the brightness had gone; they were clouded and moist. She used the knuckle of her forefinger to brush away a tear. "Oh, this time I've surely done it. I have upset you."

"No … well, yes. It's sad. Of course, I never had a father. But somehow I think having a father and losing him may be worse… I don't know."

"I don't know either," I murmured. For some reason I became teary-eyed myself.

"Oh, now it's your turn. Maybe I should not have asked you to tell me about yourself. My mistake. Sorry."

"No, no, it's fine. I … I just haven't thought about these things for some time."

"Well, we can't end the evening this way. Come, come here." She threw off her robe. "Come be with me. Put your head on my lap so we both can feel better."

I kissed her thigh one, two, three times, and placed my head where it would bring comfort to her and her warmth would bring solace to me, as she stroked my hair with her fingers.

PART III

SCHOOLED

1

When they removed my blindfold, I found myself in a room that was surprisingly well-lit. After having been led through a maze of hallways, I expected to be in the bowels of the temple, in some concealed, dark corner where mysterious things unknown to or beyond the ken of the general population took place. No. It was just a room with a table, a few chairs, and several mats. The chair behind the table had carved on its back images of swans and the rising sun. It had a red cushion. The other two chairs were simple four-legged stools. Effigies of several gods were placed along one wall. The only distinction among them being that the effigy of Dagon was on a raised platform.

I looked at the ceiling. The light was coming from two openings that were placed at a slant. Apparently, there was a structure on the roof that caused one end of the openings to be raised. I was wondering how the priests kept the rain out, when he entered the room and spoke.

"Interesting, isn't it? This room is surrounded by other rooms or hallways on all sides so the only way to get light from the sun in here is to have holes in the roof. In case you're wondering why the floor is not damp beneath the openings, there are bronze coverings that fit tightly over the openings when it rains, and because they are slanted, the water doesn't pool on top, but rather flows away into gutters."

It had been more than a decade since I had spoken to Phodan and, although I had seen him from a distance on a few occasions, this was as close as I had been to him since our last, unpleasant encounter in childhood.

"Ingenious, but perhaps I should expect no less of the priests."

We looked at each other for a long moment. A faint smile curled the ends of his lips, but his overall look was placid. He betrayed no emotion. He signaled for me to have a seat.

"If you don't mind, I'll make use of a mat rather than the stool. That might be uncomfortable."

"I understand."

I pulled up a mat while he sat down in the ornate chair behind the table.

I was less anxious than I thought I might be in Phodan's presence. It had been a couple of days since I was informed that Phodan would be the priest making a recommendation in my case, so my initial dismay and alarm had now diminished. Moreover, a sense of resignation had been growing within me over the last few days. The fact was I had killed someone. No disputing that. Under the circumstances, I would do it again. If the authorities did not consider my action justified, so be it. And if Phodan were tempted to use his position to avenge a childhood insult … well, the gods would be my final judges.

"A scribe will be joining us in a few minutes."

I didn't make a verbal response, but my face must have indicated I was curious why a scribe would be present.

"I'm going to ask you a number of questions," Phodan explained. "I already know what you did and why we are both here, although, of course, I do want to hear what you have to say about your actions. But this is a difficult case, which is why the king has asked me to consult with him." Here he flashed a smile. "So, I want to consider not just your immediate past actions, but all other relevant circumstances, such as your experiences as a soldier, your relations with your family, and so forth. It's fair to say the killing is not something you're unaccustomed to, correct?"

"Does that make me more or less guilty in your eyes?"

"It's a factor, a factor whose significance depends on my obtaining as complete a picture as I can of your history. We knew each other as children, obviously," here, another quick smile, "but since we parted ways I have not kept up with you. This is especially true after I moved to Ekron. Yes, I've heard of your exploits, but I don't know the person behind those exploits. You need to tell me about that person."

The scribe entered, a young man roughly my age, maybe around twenty. He sat on a mat also. He had with him three reed pens, a small basin for his ink, and several sheets of papyrus.

"Where do you want me to begin?" I asked Phodan.

"Why don't you start after your father's death, which is when I believe you joined the army."

⚊⚔⚊

2

"Nice distance, shithead, but the objective is to hit the enemy with the point of the javelin, not the shaft, you fucking idiot!"

The insult stung, and my face must have betrayed my emotion, because the sub-officer now lit into me.

"Oh, little big boy feeling sad? Am I making you cry? By the gods, I'm supposed to count on the likes of you in battle? Fuck. Maybe I should get your sister out here. She'd do a better job—maybe even be more of a man than you." With this he laughed and jabbed me in the chest with his right hand. "Now go get that fucking javelin and try again. And if that shaft is cracked, I'm going to peel your skin off to bind it."

Javelin throwing practice. It's more difficult to throw a spear so that it hits its target true than one might imagine, and this is especially the case with the javelin, the long, heavy spear we used as a long-distance missile in combat.

One critical element in proper spear throwing is finding the balance point of the spear—the point where one can hold the spear without it wiggling or waving about. Because of the weight of the spearhead, the balance point is not halfway down the shaft. In fact, often it is somewhere toward the middle between the halfway point and the end of the shaft. But spearheads are not entirely uniform in their shape and weight, so there is some difference in the location of the balance point among different spears.

Given sufficient time, anyone can locate the balance point, but in the heat of battle soldiers don't have the luxury of time to search for the balance point. One objective of our training was to provide us the skill that would enable us to know where to grasp the javelin immediately upon picking one up.

Of course, knowing where to grasp the javelin was one thing; knowing how to throw it once you had it in your hand was another. With the hand on the balance point, one was supposed to bring the javelin up to one's ear, holding it level, so that it neither pointed up nor toward the ground. This allowed one's vision to become the "eyes of the spearhead," as the sub-officer liked to say.

With one's eyes on the target, one would step forward with the left foot, creating about a shoulder-length distance between the feet. Both knees should be bent slightly. At this point, if possible, one could run a few steps to gain momentum and put more velocity into the javelin. However, we also had to learn to throw from a stationary position, as our circumstances might require that. Whether throwing on the run or throwing while standing still, we were told to bring the javelin back behind our ear, with the spearhead now pointed slightly upwards. We were then to bring the javelin forward in a straight line until it was slightly above our shoulder. This was the release point, the point at which we should hurl the javelin, twisting our hips slightly as we let it go. If all went well, the javelin would fly in the intended direction and strike the intended target with the tip of the spear.

It did not always go well, certainly not at first.

Repetition, repetition, repetition. And then again. We would continue with the same exercise, day after day, week after week, until the javelin became an extension of us, until we no longer had to think about what to do before grabbing the javelin and throwing it any more than we had to think before raising our arms or lifting our fingers. The javelin became as natural a part of our bodies as our limbs—but with the advantage that this particular limb could strike a foe at a great distance.

As our sub-officer liked to remind us, "Any jackass can pick up a spear and try to throw it, and perhaps if he's lucky enough, he'll actually hit something. But nine times out of ten, that spear will miss, hit the target shaft first, or drop on the asshole's foot. Only a true soldier can master the spear—can make the spear do his will, reliably."

As with the javelin, so too with the thrusting spear, the bow and arrow, and the various swords, axes, and daggers with which a soldier might be armed. We had repetitive exercises in the use of all of them. No one soldier was expected to carry all the different types of weapons into battle. Which weapons a particular soldier would carry into combat was a function both of the soldier's proficiency with that type of weapon and the need of the army for soldiers with that type of weapon. But, in part because the needs of the moment could vary, we were trained in all the various types of implements and devices that could deliver death to our enemies.

I can't say I was the quickest learner, but neither was I the slowest. And once I became comfortable with a weapon, given my size, I could wield it with more force than almost anyone else. I was still several months shy of sixteen, but I was now as tall as any mature adult, and taller than most. I was a finger over four cubits in height.

It was good that I felt comfortable with the tools of my new trade because—at that time—I had decided that being a soldier was my destiny. This was a destiny that in part had been chosen for me and in part I had chosen for myself—although my choice may itself have been the result of decisions of others. In any event, it's what happened.

After my father's death, there were a couple of issues that needed to be addressed promptly. First, who was going to continue to work in the bloomery alongside my uncle? Me? Another adult who might have some basic skills and could be trained? This was a question not just for my relatives but also for the city, as the city had an interest in determining who would be producing iron. Second, how were my mother and my sisters to be supported? For that matter, how was I to be supported? In addition to her household duties, my mother had her laundry work, but she did not earn anywhere near enough food through that work to sustain the family. Moreover, unlike some households, we kept but a few animals in our ground floor stable: a couple of goats, one sheep, and an ass. With what my father earned through the bloomery, we hadn't needed more. I considered this modest number of livestock fortunate while my father was alive. It meant less for me by way of mucking duties and our house lacked the pervasive stink of animal dung that was an invisible resident in some houses. Now, however, because of our animals' paltry production of milk and wool, we needed to think about where we would find the resources to maintain ourselves.

Of course, I could have stayed on working in the bloomery. I had not acquired all my father's skills yet, but with some additional tutoring from my uncle I could've become an acceptable smith. My income would not have matched my father's at first, but this probably would've meant only a couple of lean years for me and my family. With my mother's support, the esteemed position of smith in the city of Gath could have been mine.

But … it was apparent early on that my uncle did not want me in the bloomery. There was no animosity between us, at least none that I was aware of. It's just that he preferred to have his son, Astynath, work with him. Also, my uncle wanted to run the bloomery, to be responsible for all the important decisions himself. Naturally, I would have taken orders from him initially, but once I came into my own, I would have been his partner, just as my father was.

One circumstance worked in my uncle's favor, one against. Astynath wasn't quite old or strong enough to take on full-time the demanding work of the bloomery—leaving aside his lack of skills. This was an obstacle to my uncle's plans. However, my uncle persuaded the city administrators to allow one of Gath's bronze craftsmen to work in the bloomery. The demand for bronze had declined significantly in the past generation. Half the pieces that the craftsmen turned out were jewelry. Casting bronze was a different process than forging iron, but at least the person would have some acquaintance with handling molten metal. Along with my uncle, I was to train this new person—and then, as far as my uncle was concerned, I would become disposable, as Astynath would replace me. Disposable, that is, if I could not claim my father's share of the bloomery. Uncle could not force me out if I were half-owner.

And here was the circumstance that favored my uncle. Upon my father's death, under our laws, his property passed to his adult sons, with his widow enjoying the right to live in his house for the duration of her life. I was the only son, but I was not yet an adult, being some months short of sixteen, which was the age of majority. This meant my mother inherited everything—the house, the livestock, and my father's share of the bloomery—with my sole right being to live in the house until I was an adult. So, my uncle only needed to persuade my mother to sell, if he wanted full control of the bloomery.

She was willing to sell.

My mother wanted to leave the city. To live on a farm, a farm that she would purchase with the proceeds from the sale of her share of the bloomery. The origins of this desire have forever remained unclear to me. If she had this desire before my father's death, I had never heard it expressed.

Was this a reaction to my father's death? A revulsion against living near the site of his murder? Or was this some ambition of hers, some dream that she had silently possessed since childhood? I have no idea. All I know is that I did not want to become a farmer.

"Son, think … You'll be in the countryside. Away from all the smells, the noise of the city. And the heat and dirt of the bloomery."

"Mother, the farm will have its own smells."

"Oh, but our farm, the farm we'll buy, has some lovely citron trees. Their fragrance …"

"It won't hide the odors from the animals, especially the pigs."

"I'm so afraid you'll be hurt in the bloomery. You saw your father's scars. He burned himself badly more than once."

"Papa … Papa … that didn't bother him."

"You'll be happier on the farm. You will be in charge. You know if you stay in the bloomery, your uncle is going to favor your cousin. And I promise you, when you turn sixteen, I will give you half-ownership of the farm."

I gave no verbal answer, merely shrugging my shoulder.

"Son, I want you to think about the future. Where do you want to raise your family? As a landowner, you'll have plenty of girls who want to be your bride. Good, strong girls, who will give you many children."

This argument meant something to her; at fifteen, it meant nothing to me.

"Son, I need you. Please do this for me."

I looked at my mother. There was no doubt she was resolute in her desire for the farm, but her eyes were tired. The flesh around her eyes was tired. Her whole spirit seemed to sag. She was right that she needed me. She and my sisters could not run the farm on their own. She needed me. And for that, in that moment, I hated her.

"No," was all I could manage. But it was enough.

As I was not yet an adult, my mother could have forced the issue. But she understood that this would've been pointless. At sixteen, I could have walked off the farm. My resistance was firm enough that she strongly suspected I would do that. So, there was no farm.

But she got me out of the bloomery.

She sold my father's share for fifteen mina of silver, with three to be paid immediately and three more to be paid in each of the succeeding four years.

In addition, my sisters would receive one mina of silver toward their dowry when they came of age. Finally, my uncle committed to supply my mother with two loaves of bread and one round of cheese twice a week until he or she died. Although this did not make my mother wealthy, it was certainly more than sufficient to sustain her and my sisters.

I'm not sure what my mother envisaged for me. Clearly, she knew I was not going to continue to work for long in the bloomery. I suppose my uncle might have tolerated me, but only as someone completely subservient to him and to my cousin, and my mother knew I would not work for an extended period of time under such conditions. Did she think I was going to help her make bread and weave clothes? Or did she imagine I would hire myself out as a laborer? Or did she care what I did at all, with her only goal being to frustrate my ambitions as I had frustrated hers?

Whatever her expectations, I decided to become a soldier. I approached Commander Bellon after a couple of months of helping to train the bronze craftsman. I was still not sixteen, but Bellon was happy to receive me and no one was going to argue with him that I was underage.

⊱✦⊰

3

Fighting and destroying our enemies, heroic victories, the adulation of our people, the glories of triumph, all the while being part of a cherished community of brothers-in-arms—this is how all boys imagine the soldiering life, no?

There are moments like this, actually. Well, some moments. A few moments. But most of the soldiering life is spent waiting for such moments. In the meantime, there is training, routine tasks, garrison duty, hard labor for the city, gambling, drinking, eating and sleeping, and gambling, drinking, eating and sleeping.

Thinking back, I don't know now what I hated most—the seemingly endless hours of emptiness that was sentry duty or the incredibly filthy and nauseating task of hauling shit and clearing gutters and cesspits.

Yes, we soldiers were the ones the city relied on to take on tasks that no one else would or could do but were necessary for the good of the entire population. There were not many slaves in Gath, and those that were in the city were either female or worked in the households of the nobles and the king. Male slaves who could do heavy labor were mostly confined to the larger farms. The army did have two male slaves, A and B (we didn't give them names), but mostly they did work for the commanders and sub-officers. They did handle our shit and piss. But then we had to handle the shit and piss of the entire city.

City life had its attractions. It also had its problems. Disposing of human waste was one of them. In the winter, some residents, especially poorer ones, added their own waste to the middens they maintained for animal dung and other refuse—more material for the dung cakes they used as fuel. Other times of the year, residents emptied their chamber pots into street gutters. These individual street gutters led to larger gutters which then were supposed to take the waste to a cesspit outside the city walls. This had worked for some time, or so I was told, but from the time of my first memories, the gutters had always seemed clogged and the shit that was dumped beside a house tended to stay there. This was especially true in the summer months when we had little rainfall. To address this problem, King Maoch decreed that residents were to carry their waste to the municipal cesspit when the gutter was clogged or risk a fine. But this decree proved impossible to enforce. As a result, the soldiers were directed to clean the gutters from time-to-time, shoveling the shit into clay kraters, which were then taken to the cesspit where they would be emptied. After a number of uses, the krater itself would be thrown in with the shit.

Worse than cleaning the gutters were the occasions, fortunately few, where we had to remove some waste from the cesspit itself. The waste went to farmers who used it to fertilize. I still don't know whether this is something they wanted or it's something that the city told them they wanted, because the cesspit was getting too full. Working the cesspit to collect this waste was not only unpleasant, but dangerous. The concentrated smell coming from the cesspit actually changed the air somehow so that it became difficult to breathe. Vapors of some sort. One time a soldier passed out and nearly fell into the pit. I grabbed one of his legs as he was sliding in and managed to pull him back, with only his head being covered with muck. He was known as "Shitface" thereafter.

Someone, I don't know who, but may Dagon bless him with many years, came up with the idea of spreading a layer of oven ash on the waste in the gutters and in the cesspit, as a way of absorbing some of the odor. It did not eliminate the odor completely, but it certainly helped.

There were other public works in which we engaged which were not as disgusting but were nonetheless arduous. If the city walls needed repair or enlargement, if a new well needed to be dug, or when it came time to finally fashion a new cesspit, we soldiers were the ones who provided the muscle.

I certainly don't want to give the impression that it was all misery, just tedious routine interspersed with unpleasant or back-breaking labor. There was something to this thing about working together as a team. After I became accepted (which took some time), I took part in a constant flow of jokes, banter, and imaginative grumbling. And we created our own contests, sometimes to see who could get by with the least amount of work, sometimes to see who could accomplish his tasks fastest. All bodily functions also served as a foundation for competition: belching for noise, farting for frequency and fragrance, pissing for distance.

I even grew to like some of the routine tasks, although not the ones that seemed pointless to me, like the continual cleaning of our weapons and armor. I understood the need to remove dirt and mud, but we were ordered to clean even when there was no apparent need to. It seemed to me that many of our chores were given to us not because they were necessary in themselves but because they were seen as a way to keep us occupied and out of mischief. And now that I think about it, perhaps that was prudent. Anyway, although I did not care for the continual cleaning, I came to enjoy our exercises with weapons, especially as I became proficient with them. This too became a basis for competition and, occasionally, wagering. We bet over who could throw a javelin or shoot an arrow the farthest and we also bet over accuracy at varying distances. The wagering stopped within a few years when I began to win all the contests, but that was still in the future.

I also enjoyed our marching excursions into the countryside. These marches served various purposes. They not only trained us for the occasions when we would need to march in earnest to meet some threat, but also were a way of patrolling our surrounding area. And, of course, they were yet another way of keeping us busy.

When we marched, we didn't march in step, although occasionally we fell into a rhythm as we were hurried along and the sub-officers would yell, "Keep pace, keep pace" or "Move quickly, dog turd." As we hurried up, we seemed to naturally match each other's stride. But then we would soon fall out of step. Interestingly, the one time we tended to march in step was when we started to cross a bridge, which, I learned, is precisely when one should not march in step. Somehow it can lead to a bridge collapse.

I recall our crossing of the footbridge over the valley at Bapetrin. It was a wide enough bridge, allowing two to walk abreast comfortably. It was about forty to fifty paces long. Below us was the valley floor, the distance between the bridge and valley being about the length of eight to nine men. Through some unconscious and unwilled coordination, as the head of the column began to cross, the men fell into step. The bridge began to shake. "Break stride, Break stride, you idiots," the sub-officers barked. We did as we were told and we crossed the bridge safely. That was fortunate because otherwise Gath might have lost almost half of its standing army in an instant.

On our marches, our pace was brisk, going nearly as fast as a man could walk, even though with our weapons and other gear we were carrying much more than a typical traveler. I was bone tired during my first few marches and toward the end of these marches I was staggering more than striving, with my tunic soaked through with sweat. Gradually, though, my body acquired the strength to handle the marches without exhaustion. When that happened, I began to look forward to the marches.

There was something about being part of this moving group, this flowing force. I recall having an especially vivid sensation one time when our column—there were about thirty of us—went around a bend on a pathway up a hill. I was at the rear of the column and when I rounded the bend, the whole of the column suddenly came back into view. I cannot describe it well, but the sensation was something like being part of a consecrated power, a hallowed, collective will. The dust cloud that our striving sandals kicked up was our incense, sanctifying our steps. We were the shield of the people.

The marches also served to teach me a few things, some practical, some just bits of wisdom that were interesting. I learned to pitch a tent, how to start a fire quickly, how to build a field tannur, and, unavoidably, how to put together a field latrine (a ditch and an improvised fence rail on which one's rear end is balanced).

One thing that was not taught us on the marches was how to have sex with a woman. That was saved for the barracks, although I'm not sure the tutoring I received there was of much use.

⊷╪╀⊶

4

The city maintained a barracks near the east gate. It was one of the few buildings that had three stories. As with most residences, it had an open courtyard in the center of the building, storage and work rooms to each side of the courtyard, and taller living and dwelling space in the back. But where at the back of most residences there was a two-story living and dwelling space, the barracks had three stories. The barracks was also larger than the ordinary residence, being about twenty paces long by fifteen paces wide, with the back portion being about seven by fifteen paces. The three floors in back were connected via an interior ladder and by an exterior staircase that extended from the courtyard to the roof, passing the entrances to the second and third levels.

Two other distinguishing features of the barracks were the materials used for its construction and its double-gated entrance. Most residences were constructed largely of sun-dried mud bricks; the barracks had been constructed from stone masonry and, consequently, had much thicker walls. This allowed for the two-entryway gate, both of whose doors were thicker and wider than the doors of ordinary residences and were reinforced by iron bars. The gate also had a compact tower to one side, with a platform barely large enough for two men to stand. This gave the impression that the sentry in the tower was there less for defensive purposes than to keep an eye on us. But the barracks probably could have withstood an attack if it lasted no more than a few days. The walls were thick and the barracks had been built on a rise, so the ground sloped away from the walls at a steep angle. Also, we had our own well, which was unusual. Fortunately, we never had to put the defensive strength of the barracks to the test.

Staying in the barracks was not compulsory. In fact, maybe half of the soldiers had their own dwelling places in the city. Many were married and lived with their families. Provided they arrived shortly after first light for their assignments, the commanders had no objection. And given the lashes and beatings that fell upon those who were not punctual, tardiness was not a problem.

I chose to live in the barracks. Given the strained relations between my mother and me, this was an easy choice. Also… also… well, I did not want to be an object of ridicule. I knew I would be the target of teasing already as the youngest soldier and I did not want to make matters worse by labeling myself as a mama's boy.

The other soldiers in the barracks were mostly men for whom marriage or family life was not an option. They tended to be third or fourth sons from families that were already poor. They chose or were pushed into the army because there was no other way to maintain themselves. And army pay was not a pathway to financial independence. We regular soldiers received half a shekel a month. (My father had earned about two shekels a week, even during slow times.) Granted, in times of war, we could grab whatever loot we could carry, but that was not a source of steady income.

In the barracks, I was assigned to a room with five others: four recent recruits, all under eighteen, and a crusty veteran supposedly in his mid-twenties, although his narrow, caved-in face and a mouth that was more gum than teeth made him seem older. "Scourge" was what he was called. His given name was not revealed to me, although eventually I would learn it.

Scourge was supposed to be our mentor, counselor, and first-line disciplinarian. He was enthusiastic about this last task and performed it well.

As the most junior member of this group, I was assigned a sleeping area next to the wall where our chamber pot was kept. This was used only at night, as during the day we would be relieving ourselves wherever we happened to be, out marching, in training, and so forth. But still, it was used frequently enough that it was a considerable annoyance. During my first few weeks, Scourge seemed to have a bladder problem, as at least twice a night he would walk over me, usually treading on my legs, and, missing the pot, spray me instead. I grew to realize these nighttime visits were deliberate, as his output was minimal. It was part of my initiation. I was just glad that he could not force a shit as easily as he could a piss.

In the morning, I would take the chamber pot out to the stairs to hand to slave A, who would then take care of its disposal. One day, groggy from lack of sleep, the pot slipped a bit and some of its contents spilled.

Scourge was already awake, of course.

"You're not only a faggot, you're a stupid, clumsy faggot," was his morning greeting as he came up next to me. He pushed his face close to mine and my body tensed, involuntarily leaning back a bit. I didn't say or do anything, for fear of committing some error.

"What, are you dumb too? And are you just going to stand there? Take care of this! Now."

"Yes, yes," I backed up a bit and put the pot on the floor to get a rag, but I did this too quickly, and as the pot made contact with the floor, there was an additional spill.

"Idiot!" This sound reached my ear at the same time that the back of Scourge's hand landed on my face. This was followed by a rough push with both of his hands that caused me to stumble backward and into the back wall. I hit it hard, and my immediate reaction was one of energizing anger, so I'd already straightened up before Scourge approached me again. By this time of course, everyone else was up and was looking at us. Antenon, the comrade who had shown me the most kindness during these first days, caught my eye and furtively gestured with his right hand, making a signal to hold back. If I were to strike Scourge, I would be punished severely. However, the quickness with which I drew myself up to my full height was enough to make Scourge hesitate. He looked away for a moment, and when our eyes met again, he limited himself to barking, "Clean it up!"

I did so, eventually handing over both the pot and the filthy rag with which I wiped up the mess to A. He took them away.

Scourge was also instrumental to my introduction to sex, or, perhaps better said, my first approximation to the sexual act.

Our group, having won the lot, was sleeping on the roof the night when Scourge was inspired to become my sexual adviser. On many summer nights, the heat that built up inside our rooms during the day was so intense that it made sleeping difficult, even after a full day of exertion. Spending the night on the roof was preferable. The roof could not support the entire company, so the different rooms into which our company was divided drew pebbles from an urn to see who would have the benefit of the relative coolness of the roof. Darkest stone prevailed. There were various conditions, such as no group could have the roof three times in succession. Also, whatever sub-officers were in the barracks could sleep anywhere they wanted.

Anyway, that night was especially warm so even being on the roof provided little relief. None of us was sleeping so we talked about ... about whatever would keep us from thinking about the discomfort and frustration we were experiencing. After a while, we had gone through all the gripes about this or that and the usual bad jokes, plus some half-hearted ones about the heat, so there then ensued a silence that weighed as heavy on us as the curtain of hot air.

Scourge broke the silence.

"Goliath, there's something that bothers me about you."

"Yes?"

"Your dick. It should be bigger given how tall you are. It's no bigger than anyone else's. In fact, I think it's smaller."

Laughter. Someone, maybe it was Sethal, was quick with a rejoinder. "Scourge, sounds like you want an excuse to hold Goliath's dick in your hands, the better to take the measure of it." More laughter.

"Shut the fuck up, you fag, or I'll kick you off this fucking roof. Speaking of fags, Goliath, is that why your dick is small? I've heard that about fags. They become fags because they can't fuck women properly."

I gave no response. What was I supposed to say?

"Have you had sex with anyone, Goliath? I mean other than sheep? That could be part of the problem. The dick is like anything else, it becomes stronger when used."

"Scourge, you're full of shit," said Sethal. "Your cock isn't big. So, what's that mean? You don't have sex ..."

"Idiot. I would expect that from you Sethal, because you don't pay attention. That's one reason you're the worst shot with the bow. What I said was sex strengthens the cock. Doesn't necessarily lengthen it. But ... maybe by making it more muscular, perhaps it could enlarge it. You know me, just trying to be helpful to our comrade, Goliath."

"Oh, yes, you're *always* the helpful one."

This time the laughter was cut short by a sub-officer yelling from the floor below. "Scourge, if you and your men don't shut up, I'll have you all flayed!"

There was no more discussion that night, but the next day, during our mid-day meal break, Scourge came up to me as I was sitting on the ground with my bowl of lentils.

"Goliath, I've decided to help you, my friend."

"How?"

"Look, I know you're young so you probably haven't had much sexual experience. Nothing to be ashamed of. Have you had any?" Pause. "No matter. We'll get that fixed. You know about Yicath, right?"

I shook my head.

"Did Bellon tell you nothing about army life when he signed you up? Yicath is one of the army's whores—for us, I mean. The officers have their own whores. She's a good one for you too, a teacher. Anyway, even though the army houses her, you still have to pay her."

"I don't have …"

"No, no, don't worry. We have you covered. Hey, look, I know I've been tough on you, so…" He gave a nod and looked away. "So, I and some others are taking care of payment, but for future reference, she's a quarter-shekel for an evening, so save up."

"So, what am I supposed to do?"

Scourge threw his head back in laughter. "Well, Yicath will show you what to do, my boy, although I'd hope even you could figure it out. As to when, we have kitchen duty tonight. We can take care of that for you, so you can go off after the evening meal. I've already arranged for a pass."

He then gave me directions. Yicath lived in a small house about halfway between the east and west gates, right up against the city walls. On the side of the house facing the street there was a small niche for Qetesh, the goddess of love.

I was anxious and jittery the rest of the afternoon, desirous of being with a woman but apprehensive in the face of the unknown. I wanted the afternoon to fly by and at the same time never to end. My unease wasn't helped by the erections which sprouted up under my tunic as the evening drew close. It was not easy to hide these and when Scourge spied one he gave me a wink and a leer that made me feel queasy. I ate little of our supper.

After supper, I left the barracks with the clay disk that served as a pass and headed off, slowly, to the designated location. As I walked, I tried to reassure myself that I had nothing to be concerned about. After all, I already knew the basics, having witnessed copulation between animals. The male has a penis which becomes erect and which he then sticks in the female's opening. If a billy goat could manage this, why couldn't I? And from having stroked myself, I intuited how pleasurable this contact with a woman should be.

As I approached the house, it seemed to me that the few people I passed in the street were all looking at me and were aware of what I was about to do. This increased my nervousness. I also began to wonder whether I should have washed more. I had removed the grime from my body, including my manhood, by rubbing it with a cloth damp with water and oil. But was this sufficient? I had also cleaned my teeth with a well-sharpened twig, followed by a chew of eggshell powder and salt, but I remained concerned that Yicath might find my breath repellent. I imagined her as a wondrous beauty, enticingly fragrant with clear, unblemished skin.

I had arrived. I knocked, softly. No answer. I ventured a louder knock. This time, I heard a weak voice from the other side of the door. "Who is it?"

"Goliath. From the barracks. I was told …"

The door was unbolted and opened. On the other side was a crone, whose facial features were almost hidden under a mass of wrinkles.

"Yi … Yicath?"

"She's upstairs," the crone said, much to my relief. "Come."

I followed her up a dark staircase, with only her oil lamp providing any illumination. At the top of the stairs, there was a short hallway and on either side there was a room. I made for the left side, but the crone snapped, "Not that one, over here." As she gave this instruction, she pulled back a heavy curtain and said, "Yicath, the visitor you expected."

I turned as directed and as I headed into the room I heard a throaty voice say, "Come in."

There was a lamp in the corner of the room on a small table, but the light was even dimmer in the room than it had been on the stairs. I stood still for a moment, blinking, as my eyes adjusted to the darkness.

"Come, come here."

I followed the voice to a partially raised straw mattress, which at one end was perhaps two to three hand lengths off the floor. At the other end was Yicath.

Yicath bore no resemblance to the fantasy my lust had created. She was exceedingly thin, bony. Her breasts hung downward like teardrops. I hesitated, not knowing what to do and not knowing what I wanted to do. I wondered whether I should feed her before or instead of fucking her.

"Come, come closer. Don't be shy. I was told you had not been with a woman yet." As she said this she extended her arms out to me in an invitation.

I sat down on the bed, maybe an arm's length away, and she leaned over and pulled me toward her. She gave me an open-mouth kiss, and I accepted it with eyes closed, trying to tell myself to relax, not think about anything. But as I tried to empty my mind of thoughts, her body odor forced me to become aware of it. She smelled like a donkey which had been kept in a stable for weeks.

She broke off her kiss, mumbled for me to wait, and pulled off her tunic and unfastened her undergarment. She then directed me to pull off mine. Seeing her naked, combined with the novel excitement of disrobing in a woman's presence, did arouse me and I acquired the requisite firmness. I leaned in, she pulled me on top of her, and we kissed some more. A moment or two later, I decided to aim my spear for what I sensed was the target area, but I found no opening, poking only abdomen or thigh.

"Hold on," she said, and she shifted her body, grabbing a cushion that had been propped against the wall and pulling it under her rear end, giving it more of an upward angle. This brought some of her bush into view, which gave me some hope of success. But the second attempt fared no better, and the lack of success was deflating both emotionally and physically.

"I'm sorry. I can't."

"Don't worry. This happens sometimes. Let's try this," she said as she turned herself around, presenting her scrawny rear end to me. "Rub your cock on my buttocks. I know it sounds strange, but it works."

I did as directed, placing my dismal, limp cock on her right cheek and rubbed it back and forth. The meager flesh on her buttocks gave me little to work with, but the friction did stimulate my cock, so it began to acquire some stiffness, although its solidity was still like a piece of cheese that had been sitting in the sun.

"Try again."

"What, from the rear?"

"Yes. You may find it easier." She lowered her head and moved up on her knees, so her rear was pointed skywards.

I made my approach. It seemed like I might be entering, but it was tight.

"No, no," she said sharply. "Lower, lower."

"Yes, sorry, sorry," I stammered as I realized I had been heading into the wrong opening. I repositioned myself, thrust myself forward, and this time she reached underneath her and grabbed my cock, trying to guide it.

To no avail. I was rapidly losing whatever firmness I had obtained so Yicath might as well have been grabbing yogurt and trying to force it into a narrow-necked jar.

Back to rubbing cock on buttocks, this time trying the left cheek for freshness. Once again, it seemed to help. In fact, I was starting to enjoy it so much I decided to keep the cock on her buttocks and reach release that way. Seemed more of a reliable path to satisfaction. So, I kept up the back-and-forth motion, grabbing the sides of her rear for balance. I thought I heard a noise outside the room but I dismissed it, thinking the crone was probably walking around.

But then a moment later I distinctly heard laughter. Male laughter. I got off the bed quickly, in a panic. I was standing up with my cock fully erect and pointed in the direction of … Scourge's face, contorted with malicious amusement. His head—and Sethal's head—were poking through the curtain.

"I always knew you was a fag, Goliath. Even with a woman you go for the ass. But by the gods, man, don't be so stingy with your cock. Stick it in her—or do you like jerking off so much that you just have to keep it in view?"

"Scourge … what …"

"Caseth, get out of here you asshole," Yicath screamed at the man I knew as Scourge. "I thought you said you were the boy's friend."

"Oh, I am, I am. I came by to see if I could be of any assistance," he said with a mocking laugh. "But there are some things that are just beyond help."

By this time, by fumbling around, I found my tunic and had pulled it back on. I then started for Scourge, but Yicath reached for my ankle and caused me to stumble. Sethal came into the room quickly, interposing himself between me and Scourge.

"Goliath, don't. You'll be lashed. It's not worth it."

I pushed him aside and he fell. I looked at him on the floor. "What's not worth it? Cracking your head open? You may be right about that." I then turned back to Scourge, and saw that he had now pulled out a dagger.

"Don't come any closer, my boy. You're a big lad, but an ox's skin yields to the blade just like a lamb's."

We eyed each other for some moments. I was determined I wasn't going to back down. At the same time, as my fury abated, I began to think that the present moment was not an opportune time to seek vengeance.

As Scourge and I stared at each other, Sethal picked himself off the floor and eased his way over to Scourge's side. He tugged at Scourge's tunic.

"Come on, Scourge. Let's go. You've had your fun."

Keeping an eye on me, Scourge slowly backed out. I followed. Not that I intended to do anything now, but I didn't want him to feel he could relax. He kept looking over his shoulder as he slowly went down the stairs. When he reached the bottom, he and Sethal then hurriedly opened the door to the street and left without saying another word.

When I turned, I saw the crone was standing behind me.

"Why did you let them in?" I bellowed.

"He paid me," she said scornfully, as if I should've known the reason already.

"Maya, you shouldn't have done that without asking me," Yicath said. She had come out of her room and was now clothed.

"Why? He said he and his friend just wanted to look. I didn't know they were going to make any trouble."

Yicath responded with a hard slap. "How much did he give you?"

"Feh, just a small copper piece."

Yicath motioned with her fingers. "Give it to me, and give me whatever else he gave you. I don't believe he just gave you a small copper piece."

Maya stayed motionless. She was wearing a robe with long sleeves and she folded her arms together so that her hands were not visible.

Yicath tugged at Maya's arms. "Give me the copper, you old bitch."

They struggled, with Maya surprisingly spry for someone who had to be in her fifties.

I didn't know what to do. Intervene? To what end? To determine who should get the payment Scourge had made for my humiliation? But it seemed strange to leave while the fight was going on. So, for a few moments I just stood there. Then they both fell to the floor, kicking and punching, and rolled rapidly toward me, almost knocking me backward down the stairs. That was my signal to depart.

My departure did break up the fight, because Yicath sprung up when she noticed I was leaving. She yelled to me, "Don't forget to make your payment by next temple day."

I halted and spun around. "What do you mean 'payment'?"

"Look, just because you didn't come doesn't mean you don't owe me."

"But Scourge paid you already."

Her face expressed genuine surprise. "Huh? Caseth? No… no he didn't pay me. He just vouched for you. Said you were low on metal but you could be relied upon to make payment. Hey, I accepted you because he said …"

I had to give Scourge credit. He was a complete snake.

I didn't want any more trouble, so I said, "Fine, fine. I'll get you the payment."

I did return to the house within a few days. When Maya opened the door, I saw that she was badly bruised and there was a deep cut above her eyebrows. She called for Yicath, who eagerly accepted the quarter-shekel. Yicath turned away immediately after snatching the quarter-shekel, but I told her to wait.

"Here," I said, as I reached into the sack slung over my shoulder. "I have some bread for you. For both of you." I handed Yicath two loaves.

Yicath looked at me puzzled. "I don't fuck for bread," she said.

I shook my head. "I'm not asking you to. Just take the bread. Please."

Yicath eyed me warily, as if she suspected some trick. After a moment, she accepted the bread. I left.

As far as I could tell, Scourge did not reveal anything about my botched visit to Yicath to our fellow soldiers. At least I detected no snickering.

But I didn't have the time to reflect upon my relationship with Scourge because within weeks I received some extraordinary news.

5

One day, after the midday meal, I received a summons to report to Bellon, who, when he was on site, worked in a large room off the barracks court-yard. The sub-officer who delivered the summons gave no indication why Bellon wanted to see me, and, consequently, I was apprehensive, wondering whether I might be disciplined for some offense.

Once we arrived at the room, the sub-officer announced me. Bellon ordered the door opened, and I walked in. It was a large room, with a long table and several chairs. Bellon was seated behind the table. Still nervous,

I approached the table and stood rigidly before it. But Bellon eased my worries almost immediately. He rose from behind the table, and greeted me warmly, putting his arm around me. "Goliath," he said, "I'm pleased to tell you that one of your father's murderers has been captured."

I was too taken aback to say anything at first.

"I assume you're pleased by this," Bellon said, more as a question than an assertion.

"Yes, yes, of course," I stammered. "But how…"

"We had reports that there were some thieves sheltering in the caves in the highlands east of Ekron. The king of Ekron agreed to send a detachment to search the area, along with a few of our soldiers. Sure enough, within a couple of days they came upon a group of thieves. It was their drunken carousing that gave them away." Here he paused and gave a low chuckle. "Caves can't hide stupidity. Anyway, given their state, they didn't put up much of a fight. Most were killed quickly, but two were wounded and captured. They were taken back to Ekron; we believe one of them was probably involved in your father's murder."

"How do we know that? Did he confess?"

"Some of the loot that was found with this thief clearly came from the raid on Ayun, including a silver lion-headed rhyton, which was an heirloom of one of the families that was slaughtered. Of course, the villain denied any involvement—well, at least at first. They always do. He claimed the rhyton belonged to one of the thieves who was killed. After further interrogation, he was persuaded to be more truthful. He does admit that he took part in the raid on Ayun—although he still claims he did not fire the arrow that killed your father."

"So, it still could have been someone else?"

Here Bellon laid a hand on my shoulder. "I think we found your father's killer. I don't think there's a need to look further. He took part in the raid and in my view he's probably the one who shot the arrow. Seems like the type. But whether he did or did not, as part of that band of brigands, he's a murderer. The magistrates of Ekron have so adjudged him, and their king has approved this judgment."

Bellon squeezed my shoulder and a quick nod from him indicated he considered the matter settled and that I should as well. I must admit I didn't feel like protesting. I was happy at the prospect of justice being done and I wasn't going to argue for the possible innocence of an admitted thief.

"What will be done to him? Will he be executed here?"

Bello gave a half-frown and shook his head. "Sadly, no. The king of Ekron has asserted his jurisdiction, as is his right, and he will be executed at the next feast day in Ekron."

One thing that distinguished the five Palestim cities from the surrounding countryside was our method of dealing with criminals. In the five cities, private vengeance was prohibited. Instead, there was a formal ceremony. Executions took place in public, and the executioner, appointed by the king, inflicted the punishment—usually prolonged.

Bellon said, with some hesitation, "I could give you a pass if you wanted to attend the execution. Under the circumstances, I'm sure the commander of the Ekron garrison could arrange for lodging."

I made Bellon wait for an answer. I didn't know what I wanted to do.

"Well?" Bellon asked.

"No ... no," I finally replied. "Thank you, Commander, but I think perhaps I should stay here." A thought occurred to me. "Have you told my mother?"

"No, not yet. I wanted to tell you first. As a member of our company, I thought you deserved that. I'm going to tell your mother now. It might be good for you to accompany me."

I had conflicting emotions. I hadn't seen my family in months, not since I joined the army. Having parted from my mother on bad terms ... well, I was uncertain how she or I would feel upon seeing each other again. But I also felt a desire to see her, and my sisters.

Sensing my hesitation, Bellon said, "Come, son, you should do this. You should be with me when I speak to your mother."

We set out after I had a chance to wash my hands and face in a basin and put on my armor. Bellon said I should treat this as a formal occasion.

The short walk to my mother's house turned into something like a spontaneous procession, as word had spread through the city of the brigand's capture, and several children and a few adults excitedly walked behind Bellon and me, chatting away about the news.

My mother and sisters undoubtedly knew something was happening by all the commotion. Avram and Dedra were just outside our front door as we drew near, and when they recognized me, they pointed at me, giggling and squealing. Dedra ran back inside yelling, "Goliath's coming!" Avram waited a moment longer, flashing me a broad smile, and then she too disappeared inside.

We were at the door. A different emotion took hold of me. A confused sensation of anxiety, anticipation, and joy. Bellon signaled to me to knock. I did. Avram reappeared.

"We bring you news," Bellon intoned solemnly. "Is your mother home?"

"Yes, Commander," Avram replied just as formally, "but she begs a few moments time to make ready to present herself. You may enter and wait in the courtyard."

We did so, and Avram offered us some water, which we declined.

Within a few moments, my mother appeared on the stairs outside the second level of our house. Still in mourning, she had on a long black robe which she curled around so that it also covered her head.

Bellon and my mother exchanged greetings. Bellon cast me a sideways glance. It was a discreet signal for me to speak.

"Mother, it pleases me to see you again."

My mother looked at me and managed a half smile. She then turned back to Bellon.

"Aliya, on behalf of King Maoch and the people of Gath, I am pleased to inform you that we have captured one of the thieves responsible for the murder of your husband, Abalath, the smith. He will suffer the appropriate punishment for this horrible crime. Let me take this opportunity to offer you my condolences once again. However, Dagon, may he be praised, has seen that justice is done."

My mother seemed to shake a bit, and then with a quivering voice she said, "Thank you. May I and my family be avenged." Her voice rose and her eyes went to the heavens. "May he who caused this pain—pain that will not go away—suffer for it." She then began to weep and turned to put her head on the shoulder of Avram, who was behind her.

I stood still for a moment and then moved forward to embrace my mother, wrapping my long arms around both her and Avram. My mother turned and looked up at me and then laid her head on my breastplate.

After a few moments, Bellon cleared his throat and said, "Goliath, I leave you with your family. You can stay with them tonight and during the day tomorrow, if you want. Be at the barracks at sundown tomorrow."

Not sure what to say at this juncture, I just nodded and saluted. Bellon then left.

After Bellon departed, my mother said, "I wish I had known you would be here tonight. We don't have the proper food for a homecoming. We don't even have milk because the new lamb hasn't weaned yet."

"Mother, don't worry. That doesn't matter to me."

"Avram will go to the market for some dried figs. I can at least make you a fig cake."

"Don't bother, Mother, I'm happy to eat ..."

With a wave of her hand, she shushed me. She and Avram then went upstairs, presumably to get some copper or something else of value to trade for the figs. Meanwhile, I noticed Dedra was looking at me intently.

"What? What is it?"

"Don't you get hot under that helmet?"

I laughed. "No ... well, maybe a little. But one gets used to it."

"Can I try it on? Please."

Instinctively, I turned around to see if anyone was looking, but then I realized I was at my mother's house, not in the barracks.

"Sure, here." I lifted the bronze helmet off my head and placed it on Dedra's. The helmet swallowed her head completely. "Well, it protects you well enough, but we may need to cut out an opening for your eyes so you can see," I said as I rapped the top of the helmet with my knuckles. "Now let's see if you can carry yourself like a soldier. We're going to march."

"But I can't see!"

"We'll just pretend that we're on a night march, without a moon. Follow the sound of my voice. Ready? Let's go."

Using my deepest voice, I start snapping out commands. "Forward, one, two, three, now turn left, one, two, three, now turn right!"

Dedra was doubling over with laughter. "Keep your back straight, soldier," I commanded, "or I will have you flogged."

"That's all I need, another soldier in the house," my mother interjected, as she descended the stairs with Avram. "Take off that helmet, Dedra, it is not fitting for a girl to wear such a thing."

The faceless helmet whirled around in the direction of my mother's voice and admitted a sigh of protest, but Dedra, with my help, slowly lifted the helmet off her head.

Avram then went off to the market and Dedra went upstairs to her spindle, as she had been helping my mother with weaving when Bellon and I had arrived. This left my mother and me alone in the courtyard. An awkward silence followed as we both struggled to find the right words.

"How are you getting on, Mother?" I finally managed to say. "Is Uncle living up to his part of the bargain?"

"We have enough to eat. Could have more, but we have enough."

"The house. Is there anything in need of repair? I mean, while I'm here, I could ..."

"No, I think we're fine."

"When was the last time the stalls were cleaned?"

"I'm not going to have a guest clean my stalls!" my mother said indignantly.

"I'm your son, not a guest."

"You're a guest. You don't live here anymore."

I didn't pursue this. I didn't want to take the conversation down a path that might lead to bitter memories.

"Just relax as a guest should. Have a cup of wine. I have to go help Dedra with the weaving."

"Fine. I'll sit with you."

She looked at me for a long moment. "As you like."

I sat with my mother and sister for some time until Avram returned. Dedra worked the spindle, twisting the coarse wool fibers into usable thread, while my mother stood and worked the loom, weaving the thread itself into a garment. She was making a new tunic for Avram.

As she spun, Dedra sang softly, and soon I joined in, with the rhythm of our songs at times matching the rhythm of my mother's weaving.

Avram returned presently and she brought back not only figs, but a small portion of pork. I was surprised and delighted as this implied my mother was going to make a stew. Indeed, my mother soon stopped her weaving, saying she was going to prepare the evening meal, while Avram made some bread.

"I can make the bread, and Avram can help you with the stew or she can take over for you at the loom," I offered.

"Just sit, Goliath, we can take care of the meal," my mother responded.

"You? Make bread?" Avram said more pointedly.

"We don't live on air in the army. I've become quite good at making bread. Especially when we're in the field, it's one of the tasks I'm routinely given. If we had to, I could even throw together a field tannur for you, but of course that's not necessary."

"Goliath, please, there's no need to trouble yourself. You're a …"

"Yes, yes, Mother. I know I'm a guest. I am also still your son and a brother to my two sisters. I'm not used to remaining idle. Anyway, a guest's wishes should be respected within reason, and my wish is to make the bread for this evening's meal."

My mother and I went back and forth at least a couple more times, with her protests contending with my insistence in a ceremonial duel until finally she yielded.

Avram then asked to be relieved of weaving so she could "supervise" me and make sure I would not ruin the bread. My mother just threw up her hands. "Do what you want," she said as she walked away.

I leaned in to whisper to Avram, "Yes, pay close attention to me—and learn from the master."

I remembered where we had stored our flour, water, salt, olive oil, and honey, so I went to the appropriate pots, kraters, and amphorae to gather the ingredients. I had to ask Avram for the starter dough, however, as where that was kept depended on when they had most recently baked bread.

Once I had everything together, I mixed the ingredients based on my newly acquired military wisdom, using a ratio of something less than 3:1 for the flour and water. I used two spoons of oil and nearly as much of salt. One spoon of honey sufficed. I added the starter dough to the mix. After the dough had risen, I kneaded it, and then divided it into small balls, leaving it to rise further.

While the dough was rising, I started a fire in the tannur using kindling and dung. Afterward, I used some of the water to rinse my hands, and then when the dough was ready and the temperature within the tannur was just right, I slapped the various pieces of dough on the inside of the tannur and let the bread bake. I must confess—and Avram was grudgingly forced to concede—that the bread was delicious.

The entire meal was delicious. The pork was especially welcome, although it led to another round of ritualized dialogue between my mother and me, as she repeatedly offered me her portion and I just as often refused. We finally agreed to divide it between Dedra and Avram, who, fortunately, did not let ceremony stand in the way of their appetite.

It was autumn, so there was a chill in the air as night fell, but all four of us nonetheless decided to go to the roof to view the heavens, with Dedra, Avram, and me taking turns telling the stories that the stars silently revealed to us. My mother mostly listened quietly; she did sigh deeply when Avram told the story about the giant bellows and the invincible sword forged by the smith.

As the night wore on, I thought we might go inside to sleep, but everyone seemed inclined to stay on the roof, so I went inside to bring up more mantles to guard against the chill. I then curled up next to my sisters.

But I had trouble falling asleep. Yes, after the initial anxiety about seeing my mother again had faded, I had experienced mostly joy during my visit. Now, though, as I lay awake, I had an ill-defined feeling of unease at being in my mother's house—couldn't really call it my home any more. And what would tomorrow bring? What would we say to each other? And how would I respond if she offered me a room in her house? I felt certain she would do this. Many soldiers stayed with their families in the city. She knew this. But, though I had no love for Scourge, I felt I couldn't stay with my mother. Every day would be a reminder of our confrontation over the farm. I had no regret over my refusal to yield to her plans for life on a farm, but at the same time I felt sorrow for her and a twinge of guilt.

Despite these disturbing thoughts, I did manage to doze for a bit, but then I awoke quite early. My mother and sisters were still fast asleep. I knew if I had to see my mother face-to-face on this morning it would heighten my unease. I was already feeling a great deal of turmoil.

I shook Avram gently.

"What … What is it, Goliath?" she said drowsily.

"Shh! Whisper. Don't wake the others. Please tell Mother that I needed to return to the barracks."

"But why?"

"Just do as I ask, please."

"She'll be upset."

"Yes … Well, tell her I'll be back for a visit soon. If she'll have me."

I kissed Avram, then my mother and Dedra, and left.

I walked the dark, deserted streets to the barracks, not thinking about anything in particular. I couldn't have known that years later I would think back on this night repeatedly and wonder how different things might have turned out for my family had I decided to stay in my mother's house.

⊷⊶

6

Some months passed. Months which had now fallen into a not disagreeable routine. Drills, marches, labor for the city, labor around the barracks. The most noteworthy and happiest event was my reassignment to a new sleeping area, away from Scourge. We had to make room for a few new recruits who were put under his care, to train and test as only he could do. Antenon was assigned to the new area as well and the others in my new group ranged from amiable to tolerable.

One morning while I was working the two teats of one of our sheep, Lukioth, a sub-officer, called out to me. I stepped away from the milk stand because I didn't want to spook the ewe. They stop producing when they get tense.

"What is it?"

"There's a boy at the gate. Says he has a message from your mother's household."

"Uh ... can he wait ..." I gestured over my shoulder to the ewe. "I'm right in the middle."

"Right. I can take the message for you if you want. Look for me after you finish the milking. I'm on gate duty."

Now I was the tense one. I had trouble eliciting more milk and the ewe, sensing my nervousness, let loose a long piss. I was able to pull the bucket away just in time.

Milk duty over, I hurried over to Lukioth, who looked bored, sitting on a stool by the gate, talking to a wine peddler.

"Sir, what's the news? Please tell me," I said anxiously.

"Nothing to worry about Goliath. She just wants you to come to the evening meal in two days. That won't be a problem. You can get a pass."

"But why? Did the messenger say why?"

81

Lukioth turned his head slowly and looked at me with heavy eyes. "No. That's the entire message. Come to dinner. Probably thinks we don't feed you enough, big boy that you are."

I went back to my chores. I thought my mother probably did just want to see me. I had returned to see her and my sisters about a month after my initial visit, but I hadn't been back since. My mother probably thought that more than enough time had passed since she had shared a meal with her son. Still, something about the invitation bothered and worried me.

The day arrived and, adorned with a clean tunic, I walked to my mother's house. When I was about ten paces away, I heard a number of voices coming from the courtyard of the house. Some unfamiliar voices.

I knocked. Avram opened the door. She was wearing a formal, crimson red robe, long-sleeved and high-necked. There was a pattern of purple blue anemone along the cuff of her sleeves. This was to be an occasion of some importance apparently.

I entered. There was a table set up in the courtyard with a few chairs, in addition to several mats placed in a semi-circle in front of the table. Before I could take in the scene completely, my mother rushed up to me to embrace me. When she moved out of the embrace and looked at me, I saw her eyes were sparkling with happiness and excitement. She, like Avram, wore a formal robe. Her robe was a deep blue, almost matching in color the anemone of Avram's robe. In turn, she had a pattern of red anemone on her cuffs, although her pattern was more intricate. It seemed as though her robe and Avram were designed to be paired for some reason.

I looked over my mother's head toward the people standing behind her. I recognized Dedra, of course, my uncle and his wife, and my aunt (my mother's sister). But there was a group of four I could not quite place. Gath was not that big a city, so I probably had seen their faces at some point, perhaps at a public event, but I couldn't recall their names. There were two older women, perhaps in their mid-forties, a mature man, in his mid-to-late twenties, and a young man about seventeen or eighteen, that is, a bit older than me. The mature man had a long, oval face, quite thin. His whole body was thin; it did not seem especially well-nourished.

Then I suddenly remembered who this man was. He was a potter, one of two in the city who tried to earn their keep by large-scale production of jars, bowls, cups and so forth. Many households made their own pottery, but the wealthier households, and the palace, the temple, and the barracks, purchased their pottery from time-to-time.

The problem was that there were two potters in Gath and the craft of this man—Hannipath—was thought to be inferior to the work of the other. Swans traditionally decorate our most important vessels, and Hannipath's swans often seemed out of proportion and not uniform. This would not have mattered to the ordinary household, but to the palace it made a difference.

My mother tugged at my arm. "Son, come, let me introduce you to our guests." She did so. One of the women, Ummishtath, was the mother of Hannipath. The other was his aunt, Mareth, who in turn was the mother of the young man, Barekbal—so Hannipath and Barekbal were cousins.

They all greeted me warmly, although Barekbal's smile played across his lips only briefly and then vanished. By contrast, Hannipath's wide smile seemed frozen in place.

The guests were also well-attired, although the men's robes were more subdued in color and devoid of any pattern. They were brown with a narrow white trim around the cuffs of the sleeves. I began to feel embarrassed. I had on a plain, dull white tunic, what most people wore every day.

"Mother, I wish you had told me this was going to be a special occasion. I could have borrowed a robe."

"Son, don't worry. Everyone knows you serve in the army."

"And you still haven't told me what the special occasion is."

"Avram and Barekbal are betrothed!"

I swallowed hard. "This is news." As soon as I said this, I realized it wasn't the proper response. Some of the delight disappeared from my mother's eyes as she pulled me back from the guests.

"Son, aren't you happy for your sister?"

"Yes, yes, of course. I… I'm just surprised." I looked at the guests, especially Barekbal, and I gave as convincing a smile as I could force.

I suppose I should not have been surprised. Avram was over a year older than I was and most young women were married by her age, but with the death of my father and my departure from the household … well, I just had not given her marriage situation much thought.

I walked over to Avram and held out my hands. "Sister, congratulations! I'm very happy for you!" We hugged and as we did so I whispered in her ear, "Is this is what you want?"

"Yes, yes," she replied.

I looked at her as we pulled apart and her eyes indicated sincerity.

"Goliath, please, you must meet your new brother," said my mother as she again tugged me in the direction of our guests.

Barekbal mumbled his greeting, extended his hand, and then couldn't decide whether to shake my hand or embrace me, so we did both. He was more socially awkward than I was, and this was a standard that few could meet. I began wondering how he was going to support my sister.

As if in answer to my thoughts, Barekbal went to the table where I noticed for the first time that in addition to a platter of bread and cheese, there were two objects draped in linen. Barekbal picked up one of them and brought it to me.

"Brother, I offer this to you as a bride gift." He gave a slight bow as he did so.

I took the object into my hands and removed the linen cloth to reveal a stirrup jar, rich with elaborate black and red decorations. It bore two stylized swans on each half of the jar—no two of which were exactly alike.

"Thank you, thank you. I will treasure this."

"There's another gift for you." Hannipath was speaking. "Let me get it for you." He walked to the table, picked up the other object, and brought it to me. I could tell it was a cup of some sort. "I know by tradition, I don't have to, given your mother's independence, but …" He held out the object to me. "I thought you should have this. From one family member to another."

I looked around for someone I could hand the stirrup jar to. I caught Dedra's eye and she obliged. I then took the object from Hannipath's hands, lifting the linen covering to reveal a smartly crafted bronze cup. It had two swan head handles. I turned it around and over. This was an item of value, presumably purchased by Hannipath as to my knowledge he had no skills in bronze casting.

"Thank you. Thank you very much," I said. "But you really should not have. If anyone is worthy of two bride gifts, it is Avram," I said as I flashed a smile in her direction. "But this is far too generous…" I stopped. My mother was suppressing a laugh behind her hands. Hannipath's smile was growing even wider, threatening to move his lips into contact with his ears. He held my mother's hands in his.

"Avram has only one bride gift," Hannipath stated with a short laugh. "The second gift is on behalf of your mother."

Before I could fully grasp what he was saying, my mother stepped forward and threw her arms around me. "Son, Hannipath and I are to be married!" Still holding the bronze cup in one hand, I placed my arms around her, more to steady myself than anything else.

My mother? Marrying Hannipath? He had to be at least ten years younger than my mother. Marriage between a young man and an older woman, especially a woman whose childbearing years were probably behind her, was unusual and when it happened the explanation was usually financial. This was the thought that crossed my mind as my initial stunned reaction passed. The potter needed my mother's support.

My mother and I parted. Then it was Hannipath's turn. He did not limit himself to an embrace, kissing me on both cheeks. I was thankful he didn't call me "son."

"Well, um … this is a night of surprises … and of most extraordinary news!" I was making an effort to sound as cheerful and pleasant as possible. "Dedra, would you mind?" I handed her the bronze cup. "I need to greet our other guests." I walked toward Ummishtath and Mareth in a daze, letting custom guide my body, so that it would make the proper gestures and utter the proper words.

Time to break bread and share a meal. The betrothed couples sat at the table, facing the rest of us, who were seated on the mats. When the wine jug arrived in my hands, I poured myself a good measure.

After the wine had loosened my tongue and I felt bold enough, I asked, "Mother, so where do you plan to live?"

She seemed startled by my question. "Why, here, of course," and she gestured with both hands toward the surrounding house.

'I thought perhaps …"

Hannipath anticipated my next question.

"I'm moving out of my house so Barekbal and Avram may have it. I have but a few rooms of living space in my small home, since it also houses some of my goods and supplies. It's really too small for two families to share—especially if one family is going to be blessed with many children." Here he turned toward the younger couple and raised his cup in salute.

"Very good. May you have much happiness here," I said. I said that, yet I was thinking his happiness would be purchased with my father's resources. A rude thought, a thought uncharitable both to Hannipath and my mother, but there it was nonetheless.

Occupied by my own thoughts, the conversation drifted over me, although listening with one ear I was able to follow enough of what was said to interject an appropriate response from time-to-time.

At one point though, my inattention must have deafened me because I felt Dedra tugging vigorously at my sleeve.

"Hey, are you asleep? Goliath, could you *please* pass me the water?"

"Uh, sure," I said as I handed her the jug.

"That was only the third time I asked you."

"I wanted to make sure you really wanted it."

"Oh, so that's the explanation. I thought you had too much wine."

"No, little bird, I can handle the wine."

"Of course, you're a heroic soldier now," she said mockingly.

"The hero part is yet to come … but it will. And what are you doing with your time? Do you have some young men pining for you, ready to propose marriage?" I said this teasingly, but then I realized this could be possible. Dedra was around thirteen and was beginning to take on the shape of a woman. I suspected she had had her first blood by now.

"No, not yet. I can wait. Besides someone has to take care of the weaving and the grain grinding. Mom and Avram have been occupied with other things," she said with a smile.

"So, you're developing your talent as a weaver. That's good."

"Developing? Who do you think put those flowers on Mom's and Avram's robes?"

"Very impressive. When we decide to decorate our tunics with anemone down at the barracks, I will know who to recommend."

"Well, your tunics could certainly stand improvement in some way."

A pause. I then asked, in a whisper, "What do you think of your new father?"

"He's not my father," Dedra said a little too loudly, as I noticed that Hannipath glanced in our direction.

I leaned in a bit closer. "Right, but you know what I mean."

Dedra turned her head, looking at nothing in particular, and then turned back to me to say, "Mom loves him. So …"

"Yes, this is what's important. It is her decision."

The meal finished, the women cleared away the food, bowls, and platters and retired to the rear of the courtyard. Hannipath asked me some polite questions about life in the military to which I gave the expected, uninformative answers. Returning the favor, I asked him how his business was going. His responses were equally cordially evasive, although I was able to glean that Barekbal worked with him eight days every month. The rest of the time Barekbal worked as a laborer, mostly in the farms outside the city. Avram would not have the life of a noblewoman by any means.

Unsolicited, my uncle offered up a mixture of complaints and boasts about work at the bloomery. He and Astynath were turning out splendid work, but the city was demanding too much and paying too little.

"What do you soldiers do with all the spear points? Wager to see who can break them the quickest?" he grumbled.

After some more chatting, Hannipath and Barekbal stood up, which was a signal that the evening was coming to a close and I should be taking my leave.

Before I did, I pulled my uncle aside. I wanted to ask him something, but he got in his words first.

"Goliath, I'm glad we have a chance to talk in private. This has to do with the arrangement between your mother and me, but you should probably be aware. My pledge to her of silver, bread, and cheese was based on the belief that she would be a widow. Well, that's not going to be so, is it?"

"But the payment was based on the value of my father's share of the bloomery."

"Look, as I said, the arrangement is between your mother and me. It's not fitting for a man to support another man's wife—and she agrees."

"It's not just my mother. It's my sisters who need support."

"Avram is getting married herself if you haven't noticed, but don't worry. She will get her full mina as promised. Dedra isn't ready to marry yet, so Hannipath has time to fund her dowry. My contribution will be a half mina."

"What else has changed?" I asked with some irritation.

"The food allowance will be cut to one loaf of bread and one round of cheese once a week. I'm paying six mina of silver now to your mother instead of twelve mina over the next four years."

I did not say anything. I doubt that I had to. I'm sure my expression indicated displeasure.

"This is not something I forced on your mother. Perhaps when you have a wife you will understand. It's demeaning to be supported by someone who is not your husband. Let me add that as my gift to your mother and Hannipath, I'm taking care of the arrangements for the wedding feast. There'll be mutton as well as pork, figs, and honey cakes."

We were silent for a moment. What I wanted to ask him now seemed trivial, but I needed an answer. The wedding was to be in two weeks, to coincide with the full moon, which among our people is considered a favorable sign.

"Uncle, as you know, I don't have much in the way of money. Don't need much for myself."

"I can certainly spare some copper pieces ..."

"No, that's not what I want. I would like to have access to the bloomery to fashion some gifts for my mother and Hannipath and Avram and Barekbal. I will need to get permission for leave, but I think I can get that. Also ... well, I may need your assistance. Father taught me a few skills but ..."

My uncle seemed relieved that I wasn't asking for something else. "Of course. Don't worry. Astynath and I would love to have you pay us a visit. And together we can fashion a nice dagger for Hannipath and a bracelet for your mother. For Avram and Barekbal, well ... something practical, like a good knife."

"Thank you."

My business with my uncle being complete, I rejoined the others to offer my congratulations again, to embrace my mother and sisters, and to say my farewells. Returning to the barracks, my mood was quite different from what it had been. I had been somewhat anxious on the way to my mother's house, not knowing what to expect. Now I was more angry than anxious although the exact cause of my anger was unclear. Yes, I was annoyed at my uncle for changing the payment terms for my father's share in the bloomery. He could do this with my mother's consent, but it seemed wrong to me. But I was also angry with my mother. It had not been a year since my father had been killed. No law prohibited her from marrying again so quickly but custom dictated a wait of at least a year. And to agree to accept less for my father's share of the bloomery than it was worth! My uncle had stressed how demeaning it would be for my mother and Hannipath to take payment from him. What about cheapening the memory of my father and his years of work!

But I was also angry at myself for being angry. My mother was happy. Avram had assured me that the marriage to Barekbal was voluntary. Who was

I to question their decisions? A laborer with armor and a helmet, earning half a shekel a month, who shared a room with four others—that's who I was, nothing more.

Thinking of my quarters at the barracks reminded me of the gifts I had received. The space allotted to us was just large enough to accommodate our bodies and gear, plus maybe a few personal items. Some soldiers had cups, daggers, amulets, figurines of their protector god or goddess, but I did not recall seeing anyone with a stirrup jar. This is something that would get in the way and be stepped on or otherwise damaged within a short time. I decided I would keep the bronze cup and ask Patibal if I could store the jar somewhere for safekeeping.

Patibal laughed at my request. "What? You think you're still at home? We're not here to serve as a fucking storage facility." Seeing I was hurt by his mocking reply, he softened his tone. "Look, lad. Here's the situation. If you come into possession of something really valuable, such as silver, some jewelry—and you may the next time we sack a Hebrew town—they will keep it for you at the temple, provided you make an offering. Otherwise, your choices are to keep it with you—and you're right this jar will probably be more of a bother than it's worth—or just give it to us. Our storeroom is full of jars, bowls, pots, cups. We'll put it to use eventually." He then it held up the jar for closer inspection. "Not bad. Some effort went into this." Pause. "Oh, this must be from Hannipath's shop. None of the swans match."

As I entered the bloomery a few days later, I was disheartened by the thought that a gift over which one had labored might just be shoved aside as an annoyance. Would the gifts I fashioned for my mother and Hannipath wind up in a corner of their storeroom?

But once I got started, I managed to push that thought into the corner. I concentrated on making the best blade, bracelet, and knife I could. Fortunately, Uncle was eager to help. It would have been impossible for me to impart any design to the bracelet on my own. Uncle was able to embed a pattern of curved lines into the bracelet, which provided it with a pleasing sense of flow. The dagger blade was mostly my work—it only took me four attempts. But Uncle was the one who secured it to its hilt, a fine piece of cedar wood in which he had carved a spiral.

I was less pleased with the knife. It was the last piece on which I worked and I didn't spend sufficient time on it. I knew the process for trying to keep the finished product from being too soft on the one hand and too brittle on the other, but in rushing the work, I may have produced a less than ideal edge. But … it would have to do.

Work done, Uncle invited me to share a meal with him and Astynath. Whatever bitterness I had felt toward Uncle had faded. Perhaps it had left a mark, but any dark feelings were now gone, like heat from the iron.

The day of the wedding arrived. My mother's courtyard was packed with perhaps thirty people. My mother's livestock had been moved to a neighbor's house so they would not be alarmed by the crowd and the noise and so their bleats and braying would not disturb the festivities.

Statements of commitment before a few witnesses suffice to bind a couple, but if metal or meat is available for payment, a priest is sometimes retained, to burn some incense, say a prayer, and sanctify an offering. Either my uncle or my mother or Hannipath, or perhaps some combination of them, decided to scrape together the necessary funds or food. The deputy high priest was in attendance and he prayed to Hishara, goddess of marriage and fertility, and Qetesh, goddess of love. Then, the proper offerings having been made, my mother and Hannipath, wearing the same robes they had on when I visited, made their statements. Avram and Barekbal, also attired with the same robes they wore that evening, followed with their statements.

Gifts were then offered to the couples, mine included. My mother and Hannipath were either pleased or considerate enough to feign their pleasure. Barekbal's face was expressionless, as it had been for much of the evening, although his eyes flitted back and forth as if he were searching for an answer on how to react. Avram cried.

The food and drink came next. Ample wine. I indulged, so much so that I found myself singing with Dedra, much to the amusement of Avram. The evening accelerated apace with the wine, and soon it was time for me to take my leave. My mother had invited me to stay on a mat in one of the downstairs rooms, but I knew they would be uncomfortable with me spending the night. Fortunately, I had the foresight to arrange for Antenon to fetch me back to the barracks after the full moon had passed its high point in the sky and begun its descent. Otherwise, if I had tried to stumble back by myself, I might have wound up in a shit gutter.

'Hang on, Goliath. Gods, you've had too much to drink."

"You mean wine?'

"Yes, wine, wine."

"Well, maybe I have. I think I want I take a nap."

"Not until we get to the barracks. Wait! Don't pull on me. Can't hold the torch if you're dragging me down."

"Fine," I said as I slumped to the ground.

"Get up, get up! You know you're too big for me to carry."

"Hang on, let go, get up … too many things …"

'If you don't get up and walk, I'm going to set this torch under your ass. Now get up!"

"I need a drink."

Somehow we made it back, because the next thing I remember I was on my mat in our shared room telling Antenon not to make noise so I could go to sleep. He responded with a curse.

My stomach was queasy the next morning, but not so queasy that I couldn't keep down some bread and water, which helped settle things a bit. Anyway, it was not my physical distress that bothered me so much as the day wore on, but my brooding on my mother's remarriage. I should have been happy for her, but I wasn't. More than that—I had a deep sense of foreboding.

⟞╌╀╌⟝

7

Not more than a few months after the double wedding, I had my first combat, an attack on a settlement that the Hebrews had brazenly placed in our territory. We were victorious. Not unexpectedly, over the next two years there were further clashes with the Hebrews, in all of which I distinguished myself. But perhaps the most noteworthy occurrence during this time was I grew to my full height. I became quite tall. Taller than four cubits and a span, easily head and shoulders above anyone else among the Palestim, or, as far as I knew, among the Hebrews.

My father had been taller than average, as was my mother, but not exceptionally so, nor .was anyone aware of any relative of mine who possessed anything like my height. My extraordinary stature helped feed some rumors that I was, as my dark skin also suggested, indeed a Nubian, a race reportedly of very tall men, although no Palestim of my acquaintance had ever met one. I was aware that Scourge was one of those who relished spreading this story as it implied I was a bastard and not truly a Palestim.

Another story about the secret of my height had to do with Lost, my cat.

I had adopted the kitten I found during my initial combat, the attack on the Hebrew settlement, bestowing upon him what I thought was an appropriate name. Lost became as constant a companion to me as a cat can be, spending nights curled up beside me until he awoke an hour or two before dawn to start his wandering. He was also at my side during any meals where we had meat, insisting on sharing some of my portion and manifesting an appetite that proportionately rivaled mine. The commanders, sub-officers, and my fellow soldiers tolerated his presence. First, he earned his keep, ensuring our barracks remained free of mice and most bugs, and, second … well, I earned my keep also, and in doing so I also gained the respect of most of my comrades. Allowing me to keep Lost was considered a small indulgence. The only time Bellon raised an objection was when Lost insisted on following me on an overnight march. He soon tired, naturally—cats are built for short bursts of speed, not endurance—and then I quietly snuck him into my bread bag, having given most of my bread to Antenon to carry, where he took a long nap. Bellon wasn't amused when Lost emerged from my bag at camp, but fortunately Lost didn't make a nuisance of himself that evening.

Why did I become attached to Lost? Don't know really. Didn't think about it at first. It was just impulse that resulted in my bringing him back to Gath from that scorched Hebrew village—that and the fact that he clung to me with all the tenacity his tiny claws could muster. Later I told myself that I had affection for him because he too had lost a parent through an arrow fired for malicious amusement. But if I ever thought of distancing myself from Lost, those thoughts came to a definitive end after a couple of incidents, the first one an act of exquisite beauty, the second an act of depraved cruelty.

One day, when Lost was perhaps a year old, he and I were sitting in the courtyard after the mid-day meal. We were both relaxing, digesting. Lost, though, suddenly became attentive to something only he sensed. He bestirred himself and moved over to the side of the courtyard, partially hiding behind one of the supports of the courtyard roof. There, Lost sat quietly on his haunches, appearing to stare at nothing in particular. Then a bird swooped down a bit too close to Lost. In one flawlessly coordinated smooth motion, Lost leaped up, snatched the bird out of the air, and with a barely noticeable twist of his head snapped the bird's neck. It was one of the most graceful things I ever witnessed. How could I part with this matchless, refined hunter now? By comparison he made me and my comrades look like lumbering dullards, with all the agility of trees. No wonder the Egyptians regarded cats as divine.

We Palestim don't consider cats divine, however. To the extent any super-natural powers are attributed to them, they are magical powers, powers often said to be used for personal advantage, sometimes even for evil ends. This explains the other set of rumors about my height. Lost's arrival coin-cided with my last growth spurt, so not surprisingly those who thought cats possessed occult powers connected the two. Among the believers in Lost's powers of sorcery, there was no unanimity of opinion about how Lost con-ferred another span of height upon me, but some said I grew more during the night, when Lost snuggled against me, so somehow this physical contact transferred a power that caused my body's expansion.

I treated these stories, which of course reached my ear, with amused indifference because only a handful of the soldiers believed the stories and most who did didn't regard this as a reason for being hostile to Lost. If any-thing, some wanted to get hold of a black cat of their own.

But then there was Scourge. I never knew whether Scourge actually believed in Lost's supposed powers or he just said he did with the hope of causing problems for me or with the goal of providing justification for what he did to Lost. In the end, it did not matter.

One evening, as I was retiring, I noticed Lost was not around. This was somewhat unusual, because he liked to sleep with me, but he had disap-peared before. My first thought was he was still out roaming, perhaps look-ing for a mate. He had been mature ever since he was about eight months old. Still, I felt uneasy for some reason, so I left my room to look for him. Lukioth was the sub-officer on duty and he had no objection. We had no drills or tasks of importance the next day. Anyway, I just planned to walk around the courtyard and then, if necessary, to go outside and walk around the immediate vicinity of the barracks.

I looked in the stables first, an occasional hunting ground. Nothing. Then I decided to go to the storeroom. This was also a favored hunting ground as grain was sometimes spilled on the floor, providing an invitation to mice. I was still a few paces from the storeroom when I heard Lost's unmistakable cry, along with Scourge's equally unmistakable laugh. I ran to the storeroom door. It was barred from the inside. I pounded on it, demanding it be opened. Silence, then some muffled voices, Scourge's laughter, and again Lost's pained cry. Anger gave me strength and two kicks forced the door open, breaking the bar where it met the latch. I lost my balance as the door gave way and I fell on the storeroom floor as I entered. When I looked up, I saw that one of the new recruits was holding Lost's head down on the table where we kept our scales. Lost's hindquarters were dangling over the edge of the table and underneath Lost, holding a burning stick to Lost's scrotum, was Scourge.

Before I pulled myself off the floor and slammed my body into Scourge, I heard him say, "Trying to find out how a fag like you grew so tall. I think you swallow your cat's seed."

The noise of the door splintering and our brawl could not fail to rouse the camp. I managed only one good punch on Scourge's face, bloodying his nose, before many arms grabbed me from behind and pulled me back. "What in the name of all the gods are you idiots doing?' Lukioth shouted. "Door broken. Cat bawling. You two rolling on the ground ... You trying to fuck each other?" He turned to address some of the soldiers who had crowded into the room. "Get them both out of here. Take them to the cell and shackle them."

The cell was a small, dark area embedded in the wall near the gate. Couldn't really call it a room. Too small for anyone to stand in it, and I could barely fit in it hunched over. It was a holding area for drunk or disorderly soldiers. The shackles were used only for violent offenders. We met those conditions.

We were carried off quickly. I did manage to yell out to Antenon, who I spied in the crowd milling about, "Antenon, for the sake of our friendship, please look after Lost."

The smell in the cell was incredibly foul, being the repository of years of shit, piss, and vomit. Yes, our two slaves, A and B, were supposed to clean it from time to time but they were not especially diligent about this task and no one cared to check whether they cleaned it up or not.

But the worst part of the night I spent in that cell was not the smell, or my having to relieve myself where I sat, or the parched throat I developed.

It was having to listen to Scourge blabber on all night. He carried on without stopping, as if his very life depended on voicing a steady stream of insults, random observations about most anything under the sun, and complaints about the injustice of being placed in the cell with a "fag." It seemed he could not have a thought without saying it out loud. Responding to him would not help, of course. That would just encourage him. So, I did my best to distance myself, closing my eyes and trying to think of anything, pleasant or unpleasant, that would move my soul away from his clamor. I was awake all night.

Patibal, Agenor, and Lukioth came for us while it was still dark. Wordlessly, Lukioth unlocked the shackles. I had difficulty exiting the cell as my legs had lost some of their sensation. I had to crawl out.

Once we were outside, Patibal addressed us. "You know the punishment for fighting. You both will be lashed, but we've talked to Bellon. He agrees that we should not waste our time and strength on you. You'll do the job for us." Scourge and I both showed our puzzlement. "You're going to lash each other. Until we decide you've had enough. Each of you hates the other. You can work off some of that hate. And this will be the end of it … or you'll both be meeting the executioner."

I looked over to Scourge. He had a wicked smile and was nodding and murmuring.

Patibal continued, "We're going to do this as soon as the company gets up. You can go now to clean yourselves and take off those filthy tunics. Don't want your stink ruining everyone's breakfast. Don't bother to put on a clean tunic. Remember, you'll be flogging each other."

I got up slowly, and then made my way to my area. I was relieved to see Lost but also anguished by the sight of him. He was lying next to Antenon. Antenon—Dagon's blessings be upon him—had spread some honey on his scrotum, but even without picking him up I could see that Lost's scrotum was red, splotchy, and blistered. Lost looked up at me. He emitted no sound, but his eyes accused me with their sadness.

I removed my soiled tunic and washed where necessary. Antenon raised his head. "What's going on?"

"There's to be a show. Scourge and I are to whip each other in front of the company."

"What? No! Why? Can I help you in any way?"

"Just continue to take care of Lost, brother. I'm indebted to you." With that, naked, I went back down to the courtyard.

Patibal had two whips in his hand. Each whip was shaped the same, with a wooden handle attached to three leather thongs, maybe two cubits in length. The thongs were knotted with bones at irregular intervals, with an indented piece of bronze at the end. When I stood in front of Patibal, he shook his head slowly from side to side.

Scourge appeared a moment later and then Patibal spoke. "The sub-officers are rousing the company. We'll start when they're assembled and I'll give my instructions then."

We stood silently for a few moments. Thankfully, Scourge's stream of words seemed to have dried up.

Once the company had gathered, Patibal directed Scourge and me to stand apart five paces. He then said, "I'm now going to give each of you a whip. Don't start, I repeat, don't start until I give the signal. Also, just as you are not to start until I give the signal, you will stop immediately when I give the signal. Immediately. Understood?"

"Yes," I said.

"Can we stop whipping before the signal?" Scourge asked.

"What do you mean?"

"Do I have to keep whipping all the time?"

"Scourge, what game are you playing?"

"Sir, I just mean I may tire of using the whip."

"You understand if you stop, Goliath doesn't have to stop until I say so."

"Yes, sir."

Patibal gave his signal. We began.

Scourge was quick and lithe and recognizing that I had a huge advantage in reach, he immediately dashed in close to me, swinging his whip against my right arm, perhaps hoping to dislodge the whip from my hand. It didn't work. As he tried to give a backhand strike against my face, I landed my whip across his back, tearing out chunks of flesh. He retreated as quickly as he had advanced, and as I went after him, he danced away to my right, but the room for maneuver was circumscribed by the assembled company, and as he went around my side I placed another powerful blow on his back. To his credit, he neither whimpered nor winced. In fact, he managed a return hit as he ran away, although it landed with much diminished force.

I scored a couple more hits as he tried to circle me, eliciting shouts of encouragement from the company—Scourge had few friends. It was evident that if things were going to continue in this fashion, I would make short work of him. Scourge was no fool. A profoundly malicious man, but no fool. As I advanced again, he feinted a retreat, drawing me in closer, and then he quickly reversed course, launching himself headfirst against my lower body, clearly hoping to make contact with my most sensitive areas. But his aim was off and I also managed to turn my body just enough so that his head landed on my thigh. The impact pushed me back, but I maintained my balance. Scourge grabbed hold of both my legs, opened his mouth, and tried to bite my penis. I brought my right hand down forcefully on the side of his head. This pushed him to the ground and although he managed to sink his teeth into my thigh before he went down, I had evaded a far more serious injury.

I brought my whip down on his back and he grabbed my arm, trying to restrain me. Infuriated, I shook him loose, dropped my whip, and yanked his arm up and away with both my hands, forcing it behind his back beyond where nature designed it to go. The crack was audible and for the first time during our contest he screamed.

"Hold!" Patibal yelled. "Stop, Goliath!"

"Oh, gods, dear gods," Scourge moaned.

Patibal pointed to a couple of the soldiers. "You, you, get the limb kit." This was some splints of bark and linen cloth to place on a broken limb, in an effort to hold it in place. If the gods smiled on one, perhaps one could regain some movement in the arm or leg, but it was always crippled. Patibal then looked at me. "Take care of your own wounds, then get dressed and go see Bellon."

"Sir, I dropped my whip only after ..."

"I didn't ask you to engage in conversation. Do as I have ordered."

I went to my quarters. Antenon walked with me.

"Are you hurt badly? Your thigh is still bleeding."

"I'll be fine. It seems worse than it is because of the size of his bite. It's only the surface that he scraped away. How do I look otherwise?" I could tell I was bleeding from my lips and I was wondering if my face was scarred.

"As fiercely ugly as ever, friend."

Antenon helped me clean my wounds. He also wrapped some cloth around my thigh. "Now that's two sets of wounds I've had to deal with in less than a day," he said, nodding in the direction of Lost. "Soon enough I'll have to join the ranks of the healer priests."

"How is my companion?"

"If his wound doesn't get infected, he'll live. Whether he will ever be a father is more doubtful."

"Scourge … May he be accursed. I don't understand …"

"No one understands him. But you definitely got the better of him today."

"Right. Now I have to appear before Bellon. I suspect the commander is not happy I broke an experienced soldier's arm."

"Scourge is the one who first tried to turn the contest into a brawl."

"Let's see how that fares as an excuse."

I announced myself outside the room Bellon and the commanders used as a work area. After some moments, Lukioth opened the door and signaled for me to enter. Bellon and Sardon were seated at a table. Most of the sub-officers were in the room as well. I knew the protocol: don't say or do anything until instructed to do so.

Bellon spoke. "Come closer to the table, Goliath." I did.

"You understand why you and Caseth were to be punished today, correct?"

"Yes, sir."

"And what was the reason?"

"We were fighting, sir, and fighting between soldiers is prohibited."

"That's right. I understand he was doing something to your cat, but that did not give you an excuse to start a fight, let alone break down the door to the storeroom. If you had a concern, your obligation was to bring it to the attention of the sub-officer on duty. You've taken an oath to Dagon to protect the king and the people of the city of Gath. You're not an Egyptian and you don't have a duty to protect cats."

"Sir, all creatures are sacred to Dagon. He wants us to use them only as necessary …"

Sardon jumped out of his seat, "Shut up! How dare you contradict the commander!"

Bellon quietly laid a hand on Sardon's arm and gave him a hard look. Sardon returned to his seat.

"We don't want our soldiers to be timid, so I'm glad you spoke up. As you have been trained to do, if you ever see something amiss around the barracks or on campaign, don't be quiet. Speak up about it. Even if it is a commander who is mistaken about some fact—perhaps especially if it is a commander—you should bring that mistake to his attention, respectfully of course. But you can't make your own rules. I'm aware of what the priests say about Dagon and his concern for animals. This is why Dagon is sometimes portrayed in the guise of an animal. But just as we submit to Dagon, so too must we submit to those whom Dagon has invested with authority. The orders of your commanders, just like the laws of the king, must be obeyed. You understand that, right, Goliath?"

"Yes, yes, sir."

There was a pause. Bellon leaned back in his chair.

"You know why we decided that you and Caseth should engage each other with whips?"

"Lashing is the prescribed punishment for most offenses, including fighting."

"Yes, that's right. But there was another reason. We're aware of how tall you are and how long your arms are. How can we fail to be? Also, we have been aware that Caseth has not always treated you fairly." He paused again, to let the statement sink in. "You understand what I'm saying Goliath?"

"I think so, sir."

"Had Caseth received from you a good ten lashes or so, in front of the entire company, I think that would've put an end to any harassment of you. But it didn't turn out that way, did it? You broke his arm. Whatever faults Caseth had—and your commanders aren't blind, we're aware of them—he was a good soldier. Fearless in combat. Now... well, maybe we can use him for sentry duty at the palace."

He paused again. I ventured to say something. "Sir, do you want me to explain myself?"

"No need to. I know what you're going to say. He departed from the rules first, biting your thigh, and everyone knows ... well, it wasn't your thigh he was after. But tell me, Goliath, if in combat one of your fellow soldiers fails to follow an order, does it excuse you from following orders?"

"No, sir."

"No, of course not. You clearly still had Caseth at an advantage. You could've whipped him repeatedly while he was on the ground. But you acted on impulse. Goliath, you obviously have many of the qualities of a good soldier. You're strong, you have endurance, you're a skilled fighter, you're cooperative... but you also need good judgment and self-control. Instinct is not the same as impulse. You're trained so some actions come naturally to you, by instinct, like moving your shield to deflect a sword thrust or a slung rock. Impulse is when you let your emotions control your actions. Do you understand the difference?"

"Yes, sir."

Another long pause. "But this incident with Caseth is not the principal reason I wanted to speak with you. There's something more important. As you know, we've been in conflict with the Hebrews the last couple of years. The kings of the five cities have decided it is in the interest of the Palestim people to bring peace to our lands, if possible. Of course, we've always wanted peace; it's the Hebrews who want war. But now they apparently desire peace as well. We would like this peace to endure. For that to happen ... well, we want to make sure that disputes that are bound to arise from time-to time, such as disputes over wells, grazing rights, missing cattle, cases of rape, don't generate larger conflicts."

Bellon looked away for a moment and tapped his fingers on the table. He then looked back at me. "Are you aware of the single combats that are sometimes used to settle trade disputes in Ashkelon?"

"I've heard of them. I can't say I know that much about them."

"With the approval of Ashkelon's king, merchants who cannot settle their differences will sometimes agree to resolve them by use of dueling champions. This method seems to work. It's been used a few times to settle disputes with foreign merchants, and in that case, it's a better alternative than war. Something like that is how we plan to settle future disputes with the Hebrews. In other words, the Palestim city or cities involved in the dispute will appoint a champion to fight on their behalf against the Hebrew champion. The side whose champion prevails will also prevail in the dispute."

"The accursed Hebrews will never honor this bargain," Sardon interjected.

"I share your skepticism, but we'll see. Anyway, Maoch has decided that Gath will participate in this arrangement along with the other Palestim cities. Each city is to appoint a champion." Bellon folded his hands in front of him and our eyes locked. "In our campaigns over the last couple of years, how many of the enemy have you killed? Fourteen, fifteen?"

"Maybe. Don't know for sure, sir, because I don't keep count." I lied. I knew exactly how many: fifteen.

"By any measure, you've done well. You're always in the thick of the fighting and the fact that you have emerged from these battles without any serious injury speaks for itself. Based upon my own observations, as well as the recommendations of Sardon and the sub-officers, we want you to be Gath's champion, provided you prove yourself during training. But this decision has to be entirely voluntary on your part. You must be wholeheartedly committed to this service." His raised brow indicated he expected a response.

"I am honored by the confidence you have shown in me. With the help of the gods, I will prove myself worthy of this honor."

"Good. As I noted, you will need to undergo training. You have good skills, but your skills still need developing. You must have unsurpassed skills. Our city's fortunes will rest on your shoulders. As it turns out, a young nobleman will be joining us as a new commander. He is from Ashkelon, where some in his family are merchants, so he is very familiar with the single combats, and he's very skilled himself, especially with the sword and short spear. Hs name is Ahirom. He will be in charge of your training. He should arrive in Gath within the month. Do you have any questions?"

"Not at this time, sir."

"Very good. One thing: do not talk to anyone else about this for now. I will make an announcement at the appropriate time. Understood?"

"I will not fail to obey again."

"Ah, speaking of that … I've yet to prescribe your punishment for deviating from the rules laid down for today's combat. Cesspit duty for next fifteen days. And we will withhold your pay until we recover the costs of the storeroom door. That's all. You're dismissed."

I bowed and left the room—a poor shit shoveler and the champion of Gath.

8

"I think you can stop there," Phodan said, as he stood up. He stretched and suppressed a yawn. "You'll have to excuse me. Strangely, sitting still can be tiring," he observed with a smile. He then walked around the room a bit, finally turning to face me. "As a man of action, do you have trouble sitting still?"

I shrugged. "Not especially."

"So, you can sit still if you have to? In other words, you don't have any trouble controlling your impulses? I noticed you mentioned that Bellon observed you could be impulsive. No longer the case?"

I smelled a trap. After a long moment, I said, "Yes, as I've matured, I'd say I have gained more control over my impulses. But I still feel indignation at any injustice."

He then studied me for some time, without saying a word. His expression was unreadable. Finally, I broke the extended silence by asking, "Are we finished? Do you need any other information from me?"

A broad smile appeared on his face, as though I had just done something to make him very happy. "Actually," he said, "I have some questions for you." He then sat back down.

PART IV

CHAMPION

1

Being summoned to appear before a king means either very good news or very bad news.

Being summoned to appear before a queen … well, an exceptional summons like this was bound to produce some anxiety.

But as I kept telling myself on route to the queen's chambers, I had no reason to worry. On this, my second trip to Ashkelon, I was held in high esteem by the Palestim people. The principal purpose of the trip was to celebrate our decisive victory over the Hebrews and to display various trophies from that victory, including the Hebrews' sacred chest. The king of Ashkelon had already given me hearty congratulations, in the process bestowing upon me a dagger with an ivory hilt with two inset gems. Perhaps the queen wished to give me a separate gift.

A guard accompanied me to the queen's chambers. As we approached, he gave a silent signal to the two guards flanking the doors to the chambers. Without uttering a word, they opened the doors and I proceeded inside.

I found myself in the queen's audience hall. It was smaller than the ceremonial throne room, where the king presided, but still of imposing size, perhaps twenty paces by fifteen paces. At the end of the room I was facing was an intricately carved chair, perhaps of olive wood, with a red cushion. From my distance, I could not tell exactly what the pattern was on the back of the chair, but it appeared to be two swans beneath a rising sun. The chair was slightly elevated above the floor, resting on a stone platform. Along each side of the hall were two wooden couches, also with red cushions. These were simpler, lacking any elaborate design.

I walked maybe two paces forward into the room when the guard held up a hand next to my chest indicating I should stop. A moment later, a woman in a pale blue robe appeared from a door to the left of the queen's chair. From what Altara had told me, I assumed this was a handmaiden, but I made a slight bow anyway. The guard hissed, "That's not the queen."

The handmaiden looked me over, and then proclaimed, "Queen Tanith enters." As soon as the handmaiden had spoken, the guard placed a hand on my back and whispered, "Kneel." I did so, as did the guard. My head was lowered, but I could detect a figure gliding into the room. Once seated, the figure said, "You may rise."

Seated on the chair was a woman in her mid-thirties. Her black hair had been expertly trimmed and shaped, with strands falling evenly across her forehead and the hair along the sides of her head braided. The braids appeared to be secured by silver bands. The azurite around her eyes matched the deep, rich blue of her robe, which was embroidered with a silver-colored thread around its hem. Bracelets of silver adorned both arms. Her nose was delicate, but her thin-lipped mouth was wide given the contours of her face. Sufficiently capacious for any royal command.

She spoke, nodding to the handmaiden and the guard, "You may leave us." Both backed out of the room, keeping their face toward the queen. Both doors closed.

"Thank you for coming so promptly, Goliath. I want to ask you some questions, so come sit on the couch on my right." With a scarcely detectable movement of her hand she indicated the couch nearest her.

Once I was seated, the queen said, "I don't often have occasion to speak with celebrated warriors. The king thinks matters of combat—all that blood and gore—are too savage a subject for my ears." She smiled. "But I could not pass up the opportunity to speak to such a hero. So, you are to tell me about your experiences as a champion and the recent victory of our people over the Hebrews, a victory which I believe owes much to you, is that correct?"

"The gods saw fit to allow me to play a part in our victory."

"Well, when you tell the story don't be too modest, because it will not make for a very interesting tale. Besides, we in Ashkelon are not noted for our modesty." Another quick smile. "But I must not be rude. That's not becoming a queen. Here I am giving you instructions and I've not even asked how you are enjoying your stay in our city. This is your second trip to Ashkelon, yes?"

"Yes, Your Majesty. I was here previously to represent the merchants of Ashkelon in a combat."

"Yes, with the Egyptian. I'm looking forward to hearing about that. And your accommodations here are suitable?"

"Yes, Your Majesty. Your hospitality and the hospitality of his majesty the king have been more than I could hope for."

A pause. The queen turned her head to the side and back again, looking at me from a couple of different angles.

"I understand Commander Ahirom has been gracious with his hospitality as well, sharing with you … how shall I say this … certain comforts."

"Your Majesty, I …" My face expressed uncertainty.

"Oh, am I misinformed? I thought Ahirom was letting you bed his concubine, Altara."

I blushed. "I have had the pleasure of her company from time-to-time."

"And my understanding is Altara derives pleasure from your … uh, company as well."

"I hope that is true."

"So, the ladies like you."

"I may not be the best judge of that."

"Again, such modesty. How unusual in a hero." She did a half turn to the left, then faced me again with a malicious smile. "I understand Altara is quite taken with you. Must be some reason for that. Especially for someone so experienced as she."

"Altara enjoys my conversation."

Laughter exploded from her nostrils. "And you are a wit also. I'm sure you two must do more than talk."

"We do what people do."

"I'm sure you do. But I can't permit Altara to be the only one to enjoy your conversation. Come now, tell me of your exploits."

⊷⊷

2

A teacher will help you master a skill; a good teacher will help you master a skill by methods you may not have imagined.

Ahirom arrived in Gath about twenty days after Bellon informed me I would be Gath's champion. He was in his late twenties then—a man with hair the color of sand and blue eyes. This was unusual and suggested some of his ancestors may not have been from among our people. But, of course, I'm not one to speculate about the origins of unusual characteristics.

He also kept his hair cropped short, shorter than any of the other commanders or soldiers. I thought perhaps this was the custom in Ashkelon, but, no, he explained to me it was for military reasons.

"You want your helmet to fit as securely as possible on your head. The more hair you have the less tight the fit and the better chance that it will be askew or perhaps might even fly off."

He did have a slave available to cut his hair whenever he wished, so that certainly removed one obstacle to frequent hair trimming. He was a man with ample financial resources.

The importance of a snug helmet fit was not the only thing Ahirom taught me. He taught me the importance of—how did he put it—foundational preparation. If one wants to perform a task well, don't just practice that specific task. One must also prepare one's body and soul so that they will be able ready to respond to the demands of the task.

I understood some of this already. I recognized we soldiers went on marches not just to patrol the countryside or observe the foliage, but to harden our bodies for marches on real campaigns. Ahirom, though, had me undertake tasks that at first did not seem connected to the single combat for which he was preparing me. He had me run for long distances and lift heavy objects. He also would throw objects at me without warning, usually small pieces of pottery with rounded edges that he would carry in a bag slung over his shoulder.

After a particularly long and grueling run undertaken in mid-day heat, I had to satisfy my curiosity. Panting, I said, "Why? Why am I doing this? Am I preparing for an athletic competition of some sort? I thought I was supposed to kill my opponent, not challenge him to a footrace."

Ahirom smiled at me indulgently. "You're going to be engaged in a life-and-death struggle—a struggle for which there is no time limit. I have witnessed four combats. One ended in a few moments. One seemed to take longer than grinding grain. The victory in that combat went to the warrior who had the most endurance, not necessarily the most skill with a sword.

His opponent wearied of moving about with his heavy shield and he wasn't quick enough to block the mortal thrust. More likely than not, your combat will be over quickly, but we don't know that. I want you to be prepared for any possibility." With that, he flung another piece of pottery at me, which I barely managed to avoid. "And, yes, I want you to be able to react very quickly to whatever comes your way, whether it's a javelin, a sword thrust, a dagger whipped out suddenly, or just some sand and pebbles thrown toward your eye. Your reflexes have to be as good as those of your cat."

Of course, I also underwent the expected training for single combat, namely endless practice with the various weapons that I or my opponent might use. The major difference from standard military drills was that I engaged in simulated combat with various selected soldiers and Ahirom himself. We used javelin and spear shafts from which the spearheads had been removed and wooden swords and daggers with blunted points, although I was forbidden to use javelin shafts after I landed a hit on the side of a fellow soldier's face. Fortunately, it only knocked a couple of teeth out instead of breaking his jaw. Similarly, I was not permitted to use the heavy shafts that played the role of clubs and axes. But javelin shafts still came my way, as did blows with the substitute clubs and axes. About the only weapon we did not practice with was the bow and arrow because this weapon was excluded from single combat, apparently because having two opponents fire arrows at each other from 200 or 300 paces away did not satisfy notions of what a single combat should entail.

Intensive training went on for a little less than two months. After that, the pace slackened. Ahirom thought I was as fit as I would ever be. Naturally, we still went through exercises from time-to-time to keep my skills and reflexes sharp, as the occasional potsherd bouncing off my head reminded me.

Spending so much time with Ahirom allowed me to become acquainted with him, especially since he would often take his meals with me, unlike the other commanders. I learned his family's wealth originated with his grandfather, who was a very successful merchant. He funded trading expeditions to Egypt, Phoenicia, and Alashiya—an island in the sea which was a rich source of copper. Some stories claimed that our people came from Alashiya, leaving there because of Dagon's promise of a better life in Palestia.

When I asked Ahirom whether he thought the Palestim originally came from Alashiya, he gave an answer that I eventually learned was a favorite response of his: "The question is complex, and our time to consider it is short, so I cannot answer with certainty. It might be."

I found the caution of Ahirom with respect to such questions interesting because, as I found out, he was a learned man. Not only could he read and write, but he even spent time in the temple at Ashkelon studying histories and chronicles relating to the Palestim and other peoples. Many who have not had the benefit of an education like Ahirom's will make sweeping assertions without the slightest hesitation, insisting they are correct about this matter or that. On some issues, certainty seems to increase with the level of ignorance.

As we talked more, I came to understand one reason Ahirom was reluctant to make definitive pronouncements about various subjects. He had read or heard different versions of the same set of events—versions of these events with which most Palestim were not acquainted. One striking example of this was Ahirom's knowledge of the Egyptian story of how the Palestim came to their new land.

After practicing one morning in our usual field outside the city, we were seated under a terebinth tree, its low but widespread branches providing us with some very desirable shade.

I was thinking out loud about my eventual encounter with a Hebrew champion. Although I said I welcomed the opportunity to represent our people, I lamented the fact that we had to fight it all. "Why can't the Hebrews just leave us alone? This land is ours. Given to us by Dagon, who helped us drive away the Egyptians."

Ahirom, who was fully recumbent, his head propped up only slightly against the tree trunk, said after a moment, "You know the Egyptians tell a different story."

"What do you mean?"

"Some of the ships in my grandfather's trading expeditions were permitted to travel down the Nile, the large river that runs through Egypt. There's a large city in the southern part of Egypt which has many monuments and buildings, incredible buildings, some almost as large as Gath itself. Anyway, there is this one building there, I think it might be a mortuary temple for one of the pharaohs, that on its walls has reliefs that describe the defeat of our people."

"What?"

"Yes. In fact, depicted on one of the walls are piles of genitals which the Egyptians supposedly removed from the bodies of our soldiers."

I spat on the ground. "These are lies! How then did we get here? If we were defeated and dickless, how did we establish our five cities and populate them generation after generation?"

"That's a good question. But Egyptians say that they allowed some of us to live and then used us as mercenaries to garrison some of their forts, including the fort at Ashkelon."

"And why aren't we paying tribute to them now?"

Ahirom sat up and looked at me. He shrugged his shoulders and spread his hands, palms up. "Again, good question. Don't know how the Egyptians would answer that. They grew weak—we grew strong—something, something ..."

"But what do you think? Do you think there's any truth to this Egyptian fable?"

"The question is complex, and our time to consider it is short, so I cannot answer ..."

"... with certainty." I finished his statement for him. "I thought you might say that. I would settle for an uncertain answer. Just what do you think?"

He paused to gather his thoughts. Then looking at the ground and not me, he said, "Each people has its own stories. In these stories, they are always the favorites of the gods. They have always triumphed and will always triumph over their enemies, at least as long as they respect the gods." He dug up some dirt and grass from the ground and threw it back down. Looking at me he asked, "Have you ever heard of a people who told stories in which they were not the favorites of the gods? Have you ever heard of a king who built a monument to boast of his defeats?"

He had an edge in his voice and I found his question unsettling. "No-o ..."

His tone grew even more emphatic, making him sound like a parent scolding a child. "Do you know when people stop telling stories that describe them as the favorites of the gods?"

I shook my head.

"When they are annihilated and no one among them is left to tell any more stories. The stories that continue to be told are the stories of those whom the gods let survive." He stood up. "And that's why you need to win your fights. Not just the first one, but whatever fights you may have, so we Palestim can continue to tell *our* stories. Let's head back to Gath."

I did not have to wait much longer to find out whether I could help preserve our people. A dispute arose between us and the Hebrews. There was a settlement called Lachish which the Hebrews had established a long time ago, but which our forefathers had captured and partially destroyed, in the process killing and driving out the Hebrew settlers. This was maybe fifty years before my time. Don't know. Anyway, the remains of the settlement were near our borders; in fact, it was just east of Gath. The Hebrews wanted to resettle there. They argued they needed more space because of increasing population. However, knowing that reestablishing a presence there would lead to conflict, they sent an emissary to Maoch, notifying us of their intent and requesting permission. Maoch consulted with the kings of the four other Palestim cities and they decided that being so close to our territory the settlement would threaten our security, so they denied permission.

Both the Hebrews and we Palestim wanted to avoid restarting hostilities, so both sides decided to use our new method for resolving disputes—single combat. As Gath was the city closest to Lachish, its champion would represent our people.

I was called into the commanders' room and given the news. Bellon, Sardon, and Ahirom were present, along with a young man, maybe thirteen or fourteen. Good, solid build. Bellon introduced me to him. He was Bellon's nephew, Nikon. He was to be my shield bearer.

Some of the rules for single combat had previously been explained to me, but Ahirom now went over them again, this time in more detail so I would know exactly what to expect. We also discussed the tactics I might use.

"Prepare for the heat. The combat will take place at mid-day so neither side has the advantage of the sun," Ahirom said. "It's a shame we haven't established sufficient trust with the Hebrews to schedule the combat just after daybreak."

"Is that how it's done in Ashkelon?" I asked.

"Recently at least, yes. The combatants are aligned north-to-south and no one can move before the start of the contest on pain of forfeit." He looked directly at me. "Forfeit in this case means execution of the offending champion, not just a loss for the merchant. But perhaps a method that works well to resolve disputes among merchants may not work so well between different peoples, hmm?" He gave a quick grin. "But we have implemented as many safeguards as practical. Each champion will be accompanied to the site of combat by an interpreter and a shield bearer. The shield bearer will lay the shield by his champion's side and then, following the instructions of his interpreter, will grab and grip the arm of his counterpart in neutral territory. The interpreters will then simultaneously give a shout and the shield bearers will break their grip and scurry as fast and as far away as they can, followed no doubt by the interpreters. Combat starts as soon as their grip is broken."

"I and my opponent are twenty paces apart, yes?"

"That's correct. As we have discussed before, do pick up your shield immediately. There will be a temptation to rush your opponent or grab and hurl your javelin in the hope you can strike him before he gets his shield up. Won't work. And you'll never have a chance to reach for your shield again. Remember that your size is both an advantage and a disadvantage; it gives you a long reach and enormous strength to your blows, but it also makes you a big target."

"After I pick up my shield, though, I should use the javelin first, as we discussed?"

"Yes. Bear in mind, circumstances can change quickly, but that is almost surely the best choice. The javelin is cumbersome and will slow you down. Best to get rid of it quickly… and you may score a hit with it and that will be the end of things."

"Now regarding the ax and the sword—we discussed this, and you have not given me a clear recommendation."

"Yes." Ahirom drummed his fingers on the table for a moment. "The thing is in your hands the ax is very powerful. I doubt it will shatter his shield, but a blow might very well force him back, possibly even knocking the shield out of his hands or knocking him off his feet. But the sword is more versatile and maneuverable. You have to fend off his attacks at the same time that you're pursuing yours. I'd say go the sword. What do you think?"

"The sword it is."

The contest was in two days and much of the next day would be devoted to marching to the site of the combat. This was good. I did not want time on my hands to fret. I learned from our battles that the anxiety before fighting was far worse than any fear one might have in the midst of combat. In fact, one was usually too focused during combat to experience any fear.

Foresight is both a blessing and a curse for humans. Yes, we can plan for the future, setting aside grain, preparing for seasonal rains, and so forth. But we can also imagine horrible things and worry and dread. In this, I envied Lost, who did not seem to have the capacity to think about what might come. No wonder cats sleep so soundly.

The rest of that day I busied myself with weapons practice and getting acquainted with Nikon. And then there was the haircut.

Ahirom insisted I get a close trim. Not only did he want a tight helmet fit, but he wanted me to be as cool as possible in the mid-day sun. He had his slave come by to do the trimming, which took place in the commanders' room to avoid creating a distracting spectacle for my fellow soldiers.

Ahirom looked at me for a long moment after my locks had been shorn. "By the gods," he chuckled. "You do have a very large head. It's huge."

"Thanks. You make me feel like a monster."

"Oh, your head is beautiful, Goliath. I'd kiss your forehead if I could just reach it!"

The next day, ten of us set out for the combat site. Well, there were ten of us in the official party—the number specified in the agreement with the Hebrews. There were another forty or so soldiers trailing behind, along with several scouts. I'm sure the Hebrews were taking similar precautions. The losing party might think this single combat arrangement was a bad idea and turn quickly to the more traditional way of prevailing in a conflict.

During the march to the site and that evening, as we were encamped, I was never left alone. There was always someone talking to me, telling a story, or just making casual observations about this-and-that. Even Sardon talked to me, and, apart from orders, he had scarcely directed a word in my direction since I had become a soldier. I understood why they were doing this, but the constant flow of chatter was effective in preventing me from thinking too long about why they were doing this.

That evening, before we retired, Bellon insisted I drink a large cup of wine. One cup, and no more. As I had my wine, he told me and the assembled company various stories from his many years as a soldier. I must admit some were amusing, with perhaps the funniest one being the tale of a slave tending a jack donkey who made the mistake of lifting his tunic to relieve himself, in the process presenting his bare ass to the jack's gaze. The jack became amorous and pursued the slave around the field until the slave tripped … and, well … When the slave was asked whether he was hurt, he said only that he still felt constipated because he had not been able to take a shit.

The next morning, we had our usual bread and cheese for breakfast, but then Ahirom provided me with a rare treat: two boiled duck eggs. Before we ate, Bellon offered a short prayer for victory and poured a libation before figures of Dagon and Bel. After breakfast, some of us gambled for a bit, with Bellon generously providing the players with some copper pieces to increase interest in the gaming. We played until a point where I was ahead in my earnings, and Bellon then called a halt.

It was time to pack up and walk the remaining distance to the site, maybe an hour away. I stood up, stretched, and yawned, even though I didn't feel tired. I extended my arms outward and flexed the fingers on my hands, while rolling my neck around in a small circle, working out imaginary kinks. I let out a grunt. I heard Bellon yell, "Let's go."

It was getting hot already. As we walked, I could feel the warmth of the sand through my sandals.

Ahirom came up next to me. "You know you're going to win. I mean, I don't want you to become overconfident, but you are going to win."

"Thanks. I feel pretty good about things."

"There's something I haven't told you before. Again, I don't want you to be overconfident, but the Hebrews are terribly scared of you."

"How do you know this?"

"We interrogate some of our prisoners. Our merchants come back from their territory with stories. You're a giant, you know, at least in their eyes. Helps them explain to themselves some of their defeats. 'The Palestim have a giant among their soldiers. Five cubits high! No! Six cubits high!' I would not be surprised if some of them claim you are seven cubits high and have four arms. Needless to say, we do nothing to discourage these stories."

"With my luck, if I had four arms, I'd just be assigned to cesspit duty more often."

Ahirom chuckled and patted me on the shoulder. "Point is that the Hebrew champion will feel defeated as soon as he sees you. You will be six cubits high in his eyes."

We arrived at the site. The Hebrews were on the rise opposite us. The interpreters from both sides walked into the dry creek bed separating the parties, which is where the combat would take place. They talked. They came back, and then went back down, this time accompanied by their respective commanders. More talking. Bellon and our interpreter walked back up the hill. "It's all set," Bellon said. "May Dagon and Bel watch over you and us, Goliath, and may they provide you and our people with victory. On to victory!"

"On to victory!" echoed all the voices in our small force.

One last hand on my shoulder and a silent nod from Ahirom and I began my descent.

"Is that shield too heavy for you," I asked Nikon, for want of anything better to say.

"Not at all, sir."

"So, do you think you might want to be a soldier in a few years?"

"Yes. I mean, I would like to be a commander."

"Yes, of course, like your uncle."

As we were walking down the slope, I looked at Nikon or the ground in front of me. I couldn't bring myself to look straight ahead.

We stopped. Out of the corner of my eye I saw that the Hebrew champion and his shield bearer had stopped also. We were twenty paces apart. I swallowed hard. I shuddered. My hands trembled. I began breathing rapidly. I then looked across to the Hebrew champion and I regained a bit of my composure. If I was afraid, he seemed to be in full panic. All the color had drained from his face and he was visibly shaking.

He said something, but I couldn't make it out. His voice was weak and of course he was speaking in Hebrew. I then heard him say something like "dog" in our tongue. "Dog?" I said in the loudest voice I could manage. "Is that the best you can do? Well, you need not worry about learning any more of our language because in a moment you will have no more use for it." Nikon and our interpreter laughed. I felt better.

The shield bearers then lay down their shields and walked toward each other. They gripped each other's arm. Almost instantly thereafter, the interpreters yelled, and their grip was broken.

I immediately grabbed my shield while continuing to look at the Hebrew, who was doing the same. Apparently, he had received similar advice because he was also going for his javelin, which was strapped between his shoulders. He had his javelin out first, but here he made his critical mistake. In his rush, he did not position himself properly for his throw and he released the shaft at an unfavorable angle. The javelin went up into the air and fell to the earth well to my side, maybe ten paces behind me. I made ready for my throw. Recognizing his plight, the Hebrew rushed toward me, hoping to close the gap between us and engage me before I could hurl my javelin. In this he failed. I released my javelin. He did have his shield up, but the force from the javelin knocked him backward and off his feet. I was on top of him quickly with my short spear which I plunged into his neck and wrenched viciously upward. Windpipe, gullet, and bone were all exposed briefly before a flood of blood obscured them. The combat was over.

I raised my bloody spear over my head and faced the Hebrew company on the hill, removing any doubt as to the victor. I then turned around slowly to face our contingent, who were letting out a resounding cheer.

The Hebrews honored their agreement. They did not resettle Lachish. However, within a couple of months, another dispute arose, concerning access to a well. The well, which was roughly equidistant between Ekron and Gath, was within our territory, as the Hebrews conceded. But they had established a settlement within their territory a little over two hours walk from the well. The settlement had its own water supply from a stream, but this stream was more like an intermittent rivulet and the expanding settlement wanted a reliable supplementary source. The Hebrews argued that they would not abuse the well privilege. Given the distance between the well and their settlement, it was too remote to be used frequently. Our leaders, though, did not think assisting the nearby Hebrew settlement to prosper and grow was necessarily in our interests. They scheduled a second contest.

Having prevailed in the first challenge, I was more relaxed on my way to the second one. But once we arrived at the combat site and looked over to the Hebrews, we had a surprise.

"What's that hanging over the Hebrew champion's shoulder?" I asked. "It looks like a bag."

Ahirom said, "You know my eyesight is poor. I can't make it out."

"It is a bag. Looks like a bag with stones," Nikon said. "He has a sling."

I turned to Ahirom. "A sling? Is that permitted?"

Ahirom pursed his lips. "Hmm. Well, the only weapon prohibited is the bow. Does he have any weapon other than the sling?"

"It appears he has a sword," Nikon said.

Ahirom grabbed hold of my arm and brought his face close to me as I inclined my head to catch his words. "Look, don't let this rattle you. It's obvious what his tactics are. He hopes to be able to keep you pinned down so you can't close with him and somewhere along the way score a lucky hit, knocking you out. He'll then finish you with the sword. Don't lose your focus. Keep maneuvering your shield to deflect his rocks. Once he's run out, he's finished. As you know from our skirmishes, slingers can be deadly in a large group, but a slinger on his own …?" Ahirom shook his head. "I think it's a sign of desperation."

I will say this for the slinger. He was cocky. Or foolhardy. When the shield bearers broke their grip, he did not reach for his shield but instead immediately started flinging his rocks. He was hoping to strike a mortal or disabling blow quickly. In this he was disappointed. I blocked four stones in quick succession, with only one making contact after it bounced from my shield onto my shoulder. It then occurred to me that I should close on him while I was deflecting the rocks. The distance helped him not me, as once I was within a few paces he would not be able to use the sling effectively. In fact, he panicked as I drew near and instead of picking up his shield, he started throwing rocks from his bag with his hands and then he took off running. He was fast. Desperation gives men wings. But after it was clear that he would not be welcomed back behind his own lines, he had nowhere to go but to run up and down the hill, pausing every now and then to throw a rock. I kept pace with him, the length of my stride compensating for any deficit in speed. He eventually ditched the bag realizing that it was a hindrance and was slowing him down. This did allow him to pick up some speed and he was far enough ahead of me at one point that he could circle back and pick up his shield, but as he did so his right foot gave out and he slipped, falling headfirst to the ground. He brought his head up just in time for it to meet the tip of my spear which I drove into his skull, entering by his left eye.

When I turned to face the Hebrews, they looked disgusted. One of them was yelling at another in their company, presumably the one who suggested using a slinger.

By contrast, our company was giddy with joy, and I confess I had a touch of exuberance myself. I ran up the hill to be embraced by Bellon and then everyone else in turn. I lifted Ahirom above my shoulders as he laughed maniacally. We were all laughing and shouting.

We were too exhilarated to stop on the march home so we arrived in Gath late at night. We woke up the barracks. Bellon gave the news and ordered two rounds of wine for everyone. We had more.

It was that night when Ahirom first mentioned Altara to me, although not by name. We were still sitting in the courtyard, although the celebration was winding down. He was deep in his cups, when he turned to me, laying a hand on my shoulder and said, "You know, big boy, you really deserve a reward for this victory."

"Bellon is giving me five shekels of silver."

He made a dismissive sound with his lips, waving his right hand about. Slurring badly, he said, "Das nusing, nusing." He looked up at me with bleary eyes. "Ya know, I travel back to Ashk'lon now and then. Right?"

"Actually, I didn't know that. I thought you just went to your farm."

"Well, that too … but in Ashk'lon there's a woman you see … beautiful woman …" Here, with his right hand, he sketched in the air a rough outline of a woman. "Beautiful. Anyway, old friend, I can arrange…" He didn't finish the thought.

"Yes, you were saying?"

"Well, you know, I keep her, so … if ever…" He waved his right hand about in some vague gesture and then leaned over, his head slowly approaching the ground. I pushed a cushion under him. I stumbled to my quarters where I found Lost waiting for me. He licked my face by way of congratulations.

The next day, after the mid-day meal, I spied Ahirom as he was coming out of the commanders' work space. His allusions the previous night to a woman had aroused my interest, as one might expect. I decided to approach him.

As I came closer to him, I could see he did not look well. His face was ashen and I could detect the sour smell of vomit on his breath from a couple of paces away. "Good day, sir. I hope you're well," I said half-jokingly.

"No, I'm not," he said with a note of irritation. "What do you want, Goliath?"

"Last night ... you mentioned something about a woman in Ashkelon ... about how you can arrange for me to meet her."

"Did I?" His eyes narrowed and he looked away. Then looking back at me, he said, "I don't remember that."

"Well, sir, I don't mean ..."

"Look, Goliath, maybe we can talk about this some other time. I need to get back to my farm."

And that was that—at least for another year.

That winter I had my third combat. The city of Ekron had executed a Hebrew who the Hebrews claimed had been wrongly accused of rape. This particular Hebrew had some sort of religious function, so in their community he was regarded as an important person. Ekron had their own champion, but he was untested, so their king asked Maoch whether I could represent their city. This was an honor for Gath and Maoch, so he agreed. No one thought to ask me.

Winter is our rainy season and we had showers throughout our march to the combat site. Breakfast the morning of the combat was wet and miserable, as the rain intensified. In contrast to the two prior combats, no one talked much as we approached the site, with the only sound at times being the rain plunking against our armor.

The dry creek bed was no longer dry, but rather a morass of mud. I thought the winner might be whoever does not get mired down. Perhaps my size would cease to be an advantage.

As it turned out, this third time, the Hebrews decided to try to find someone who might approach my size, at least in terms of height. Their champion was over four cubits tall, but he was also quite thin. He did not appear healthy. It was as though his body had drained the energy from his limbs and torso, channeling it into his stature.

He did put up a good fight, however. At the start, both of us went for javelins and both of us missed. We then strode toward each other, swords drawn, treading carefully so as not to lose our footing. I noticed his sword was iron, indicating he had it either procured it from some Palestim— perhaps the corpse of a Palestim—or the Hebrews had learned the process for forging iron. In any event, it held up well as we traded blow for blow. His reflexes were good, but as we continued I could tell he was getting tired. Instead of lifting his feet, he was shuffling through the muck. His shield was moving just a little too slow and his sword was getting too close to his body as he deflected my thrusts. And then he failed to parry when I brought my sword down upon his right shoulder, cutting a huge gash. His sword dropped. Courageously he struggled on, using his shield to ward off my blows, which now increased in tempo, as he tried in vain to control his right hand enough to pull his dagger. The combat ended when the edge of my sword landed a hard blow on his helmet. His knees buckled and his shield dropped enough that I could thrust my sword into his throat. When I pulled it out, he fell into the mud, his blood, the muck, and the rain forming a hideous puddle.

I earned twenty shekels of silver—and the following spring a trip to Ashkelon and my first kisses from Altara.

⊷⊷

3

The journey to Ashkelon from Gath can take two to three days, depending on one's pace of travel. We had merchants traveling with us, their mules laden with goods, so our trip lasted three days, two of which were oppressively hot and dusty. By the third day, however, a cool breeze could be felt coming off the sea.

The sea. The sea. Yes, I had heard people describe it, but to see it, to smell it, to hear the sound of its waves crashing on the shore, to dip one's hands into its salty, blue-green waters … Knowing of something and experiencing something, well, sometimes they are as different as contemplating a cup of wine and drinking it. Knowledge without direct experience can inform, but somehow it seems thin, insubstantial, whereas some experiences flood the senses. Love is like that too, right? One can hear talk of love, one can observe how people in love behave, so one can have some understanding of love without being in love, but still … it's not quite the same, is it?

I think my memories of Altara and of the sea shall ever be conjoined, and not just because I encountered them around the same time. Perhaps love and the sea have something in common. Both come in waves that overpower one, which then recede briefly, only to return again with majestic, breathtaking force. Desire sweeps one away like the tide.

⊫≼╂╀≽⊨

4

The queen snapped at me, visibly irritated. "I didn't ask you here to prattle on with your boyish, lovesick sentiments. I want to hear about your exploits as a champion."

She stood up. I followed quickly.

"My apologies, Your Majesty. Do you want me to leave?"

She eyed me for a long moment. "I still haven't heard of your combat in Ashkelon last year or how you captured the Hebrews' sacred chest. Stay and tell me about these, but don't let your thoughts wander."

"Yes, Your Majesty. I will not mention Altara again."

"I didn't say you should not mention her, but ... keep to your story. Don't dwell on your emotions. It's unmanly." She returned to her chair and motioned for me to do the same. "Continue. Tell me about the Egyptians' champion."

⊫≼╂╀≽⊨

5

I was going to Ashkelon as the result of a dispute between a group of the city's merchants and an Egyptian trader. Trade between Egypt and Palestia was not frequent, but usually three to four voyages were undertaken each year. Egypt sent us papyrus, gold, and incense—basically luxury goods— and in return we sent wood, ironware, and wine. In a recent trade, a couple of Palestim vessels went to Egypt with merchandise based on the security of a vessel laden with papyrus and gold that was moored in Ashkelon's harbor. The goods on the vessel would be released to the Palestim merchants once word was received from Egypt that the Palestim merchandise had been delivered. Word was received, but when it came time for the Egyptian trader's goods to be handed over, he claimed he had been robbed. Thieves had somehow gained access to his vessel and spirited away most of his gold.

Ashkelon's merchants believed the trader had arranged for the gold to be taken away and had either stored it somewhere or had it taken back to Egypt. They seized the vessel. They also wanted several of the Egyptian's fingers to be removed, but the king refused, although he did order the trader to be detained under guard in some back room of the palace.

In former days, Egypt might have resolved the dispute by sending a fleet to sack Ashkelon, but Egypt was not the power it once was. Nonetheless, the king was loath to create animosity between Palestia and Egypt. He proposed to the Egyptian trader that he submit the dispute to trial by single combat, with the understanding that if the Egyptian prevailed, he would be free to leave with his ship, minus the goods that remained on board, but that if he lost, the ship would be forfeit and he would have to stay in Ashkelon three more months, at his own expense, while the search for the missing gold continued. Under the circumstances, the Egyptian trader found these terms acceptable. Also, the Egyptian could arrange to have someone from Egypt represent his interests in the contest if that was his preference. That was his preference. The merchants of Ashkelon petitioned Maoch for my services. He granted their petition.

Ahirom accompanied me to Ashkelon. He was in high spirits, confident after my three victories that I would triumph again. Also, he was looking forward to spending time with his friends and acquaintances in Ashkelon, or so he said. I learned that he traveled to Ashkelon about six times a year, usually on horseback, although on this trip, since I did not ride, he walked with me most of the way, occasionally making use of one of the mules.

In Ashkelon, Ahirom arranged for me to stay in my own room at the city's barracks. Staying at the barracks would allow me to go through some drills with Ashkelon's soldiers in preparation for the combat.

Ashkelon's barracks were larger than Gath's, with a steep glacis that made an approach from the side facing the sea nearly impossible. My room was on the third level, facing the sea. In contrast with my quarters at Gath, I had a table and chair and a raised mattress of straw and goat hair. The benefits of being a champion.

In the two days that I had before the contest, I went through the necessary drills, but I was distracted. My thoughts were overwhelmed by all the novel experiences that Ashkelon offered. Not only was there the sea itself, but also all that went with the sea. Ships— which I had never seen before;

the creaking piers jutting into the water, piled high with trade goods and an assortment of fish; the gulls, with their black heads sharply contrasting with their white bodies, circling and diving over the harbor. The city itself was very different from Gath; it was three times the size of Gath, with many houses spilling outside its walls. It was impossible to get lost in Gath, but in Ashkelon, although one always knew in which direction the sea lay, one might wander in its narrow, crisscrossing alleys and streets without a clear sense of direction for some time—as I found out.

The evening before the contest, Ahirom invited me to his residence in the city to share a meal with him. The house was smaller than I had imagined given Ahirom's wealth, but as he explained to me, he had sold his larger residence when he purchased his farm outside Gath. Now that he visited Ashkelon only every other month, a modest residence sufficed. As it was, the house was richly appointed with some sort of furniture in every room. Moreover, he had fashioned a sort of dining area on the roof over the left side of his courtyard. In addition to a table and chairs, he had two small couches with goat hair cushions which could be removed when it rained. He had a servant who managed the residence during his absence, along with two slaves, a brother and sister. The slaves were from a land unknown to me far to the north. Ahirom's father had purchased them at the Phoenician city of Dor.

There were two offering tables, one for Dagon and one for Bel, near the dining table. Before we began our meal, Ahirom uttered a short prayer and poured a libation into the bowl on each table.

"With the help of the gods, I've no doubt that you will emerge victorious tomorrow," Ahirom said.

"May it be so."

"There is one thing you should know. I saw the Egyptian's champion today."

"Where?"

"He's being housed in an annex to the palace."

"He gets to stay in the palace?"

"An annex. His room is no larger than yours. He's there for security reasons. If we placed him in the barracks, there might be an unpleasant confrontation, not with you, but with some of the soldiers."

"I understand."

"Anyway, he's … he's quite tall and striking. Not quite your height, but not far from it, and unlike that last Hebrew champion you faced, he's filled out. He's in good shape, with a torso as taut as yours. Also, he's a Nubian. Black as night. Much darker than you. He has a shaved head, but curiously he has a beard. Don't know if that's the custom in his country or he wears it that way for affect, perhaps to give himself a fierce look. If so … well, it's well-designed.

"Why are you telling me this?"

"Don't want you to be surprised … or …" He searched for the right word.

"Shaken?"

"I don't think anything could shake you, Goliath. It shouldn't. Still, seeing someone so different for the first time … it could affect your concentration."

"Thanks for the description. I'll be prepared."

But I was not prepared for what I saw the next morning as I approached the field of combat. The Egyptian champion had on little armor—just a helmet and arm guards that extended from his shoulders to his wrists. This gave me some pause as I had on more armor than usual. Underneath my corselet, I was wearing a bronze coat of mail. Ahirom had suggested this extra layer of protection as the combat would take place in the early morning, pursuant to the custom in Ashkelon, and I did not have to worry about the heat.

More surprising, though, was the absence of a shield and the Egyptian's choice of weapon. In his left hand he held a large circular net, large enough to drape a body. The net appeared to have iron weights along the edges. In his right hand he held a spear. There also appeared to be a dagger fastened to his girdle. No sword or javelin.

"Have you seen this net used before?" I asked Ahirom. "What tactics should I use to defend against it?" His suddenly solemn face drained of color gave me my answer.

"Wait," Ahirom said, as he grabbed my arm. "I'm going to talk to the arbitrator."

The rules for single combat were different in Ashkelon. In addition to the earlier start time, there was an arbitrator chosen by both sides, typically a member of the merchant community who did not have a personal stake in the dispute. This arbitrator would give a hand signal to start and stop the combat. He would also confirm the death of the defeated champion. When Ahirom had mentioned this function to me, I remarked that hardly seemed necessary. He explained it was the custom for two reasons. First, merchants are not an especially trusting group. They demand proof. Second, there would be a crowd witnessing the combat from a distance. They needed to know when the combat was definitively over.

Yes, we had spectators that day. Perhaps several hundred. This could not be avoided. Unlike the barren setting for the contests with the Hebrews, Ashkelon's field of combat was a short walk from the city walls, on a plateau overlooking the sea. A duel to the death was of no small interest to a substantial portion of the city's population, even though they had no personal stake in the controversy. A detachment from the city's garrison kept the crowd at a distance, perhaps 150 paces from the combat area. The crowd's enthusiasm and lung power were not adversely affected by their impaired vision. They were yelling as soon as they spied me approach the field of combat, and now that there was an unexpected pause in the proceedings their shouts grew louder.

Ahirom's conversation with the arbitrator was animated and prolonged, in part because within a couple of moments, both the Egyptian trader and some of the Ashkelon merchants with whom the trader had the dispute joined the discussion. Raised voices and much pointing. Meanwhile, the Egyptian champion and I looked at each other. He narrowed his eyes to the point of squinting and bellowed out something like, "Enjoy these last few moments. You die today." He had some knowledge of our language, or perhaps the trader had taught him to recite this phrase. I put on a mask of boredom, dismissing his comments with a wave of my hand, and replied, "Bark away little doggie, you have no bite."

Ahirom returned and motioned for me to turn around and speak to him. I leaned in.

"Can't do much about the net. The net isn't expressly prohibited, probably because no one has used it before. I was able to persuade the arbitrator that the net should be treated as a shield substitute, so he will have to place it on the ground before the combat starts, just as your shield will be placed on the ground. Anyway, look, by way of tactics, all I can say is avoid the net. He can't do much otherwise with a spear." Ahirom grasped my arm firmly and looked into my eyes. "May the gods smile on you."

The Nubian and I faced off. The arbitrator dropped his hand.

I picked up my shield and prepared to release my javelin, but before I could get a proper grip, the Nubian ran toward me and cast his net. I moved back quickly on a slant, and tried to position myself again, but the Nubian was able to yank his net back almost in an instant; he had a drawrope tied around his wrist. He cast again, and again I moved back on a slant, avoiding the net. Realizing I would not have time to position myself for a throw, I dropped my javelin and reached for my short spear. As I did so, my adversary closed and jabbed away at me with his spear, forcing me to block his thrusts with my shield. He then cast his net again, hoping to snare me while I was engaged, but again I was able to avoid it— barely.

I decided to rush him, hoping to strike his unprotected body in the interval between his throws, but he was too adept with the net, and he was able to sling it before my spearhead reached, although not with much force. The net caught my shield. He tugged it in violently. To avoid being drawn into him with my left arm trapped in his net, I had no choice but to let go of the shield, which he snapped away. An audible gasp went up from the crowd. Simultaneously, we both thrust our spears. I did land a glancing blow on his left shoulder but the spearhead failed to penetrate. His thrust was deflected by my armor. I thought I could strike again while he maneuvered the shield out of his net, but he deftly expelled the shield in a moment while parrying my thrust with his spear.

I was now afraid. The Nubian had the advantage. If I were quick enough on my feet, I could keep dodging the net, but for how long? Eventually, weighed down by my armor, I would tire.

It then occurred to me that if his net could snatch away my shield, then perhaps the process could work in reverse: provided I had the right angle, I could snag his net on my spear and yank it off. I would have to take some risks to make this maneuver, but that was better than dancing to his music until I died.

As he cast the net again, instead of moving back on a slant, I moved forward on a slant to his left side, throwing myself to the ground and then rolling away quickly, until I was positioned under his left hand at which point I thrust my spear upward with both hands, hooked the net on my spearhead right where it met the drawrope, and yanked it forward. The net came off his hand. He stumbled forward and went to his knees. This was good—because my spear had become entangled in his net.

I leapt up and drew my dagger, all in one motion. I was upon him before he could react and pushed him to the ground. He landed on his right side. I was able to plunge the dagger into the left side of his chest, but the wound was not fatal. In the meantime, he shoved his spear toward me, hoping to strike me in the side, but with his right arm on the ground, his angle was too high and the spear skittered along on the surface of my armor. He grabbed my right hand with his left, hoping to force the dagger from my hand. He failed, but he did manage to stay my hand. He then dropped his spear and tried to slide his body so he could face me full on, simultaneously groping forward with his right hand, hoping to reach the dagger, or possibly just tear at my face, but I countered with my left, pinning him down.

It then became a trial of strength. Slowly, inexorably, straining with all my might, I moved the dagger down toward his neck. His body bucked defiantly, as he tried to use his legs to lift himself up or move me off. To no avail. Terror doused the fire in his eyes; my blade extinguished his flame completely.

Exhausted, I pushed myself up. The arbitrator came over and confirmed the result with an emphatic nod toward the disputing parties. The crowd let loose a cheer.

Ahirom rushed up to embrace me. He was trembling. "Don't tell me you were concerned," I whispered hoarsely.

He chuckled. "I must admit it … But now I feel ashamed. I should never doubt you. You're a warrior without equal."

Ahirom insisted on a celebratory mid-day meal at his residence, with a large number of guests matched by an equally large number of servings of wine. Ahirom invited his father, Melqath, and introduced me. Melqath was in his late fifties, with thinning white hair; he had light eyes like Ahirom, although they were greenish-blue rather than pure blue. He maintained a reserved, formal bearing. His greeting was formal too, almost cold. I noticed he had no drink with him.

After we parted, I said to Ahirom, "Your father doesn't seem to like me."

"No, that's not it," Ahirom assured me. "My mother died last year and now he doesn't like to go to events, unless business requires it. Don't let him spoil your mood. Drink up!" I did.

At some point during our rounds of drinking, Ahirom planted himself beside me and kissed my cheek. His breath was fishy, no doubt as a result of the half-eaten fillet of grouper he held in his right hand. "I can't tell you how proud I am … how happy you made me."

"Well, you can imagine, I'm also glad it turned out well."

He looked at me. "I have a confession to make," he said.

"Yes? What is it?"

"First, I want you to know I'm going to give you two mina of silver."

"That's very generous. Thank you."

"Well …" He gave a half-smile. "I made five mina today."

"How?"

"By wagering on you."

"With whom?"

He took a swig of wine. "The merchants. The merchants who had the dispute with the Egyptian trader."

"What? Why would they bet against me? I was fighting for *them*."

"That's how merchants think. They want some insurance against possible losses. Make no mistake, they wanted you to win. That ship even without the gold is worth much more than five mina. But … if things did not turn out well, they did not want a complete loss."

I looked down at my cup, still having difficulty comprehending this information.

"Look, I didn't mean to make you sad. This is a day to celebrate." He put his left hand on my shoulder. "Goliath, I haven't forgotten that some time ago I promised to … to introduce you to a special woman. She's my concubine. Her name is Altara. I want you to spend this evening with her."

I turned my head and looked at him out of the corner of my eye. I said nothing.

"Look, I know this day was trying, but trust me, this will relax you."

"Well, if you are going to twist my arm …"

"Ha! Fine, then. Stay here this afternoon. Take a nap. I'll clear this crowd out in a bit. Then I'll have my slave Tamreya give you a nice hot bath. She'll scrub you with some natron—want to make sure we have all that blood off you—and put some oil on your body. And I have another surprise. I've had a tunic made for you. White wool! Very nice! You'll see." He pounded my shoulder with his hand. "Took the wool from half the sheep in Ashkelon to make it!"

6

I paused and looked up at the queen.

"Yes," she said, "why have you stopped?"

"At this point in my story I would speak of Altara and you had said …"

"Oh, go on. You won't be happy unless you can talk about her. Just avoid sentimentality. I would be more interested in the details of your … conversation."

⊰⊹⊱

7

Ahirom's male slave accompanied me to Altara's residence—or I should say the residence supplied by Ahirom. When Ahirom had his larger house, Altara had lived with him, along with his wife and children. But now that Ahirom occupied a smaller abode and was only occasionally in Ashkelon, he thought it better for Altara to have a separate residence.

The house was a small, narrow two-story building, situated on a rise that separated it from adjacent buildings. I could tell from the outside that it did not have a courtyard. No need for one. Ahirom would not have his woman grinding grain or milking ewes. Although the building was small, it was well-built, constructed with dressed sandstone, as were the other nearby buildings.

A woman with a pleasant smile opened the door. She was in her forties. She introduced herself as Munika, although I couldn't be sure of her name as she spoke with a foreign accent. She invited me in and brought me down a hallway to the rear of the building. A door opened onto a small open area bounded by a low stone wall. A hearth was in one corner and in the other was a table with two chairs. One could almost make out the sea if one looked west.

"Please, sit down and refresh yourself." Munika nodded to the cup of wine on the table. "I'll be back in a moment."

I was still standing when Munika came back with a basin of water, a cloth, and a bar of natron. "Sit, sit," she insisted. "I wash your feet."

"But I just finished bathing."

"Street dirt," she said.

I held out my feet. "Oh, my," Munika exclaimed. "I might need another basin. I've never seen a foot so large."

Munika proved capable of meeting the challenge of my hooves and when she finished, she said, "Come inside now. I'll take you up to Altara."

Back inside, we ascended the staircase, which was well lit, with two oil lamps in niches in the wall. As soon as we reached the top of the stairs, I heard a lilting voice call out from the room on my left, "Welcome, Goliath, please come in." I pulled the curtain aside and entered.

Altara was seated at a table which had a lamp. She held a highly polished bronze mirror in her left hand while she applied malachite to her lower eyelids with a small ivory stick. "You'll have to forgive me. I should have been ready for you. Please have a seat on the couch if you wish."

"I... I..."

"Or you can continue to stand if you want. Whatever pleases you."

Altara finished applying the malachite and turned to face me. "Oh … you are tall. I'm glad Ahirom likes high ceilings." She walked over to me and placed her two hands on my right arm. I never felt hands so soft. "Come, sit on the couch. Otherwise I may need to climb on a stool to talk with you."

I sat. Altara sat down next to me. It was now twilight, with darkness increasing rapidly, but the remaining sunlight entering through two windows and the light from the lamp revealed that Ahirom did not deceive me. Altara was beautiful. Her hair, the color of carnelian or copper, was pulled back, permitting a full view of her softly sculpted face, from her green eyes, which blended smoothly with her malachite, to her inviting lips. Her thin white linen robe traced a slender body that was unmistakably female. A scar that was half a finger in length and ran down her right cheek to the edge of her mouth caused the corner of her lips to fold inward, but somehow this made her more attractive—it prevented her beauty from being the inert beauty of a statue. It was a flaw that proved her to be flesh.

But it was her touch that put me in her power. When we sat, she placed her left hand on me again, her fingers whispering across my arm. Her touch both energized and paralyzed me, causing my heartbeat to quicken while binding me to that spot, unable to move.

"You had another triumph today, I hear," she said. "That must make you feel good."

My thoughts a prisoner, I was unable to say anything but the truth. "I feel … I feel like I would gladly trade twenty victories for the pleasure of sitting next to you."

She flashed a smile and let loose a short laugh. "Oh, you're too kind. Thank you." She then leaned forward and pulled my head down until our lips met. We kissed and then we kissed again and again, my lips greedily seeking to drink her in, while her tenderness held my desire in check. She was fragrant, wearing a perfume that mixed myrrh with sweet cane.

"If you want, we can lie down on the bed," she said as she ran a finger along the outside of my thigh. I picked her up and carried her over to the bed.

It was then that we realized we had a problem. Her mattress sat on a wooden platform, with finely carved panels at both ends. It was difficult enough for me to fit on the mattress given my width, but my length made it impossible. As I tried to lie down, my lower legs dangled awkwardly in the air propped up against the bottom panel. I was a ramp leading nowhere.

"I'm so sorry," she said. "I should have taken care of this before. We can take the mattress off or…"

"No, no that's fine," I said as I slid off the bed onto my knees. "Just let me kiss you. Let me kiss your lips, cheek, ears, neck … May I…" I motioned toward her robe which together we then removed. The sight of her inflamed my desire, sending heat coursing through my veins.

Kneeling, I drew Altara closer to me, seeking her mouth again. Then, as promised, I refused to ignore her waiting cheek, her patient neck, or her lonely ears, spending some moments with each. I worked my way down from her shoulders, pausing a good while at her breasts, which unobtrusively requested my attention. I laid my lips across her belly as her hands caressed my head.

She had on an undergarment, a short skirt across her hips, which was fastened by a fibula. I fumbled with it until she said, "Let me." Her breathing was becoming as heavy as mine.

I then journeyed to her legs, letting my lips feel the warmth of her thighs. I kissed every part of her body that I could see and then I used my lips to see where my eyes could not.

Her previous fragrance of myrrh and sweet cane was now replaced by a full, feral, fecund scent. Sheep's milk, but richer.

Lacking experience, I let Altara's responses be my teacher. I learned that it was not her opening, but a knob above her opening that was most sensitive to my tongue and lips. Her low moans and the trashing about of her thighs guided my movements and in expressing her pleasure she also gave voice to my increasing ardor. After some time, the moans increased in intensity as her hands dug into my scalp. Her thighs then suddenly pressed against my ears, as her lower body quivered and twitched. She was saying something. I couldn't make it out.

I didn't know whether to stop my caresses with my mouth or continue, so after a pause I continued. Altara laughed. "Oh, gods," she said, "you're tickling me."

I raised my head. "Do you want me to stop?"

"Yes … no … yes … oh, no." She laughed again. "Come, kiss me … here," and she motioned to her mouth.

We kissed and then she said. "I was supposed to give you pleasure."

"You have."

She then closed her eyes and whispered, "Fuck me."

"How…"

"Yes, that's right. Our problem. Hold on. Up for a moment." She pushed me off, got out of the bed, and started tugging on the mattress. "Help me get this on the floor."

We yanked the mattress off the bed and she grabbed a cushion that she had used to prop up her head and threw it on top of the mattress. Altara then looked at me, and laughing, said, "You need to remove your tunic or you're going to stretch it beyond all repair." In saying this, she put her hand on my bulge.

I disrobed. Altara began to lie down and then stopped suddenly. "Wait, before I forget … gods, I am … Why didn't I think of this before? Look, you can't put your seed in me … I can't have a baby. Sorry. You understand?"

"Yes … I understand. So …"

"Just when you feel release coming, pull out and spread your seed on my belly."

We then lay down and she used her hand to guide me into her opening. I thought: this is why men want women. I had pleasured myself with my own hand for years, of course, and had forced myself on that Hebrew girl, but this sensation … wine compared to water.

It didn't take long. The ferocity of our desire didn't permit it. Our bodies rose and fell in unison, moving fast, then faster. She clutched at me and pulled me in deeper. After some moments I felt the shuddering begin, and I pulled my hips away from her body, making my seed dodge her opening, just like I had trained my body to move away from a blade.

Desire abated, we lay together, slowly, tenderly kissing, our hands holding and caressing, working against time to maintain our unity. We talked—about what I cannot recall—and giggled until Munika's barely audible voice said, "Altara. Altara."

"Yes?" Altara raised herself up on one elbow and turned toward the curtain.

"It's night. The moon shows it's late."

"Fine. Thank you." Altara turned back toward me, putting her hand on my cheek and sighed. "You have to go."

"Must I?" It was a question to which I knew the answer.

"Yes, you can't ... You must return to the barracks, I believe."

That was my understanding, but I had not told her. I suppose Ahirom had.

"Munika will bring a basin and you can wash up before you leave."

"Don't think I want to," I said as I reached for my tunic. "I don't want to wash you off."

She also dressed. Before I walked out of the room, I cupped her hands in mine. "The gods willing, I will see you again, but before I pray that I be granted this request, I need to know whether you want this as well."

Altara did not answer right away. She looked down for a moment and then said in a soft voice, "Yes."

I turned to leave. Before I descended the stairs, I heard her run to the curtain and call out, "Don't just ask the gods. You need to ask Ahirom as well."

I walked to the barracks, still bathed in her scent. I couldn't sleep that night. Altara had awakened a passion in me that would not let me rest. In the morning, I thought for a while that I had been able to suppress this passion, as I answered questions from the soldiers and the sub-officers in Ashkelon's garrison regarding my victory over the Egyptian and my thoughts strayed for some moments from Altara. But while I was still engaged in some bantering on the topic of my combat, a renewed wave of desire passed through my body, seizing my thoughts and speech. I had defeated the Egyptian champion, but this passion had captured me. Too abruptly, I broke off our conversation, mumbling that I recalled I had some business to take care of. I went to my room to gather my thoughts, and then I went back to the courtyard, a goatskin with wine in my hand. I stopped by offering tables for Dagon and Bel and poured a libation while pleading for their favor. I then thought I must make an offering to Qetesh, goddess of love, and like a madman in the grip of brain fever, I went from soldier to soldier asking where I might find an effigy of Qetesh appropriate for prayer and an offering. One soldier did have a figure, which I borrowed, but before I poured the libation, I needed to borrow a bowl into which to pour the offering. Then I decided I could not make an offering by pouring wine from a goatskin. I needed a proper vessel, so I went to the kitchen and asked for a ewer. It was in such a frenzied state that I passed the early part of the day.

Libations and prayers completed, I sought out the commander on duty and asked for a pass, explaining I needed to see Ahirom. He looked at me quizzically for a moment, but then handed me the clay disk, cautioning me only that I should return before the evening meal as the prevailing merchants planned to come to the barracks to present me with a gift.

I left. I hurried through the streets to Ahirom's house. His male slave opened the door and went to fetch Ahirom.

"By the gods, man," Ahirom said as he slowly emerged from his upper level and walked toward me. "What are you doing here? It's not even close to mid-day. Oh, and look at you. It looks like you haven't slept."

"In truth, I haven't. Not much."

"I was hoping to relax you, not set you on edge. Something troubling you?"

"I'm not on edge. I'm ..." I couldn't find the words.

"Fine. Why are you here?"

"I need to see Altara."

Ahirom threw back his head and laughed. Shaking his head from side to side, he said, "Oh, gods, what have I done?" Then, looking at me, he said, "I don't know if ... well, when did you want to see her?"

"Now."

Again he laughed. To no one in particular, he said, "So the mighty warrior has fallen." Then to me, he said, "Well, that's not possible. She's at the palace today. I don't know if I told you, but I persuaded the queen to allow Altara to be one of her attendants. She's at the palace every other day and then on special occasions. This was no small feat, mind you, given Altara's ... status."

"Then this evening."

"The merchants are coming to the barracks this evening to bestow a gift upon you. Meant to tell you that yesterday."

Silently, I prayed to Qetesh.

"Oh, Goliath … your expression … don't think I would've seen such agony on your face had the Egyptian removed your balls." He put his right hand on my shoulder. "I don't know if this is good for you or bad, but … fine, fine. I can't say you don't deserve this. I will arrange things. I will have the merchants come tomorrow night and I'll get word to Munika, who will let Altara know."

"Thank you, thank you."

With his hand still on my shoulder, he looked at me intently and said, "But this is the last time. We return to Gath in two days, and Altara will be … otherwise engaged for the remainder of our stay in Ashkelon." As he said this, he squeezed my shoulder tightly. It did not seem playful. "Now get back to the barracks. Find some companions to do drills with you or offer to help them with some tasks. Then get some rest."

That evening, Altara was waiting for me at the top of the stairs as I entered her residence. I bounded up the stairs and we embraced. Still locked in an embrace, we went into her room. Her mattress was already on the floor. We made good use of it. The mattress did not stay there the entire evening, however, as I wanted to kiss Altara intimately again, and I needed her on the bed for this. My neck would not permit it otherwise. One of the difficulties of size. She did not refuse my request. Like a bee at a blossom, I drank her nectar—until the blossom closed.

Our desires temporarily sated, I leaned back against the wall. Altara told me to get a mat that was on the other side of the couch as I would be more comfortable. I complied, although I don't think I would've noticed had I been sitting on nails.

We were silent for a while, and I grew anxious, worried about saying something wrong and equally worried about saying nothing. Impulsively, I made ready to leave, but she called me back imploring me to stay and sit.

Then we talked. She asked me about my family, my time before I was a champion, and I told her about the bloomery, my parents, my sisters, Phodan, my father's death. This was the first time I had related these events to anyone, at least in any detail. This was the first time anyone had seemed interested in them.

Desire then returned for both of us, and we reversed the order that we followed earlier, with Altara on the bed, and then the mattress on the floor. After we made love, we entwined our legs and held each other tightly. I kissed her eyes, perhaps the one part of her that my lips had missed.

"You've got malachite and kohl on your lips now," she said, laughing, brushing off my lips with her finger.

"I want to taste all parts of you, even the parts you've added. You think they make you beautiful, but you have beautified them." I kissed her eyes again, flicking my tongue lightly on her lids. She giggled. Then I kissed her ears in turn, her cheeks, her neck, her fingers, her hands, her ...

"Stop, stop," she said. "I can't take any more."

"I will stop if you tell me about yourself. It's your turn now."

"Mmm ... well then, maybe you should continue kissing me."

"No, no. As much as I would enjoy that, I want to know you. Your history is part of you too and I can't embrace that unless you share it with me."

She paused to gather her thoughts. She looked away from my face. "My first memories ... let's see ... I was a servant—slave actually, although I did not know the difference then—on the farm of Ahirom's father, Melqath. He has a big farm. Wheat, barley, olives, goats, sheep, pigs ... most everything I suppose. Although he stopped raising pigs. Too much trouble." She turned to me. "Did you know pigs can't sweat?"

"No, I didn't. Never been on a farm myself, and we didn't keep pigs at our house."

"Yeah, it's strange. Anyway, at the farm I lived with my mother and my aunt. We shared a room with other female slaves. I think there were ten of us. Not sure when I was first put to work. Five, six maybe. Fed the animals, things like that." She looked up at me again. "You sure you're interested in this?"

"Yes, I am," I said as I kissed her nose. "So, your father ... he died when you were young or before you were born or ..."

"Before I was born, so my mother said. She was pregnant with me when our city was taken and we were enslaved."

"Where's your family from anyway?"

"Thrakia."

"Never heard of it. Where is it?"

"To the north. Across the sea somewhere. Don't really know myself."

"Is that where Munika is from? I noticed she speaks with an accent."

"Munika is my aunt. I guess I haven't told you that. But then, we haven't spent much time talking until now," she said laughing.

"Do you speak Thrakian, or whatever it's called?"

"Only a few words. My mother wanted me to learn your language, so she usually spoke only Palestim around me."

I picked up one of her hands, and after kissing it, said "You must not have worked on the farm for too long. Your hands are very soft."

"Stopped when I was nine. They freed my mother, which meant freeing me. Still don't know why they did this."

"But that was a good thing obviously."

"I suppose so. All it meant at the time was that I stopped working the farm and they moved me to Ashkelon to work in Melqath's city home. Cleaning. That sort of thing. My mother remained on the farm."

We had thrown a mantle over ourselves and Altara began picking at the mantle with her fingers as she spoke. "Didn't see my mother after that. She and a bunch of others got sick that winter. The flux."

"I'm sorry."

We were both quiet for a moment, and then Altara started speaking again. "So ... they allowed Munika to move to the city as well. That was nice. She taught me how to weave and I was doing a lot of that when ... well, as you know, Ahirom took an interest in me." She moved her hand gently across my chest, propped her head up on my shoulder and gave me a smile. "That's my story. Been Ahirom's concubine since I was fourteen. Over five years now."

"I know there's more to it than that. Ahirom told me you work in the palace, as one of the queen's handmaidens."

She threw her head back and laughed. "Is that what you call it? Every other day I have to be at the palace before dawn so I can empty her piss pot. Then I get to fetch whatever she wants and clean up her room."

"You don't like it?"

"Maybe I shouldn't complain. Gives me something to do. I think that's why Ahirom arranged for it. When he moved to his farm outside Gath last year, he knew I was going to be alone most of the time, except for Munika. When I lived with him and his family, I helped look after his children. I liked that."

I thought about asking her whether she liked her arrangement with Ahirom, but thought better of it. Wasn't my place to question it.

"Anyway, the queen is nice enough. It's the other attendants who are the problem. They treat me like dirt. You know, I'm a whore." She nestled closer to me. "I think they're jealous. Ahirom is one of the richest men in all of Palestia." She moved her face against my neck and gave me a lick. "And I enjoy fucking. And now I've fucked the greatest warrior in all of Palestia." Her hand went under the mantle and worked its way to my groin.

"I think you're going to be disappointed. In some things, women are stronger than men. A couple of times in an evening I can manage, but beyond that ..."

"Oh ... I think I could help you find your strength again." She stroked me gently back and forth but to no avail. Not enough time had passed. I moved her hand away.

"Just hold me," I said. You know that soon ..."

"Don't say it." She put a finger to my mouth. "I don't want to think about it."

We lay together quietly then, occasionally sharing kisses, sharing words. Until Munika told us it was time.

I dressed silently. Altara remained on the mattress, her head turned away from me. I walked to the curtain.

"I ... I must go."

"Wait," she said, as she rose from the mattress, still naked, to embrace me. We kissed for a long moment, neither one of us wanting to let go.

"Goliath," Munika whispered from somewhere behind me.

"Yes, I know." Then, looking at Altara, I said, with my voice breaking, "I pray that the gods let me see you again."

"May the gods grant your prayers."

I started down the stairs.

"Wait, wait," Altara said. "I need to give you something." I returned to the room. Altara was sitting at her table fumbling for something. She picked up a knife and cut off a strand of her hair. She ran back toward me. "Keep this," she said, as she pressed the lock into my hand. Then she ran to the corner of the room behind her bed. She returned quickly with a finely crafted earthenware effigy of Qetesh, showing her nude and standing on two lions. "Take this," Altara said. "Qetesh has never failed me."

"But what will you use?"

"I can ask … I'll be able to find another figure. Now hold my hair and Qetesh as you kiss me."

⟪⊱⟫

8

News of my triumph over the Egyptian reached Gath before I did, and I received a very warm welcome from Bellon and my comrades once I returned. The welcome included a mina of silver from Maoch. No, the king did not give it to me personally—Bellon gave me the gift in the king's name—but it was still gratifying to have my accomplishments recognized by the monarch.

Bellon also offered me my own room at the barracks. However, not wanting to cause any resentment among my fellow soldiers, I told Bellon that although I was very grateful for the offer, I thought I should share my quarters with at least one other soldier. He saw the wisdom in this, and Antenon became my roommate—along with Lost, of course.

The respect I now enjoyed along with the increase in material comforts pleased me, but they could not dull the pain I felt over my separation from Altara—a separation that as far as I knew would be permanent. The first few weeks back were torment, with her absence burning inside me, searing a hole in my very vision so that when I looked at something for more than a few moments, Altara's image would appear.

Compounding my agony was my inability to unburden myself by sharing my predicament with anyone. Much consolation comes from simply telling others of one's sorrows and frustrations, as though the telling itself somehow dissipates the pain. Ahirom had not sworn me to secrecy, but beside the fact that I knew he would not appreciate me talking about his concubine, there was my disinclination to talk about my yearning for the commander's concubine. It would make me look ridiculous at best. Lost alone heard of my desire for Altara; he could keep a secret and if he considered me foolish, he did not so indicate.

But given our companionship, I could not conceal completely my emotional pain from Antenon, so I told him some half-truths.

One evening, as I was offering yet another prayer to Qetesh, Antenon entered our room. "Goliath, if you spend any more time holding and kissing that effigy, I'm afraid you'll find yourself engaged in a sacrilegious act that I don't even want to think about."

I gave an embarrassed half-chuckle to acknowledge his presence and hurriedly whispered the conclusion to my prayer.

"You met someone while you were away. Am I correct?"

I turned to face him, still on my knees. "Yes, but I hope you understand. I don't really want to talk about it. I can't talk about it. I know you're my friend, but ..."

He sat down, his back against the wall. "No, that's fine. A friend knows when to offer assistance and when to refrain from offering assistance. You know I won't judge you, but if pains you too much to talk about it ... sure, no problem."

"Well, it's a delicate situation. Also, an impossible situation. Which, as you can probably tell, is why I'm not particular happy."

He raised his eyebrows and coughed into his hands a couple of times, trying to clear his throat for the proper words. "If it's a married woman ... again, you're my friend, and I'm not going to judge you, but ... the gods can forgive an act of passion but to plan to make away with another man's wife..."

"No, no, it's not that. I really can't explain, but I hope you know I would not take another man's wife. But, there's this complication ..."

"She's ... What? Promised to someone?"

"In a way. Yes, you could say that I suppose."

"Depending on the formalities, the promise may not be binding. What stage ..."

"The thing is I don't know for sure what her heart wants. And then ... How could I sustain her? And she lives in Ashkelon." My gaze fell on the effigy of Qetesh.

"I can see why you pray so often. Friend, I'd try to lift your spirits by suggesting female companions in Gath but ..."

I gave him a hard look.

"But I know you would not be interested." Pause. "Given the selection, I can't blame you."

After a few moments of silence, Antenon slapped his knee and said, "The only way to find a good woman, either to settle down with or to pass the time with, is to have money. We're not at war, so we need to gamble more." Antenon punctuated his counsel with a laugh. I knew he was only half-serious, if that. We both had enough common sense to realize gambling was not a reliable path to wealth.

However, it was a useful path for diversion, so for a while I threw myself into the soldiers' games even more than usual. Dice, studded knuckle bones, engraved shoulder blades—anything that could be juggled, thrown, and wagered upon was used. We also played simplified versions of mancala—most of my comrades did not have the same cognitive powers as Phodan. But after a while, the gaming lost its appeal, in part because I began to be concerned about losing, which is an attitude sure to drain the enjoyment from gaming. It's not that I was actually losing—in fact, perhaps after a couple of weeks I was up a bit—but I was worried about squandering what money I had. I had earned a fair amount through my various challenges—perhaps four or five silver mina, not counting the value of the various tangible gifts such as cups and daggers—what if I earned more? Could I possibly offer to … what? Buy Altara from Ahirom? Every time this thought entered my head, I tried to dismiss it as unrealistic, but like a hungry dog it kept returning no matter how many times I shooed it away. Yes, the likelihood of acquiring enough wealth to make an offer that Ahirom would not find laughable or insulting seemed small, but then if I lost what money I had, the difficulty would be all that greater.

As an alternative to gaming, or drinking, and in an attempt to find something to keep my thoughts from drifting back to Altara, I turned to visiting my mother and sisters more often. In saying this, I recognize how unfeeling, how cold this might seem. It's as if visiting my mother was just slightly better than utter boredom. But I don't think I was unique among young men in not being especially keen in spending time with my mother.

I did miss seeing Avram and Dedra, especially Dedra, the baby of the family. She'd always been someone I could tease good-naturedly, with repayment swiftly and just as lovingly delivered. So, it disappointed me that she seemed to be in a solemn mood each time I visited her, my mother, and Hannipath during this period of time. On one occasion she seemed very troubled, scarcely said a word, and then left the meal abruptly.

As she did not seem to be ill, I thought perhaps she was despondent over something. What could it be? It occurred to me her sadness might be due to her not yet finding a husband. She was now almost seventeen—a bit past the prime of her marriageable age—so when I had the opportunity, I discreetly asked my mother how matters stood in that regard.

"I leave such things to Hannipath. It's the job of the man of the house to find a suitable husband for his daughters."

I thought, but did not voice my thought, that perhaps this was the problem. Since Dedra was but a step-daughter, perhaps Hannipath felt less of an obligation to make an effort to find a proper match.

I felt awkward around Hannipath and I was reluctant to bring the issue up with him directly, but one evening when I was visiting, he asked me to help him replace a wooden beam that was used as a roof support. For some reason, perhaps because we were alone, perhaps because I thought he would be more receptive to my inquiry as I was assisting him, I broached the subject, asking about the status of Dedra's prospects.

"She has had a couple of suitors, but I did not think they were suitable. Not in a good financial position themselves, plus they wanted a significant dowry." He said this without looking at me, his eyes fixed on the beam.

"What was their position?"

"One was the second son of a small farmer; the other the third son of the man who operates the olive oil press that supplies the temple and some of the nobles."

"What did Dedra think of them?"

He looked at me, then looked away quickly again. "Oh, you know … girls like the attention. But this is an important decision. This is a decision how she will spend the rest of her life."

"What was the size of the dowry they expected?"

Hannipath took a long while in answering. Then he mumbled, "A mina of silver."

My uncle had already pledged a half-mina, which meant Hannipath only had to supply another half-mina. He had now had almost three years to gather and set aside this sum. The house was not overflowing with luxuries, but he and my mother appeared well-nourished, and from visiting with Avram and Barekbal, I knew the pottery business had become more successful and was bringing in some steady revenue. Not a lot, but some.

We worked in silence for a while, and then I told Hannipath, "If it will help find a suitable match, I will contribute a half-mina myself."

No answer. We finished fitting and trimming the beam. Then Hannipath said, "You don't have to do that."

"I want to do it. Dedra's happiness is important to me and I don't want her to miss an appropriate match for lack of ..." I stopped myself. I had to be careful not to insult him.

"Fine," he said flatly. "When the time comes, I will let you know."

While Dedra seemed glum, Avram seemed, if not overflowing with joy, at least content with her situation. She was with child when I visited her and Barekbal and that may have contributed to her generally cheerful mood. Their first infant had died from a wasting disease within a few months, but this was not unusual. There was even a saying that "the firstborn belongs to the gods." But the second-, third-, and fourth-born seemed to suffer the same fate as often. Anyway, like most parents with a child on the way, Avram and Barekbal were optimistic and hopeful.

Barekbal seemed more at ease. Less shy. He was growing into his marriage, and the increasing success of the business he shared with Hannipath gave him some confidence. One tangible benefit of the upturn in business was that he was now able to spend most of his days at the workshop instead of in the fields. His extra work as a farm laborer was mostly confined to harvest times.

Barekbal was eager to show me one reason for their success, which was a new style of pottery that imitated the look of bronze tableware. This new style gave those who could afford it a reason to buy an additional set of jugs, jars, and bowls even if they didn't really need them. Barekbal took me over to the workshop which was about thirty paces from the house, basically next door but with enough open space in between to keep some of the fumes and odors out of their living space. The workshop was a spacious, stand-alone, one-story building. Inside were an area for treading the clay, potter's wheels, a kiln, a cistern, and a storage area. The new technique for creating the imitation bronzeware involved the use of a slip, which was a mixture of fine-grained clay, ochre, and some other materials. This was applied to the shaped clay, which was then burnished by a bone tool designed for that purpose, before being fired in the kiln. Barekbal explained that Hannipath had learned of this method from a merchant from Gaza who had stopped by the shop. The other potter in town had no knowledge of it, which at least for a time gave Barekbal and Hannipath a marketing advantage.

I shared a couple of evening meals with Avram and Barekbal. They supplied most of the food, but I bought some fig cakes for one meal and some pork for another. The latter was especially appreciated.

We talked of my exploits, of course, but I tried, politely, to move the conversation to other topics. In particular, I said as little as possible about Ashkelon. With respect to family matters, Avram confessed she had not found much time to spend with Dedra. The demands of her own household prevented it. Looking at her hands, I could confirm the truth of her statement.

Barekbal thought that one reason Dedra might lack prospects was that Hannipath had been too busy—or maybe had other things on his mind.

"What do you mean," I asked.

Barekbal studied his hands for a moment, and then said, "He's ... I don't know quite how to say this. Look, some days, he seems quite happy, cheerful, full of energy. Other days ... he ... he seems dispirited or preoccupied. Won't talk much. Sometimes I have caught him staring at nothing when he's supposed to be painting some pottery."

"Any connection between these moods and business?"

"No, that's it. We could be having a good day in terms of sales or quality of product turned out and he still seems troubled."

"Maybe it's something at mother's—their—household," Avram said. "Sick sheep?"

"How about mother's health?" I asked. "She seemed fine when I saw her. But ... well, she is getting on in years. Perhaps some recurring malady?"

"Don't know," Avram said. "I have not noticed anything either. But recently I've not been there much more often than you have been, Goliath."

"So how long has this pattern of back-and-forth behavior been going on?" I asked.

Barekbal shrugged. "Can't say for sure because I only noticed it when it became apparent it was a pattern. So... maybe six months. A year at most."

We were all silent for a moment. Then I ventured, "Could just be the strain of running both a household and a business, especially a business where trade has picked up." Lacking any other explanation, this was tacitly accepted by all as the end of that particular topic.

So, family visits gave me some matters to worry about, which perversely I welcomed. These new concerns combined with the passage of time allowed me to go hours, if not days, without pining for Altara. I still prayed to Qetesh, but this was now more the result of habit than fervor.

Then, after perhaps three or four months back in Gath, something happened which caused slumbering thoughts of Altara to bestir themselves. Ahirom invited me to spend a couple of days with him at his farm. I could not refuse. If I hoped to retain any chance of seeing Altara again, I needed to maintain good relations with Ahirom. At the same time, I dreaded the prospect of being constantly reminded of her— reminded that she was not that far away yet still unreachable, with both the means and the obstacle to my seeing her being my host.

But, as the trip started, my brooding was shoved aside to make room for a new experience—riding a mule. I had ridden the family donkey when I was a boy, but, given my size, that had stopped when I reached adolescence. I demurred at first when Ahirom told me we were both going to ride to his farm, explaining I was concerned the mule could not bear my weight.

"Don't worry. You'd be surprised at the weight a mule can carry—up to one-third of their own weight. They're stronger than horses you know, and the mule you're riding is the largest one I have, maybe the largest in Palestia. His mother was a very large mare. Just make sure your feet don't drag the ground."

"I'm not bothered about walking."

"*I'm* bothered by your walking. I'm riding and I'm not going to have you trailing behind like some slave. Plus, you'll slow us down. We can be at the farm just past mid-day if we ride."

So, I climbed on the poor animal Ahirom had decided to challenge with my mass. I can only hope the mule was more comfortable than I was. My backside let me know that it had been years since I had ridden. When the mule whimpered, I thought, "He's speaking for both of us."

Fortunately, as Ahirom had predicted, we arrived at his farm a little after mid-day, before soreness changed to real pain. As I slid off the mule, it brayed, repeating its deep-throated honking quickly as though it were breathing rapidly. Probably was.

The farm was situated almost due west of Gath, although a bit to the north. It wasn't far from a junction for a trade road joining Ekron, Ashkelon, and Gath. As Ahirom pointed out the expanse of his farm, swinging his arm from the valley below, where fields were cultivated, to the plateau where his pastures and farm compound were located, I was duly impressed with its size. Not that I had vast knowledge in these matters, but it was the biggest farm I'd ever seen.

The compound was also large, with several outbuildings in addition to the main residence. Like a good commander, Ahirom thought defensively, and the compound was bounded on one side by a slope leading from the plateau to the valley. On the side facing the plateau, there was a deep ditch and a wall. The wall was taller than a man, but not by much, so it could be scaled, but like the other defenses it wasn't designed to make the compound impregnable, just a difficult target for brigands. The compound had both a well and a cistern, so water supply would not be a problem if for some reason no one could leave the compound for several days. Defensive manpower was thin—Ahirom had three free men who had been properly trained in the use of weapons and four slaves who he would trust with a bow if necessary—but as Ahirom explained, there was no point in preparing to take on the whole Hebrew army. His objective was to make sure his family was safe from the ordinary threats faced by isolated farms.

He did make his family's residence as much of a fortress as possible, however. The outside wall was of stone, not mud brick, and the one entryway had double doors, both heavily bolted. The most imaginative defensive measure, though, was a hidden hatch in a storeroom that led to a tunnel that connected with a cave that eventually opened on the slope leading to the valley. While climbing the slope, the cave was barely noticeable as its opening was obscured by a rock. The tunnel was very narrow—barely large enough for a normal-sized man to squeeze through. Not being such a man, I couldn't fit in the tunnel nor did I try too hard for fear of becoming stuck. After my half-hearted effort, Ahirom chuckled and said, "Well, I suppose if you are ever here during an attack, you'll be among the last defenders." To which I boasted in reply, "If I'm here during an attack, no one will need to make use of that tunnel."

I met his wife and children at dinner. I'm not sure what I expected. I certainly didn't think his wife would be plain and ordinary, but I was still taken aback at how beautiful she was. More beautiful than Altara? Impossible to say. It would be like comparing two exquisite gemstones that were cut slightly differently. Elissa had hair the color and shine of onyx. Her features were sharper than Altara's: an aquiline nose, high cheekbones, and a square jaw, so her face was more commanding than inviting, but it drew one's attention nonetheless. With respect to her form ... well, it would not be fitting for a guest to dwell too much on the body of his hostess. Suffice it to say that it was pleasing. The thought did occur to me that Ahirom had a surfeit of female beauty at his command—couldn't he spare his mistress?

Ahirom's children, Apphia, a lively girl older than five, and Melqath—named for his grandfather presumably—an inquisitive boy just short of four, peppered me with questions during dinner. Ahirom had obviously been filling their heads with tales of my exploits, perhaps embellishing them in the process.

"How big was the Egyptian's net? This big?" Melqath asked as he spread his arms as wide as he could.

"It was large enough to cover me."

"Was it large enough to cover this table?"

I looked at the table. "Yes, I ..."

"Was it large enough to cover this house?"

"No, I don't ..."

"This farm?" Both children laughed.

"Do you get covered in blood when you kill people?"

"Apphia," her mother interjected, "don't be gruesome."

"You live on a farm and you know animals bleed when they are cut," I answered. "If you're close to them when they're cut... sure, you'll get some blood on you."

"Are you the strongest man alive?"

"Don't know, I have not ..."

"I'm going to be the strongest man when I grow up."

"I'm stronger than you are," Apphia rejoined, giving a slight shove to her brother to emphasize her point.

"No, you're not."

"You can see, Goliath, what important debates we have here at the dinner table," Ahirom said.

"Oh, I can recall somewhat similar debates during our family dinners, although usually it was arguments about who worked the hardest that day."

This led to some questions from Elissa about my family, their current whereabouts, and so forth. I made similar inquiries. Her family was of merchant stock, like Ahirom's. Indeed, their grandparents had been partners in some trading ventures. Her mother was dead; father lived in Ashkelon with a second wife. I didn't ask whether she preferred the farm to Ashkelon or the other way around. I didn't have to. "Now I find myself a farmer's wife," she said with a hint of scorn in her voice.

"I hope that's not all you consider yourself to be, darling." Ahirom responded with a smile. "Even here on the farm you're more of an overseer of an estate than a farmer's wife."

Elissa smiled and nodded and then said it was time for the children to go to bed. There were protests, causing Elissa to lament, "I wish Altara were here to help me with this pair." At the mention of Altara's name, Ahirom and I caught each other's eye and then we both quickly looked away.

After a few moments, Ahirom suggested we go to the roof and enjoy some wine. He said Elissa would join us later.

We reclined on our elbows on some mats, propped up by some cushions. There was a small couch on the roof as well, but Ahirom said he was saving that for Elissa.

After Ahirom poured me a cup, I said, "The gods have looked with favor upon you Ahirom. Not only do you have this farm, but you have a beautiful, gracious wife and two healthy children."

"Thank you. And, of course, thanks be to the gods." He poured a small portion of his cup over the side of the roof as a libation. "Having a family is a gift from the gods." He paused. "Perhaps this is a gift you should seek. I know common soldiers don't always think about taking a wife and starting a family, but you are no common soldier. You may have the resources to support a wife and child now. If not, perhaps if you … no, I mean *when* you continue to win your challenges, you'll have enough within a couple of years."

"But that's also a problem, isn't it? What if I don't come home from a challenge? Don't think I want to burden a young woman with being a widow, especially if she also has to deal with a child."

"I would not deny that's a risk. But you and I both know I'm just as likely to be carried away by some catarrh caused by the winter rains. One cannot plan one's life around possible misfortunes."

I shrugged and looked at my cup. "Maybe. But I know my father's death had much influence on the direction of my life."

"Yes, of course. But your life shows how resilient children can be. I know you didn't become a smith as you wanted, but, on other hand … well, now you are the most famous warrior in all of Palestia."

We drank for a moment or two looking at the stars. Ahirom then continued. "Our children are really the only way we can approach the gods."

"How so?"

"They are our creation and they are also the closest we can come to immortality. Some small part of us lives on in them."

"You don't believe our souls live on?"

Ahirom tilted his head to one side. "That's a difficult question to which no certain answer can probably be given."

"Yes, but you must have a thought."

He paused for a moment then asked, "Goliath, where is yesterday?"

"I'm not sure what you mean."

"Where is it? It was something very real, wasn't it? We both lived it. In fact, we both talked to each other yesterday, right?"

"Yes, things happened yesterday but now yesterday's over, so…"

"Right, it's over. But where is it?"

I could tell Ahirom was now in one of his strange, questioning moods. I enjoyed listening to him talk on such occasions, but I did often find his questions baffling. I tried to think of a response that made some sense, but failed, and I told him so.

"Well, answer me this, Goliath. Can you change yesterday?"

"Do you mean can I redo or undo something I did yesterday?"

"No, I don't mean that. Of course you can do that, but that is something you're doing today. No, my question is can you change what happened yesterday?"

"No, of course not."

"So yesterday is somewhere, we know not where, but we do know that whatever happened yesterday, or the day before, or the day before is frozen, like water when it becomes very cold. There's no movement, no change. It's no longer part of the flow of life."

"I suppose you could say that."

He then turned to me. "If we had some soul that survived our death, wouldn't it be like that? It would be in some place that we cannot describe or understand, and wouldn't the *soul* itself be frozen, impossible of undergoing change, because it represents the past?"

"I don't know… I can't dispute what you say, but I need to think about these things. You're a learned man. I'm not."

"I don't think one needs to read a lot of history or priestly writings to think about these matters. Just reflect on them. But I agree these are difficult issues." A pause. "Then there's the question of what does it mean to say the soul of a man survives. What do we mean by the soul?" He turned to me again.

"Um ... it's ... it's the person, in spirit."

"The essence of the person?"

"Yes, I suppose so."

"Does a person have an essence, something that when one encounters it one would say, yes, yes, that is what this person is?"

"Give me a moment. Maybe more than a moment."

"Sure."

My head was reeling with confusion. But at some level I found this enjoyable. Talking with Ahirom was like working one's way through a puzzle.

"One's memories ... that's important. It's ... it's how we know ourselves. I'm the person who worked in a bloomery, watched his father die, then joined the army, and so forth. The soul contains our memories."

"Is that all?"

"I don't know. Maybe, but if spirits are visible, then to recognize ourselves and other spirits, somehow our souls must resemble our bodily image."

"So, the soul is like a shadow of a person and it contains one's memories?"

"Something like that."

"You don't remember everything that's happened to you, do you?"

"No. Maybe that's a good thing."

"Maybe. But if you forget some things, does that mean your soul has changed or that you've lost part of your soul?"

"No. Well ... I'm not sure."

"I have a better question. What if you forget everything? You know, there are some people who suffer from this misfortune."

"Is that true? They don't remember anything? You have met such people?"

"No, I can't say I have. But I've been told this. It can happen following an injury to the head."

"Perhaps it's not true."

"Mmm. I was told this by a friend of my father's. Anyway, we can imagine it or... consider young children. Do you remember things that happened to you when you were an infant?"

"No."

"So, does that mean young children don't have a soul?"

"No, I don't think so. I think I understand the point you're making. If the soul contains our memories and we have no memories, then what's left of the soul?"

"Yes, something like that."

"The soul is not just memories."

"What is it then?"

"It's … it's where memories are kept. Also, it's where feelings are kept. Anger, love, hate, these are also in the soul."

Ahirom got up and walked around the roof. He stopped, looked at me, and said, "What if we are just our memories, our feelings, our thoughts? Why think there's something in addition to that?"

"Our memories and our thoughts must reside somewhere. How can they be connected otherwise?"

"They are connected day-to-day, moment to moment, by our desires, our plans, our intentions … and memories themselves are part of this stream, which moves along through days, months, years … but the stream is all there is. There's nothing beyond the stream."

I was thoroughly perplexed. Also, I began to experience a strange sensation. An unpleasant sensation. A queasiness. A dizziness. I felt the world had become unstable.

"Is Ahirom filling your head with his mystical musings?" This was Elissa, who had now joined us on the roof. "If you give him any more wine, he'll start asking you such obscure questions that you will think you're in a foreign land." She eased herself onto the sofa. "Darling, I hope you're not boring Goliath. He may not want to come back, and we don't receive that many visitors."

"Oh, I'm not bored. Confused, maybe, but not bored."

"Well, I don't want to talk about souls. I have one. I know it. That's all. Even if Ahirom doesn't think so."

Ahirom sat down again. He looked at Elissa and then at me. "Maybe we have had enough questions for this evening."

"I enjoy questions," Elissa said, "but maybe easier ones. Let's look at the stars and ask each other what they look like."

Ahirom said, "You know with my eyesight, the stars seem blurry around the edges and larger."

"All the better," replied Elissa. "You'll see things that we won't."

I pointed to some familiar constellations. "That's the bear. That's …"

"Oh, I know, Goliath," Elissa interrupted. "I know how we usually group and name them. But I want us to look at them again and imagine different shapes and stories. Look at this group here. Looks like a horse, doesn't it?"

"More like a dog to me," Ahirom said.

"A dog, no. It has a horse's face, not a dog's face. See how long it is. Anyway, Ahirom, it's your turn. Pick out some stars and tell us what you see."

"Over here," Ahirom said. "There are some stars close together, falling almost in a straight line. To me they look like coins dropping from a man's purse."

"Leave it to you to see money in the stars," Elissa said. "Now, Goliath, it's your turn."

I leaned back, with my thoughts still besieged by Ahirom's questions. I moved my eyes over the heavens, but I could not seem to bring anything into focus.

"Don't take too long, Goliath. Just tell us what you see."

"A woman."

"A woman? Where?" Elissa asked.

"Over here. You see, those two stars are her shoulders. Then the stars beneath them are closer together, so that's her waist. Then the stars beneath them spread out further again, so those are her hips."

"But she has no head?"

"No-o-o, that's true, but …"

"Goliath likes to keep his women quiet," Ahirom said. "A wise man."

"Or perhaps it just means that women lose their heads over him," Elissa suggested.

With such lighthearted conversation, we passed the remainder of the time that evening, until the increasing chill informed us it was time to go to bed.

The next day, Ahirom took me all around his property, from the flocks in the pastures to the grain in the fields. This took some time as he deferred to my desire to walk instead of ride. We did not talk much. For myself, I was deep in thought, still mulling over Ahirom's observations and questions from the night before. About halfway through our walk, as we paused to look at his olive trees, Ahirom turned to me and said, "Goliath, you know…

last night … I like to think, ask questions. Doesn't mean I don't believe we have souls."

"Yes. Understood."

"Some people might not understand that, so please do me the favor of not telling others, especially our comrades in Gath, what we discussed."

"I won't." Then I added, with a smile, "I doubt if I followed enough of what you said to repeat it anyway."

The rest of the day was at leisure… or as much leisure as two energetic children would permit. Apphia and Melqath had to show they could defeat the mighty warrior from Gath, so they spent some time climbing on top of me, pummeling me with their fists and stabbing me with the sticks they used as swords. I swung both of them around several times, tossing them gently into the soft earth of the pasture. Only once did I inadvertently cross the boundaries of our play-fight. At one point, I put on my fiercest look and sneered at Melqath, "I will destroy you utterly. I will rip you apart, tearing you into small pieces, so your body will become morsels for the birds." At this, he started crying and ran away. As he informed me once Apphia had consoled him and he had regained his composure, I was not playing fair. So, a new rule of our game was that I could no longer put on an "ugly" face and make threats.

I took my leave the next morning. Ahirom would stay on at the farm for a few more days. As I made ready to depart, Ahirom said, "My man, Artasas, will accompany you for the first part of your return to make sure you get headed in the right direction."

"Thanks. No need to bother, though. I can remember. Plus, Gath is more or less due east."

"It's no bother. And why take the chance that you might become disoriented? Don't want you walking in a circle and winding up back here," he said with a smile. He then handed me the spear he was carrying. "Take this," he said.

"Why?"

"Why not? I know you can carry it with ease. All you have with you right now is a dagger."

"Traveling during the day. Don't think I need to worry about thieves."

"I agree this area is fairly safe. Still … I don't think I've mentioned this to you, but there have been reports of Hebrew patrols outside Ekron."

"Really? Outside Ekron, but not outside Gath?"

"Yes. The patrols are coming from the north, apparently, which … well, it's not good news. There have been rumors that the Hebrews in the hills to the east have united with the Hebrew clans to the north."

"Doesn't mean they will attack."

"No, it doesn't, but people don't usually do something without a purpose. If I buy a sheep, I'm not just going to let it wander off on its own. I'm going to use it for milk and wool. So, if the Hebrews are joining forces, has to be with some objective, I would think."

I took the spear. "Perhaps we'll find out soon if they have some objective in mind."

⚔️

9

We had to wait only a few more weeks before the Hebrews made clear their intent.

Perhaps the clash could not have been avoided. Our settlements had been spreading northward along the coast; the Hebrews in the north were expanding southward. We were not disposed to discuss our competing interests. Also, the Hebrews were no longer inclined to use the contests between champions as a way of resolving disputes. First, they had lost all such contests. Second, they now thought they had overwhelming numbers.

They did overwhelm the first Palestim settlements they encountered. They had the advantage of surprise as well as numbers. However, they then stopped their advance. Not clear why. One possible explanation was that winter was upon us and with it, the rains. Whatever the explanation, it was a welcome pause as it allowed the five major Palestim cities to consult one another and coordinate their action. For the first time an army was to be fielded that represented all five cities, in addition to contributions from numerous settlements. Altogether, perhaps 1800 foot soldiers were to be assembled, along with over 100 cavalry and about 20 chariots. This was, for us, a very large force, but we would need it, as the Hebrews were said to have as many as 5000 men under arms.

The number of combatants, by itself however, does not indicate the size of our enterprise or the complexity of arrangements necessary to mount our campaign. Arrangements had to be made for the provision of our forces. For the first part of the campaign we would be traveling through our own territory, so we could not live off the land by seizing food from villages and farms. Accordingly, an immense assembly of animals—mules, donkeys, oxen—had to accompany the army. On the carts these animals pulled or on their backs were all manner of things that the army might need, including grain, salt, cheese, goatskins filled with water or wine, amphorae with olive oil, tools, tents, mantles, lamps, torches, additional weapons, shields, helmets, armor, and sandals. In addition to the working animals, there were also a number of sheep and goats, which would be slaughtered for meat at various points during the campaign, and spare mounts for the chariots and cavalry.

There were also about nine or ten carts dedicated to household items for the two kings and numerous nobles who were with the army. Maoch, as the senior king among the five major cities, was with us, as was King Achibel of Ashdod. They would have joint control of the expedition, although they were expected to defer to the advice of the military commanders. These carts carried bowls, jars, cups—often of silver—as well as robes and other items of clothing. There were also a few jars of scented oils. Some nobles took concubines with them. Not Ahirom, however.

Civilians, usually older men, along with about thirty slaves and a squad of soldiers staffed the supply train under the direction of one of our commanders—who happened to be Ahirom. Everyone recognized that Ahirom had a gift for planning—seldom would he overlook even the smallest detail—so he had a large role not just in organizing the logistics of the campaign, but also in developing our overall strategy. His one weakness was his eyesight, which prevented him from being a field commander.

It took several weeks to make the necessary arrangements and coordinate the movements of the various detachments, so it was spring before our campaign got underway. The detachment from Gath was told to carry enough supplies for three weeks. It would take us three or four days to march to the assembly point north of Ashdod and Ekron and then we expected to be in the field maneuvering for about two weeks. After that, we would be victorious and free to exploit Hebrew territory or, if things went badly, back behind the walls of our own cities.

When we arrived at the assembly point, most other contingents were already there. The field where we were encamped was thick with soldiers. It was a very impressive sight, a sight which was accompanied by a very powerful odor—of human and animal sweat and excrement— and the din and commotion of a few thousand yells, curses, bleats, brays, clangs, thuds, belches, and farts.

We stayed at this encampment for just two nights, which was good because most of the soldiers, including me, were restless and eager to engage the enemy. On the third morning, after the requisite offerings and prayers, we set out—although the commencement of our march was less like a runner starting to sprint than the slow uncoiling of a snake. The sluggish sequence of all the different units falling in line was repeated in reverse at the end of the day when we fell out of line. As result we made much less progress than I had thought we might. The slow pace of our march frustrated us, the heat from both sun and sand burned us, and our water and food rations left us thirsty and hungry, so some of our initial enthusiasm waned over the first few days.

Our commitment and ardor reignited, though, when we came across a Palestim settlement which the Hebrews had sacked and burned the prior winter. The butchered corpses, now largely ash, scorched bone, and bits of clothing that the birds and dogs had disdained, lay scattered throughout the town, with occasional clumps where parents had tried to protect children. Four individuals—they appeared to be men—had been crucified. Why them? Not clear. No text was left behind as explanation. Did they resist too long or give up too easily? Our commanders decided we would provide a hasty burial for the remains. No one protested. It was the right thing to do. Before we left, King Achibel spoke to us briefly. His face dark with anger, his voice resounding with rage, he said, "Remember this! Remember what you have seen here! Avenge their deaths! Destroy these wild beasts!" We answered with a deafening roar.

Our anger still had not dissipated two days later when our scouts came galloping back with a report that the Hebrew host was only a half day away, north of the former settlement of Aphek. This was news, but the more surprising bit of information was that the Hebrews were advancing toward us. This suggested confidence on their part as the land between us was mostly flat plain interrupted by the occasional hill or stream. Had the Hebrews withdrawn northwest they would have positioned themselves in more defensible terrain. Apparently, the Hebrews wanted to attack us and drive us away before *we* reached the hill country.

We marched for a while longer and were then ordered to set up camp with our position partially obscured by a high hill that ran along the center of our encampment. We did not expect the Hebrews to attack at night—a tactic as dangerous for the aggressor as it was for the defender—but just in case, the hill would channel their forces along its sides, potentially dividing them and exposing their flanks. In addition, by placing sentries on top of the hill we should have sufficient warning of any assault.

Before I bedded down next to my companions, a messenger came for me, instructing me to report to the command tent. My first thought was that perhaps the Hebrews had offered to resolve maters through single combat, but I quickly dismissed that as improbable. They had the numbers and appeared eager for battle. On our side, I could not imagine we would agree to single combat after seeing the devastated Palestim settlement. We wanted to destroy the enemy—all of them.

At the command tent, both kings were present. I immediately went to my knees and Maoch almost as quickly said, "Up, Goliath. No time for ceremony. You're here to listen to some of our decisions regarding tactics. Then I hope we can all go to bed."

As I got up, I noticed Ahirom was in the tent, with several other commanders. There was also a common soldier, heavily muscled and bull-necked. Not tall, but with very broad shoulders.

Ahirom spoke. "Goliath, for the battle tomorrow—and we are almost certain there will be a battle tomorrow—we have decided to use a new tactic. As you know, the custom has been that our boldest, strongest warriors place themselves in the vanguard of the attack. But after some discussion," here he flashed a half-smile and gave a nod to the other commanders, "we have decided that we are not going to do that tomorrow."

"Why?" I asked surprised. "It's an honor to be in the vanguard. I was hoping to be in the forefront for Gath."

"I understand. But it is also an honor to be triumphant. We want to use the tactics that will most likely secure the triumph for us. The problem with placing the best men in the vanguard, especially when facing an army that outnumbers you, is that many of them are likely be killed. And, yes, they may take down four or five Hebrews with them, but it will not be enough to make a difference between victory and defeat. So instead, for this battle, we are creating what I call a tactical reserve. Our best men—about fifty of them—are going to constitute the reserve. We will not deploy these men at the beginning of the battle, but rather will send them into the fight at the point when and where we think they will have the most favorable effect. Gods willing, that will be at the crucial point when we can secure victory."

"I'm here because I am to be one of those in this unit?"

"Yes, but you're here for another reason as well. We commanders have our own ideas about who should be placed in this reserve, but we have you here along with Bethpal, the champion for Ashdod, so you can give us your recommendations." Ahirom made a hand motion in the direction of the heavyset soldier. We nodded to each other by way of greeting. "You are familiar not only with the soldiers from Gath, but to some extent the soldiers from Ashkelon. Bethpal has some familiarity with Ekron's soldiers."

"Do you want our recommendations now?"

"Yes, we want to notify those selected tonight so we can assemble as promptly as possible in the morning."

I gave my recommendations as did Bethpal. I included Antenon, which resulted in a brief discussion. The commanders from Gath—Bellon, Sardon, and Ahirom—considered him a solid, sturdy soldier, but didn't think he had extraordinary skill as a combatant. I wanted him with me during the battle so I exaggerated his abilities. I doubt, given the commanders' skepticism, that they found me persuasive on this point, but they agreed to accept my recommendation because I made it clear I would not be at my best if I did not have Antenon at my side.

After the decisions on inclusion had been made, I left with Ahirom, and Bethpal left with the senior commander from Ashdod, to notify the soldiers of their selection. Once I had Ahirom alone, I asked who would be commanding the unit.

"I will be," he replied.

I thought about how to phrase my concern delicately. "But, sir, respectfully... You don't have especially good distance vision. How..."

"Yes, I know that. At fifty paces, I might not be able to distinguish friend from foe. You, Patibal, and Bethpal will be my eyes. I will make my tactical decisions based on what information you provide, and, of course, based also on messages I receive from other commanders." He turned to look at me. "What you report will be especially important, so I want you at my side."

"I'm glad you have the confidence in me, but why would my reports be any more important?"

"Your height, Goliath, your height. You may be the only one who can actually see over the lines of battle."

We notified the soldiers who had been selected, and then I returned to my area to sleep.

I was awakened before dawn, sometime before the bulk of our forces. Patibal, Antenon, and I, and three others from the Gath contingent, walked to the assembly point for our reserve unit, which was a small patch of open ground near Ahirom's tent.

Ahirom gave his instructions to us. "At the beginning of the battle, we will be stationed at the rear of our battle lines." This elicited a groan from some of the men. "Don't worry," Ahirom assured them, "you'll have plenty of fighting before the day is through. When I do order the advance, I will give you precise instructions on the formation you are to adopt. More likely than not it will be in a four-column formation, which I know you've all been trained in. It's a dependable formation both for attack and, if necessary, defense."

Ahirom had just completed his instructions when horns for the Hebrews sounded. This was answered by our trumpets and drums. Our combat troops hurried to get in formation in preparation to march out to meet the enemy. Our baggage train would remain behind the hill where we had made our camp.

We marched out into a narrow plain. Low hills were on our right. A stream was on our left. The stream was small and shallow enough that one could wade across it, but the banks on our near side were sufficiently steep to impede a maneuver on our flank. There was a fairly large hill behind the center of the Hebrew lines, just as there was a hill behind us.

The narrowness of the plain disadvantaged both sides to some extent. We had cavalry and chariots, whereas the Hebrews had but a few horsemen; we could not take full advantage of this disparity given the confined area for maneuver. On the other hand, the narrow frontage meant the Hebrews could not take advantage of their superior numbers to envelop our forces.

Their forces cramped, the Hebrews stacked their attacking units—soldiers with javelins, spears, and swords—many rows deep. In the center, where they concentrated their forces, they were more than twenty rows deep.

Behind them were archers. The Hebrew ranks were so numerous that the rows of archers even extended onto the hill at the rear of the Hebrew lines.

One distinctive feature of the Hebrew forces was their large contingent of slingers. The Hebrews might not have many iron weapons, but living in the hills, they had plenty of rocks. A single slinger could not do much damage, but massed together they could break up an attack. The Hebrews stationed the slingers on their flanks.

To some extent, the disposition of our forces mirrored the Hebrews, although our forces had a different composition. Our main body of soldiers, armed similarly to the Hebrews, with javelins, spears, and swords, extended the width of the field, but they were concentrated in the center, with their ranks thinner on the flanks. Behind them were archers. Also on the flanks were our chariots and cavalry, although a number of our horsemen were everywhere during much of the battle, scouting or delivering messages.

The Hebrews attacked as soon as their units had taken the field. Their indiscipline showed immediately. Some in the front row stopped to hurl their javelins while others ran on toward our lines. The archers, even the ones far back from the field, let loose their arrows from where they stood instead of moving up behind their attacking units. Consequently, most missiles missed their targets, and those that did find flesh pierced Hebrew hide almost as often as they did Palestim skin. Meanwhile, our archers waited until the Hebrews were within range before letting loose a devastating volley.

Nonetheless, our lines in the center were forced back by the brunt of their attack. Fierce fighting face-to-face was taking place perhaps no more than a couple of hundred paces from those of us in the reserve unit and we could hear the curdling cries and screams of our comrades. It was all we could do to hold ourselves back, but Ahirom's instructions had been clear— no movement until he ordered us into action.

A strong force of Hebrew slingers tried to move around our left flank, on the other side of the stream, hoping to pelt our soldiers from the side, but our archers turned their attention to them and they were forced to withdraw. As they did so, half of our chariots went into action, followed by many of our soldiers and archers on our left. They hit the Hebrew right hard, sweeping the enemy before them, slaying many slingers and other Hebrew soldiers. For a moment, it looked like we might cause the Hebrew right to run away in a rout, but then concentrated volleys from the Hebrew archers stopped our progress. The four remaining chariots turned back and both sides proceeded to engage each other in close combat.

Opposite our right flank, the Hebrews, intentionally or not, decided to add their weight to the attack on our center. Their lateral movement exposed their side, and much of our right, including a detachment of our cavalry, moved forward to attack.

When I reported this movement to Ahirom, he cursed, saying, "Too early, too early for the horses, damn it."

He was right. The Hebrew slingers saw the horses approach and made a swift adjustment, turning to face them and fling their stones. Shields render rocks almost useless, but one cannot shield a horse in full gallop effectively. The stones hit several our horses square on, causing some to bolt and others to fall to the ground, along with their riders. Our attack faltered, but fortunately our troops were able to fall back in good order.

I must confess that events happened so rapidly that, even in the rear, I was so confused by the noise, dust, and turmoil of battle that I found it difficult to provide Ahirom with a proper stream of reports. He, on the other hand, seemed to have no trouble processing not just my information, but also the constant flow of messages he received from other commanders. He acted decisively when I passed on the latest about the Hebrew attack in our center.

"Ahirom, I'm afraid our lines are beginning to give way in the center."

"How many rows are left before the Hebrews reach our archers?"

"Four... maybe."

Ahirom placed himself in front of our reserve unit. "Men, this is the moment you've been waiting for. In your hands lies our fate. Advance in four-column order as we discussed at *that* point." Here he signaled with his left hand. "You must drive the enemy back. Antenon, you stay behind with me. I need your eyes. The rest of you ... On to victory!"

Like wild horses suddenly let loose from restraining ropes, we dashed forward, bellowing, Bethpal and I leading the way. As each row in our unit came to a point about twenty paces from our front, we paused to hurl our javelins at the enemy ranks, making sure we aimed over the heads of our comrades. Many hit home. We then drove into the Hebrews, with the first enemy I met tasting my spear—as I plunged it into his mouth. I was so frenzied I managed to yank it back quickly, even though the spearhead was hooked behind his jaw. His jaw gave way, not my spearhead.

I turned and saw another Hebrew advancing toward me, although his courage seemed to give way as he neared. His spear thrust landed lazily on my shield. Felt like no more pressure than a fly on my arm. I thrust my spear into his thigh and as he went down, my sword shortened his height by the length of one head.

By this time, some of the Hebrews were moving away from us rather than toward us. I caught one in the upper back with my spear, thrusting it through his mail, and he tumbled forward, unfortunately taking my spear with them. No matter. I advanced with my sword, with wide sweeping and slashing movements. Gashes and gaps opened in Hebrew bodies, followed by gaps in the Hebrew lines, as the enemy recoiled.

With the enemy retreating, I was able to pause for a moment to catch my breath. Movement to my left caught my eye and I turned to see that our left flank had pressed forward far enough that our soldiers had reached the ranks of the Hebrew archers, most of whom had no weapons for close combat. They were turning and running away. Our chariots swept forward again, this time with full force, scattering the archers and remaining slingers. Our left then swung around behind the Hebrew center, partially enveloping them.

I felt a tug on my arm and I got ready to swing my sword around before I heard Ahirom say, "Hold, Goliath! It's me."

I turned to see Ahirom and Antenon standing next to me. "I thought you needed to stay at the rear," I said.

"I am at the rear," Ahirom said. "If you haven't noticed, our lines have advanced forward quite a bit." He then said, "Look to the right. Antenon has told me the Hebrews there are now disordered and our cavalry is this time racing forward at the right moment."

"Yes, that's correct. Some of the Hebrews are holding firm, but the rest have turned tail."

"Good. Gather together some men of the reserve and let's head over there. We can strike a decisive blow and break their lines completely. If so, our cavalry may be able to encircle their center."

We gathered about twenty men and took off at a trot, moving about forty paces to our right and up. Here we met a thin line of Hebrew soldiers still valiantly holding their ground. We engaged; they held their ground no longer. Behind them, the archers and slingers who were still on the field broke and ran in different directions—some to the center, some up the hill at the rear of their lines, some to the right. Ahirom told us to continue to push as many as we could to the center, so we could complete the encirclement, letting our cavalry pursue those who went off running in different directions.

Within a few moments, I was greeting one of our charioteers who had come over from our left. The encirclement complete, the Hebrews were trapped.

Our own lines were thinner at the Hebrews' rear, so many of the Hebrews, recognizing their plight, turned and desperately tried to hack, cut, stab, and bludgeon their way out of the trap. In this, they were aided by arrows and rocks that suddenly began raining down on our backs. Now we Palestim who had completed the encirclement were being attacked from two sides. A number of Hebrew archers and slingers who had escaped had regrouped on top of the hill at the rear of their lines. They seemed to have rallied.

I noticed some of the Hebrews on top of the hill were blowing horns and others were lifting some ornate chest high over their shoulders, moving it around, obviously trying to show it to their troops. It did seem to inspire them.

I told Ahirom what I saw, asking, "What the fuck is that?"

"It's their sacred chest. They carry their war god around in it."

"What if we captured their god?" Wouldn't that ..."

"... end it? Yes, probably. But how do you propose to do that?"

"Let me take maybe ten to fifteen men, along with some cavalry to screen us at the beginning so we can get started on the hill before they turn their weapons on us."

He looked at me for a moment. "Let's do it. I'm going with you."

"But ... will you be able to see ...?"

"I'm not blind. Anyway, I'm following you and when we're close to them I'll be able to distinguish the Hebrews by their stink if nothing else."

Ahirom sent Antenon off at a run with a message to a mounted sub-officer, who then trotted over to speak with Ahirom. I gathered maybe twelve of our reserve plus some other soldiers who, having heard of our plan, insisted on taking part. We then launched our improvised attack. We foot soldiers scurried low, shields up, to the right of the Hebrew hill. About seven or eight mounted soldiers, with archers also on the back of their horses, rode by us and then in front of us. They rode about halfway up the hill but instead of continuing all the way up, which would have been difficult in any event, they rode to the back of the hill. This drew away some of the Hebrews on the crest, who ran toward the back of the hill to forestall a possible attack on the rear. By this time, scrambling up as fast as we could, we were more than halfway up. We were then spotted and the anticipated cloud of arrows and rocks began to cover us. May Dagon give long life to those who fashioned our sturdy, unyielding shields! We reached the crest with the loss of only three men.

There were about thirty Hebrews on top of the hill, not counting a few older men without weapons who were gathered around the chest. So, they had the advantage in numbers, but we were better armed as this Hebrew remnant was almost all archers and slingers who carried no blades except daggers. I took out one archer on the other side of the chest immediately with a well-placed javelin throw. Our attacking party then split in two, seven in each group, with each group forming a semi-circle, the better to defend ourselves against the rocks and arrows that might come against us from different directions. One rock did strike me with a glancing blow on the side of the head. Later, I'd have a lump and that spot would be sore for some time, but in the heat of the battle it did not even cause me to wince. We proceeded to cut and slash our way toward the Hebrews' chest. A few of the Hebrews took off running, but most stayed to defend their chest using what they could—their bows, their slings, their arms—in a desperate effort to parry our blows. Two older men with armor—their commanders? their chieftains?—did have shields and swords and one of them confronted me. He was skilled enough to deflect my thrusts and slashes for a moment or two, but no more. My sword cut across his exposed neck, tearing it open. He fell to the ground, grasping his throat, with his last words muffled by a bloody gurgle.

I was now almost at the chest, but as I looked up I noticed Ahirom banging away at a shield a Hebrew had picked up from one of our men. No worries, I thought. Ahirom could handle him. But then I saw that about fifteen paces behind Ahirom an isolated archer was starting to raise a bow in his direction. "Ahirom! Get down!" I yelled. No longer having a spear, I grabbed what was ready to hand, namely a rock. I threw it at the archer and it struck him in the chest with enough force to knock him off his feet. I was on top of him in an instant. My sword met little resistance as it went into and across his belly, spilling his coiled guts into his hands. I turned back to Ahirom, who had thrown himself forward on top of the Hebrew and was now engaged in a wrestling match. I raised my sword above the pair—unintentionally dropping some viscera onto Ahirom's face—waiting for the right moment to strike. The Hebrew rolled over, halfway on top of Ahirom, revealing his right thigh. I drove my sword into it and pulled the sword down his leg. Impulsively, he let go of the shield to reach for his leg and then I finished him.

I turned back to the chest. One of the old men without a weapon stood in front of me, spread his arms skyward, and began intoning some sort of chant. Presumably this was an appeal to their gods. I was not one of their gods, so I ignored his plea, killed him, and pushed him out the way. The chest had some staves attached to it, which is presumably how the Hebrews carried it around. I lifted the staves at my end. I was able to tilt it upward, but was not able to elevate it enough so those on the battlefield could see. A couple of my comrades came forward and grabbed the staves at the other end. We then lifted it as high as we could, letting out a yell in the process. The rest of our contingent joined in. We screamed, "Dagon be praised!" One of our men grabbed a discarded Hebrew horn and blew through it. It sounded like the bellowing of a cow in distress, but along with our yells it was enough to draw the attention of many of those below. We then turned the chest over on its side and together we threw it to the ground, letting out another roar and raising our arms in triumph. For good measure, a couple of our men stepped forward and pissed on it. I wondered how they had enough water to do that as my throat was parched.

The Hebrews below already sensed they were defeated. Now they became demoralized. Those that were not yet encircled abandoned the field in headlong flight. Many who were encircled dropped their weapons and let themselves be slaughtered where they stood. Some fought on with a tenacity born of desperation, but as the circle around them grew tighter many had difficulty even finding sufficient room to raise their shields and swords. Others were trampled underfoot by their own comrades. The battle had become a butchering.

I looked away from the massacre to face my comrades on the hill. We all looked at each other for a long moment and then burst out laughing. We grabbed each other and embraced. We told each other, "We did it. We did it." I was relieved to see that Antenon seemed to have escaped serious injury. He was bleeding from some cuts on his face and hands, but his wounds weren't serious.

I felt a hand on my shoulder. Ahirom. After I turned to face him, he said, "What can I say but thanks. Thanks and forever thanks."

"I take it you're not thanking me for the bit of Hebrew belly I dropped on your face."

A smile. "No, although in this instance I will consider the tang of bowel in my mouth as the taste of victory." He shook my shoulder. "Whatever you want; whatever you want. I owe you my life."

"Oh, I suppose I'll think of something." Of course, I already knew what I would ask for.

"Speaking of reward," he said, "did you have a good look at the Hebrews' sacred chest?"

I thought for a moment. Actually, I had not had a good look at it. Too busy fighting. So, I looked at the chest on the ground. "It … it's got some gold on it."

"I'll say. It appears to be almost entirely gilded with gold. The lid looks like it's made of solid gold, as are the two figures of a god on the lid." He looked at me. "This is very valuable. I'll make sure you and the other men get to share in this booty."

Ahirom then turned to the other soldiers. "Men, don't do any further damage to the chest—and that includes sanctifying it with your piss. As I was telling Goliath, this is a valuable trophy. We need to take it and present it to the kings."

"The lid's off," one soldier said. "Can we at least look inside? Might be some jewels or an effigy made of silver or gold."

"Yes, of course," Ahirom replied, "but let me take a look with you."

We righted the chest and lifted off the lid, which was already partially askew. No effigy inside. Only a couple of stone tablets. Each tablet had the image of a bullock with a sun disc at the top with some writing underneath. I lifted one out of the chest and held it up for Ahirom, who knew some of the Hebrews' tongue.

"What does it say?" I asked.

"Mmm. Well … I can only make out a few words. Something about 'don't murder' and 'don't steal'. Appears to be a set of rules. Common rules that all peoples have. Strange that they would feel the need to keep this in their sacred chest."

"They're too stupid to remember them otherwise," one soldier volunteered, to general laughter.

We carried the chest down the hill. The battle was over and our fellow soldiers greeted us with loud cheers as we passed. Ahirom grabbed a horse from one of our cavalrymen and rode off to inform the two kings, Maoch and Achibel, of the capture of the Hebrews' chest. During the battle, they had been in a tent well to the rear so they would have been aware of the general course of the battle, but not necessarily our special prize.

When we arrived at the kings' tent, they were both seated on cushioned chairs. We laid the chest before them and kneeled. Achibel told us to rise. Ahirom then explained how our boldness and bravery had resulted in the capture of the Hebrews' most sacred treasure. He did me the favor of mentioning me by name, as the soldier who had suggested the intrepid assault on the Hebrews' hill.

Achibel then spoke. "The gods have smiled on us today and we thank them for this victory. All who fought today have done our gods honor and they will be rewarded for their courage. We are especially pleased that we now possess the Hebrews' vaunted chest—the chest that they have boasted made them invincible. Maoch and I have decided this chest will be displayed in turn in all of our five great cities. This will demonstrate to our people that as long as we trust in our gods, we can defeat the Hebrews. You men," and here he looked at our party directly, "are welcome to accompany the chest on this tour. You will be honored with a feast in each city."

There was still much work to do that day, as we needed to bury our dead and care for the wounded—as best we could—as well as forage among the Hebrew dead for any valuables and plunder their baggage train. But exhausted as we were, we still had our fill of wine that evening.

I sought out Ahirom before I had too much to drink. I wanted to make sure I was sober enough to make my request clear. I found him sitting in a small group of commanders.

"May I?" I gestured to the ground next to him.

"Of course! Today's foremost hero! Sit, sit."

Their conversation, which focused on analysis of the day's battle, continued for a while. I listened mostly, but when there was a break, I leaned over to Ahirom and asked, "Can I talk to you for a moment?" I signaled with a nod of my head that I wanted us to speak away from the group. We stood and walked back a few paces.

"What is it?" Ahirom asked.

"I hope this doesn't strike you as impertinent, but ... well, earlier today you had mentioned a reward."

"Oh, of course. Don't think I have forgotten. You saved my life. But I'm afraid I don't carry much silver with me on a campaign."

"It's not silver I want."

He looked at me. Then a half-smile of recognition appeared on his face. "Yes. I understand. Altara. Right?"

"Yes, please. I would like to spend some time with her again."

"I can't refuse you can I?" He paused. The smile disappeared. As if trying to persuade himself he said, "Well, this probably makes some sense. You're going to be in Ashkelon soon anyway, when the chest is taken there. So ... Yes."

"How long will the chest be in Ashkelon?"

"The plan is to display the chest for ten days in each city."

"Could I ... could I spend more than a couple of days with Altara?"

Another pause. "I suppose I have to ask myself how much my life is worth." He searched my face. "Six days. You may have six days with her."

⚔⚔

10

"And so here you are in Ashkelon," the queen said.

"Yes, Your Majesty, here I am."

"I must say I'm quite impressed with your devotion to Altara, although it does strike me as a bit ... how shall I put this? Obsessive?"

"Forgive me. I don't know quite how to respond to Your Majesty's concern."

"Oh, it's not a concern. Merely an observation. From what you said yourself, you don't get to see Altara that frequently."

The queen rose from her chair and walked down from the platform. I stood up. "Sit, sit. I just need to stretch my legs." She walked past me, glancing at me as she did so. She stood still for a moment, then turned around and faced me. "You know, I recognize that Altara is quite lovely, but there are other beautiful women in the world. A hero like you ... let's just say

I don't think you'd have much trouble finding other women who would like to engage you in—what was the charming word you used—conversation."

"Perhaps that's true, Your Majesty, but although extra mantles may keep one warm in the winter, they are no substitute for the summer."

She now walked quickly toward me so our faces were no more than a hand's length apart. I saw the spots where the cream used to color her face had begun to streak in the heat of the day. Her breath was not unpleasant. "Do you find me attractive?"

No good answer here. Think. "Your Majesty, I'm a soldier. I work with weapons not words. Forgive me, but I could not begin to describe you."

She stepped back. She fixed her gaze intently on me, trying to discern something … what, my true meaning? I knew I couldn't look away immediately nor turn this into a staring contest. I held her gaze for a moment or two then looked respectfully away. I could feel her eyes upon me for another moment and then she too broke off. When I looked up, she was placidly looking sideways with a detached air, as if she were observing some mundane scene, such as children at play. She then looked down, appeared to inspect her robe, and began brushing it forcefully, as though to remove some dirt, real or imagined.

"I thank you for telling me of your adventures, Goliath. Your stories were interesting enough, but you may go. I've heard you and seen you—and now you're beginning to bore me. Go, go kill something."

I bowed and made as graceful an exit as I could, walking slowly backwards. The doors opened behind me without any further order from the queen, as though the guards could pick her desires out of the air.

<hr />

11

The first two days I was in Ashkelon were taken up with the requisite ceremonies attendant on the celebration of our victory and the triumphant procession and display of the Hebrews' chest. All very nice. The cheers, the praise, the adulation, the gifts. But throughout these two days my thoughts kept wandering back to Altara who was now achingly close—in the same city! It was all I could do to restrain myself from breaking away from the ceremonies and running to her house.

Not surprisingly then, on the evening of the third day, when I was finally free to see her, my passion did not permit any more patience. When Munika answered the door, she told me Altara was not quite ready to see me. She was working on her hair. Munika asked me to wait downstairs. Laughing, I replied, "No." I bounded up the stairs with Munika calling out from behind me, "Altara, Goliath's coming upstairs. He says he can't wait."

As I headed into Altara's bedroom, a cushion came flying out and hit me in the face. "Get out of here," Altara yelled. "I'm not ready."

"Why? How could you make yourself more beautiful than you are?"

"Munika is helping me braid my hair. We're not finished yet."

I stepped forward. Altara was seated by her table. Several strands of her hair had been pulled back in crisscross fashion forming braids on both sides of her head, but her hair in back, behind her ear, was still hanging loose.

"I see," I said. "Well, let Munika show me how to braid your hair. Then I can be with you and we can finish your hair at the same time."

Altara burst out laughing. "What …you braid my hair? I don't know what will look more ridiculous. The mightiest warrior in our land styling a woman's hair or my hair after you have finished."

"Munika will guide me and I think I've proven I'm fairly nimble with my hands."

She looked back at me with a wry smile. "Yes, and I know how persistent you can be. Fine, but let Munika show you before you do anything."

"Altara," said Munika, who was standing behind me, "we're almost finished anyway. Just a couple more braids on each side and then we connect them in the back."

I sat on the floor next to Altara and Munika stood behind her working her hair. "You see, Goliath," Munika said, "you cross the strands so, making sure the strands are evenly sized." I watched Munika attentively—although I did look away for a moment as I bestowed some kisses and nibbles on Altara's ankles. "Now," Munika said after some time, "we have only one more braid left on this side before we pull the braids together. Come, try it."

I knelt next to Altara who was giggling through her hands. Suddenly she said, "Please don't forget you're not on the battlefield. I don't want you wrenching my head off like I'm a Hebrew."

"I don't think you have to worry about that." I took hold of some strands of Altara's hair. The hair was slightly damp and very fragrant. She or Munika had oiled it.

"Too much," Munika said. "Let go. Start over." Munika now placed her hand over mine to guide my fingers. "Good. That's right. Now cross the strands. Yes … Let me just …" Munika made an adjustment. "Now we just need to connect the braids in the back and fasten them together." Munika did this.

"Is that it?" I asked.

"We need to brush the braids to smooth them out, and also the unbraided hair in the back." Munika picked up a brush from the table. It was a fine piece with a bronze handle. Looked like horsehair bristles. Undoubtedly a gift from Ahirom.

Munika started brushing. I then said, "Let me. I think I can do this." Munika and Altara looked at each other. "Yes, let him," Altara said quietly.

I moved the brush through Altara's hair as delicately as I could, applying gentle pressure. After some moments, unable to resist any longer, I began alternating my brushstrokes with kisses delivered to her ears and neck. When I did this, Altara moved her head back, leaning into my lips, and moaned softly. Munika said, "I think I will leave you two now."

"My hair?" Altara said. "Does it look …"

"It's good. Perfect," Monica replied. "And somehow I think later this evening you will not be thinking of your hair anyway."

Munika left. I continued my strokes until Altara grabbed my hand and began kissing my fingers. Then she turned to face me. "I missed you," she said. With that, we kissed, the beginning of an embrace that would in one form or another last the rest of the evening.

We moved to the bed—which Altara had thoughtfully altered since my last visit. The panel at one end had been removed. As we lay together, our mouths began searching for each other, as our lips moved restlessly over each other's body. Gradually, my mouth came to rest on her succulent pink flower, and I buried my head in its blossom. My tongue caressed her bud and Altara writhed, quivered, and gasped. Soon, I felt the convulsive movement of her thighs. Then, rolling over, Altara used her mouth as greedily on me, and her hair fondled me as lovingly as I had brushed it. It was my turn to moan and tremble, and then I arched and emptied myself in her mouth. She continued to lick me gently through the last spasms, and then rose to kiss me, mouth open, so I could taste and swallow my own seed and she could drink her own wetness. We moved our mouths slowly over each other so we could savor our own passion, as well as the passion of the other. In the madness of our desire, our bodies completely intertwined, we wanted to consume each other thoroughly, so there would be no separation, no distinction between us.

Striving with wild intensity to lose ourselves in each other, we continued to make love for as long as I could manage. Love and lust pulled me into her, and love and lust impelled her to envelop me.

Later, as we rested, Altara laid her hand on my chest and I nuzzled her. We murmured for a while, saying something, saying nothing. At some point, I ran my finger along her scar and kissed it.

"That horrible thing. I'm so ashamed of it. When I go out, I pull a shawl tightly around my face so no one will see it."

"I don't think it looks bad at all. Wait. Actually, I'm wrong. Why did I say that? It makes you look more beautiful. It's … it's something that makes your beauty stand out more, if that's possible."

"You're just saying that because … well, you say you love me."

"I do, but no, it's not that. You know I have scars too. They don't seem to bother you—or do they?"

She looked up at me. "That's not the same thing. Yes, your ear is … is …"

"Deformed? Mangled? Monstrous?"

"No!" She playfully slapped my chest with her hand. "It's different for you. For you, it's a mark of honor. You're a warrior. You're supposed to have some battle scars, my scar… it's nothing to be proud of."

"An accident when you were young?"

"No. Hardly an accident. Ahirom's mother cut me."

"What?" I half sat up in the bed.

"This was when Ahirom started to take a liking to me. She didn't approve."

"Gods. What did you do?"

"Nothing. What could I do? But she never did it again. Melqath, Ahirom's father, had a long talk with her and Ahirom the day it happened. What they said I don't know, but after that … after that, she didn't like me, but she never struck me again."

I didn't pursue the topic further. Altara didn't seem comfortable talking about it and I wasn't sure I wanted to know more about the incident myself.

Any reference to Ahirom just reminded me of the constraints on my relationship with Altara.

We talked for a while longer. Then I had to leave. I was going to be seeing Altara for several more days, but I could not stay in her house overnight. Ahirom's orders. He thought if I were seen leaving her house in the morning, too many tongues would wag. I was staying at his house in Ashkelon, and I had to be back some time before dawn, and then leave for the barracks from his house. A tiring deception, but I would have run every day from Gath had it meant I could see Altara.

On the third evening I spent with Altara, we did not make love immediately. To prepare me for this departure from our practice, she had told me the evening before she was going to have a surprise for me.

When I entered the house, I heard a flute playing. I looked at Munika and she nodded at me with a broad smile. Then, as I climbed the stairs, I heard Altara call out, "You *always* come early. I haven't finished practicing."

I entered her room. Altara had in her hands an ivory flute with double pipes. She was wearing a pale blue robe, presumably the same robe she wore when she attended the queen.

"I'm impressed. I didn't know you played."

"I have many talents, only some of which you are aware," she said with a coy smile. "Actually, I play for Queen Tanith sometimes. She seems to like it." Munika entered the room. She signaled to the mats on the floor. "Goliath, with permission."

"Oh, please join me." We both sat down. Altara played four different songs. Three joyful tunes, often played at festivals or banquets, and then a mournful tune. After this last one, Altara sat on the bed. Abruptly, Munika got up, left the room, and crossed the landing.

"Where ... Is something wrong?" I asked.

"No, I think I know where she's going," Altara said.

Munika returned in a moment with a tambourine in her hands. This was an instrument unknown in Gath, but I had seen it used in Ashkelon. Munika started to sing and dance, striking the tambourine during pauses and to give emphasis to certain words while singing. She was singing in a foreign tongue, presumably Thrakian. Once in a while, Altara would join in tentatively, although I could tell her pronunciation didn't quite match Munika's.

"Very nice, very nice," I said when Munika finished. "What's the song about?" I looked at both of them.

"It's … it's a love song," Altara said. "I think."

"It's a song about the longing for an absent lover and the pleasure of reuniting with him," Munika explained. Altara and I looked at each other in silence.

"Goliath, you should sing something for us," Munika said.

Altara's eyes brightened. "Yes, yes."

"Oh … I have no musical talent. Really. I can't sing."

"I don't believe that," Munika said.

"Sing, sing, sing" Altara insisted, clapping her hands.

I was embarrassed. Didn't want to sing, but felt I had to. Then I had trouble thinking of something to sing. The first songs I thought of were the ones my mother sang to me as a child. About little lambs and so forth. Not suitable. Then I thought of songs from religious festivals. No. Dirty ditties from army life? No. There was a marching song, about our homeland, absence from family, return to one's wife … a little coarse in places, but … I began to sing. My voice cracked from nervousness at first but I continued almost to the end. Then Altara said, "Goliath, you're right." "What?" "You can't sing," she said laughing. "Oh, thanks, thanks," I replied.

"Altara," Munika scolded, "you shouldn't say that."

"I'm teasing, I'm teasing," Altara said.

"Well, you don't have to worry. I will never sing for you again."

Altara came over to me and tried to kiss me, but I turned my head away, so her kiss landed on my cheek instead of my lips. "Anything you sing, anything you say is the most beautiful music to my ears," Altara said. "Forgive me. I was just joking."

I stood up, turned my back on her, half feigning anger, half feeling anger. Silly to be upset over something like this, but who wants to look like a fool? For some reason, I had a sudden memory of my humiliating encounter years before with Yicath.

Altara hugged me from behind. "I'm sorry. Please forgive me. It was a cruel remark. Wasn't thinking."

I turned around. Looked at her. There were tears in her eyes. Now I thought my reaction was even sillier. Why spoil this evening when we had so few together? I took her hands in mine. "It's fine. Don't know why I … Just forget it. Maybe I want everything I do around you to be perfect. It bothers me when it's not."

She looked down at my hands. She brought them up to her mouth and kissed them lightly. Then she lay her cheek on them. "You are perfect ... better than perfect. What did you say about my scar? Somehow it makes me more beautiful?" She met my eyes. "So too with your singing. It makes you who you are. I don't want a god as my lover. I want you."

This tiff was the closest thing we had to a quarrel during those few days in Ashkelon—although our conversation on the fifth evening was serious and tense. We had made love again and we were lying on her bed as the dark of the night filled her room. Her fingers nervously picked at the mantle she had pulled over us. She said, "Tomorrow is our last evening together."

"Yes."

"Until ...?"

"I don't know."

"I want you, but I can't bear these absences."

"What do you want me to do?"

"I don't know, I don't know."

We were both still and quiet for a moment. Then I said, "I could support you now. For my role in the battle at Aphek, the five cities have rewarded me with twenty mina of silver—a third of a talent. It's being sent to the temple in Gath for safekeeping. That's more than enough to purchase a house, or have one built, and keep us in food for years. You'll never have to grind grain." I paused. "We could have children if you wanted." We looked at each other.

"I'm not sure ..."

"Or not."

"Am I to be your concubine or your wife?"

I hadn't thought about this question. I simply wanted to be with Altara. But I answered without hesitation, "My wife."

"Will that hurt you in any way? I mean, your standing with the army?"

"Meaning?"

"Meaning in the eyes of some, I'm not much better than a whore. I'm a kept woman, or have you forgotten?"

"Makes no difference to me. Shouldn't make any difference to others. To sustain yourself, you have provided pleasure to a man; I sell my body to impose pain and deliver death. Don't see why my service is any more honorable."

"And Ahirom?"

"Yes … and Ahirom." Now I was beginning to feel stupid and exasperated with myself. I realized I had only the vaguest idea of Altara's legal status. She was a freedwoman who had become a concubine. I knew that men could dismiss their concubines provided they continued to support them with a minimal level of sustenance, just enough to avoid outright destitution. And could a concubine leave her man? I would think so, but I couldn't think of an instance where that happened. Concubines were dependent on their men, which is why they were concubines.

"Did you make any commitment to Ahirom when you became his concubine?"

"I agreed to be his concubine, if that's what you mean."

"No, I mean anything beyond that."

"No. There wasn't really a lot of discussion. We … he had already had me. Fucked me in his room one evening. Didn't think I could refuse him and … well, I wanted it myself. I'm pretty sure that's why I was cut by his mother. So, as I said, they had some big family discussion and sometime after that Ahirom came to me and said we could still be lovers. But he was honest about it. Said we could never marry but he would take good care of me." She looked at me. "I mean, I knew that of course. Knew this rich man wasn't going to marry a former slave working in his parent's house. And he was already betrothed at that time to Elissa. So … I agreed. And Ahirom has been good to me. When he had his original house—it was huge—had two rooms to myself. He arranged to have a musician teach me the flute and …" She shrugged. "Yes, Ahirom has been good to me."

This last statement hung in the air for a while. I didn't quite know how to respond. Was thinking of saying, "If you want to stay with Ahirom …" but fortunately I came to my senses and realized this would be a mistake. Instead, I turned to look at Altara, put my left hand on her face and brushed some of her hair. "I love you. I want to be with you. I want you to be my wife. You will never want for anything. Before the gods I swear this. In my house— in our house—you will set your schedule, coming and going as you please. You will be the mistress of the household, beholden to no one."

She answered me with a kiss, and then another.

We enjoyed each other's company for some time thereafter, but as reminder of the constraints under which Altara remained, Munika eventually came to the room to inform me it was time to depart.

As I was dressing, Altara said, "I hate this. I want you to stay."

"So do I. But it need not be like this forever. It won't be like this for much longer." A thought occurred to me. "You don't have to be at the palace tomorrow, right?"

"Yes, that's right."

"What do you do on the days when you're not at the palace?"

"Weave. Go to the market with Munika. Maybe play my flute."

"When do you go to the market?"

"Before mid-day."

"If it please you, let me come by in the morning. We'll go to the market together."

She looked at me skeptically. "Can you do this?"

"I've no duties now. All the ceremonies are over. The other soldiers who are with me spend their days gaming, drinking …" I was about to add "whoring" but stopped myself. "I've had my fill of those activities and there are only so many weapons exercises I need to perform to maintain my skills."

"What will Ahirom say if people see us?"

I walked back over to the bed where Altara still lay. "I don't care what Ahirom says. He won't be controlling our lives soon. Why not start now?"

The next day, I arrived at the house mid-morning. I simply told my comrades and the sub-officer on duty that I was going for a walk around the city. Wanted to get a good look at Ashkelon and feel the sea breeze on my cheeks as our group would be leaving soon. This was true. No need to add that I would be accompanied by a woman.

Or women. Munika went with us. This was proper and prudent. Once past childhood, single women did not venture out alone, except for certain discrete tasks, such as fetching water, and a single woman would definitely not appear in public with a man not her father, brother, or husband—or master.

But one cannot fail to attract attention when one is just a hand short of five cubits high and celebrated as a heroic warrior. Many greeted us, especially once we reached the marketplace. And although most maintained polite distance, a few were forward enough to ask why I was about in the city and who was accompanying me. When I answered, I silently congratulated myself on having anticipated these questions beforehand. I explained that I was with members of Commander Ahirom's household and left it at that.

Munika certainly looked like a servant Ahirom might have and as for Altara, she had her shawl drawn so tightly around her head that her face was invisible. She looked more like a shade than a live person, and sometimes I wondered how she could see where she was going.

After we left the marketplace, where Munika had picked out some cheese, figs, raisins, and squash and a wine noted for its agreeable taste, we stopped by a wall that overlooked the harbor. I could tell Altara was nervous. I had seen, and felt, parts of her body quiver, but I had never seen her right hand tremble so. I placed my left hand on top of it. "It will be fine," I whispered.

"I'm afraid. Word will get back to Ahirom."

"And what if it does? I've done nothing to embarrass him. I'm staying at his house—or at least I'm supposed to be staying at his house—and I accompanied members of his household to the market."

"I …"

"Shh. Let's look at the ships. I don't get to see them in Gath." There was one just coming into the harbor, the coordinated movement of its oars seeming to lift it so that it was gliding on the surface of the water. "You've never been on a ship, right? Or have you?"

"No, I never have."

"I would like to travel on a ship one day."

"Where to?"

"Not sure I have a destination in mind. I would just like the experience of being on a ship at sea. But if I had to choose some place, I would like to go somewhere where it's peaceful. Where I would not have to fight. Where I could spend my time with you."

"Goliath, that's a nice wish, and may the gods grant you that," Munika said, "but is there such a place? My only trip in a ship was in chains, taken as a slave after our city was sacked by the Tablians." She then uttered something in her own language, probably a curse. I could not blame her for having this sentiment, but I did wish she had not chosen to express it at this time.

On the trip back to Altara's house, I had to wonder whether I had made a mistake in going on this excursion. I wasn't concerned about Ahirom's reaction; I was concerned about Altara's. I was worried that I had agitated her. But she was calmer on the walk back. Her hand had stopped shaking.

Once inside her house, Altara's demeanor changed almost instantly. She threw off her shawl, shook her hair loose, and smiled broadly. Then she began to laugh, laugh hard. I could see the anxiety drain away from her body rapidly, like water from an upturned goatskin.

"Gods, we did it," she said, as she took hold of my arms.

"Yes, we did. First of many walks together, I hope."

She stood on her tip toes, tugged at my arms so I would bend forward, and gave me a kiss on my forehead. "That's all you get for now. So run along and when you return this evening, we will have a splendid meal ready for you."

I left and had walked a few paces away from the door, when Altara stuck her head out and said, "And don't come early like you always do. I want the meal to be ready."

I arrived early.

And I left at dawn, having spent the night. I did not return to Ahirom's house.

PART V

CHOICES

1

There are some things we can't tell others. Not because of shame, but because it's too painful for us to talk about them.

2

I could not confront Ahirom right away because we still had to take the Hebrews' chest to Gaza for our triumphal procession there. Then it was on to Gath, the last of the five cities to host the chest. Ahirom was present for the ceremonies in Gath, and it was my plan to speak with him as soon as these ceremonies were over. But the gods had other plans.

An affliction began to overtake Gath—an affliction that I later learned carved out a destructive path through our other cities. The malady crept up stealthily, signaling its presence at first with no more than a cough, but within a day or two those touched by this pestilence became feverish and their joints were racked with pain. Soon breathing became difficult for them; phlegm clogged their throats and chests; their bodies shook from ague. No remedy seemed to work, neither prayers nor sacrifices; neither poultices nor herbs.

The oldest and the youngest were stricken more often. We lost Maoch and Bellon, our king and our senior commander. I grieved over the deaths of both, but especially the death of Bellon. He had been like a father to me—a guide who was stern, but fair and forgiving.

As with other instances of pestilence that afflicted our people from time-to-time, there was no agreement about its cause. Some attributed it to the gods' anger, saying it was a punishment for our pride and a failure to give proper credit to the gods for our victory. Others claimed that the Hebrews had put a curse on their chest. This explanation gained more adherents once we learned that other cities where the chest had been displayed were affected. Still others claimed that there was a miasma in our cities that had become noxious. Those who favored this explanation pointed out that there were fewer people affected in the countryside.

Ahirom was one of those who favored this last explanation, and after paying his respects to the bodies of Maoch and Bellon, who died soon after the pestilence took hold, he left Gath to stay with his family on his farm. About a week or so after he departed, Patibal came to me and said he had an order from Ahirom instructing me to go to his farm as well.

"I would rather not leave my mother and sisters at this time," I protested.

"You don't have a choice," Patibal said. "This is an order from a commander, not a request. Sardon is aware of the order and he has approved it."

"And is there any explanation for this order?"

"You are the champion of Gath, and perhaps the best warrior in all of Palestia. We need to preserve your strength—and your life."

"How long will I be gone?"

"I suppose as long as necessary. Until Ahirom decides the danger has passed."

So, I made ready to go to Ahirom's estate. Before I left Gath, I stopped by to check on my mother and sisters. All seemed well; I was concerned when Hannipath and my mother said Dedra was not available to see me, but my mother assured me she was not sick. I also made arrangements with a merchant traveling to Ashkelon to have a message taken to Altara. Naturally, I was worried about her health and assumed she was similarly concerned about mine. The message was concise: "I am well. I hope you are too. I'm going to spend some days at Ahirom's farm. Will give you news when I return to Gath." The merchant vowed he would have a boy deliver the message as soon as he reached Ashkelon.

Then, before I set out, I did something on a whim. As a result of the campaign against the Hebrews and then the subsequent visit to the different cities, I had not been spending much time with my companion, Lost, and he seemed both morose and thin when I arrived in Gath. I decided to take him with me. I took a quiver and fastened some strips of cloth across its opening, forming a grid. The strips were close enough together to keep Lost from jumping out, but also far enough apart to let him breathe easily. I knew enough about cats to realize he wasn't going to like this strange, unfamiliar break in his routine, but I thought he would benefit from being with me—plus the farm would provide him with plentiful hunting grounds.

Ahirom's only remark on seeing that I had brought Lost was, "We have not made arrangements for another guest," to which I replied, "Don't worry. He can sleep in my room." It took Lost a few days to stop running away and hiding from the children, but eventually he warmed up to them and he even brought them a headless mouse one morning as a token of friendship.

Lost probably felt more at ease around the children than I did around Ahirom. In one sense I was glad he had ordered me to the farm because this provided me with an opportunity to speak with him. But it also meant I needed to spend several days in proximity to him while holding my tongue—to avoid any serious unpleasantness during my stay I did not plan to say anything about Altara until I was ready to return to Gath. This forced silence on an issue close to my heart ate away at me. I did my best to maintain a mask of relaxed cheerfulness, but I did not know whether I was convincing. By coincidence or by design, on a couple of evenings, Ahirom and Elissa broached the topic of my unmarried status, pointing out that because I had recently covered myself with glory, and a not insignificant amount of silver, I would have no trouble finding a suitable mate, including someone from a family that was financially secure. A daughter of a nobleman's family was "not entirely out of the question," according to Elissa. I feigned mild interest, so as not to be impolite.

After seven days, word arrived from Gath around mid-day that the pestilence was fading away. Only four individuals, three infants and an old man, had died the previous day. It was agreed I would return to Gath the following morning.

I told Ahirom that I wanted to speak with him that afternoon. He agreed, giving no sign of disquiet or concern. He told me he would be reading a text that afternoon, and to get the benefit of sunlight he would be seated on a platform that extended out from the third floor of his home. It overlooked the rocky hillside that sloped away from the one side of his house.

"What are you reading?" I asked him as I joined him on this platform.

"It's a text by a priest in Gaza discussing the heavenly bodies, their movements, their nature."

"Are you finding it interesting?"

"Yes, it contains some interesting speculations. For example, this priest believes that the evening star and the morning star are actually the same heavenly body and that this body's appearance at different times of the day reflects its position relative to the sun." He laid the text on a small table next to him. "But I assume you're here to talk about more earthly matters," and with this he signaled for me to sit on a chair opposite him. I was a bit concerned that given my bulk, I might either break this chair or that it would topple over, sending me off the platform, but it proved to be sturdier than it looked.

"Ahirom," I began, and then my throat clenched.

'Do you need some water?"

"No," I managed to squeeze out in a barely audible voice. Not a good start. Now that I had lost the chance to bring up my topic subtly, I decided to launch a sudden, frontal assault. "It's about Altara."

He looked at me intently. "If you're going to tell me you went to the marketplace with her, don't worry, Munika ..."

"No," I interrupted. "It's not about that. I want to marry Altara."

As a large cloud passing over the sun can change the appearance of things, so my words as they passed over Ahirom's ears changed his appearance. His brows drew together, the muscles in his face tensed, and his coloring became darker. He said nothing for a long moment, but started wringing his hands. Then he said, "I blame myself for this. I knew you were inexperienced with women, but I didn't give enough consideration to how spending an evening or two with someone like Altara might affect you. You're smitten; that's obvious. But can't you see that's because she's your first lover."

"No, I ..."

"Let ... me ... finish," he said emphatically as he leaned forward from his chair. "You've told me the story of how you found your cat when he was a young kitten and how he has bonded with you, unusually closely. It's clear it's because you were his first affectionate contact after the short time he had with his mother. Can't you see the same connection is at work between you and Altara? You want to cling to her because she's all you know of women."

I felt the resentment and anger rising within me. He was talking to me as though I were a child.

"I don't want to hear any more of this. Again, I don't blame you; I blame myself, but no more of this. We've had a pleasant time together the last few days, and we will be working closely together in the future. Please don't ruin matters by ... by dwelling on this obsession."

I gathered my thoughts, told myself to speak calmly, and then pressed ahead. "You are mistaken about my love for Altara, and you are also over-looking her love for me. This is something we both want." The storm clouds gathering on his face grew thicker.

"Listen to me carefully, Goliath, this is not going to happen."

"It will happen. Altara is not your slave. She is free to leave your ... your arrangement."

The storm broke and lighting now struck. Ahirom stood up and glared at me. With his voice raised, he said, "She's not free to leave, and I'm certainly not going to give her permission to take up with a common soldier, however overgrown he might be."

I stood in turn. We were less than a pace apart. "What do you mean she's not free to leave?" I barked. "Under our laws ..."

"I have a closer connection to Altara than you realize."

"How ... What do you mean?"

"She's my half-sister."

I was struck dumb. After a moment, I stammered something. What, I cannot recall.

"So, if I wanted to assert a guardianship over Altara, I think the magistrates and the priests in Ashkelon would see things my way. But I don't want to do that. Among other reasons, Altara is not aware of our shared blood and ... well, it may be upsetting to her."

"So, your father ..."

"Yes, my father."

A memory of my meeting Ahirom's father appeared in my mind. The greenish-blue eyes.

I did not know what to say. I did not know what to think. But I had a terrible sinking feeling. I had resolved to confront Ahirom; I had done so. I had expected him to resist, but I had not expected … this. His revelation made a mockery of my resolve, ambushing my plans, killing my hopes.

"What I've told you is not known to anyone outside of my family. If you tell anyone, I will have you gutted like a sheep and have your head placed on a spike. Your enormous head will make a lovely ornament for Gath's walls."

For the briefest moment, a thought flashed before me. I could push Ahirom off this platform onto the rocky slope below. A quick glance confirmed there was no one within sight. But I did not do so. Still not sure what held me back.

Instead, I turned abruptly and walked back into the house, down the stairs to my room. I could feel the blood throbbing in my head. I wanted to beat the walls, smash the furniture, and the fact that I could not do so frustrated me and infuriated me more.

I started to run, bursting out of the door to the main house, careening through the gate to the compound, into Ahirom's seemingly endless fields. No goal, no destination. I just needed to run. I ran and ran, tears streaming down my face, my mouth moving on its own, keening eerily. After some time, I fell to the ground and began to tear at it. Moaning, I called out to Qetesh, begging for her intervention. With no wine for a libation, I bit my thumb hard, drawing blood, which I dripped onto the ground. "Qetesh, hear my plea. Please, please, please, let me be with my love. Let me be with Altara."

I don't know how long I was in the fields, but the sky was turning crimson when I walked back into Ahirom's compound. Elissa was near the door to the house, saying something to Apphia as I approached. She hurried Apphia into the house and then turned to face me.

"We were getting a little worried. Ahirom said you went out into the fields to take a last look around before you left us, but we were concerned that something may have happened to you."

"I'm fine," I said.

"Did you cut your hand?" Elissa asked as she noticed my thumb.

"It's nothing."

"Well, we have delayed the evening meal, hoping for your return, so I'm glad you have arrived."

"I'm sorry for that. Give me just a moment to wash up."

The meal would have been eaten in stony silence had it not been for the constant chattering of Apphia and Melqath. Some nights I found this annoying, but this evening I welcomed their stream of questions and observations as it made the meal bearable.

Lost ambled into the room at one point. I fed him scraps from the table by hand, an interaction which I knew the children enjoyed watching. At one point I moved my hand too quickly behind Lost's eyes, and he instinctively lunged and bit it.

"Why do you keep that thing if it bites you without provocation?" Elissa asked.

"How is that any different from the company of humans?" I replied.

When the meal was ending, Ahirom and Elissa exchanged glances. The unspoken message was clear; there would be no communal gazing at the stars tonight. Elissa left with the children, leaving me alone with Ahirom.

Ahirom cleared his throat. "I regret what happened today," he said. "It was inappropriate for me to threaten a guest in my house." I said nothing. "I don't want to talk any more about … about that topic. It's painful for you. It's also painful for me. You are a comrade. In some ways, I've treated you as a brother, which is why…" He left this thought unfinished. "But without going over that well-plowed ground, let me just say that it would be good for you to meet some other women, women who it would be suitable for you to marry. We can arrange that. Elissa and I would be happy to have you back at the farm so you can meet these women and their families."

I drew a deep breath. "Let me think about this. And now, I think I'll retire for the day."

The next morning, Ahirom walked with me to the gate of the compound to bid me farewell. "I do hope you will give careful consideration to what I proposed last night." He extended his hand. I took it.

"I will," I said. And I did, although not for the reasons Ahirom had in mind.

⊱⊰

3

There is no reasoning with a man or woman in love. Talk of what is practical or prudent, right or wrong, falls on deaf ears. "Good" and "evil" are words without meaning in the domain of love; they have reference only to conduct in a faraway country ruled by other gods.

I had never been one to put much stock in sorcery—in curses, enchantments, philters, and potions. Why trust man's magic, when we can turn to the gods in supplication? But to a man in love all possible measures to secure the object of desire become necessary measures.

The sorcerer in Gath lived in the part of the city where the poor folk lived. One story houses with two rooms, or perhaps only one large room, with a hearth in the middle of the room and an opening in the ceiling. The people here had no kin, or no kin who recognized them. They worked as laborers or servants or, as rumor had it, thieves.

I startled the inhabitants of the dark, squat house as I entered. Someone in a corner yelled, "Giant!" "It's all right, all right," I assured them. "I mean you no harm." As my eyes adjusted to the darkness, I saw a man seated on a mat near the hearth. He was looking down, the focus of his attention being the earthen floor. "The sorcerer?" I asked. Without moving his head, he jerked his thumb to a door at the back about five paces from him.

As I approached the door, my nose picked up the stench of sickness emanating from behind the door. With some trepidation, I knocked at the door.

"Who's there?"

"Goliath. Of the army. I am …"

I heard the bolt being lifted. "I know who you are. Come in." The door opened.

The sorcerer had a whole other room, although not quite as large as the room facing the street. There was a pot simmering on his hearth, which was the source of the smell. Other than a hole in the ceiling above the hearth, the only other source of light was a small window on the back wall near the ceiling. Nonetheless, even though the light was dim I was able to get a good look at his face. It was heavily lined and one eye seemed to be partially closed as a result of an infection that turned his eyelids red and exuded pus, some of which had dried on his cheek. He walked in front of me to pull out a mat for me to sit on, and as he did so I noticed his breath was foul and what teeth remained in his mouth were badly decayed. I did wonder if this man could perform magic, why couldn't he restore himself to health?

"Sit. How can I help you?" he asked.

"I need a potion, or something, that will stop another man caring for a woman."

The sorcerer sat across from me. "This is a complicated matter," he said. "Do you want this man dead?"

"No," I said emphatically. "The man …"

"Because that would be easier. What you ask is complicated."

"But it is what I want."

"This would be costly."

"How much?"

"First, let's discuss the matter of delivery of the spell. Potions can be effective if they are used properly, but many who ask for potions are disappointed, because they never find the occasion to use them or the potion isn't ingested in the appropriate amount. And then they blame me! Would you be able to ensure that this man drinks a cup full of the potion?"

"Do you mean an entire cup full? Can't I just drop some of the potion into his wine cup?"

"No," the sorcerer said firmly. "I told you this is a complicated matter. It would require a significant amount of a strong potion."

I thought that if the potion were going to smell anything like what was in the sorcerer's pot, I would never get Ahirom to drink it. "If I don't use a potion, what else can I do?"

"Sympathetic magic," he answered quickly. "Thirty shekels."

"Agreed. Now what does this entail?"

"Do you have with you some item belonging to the beloved? Perhaps some article of clothing? A gift she has given you?"

I had had an amulet fashioned to contain the hair that Altara gave me. I wore it around my neck. I removed it and held it out to the sorcerer. "A lock of the woman's hair is inside the amulet."

"Wonderful. That will do nicely." He then stood up and walked to the corner of the room where he began to rummage around some articles.

"Do I need to remove the hair from the amulet?"

"Not necessary," he said without turning around, as he continued to move objects apparently at random. But then he did face me and asked, "You do have the silver with you, correct?"

"Yes, yes."

"Aha," he said suddenly. He plucked out of the jumble of objects a small bag in which something was squirming. With a withered hand, he held out the bag to me.

"What's in the bag?" I asked.

"A lizard. This will represent the other man."

"Will that do?"

"Why would I use it otherwise? I've been practicing the magical arts for ten years. I know what I'm doing," he said impatiently. "The other man is always represented as a lizard."

"Fine. What do we do now?"

"This is what you are to do. You are to take the lizard out of the bag. Hold the lizard firmly in your left hand. With your right hand, bring the amulet close to the lizard's forehead, then his eye …"

"Which eye?"

"Doesn't matter. Then bring the amulet close to one of his arms. Again, doesn't matter which one."

"Is that it?"

"No, that's just the beginning. You will then hear me chant. When I finish the chant, you are to break the lizard's neck and turn its head completely around. I will chant again, and again when I stop you will do something else. This time you will remove the eye before which you have placed the amulet. Again I will chant, and after I finish this time you will take the arm that was next to the amulet and force it into the lizard's mouth. Do you understand these instructions?"

"Yes, but …"

"Do I need to repeat the instructions?"

"No, but I would like to understand the purpose of what I'm doing."

The sorcerer sighed and then said, "By turning the neck around, you're turning the man away from your beloved. By removing the eye, you will ensure he will turn a blind eye to your beloved. By stuffing the lizard's mouth, you will ensure he will not speak to you again of your beloved."

We performed the ritual. Then I realized I didn't know what to do with this dead, deformed lizard, so I asked.

"You are to bury it near his house, of course. You do have access to his house, don't you?"

"Yes, but it still may be some time before I am at his house again. He lives in the countryside. Won't the lizard rot in the meantime?"

"You can just gut it so it will not decay as rapidly. Then dry it in the sun, making sure no flies get near it."

"Gutting it will not affect the spell?"

The sorcerer shrugged. "It shouldn't."

In possession of my means of placing a spell on Ahirom, I now sent a message to him indicating I was ready to accept his offer to meet some potential mates. A response came quickly. Ahirom would schedule something within fifteen to twenty days.

In the meantime, the lizard slowly decayed in my room at the barracks. It started to smell so bad that Lost ceased to bother it. Antenon, who, being a friend, had accepted without further inquiry my explanation that the lizard was needed for a spell, told me I would have to sleep elsewhere or buy some incense to mask the odor. I did the latter. Fortunately, by the time it came to travel to Ahirom's farm, the lizard had dried out enough that the smell was mostly gone. It was now a desiccated husk, which caused me to worry that the spell might not be effective.

At the farm I made polite conversation with the families of the potential brides, and even sometimes with the women themselves—although as they were never left alone in a room with me, we really said very little to each other. That suited me fine as my thoughts were elsewhere. On my last night at the farm, I stayed up until I heard no one else stirring and then crept as quietly as a man my size could to the outside. Ahirom had a sentry posted at all times, but he faced outward so I had hopes he would not notice me. If he did, I had already prepared an explanation in the event he or someone else saw me digging in the dirt. I would explain that I was not able to sleep and had gone outside for a walk, when the chain for my amulet had broken and I was now searching and digging for it on the ground. But no one saw or heard me. Undisturbed, I quickly buried the lizard—one advantage of big hands. I had to bury the lizard close to the stable so the broken ground would not attract too much attention, but the sorcerer had said nothing about distance affecting the spell, as long as the lizard was in Ahirom's compound. The next morning I returned to Gath and waited for the magic to work.

4

Doubts assailed me after I returned to Gath. Not only did I worry that the spell might not work, but I also wondered whether in relying upon the spell

I had made the right choice. Ahirom had threatened to assert a guardianship over Altara based on his family ties with her, but would he really risk doing so? Granted, she was not a full sibling and our laws did not punish sexual relations between siblings anyway— unlike parent-child incest—but still, having a family connection to a concubine was not likely to enhance his reputation. In addition, he could lose Altara's affection. Perhaps I should have simply proceeded to marry Altara, treating his threat as no more than posturing.

As the days went by, another problem started to weigh on me. How long could I put off informing Ahirom of my impressions of the women I had met at his farm? I would need to say something soon. How long did it take the spell to work? And one night another troubling thought occurred to me: how would I know whether the spell had worked? In my haste to acquire something from the sorcerer, I had neglected to ask some important questions.

Being in love is like being drunk. In the intervals when one's mind clears, one can have misgivings about actions taken while intoxicated.

It was while I was mulling over such matters that a boy came to the barracks, very excited. He asked for me. I recognized him as someone from my old neighborhood.

"Goliath, you must come quickly. There are screams coming from your mother's house." Lukioth gave his consent immediately, adding that he would send a few soldiers along presently, and I ran with the boy to my old house.

A crowd of around fifteen people had gathered outside the house, drawn by the wailing coming from inside. I recognized my mother's voice. Some in the crowd had pounded on the door, but no one responded. Suddenly, the door opened and Hannipath appeared riding a donkey. "Make way," he yelled. "I need to ride for help."

Some in the crowd began to move to let him pass, but I yelled out, "Hannipath, stop! What's wrong? Is it my mother?"

Hannipath's head whipped around, apparently startled by the sound of my voice. His eyes were wide with terror. Before he could answer, another wild wail came from inside the house, which then broke up into spasmodic sobs.

"Gods, man," I said. "Tell us what's going on."

"Must go," was his murmured response, and he dug his heels into the donkey's side to urge the beast on.

Some deep instinct, some animal sense of menace, caused me to run up and take hold of the donkey's reins. "Someone else can get help," I said. I turned to some of the others. "Go to the temple. Fetch some healer priests." Two or three young men ran off. Turning back to Hannipath, I said, "I need you to tell me what's going on." Now that I was close to him I could see he had some deep scratches on his face. The blood dripping from them confirmed they were fresh. Hannipath said nothing. His reply was to jump off the donkey. He started to run, but then tripped. "Grab him," I instructed the crowd. Slowly, I began to discern what was going on. Hannipath must have beaten my mother. By the sound of her sobs, and the scratches on his face, he must have beaten her badly. It was accepted that a husband could discipline a wife, but there were also limits that had to be respected. If the wife being punished were one's mother or sister, those limits were stringent.

I rushed into the house and looked around quickly, then noticed my mother on the courtyard roof. She was on her knees, wailing and sobbing, her body swaying back and forth. I was up next to her in an instant. "Mother, Mother, tell me what's the matter." I pulled her head up, expecting to see bruises. Her face was covered in tears, but I saw no marks.

She grabbed me, clawing and clutching at my tunic, babbling incoherently between her sobs. I couldn't understand her at first. Then slowly I began to make out one word; she repeated, "Dedra, Dedra."

A cold sickness swept over me, penetrating both body and soul. In vain, I tried to deny the horrible realization that my mother was not bemoaning her injuries, but rather something that had happened to Dedra.

I ran into the upstairs rooms. It did not take me long to find her. There, hanging from a beam, was Dedra, her noose fashioned from her girdle. She had looped the noose in the gap between the beam and the ceiling. I ripped the girdle from the beam, catching her lifeless body as it fell onto my left arm. Her face was drained of color and distorted, eyes bulging, tongue protruding from her mouth. She was thin, almost skeletal—except for her belly. The swelling was unmistakable. Of course, the baby she was carrying was dead also. I wrapped her body in a mantle, making sure to cover her face, said a prayer over it, and then dashed out. I didn't pause for the ladder; I jumped into the courtyard and made for Hannipath.

He was sitting on the ground, still just outside the door to the house, surrounded by a few men. When he saw me, he bolted upright, and started to run away, but my hand grabbed the back of his tunic. Yanking him back-ward, I pulled him to the ground. I then straddled him, pinning his arms against his body, and let my fists begin their work. This is one occasion when I wished the gods had not given me such strength because the work was fin-ished all too quickly. The third blow had crushed his skull; by the seventh, his face was unrecognizable. Afterward, my hands hurt.

When had the first order been given for me to stop? Don't know. But it must have been some time before I finished because when the soldiers finally managed to pull me off Hannipath, Patibal was yelling, "I ordered you to stop, damn you!"

I stood up. A soldier put his head next to Hannipath's chest and then his hand over what was left of Hannipath's mouth and nose. "The man's dead," the soldier said.

I started to go back into the house, but Patibal grabbed me. "Stay here, Goliath."

"I want to check on my mother."

"One of the men will check. You're not going anywhere. You just killed someone."

⊷┼┾

<h1 style="text-align:center">5</h1>

Standing still, I now had time to think about what had happened instead of merely reacting. What Patibal had stated was already known to me at some level, but this truth now bore into me. I had killed someone. Moreover, not just anyone, but my step-father. My body started shaking and I began sobbing.

A soldier returned with my mother, who was still weeping and difficult to understand, so Patibal received no clear answers to the questions he put to her. Speaking through my sobbing, I tried to explain. "This man," here I pointed to Hannipath's body, "has been raping my sister."

"How do you know this?" Patibal asked.

"She was pregnant."

"Where's your sister now?"

I didn't have the strength to say.

A soldier spoke up. "There's a woman's body in one of the upstairs rooms."

"Is that your sister?" Patibal asked.

I nodded.

"I can't sort this all out on my own," Patibal said. "I'm taking you and your mother to the magistrate." He turned to one of the soldiers. "Go to the temple, find the priests ..."

"They're already on the way," someone in the crowd said.

"Fine," said Patibal. He continued with the soldier. "Then wait here for the priests. They will perform the sanctification of the house and arrange to take the bodies to the mortuary. Make sure no one other than the priests enters the house."

Patibal and one of the soldiers walked with my mother and me to the palace, where the magistrate on duty would be found. As we were walking, I wanted to ask my mother how it all happened. When did Hannipath begin forcing himself on Dedra, and so forth, but she wasn't in shape to talk. Also, as I considered our situation more, I thought it might not be prudent to discuss these matters in front of Patibal.

Gath had three magistrates, nobles who were literate and had some skills with record-keeping. Their principal duties were to oversee tax collection and commercial transactions for the palace and the city, but they also resolved some disputes and imposed fines and punishment. In serious cases, however, the king and the chief priest had to be consulted.

The room in which we were taken to meet the magistrate was large, maybe six paces by eight paces. It had three tables. There was a table with some parchment and a couple of papyrus scrolls with a few chairs in front of it and one behind; another table on which were stacked clay tablets and papyrus scrolls; and a third table with the bronze pans of a scale and a collection of maybe twenty weights. A stanchion with a banner representing the king—two swans facing each other under a rising sun—was behind the table that had chairs. A sentry was posted by the door.

Patibal instructed my mother and me to take a seat in the chairs facing the one table. I declined the chair and, not finding a mat, just sat on the floor. Patibal then went to find the magistrate.

Presently, Patibal returned with the magistrate. The latter was wearing a white tunic with black and red stripes on the sleeves. He had a purple mantle draped over his shoulder. I thought he was the uncle of Sardon, but I wasn't sure. He sat down in the chair behind the table, cleared his throat, and stated, "I am Adamaos. Patibal has already summarized some of the events of today, but I must also hear from both of you what happened. He looked at my mother. "You are Aliya, correct?" he asked. My mother still could not talk but she nodded her assent. "Do you want some water?" No answer. "Get some water," Adamaos called out to the sentry.

"Sir, may I have some water too, perhaps in a basin?" I showed him my hands as I did this. They still had blood on them.

Adamaos drew back, his face showing revulsion, and then got up out of his chair and went to the hall outside yelling for Patibal. I couldn't hear what was said, but Adamaos's tone suggested anger.

"Some water and a cloth for you are on their way," he said to me as he returned to the room. Settling back into his chair, he said, "Now, Goliath, you killed this man, Hannipath, is that right?"

"Yes."

"His relationship to you?"

"He's my stepfather. My mother's second husband."

Adamaos leaned back in his chair. "You understand the seriousness of what you've done?"

"Yes."

"Why did you do it?"

At this point, the water and cloth arrived. With a nod, Adamaos indicated I could go ahead and clean myself. This was fortunate because it gave me a moment to gather my thoughts. Having had time to reflect, I gave a fuller answer to Adamaos than I had given Patibal. "First, you should know that Hannipath has been acting strangely for some time. Moody, jumpy, as though he was anxious about something. You can ask his cousin, Barekbal, the potter, to confirm this. Next, Dedra has been sad, despondent for several months, and last month when I went to see her, Hannipath told me I could not. Then today... well, today, Hannipath was trying to run away when my mother was calling out for help. I went into the house and …" Here my voice broke. "Dedra was hanging. She was dead. She also was pregnant and …"

Adamaos interrupted me. "So, you assume that Hannipath impregnated her. You also assume he raped your sister, in other words, you assume Dedra did not consent to sexual relations with her stepfather, correct?"

"Yes."

"Do you have any evidence to support your suspicions?"

I hesitated. "Dedra would not …"

"Dedra is dead, and you just said you have not spoken to her in some time. How do you know you have not killed an innocent man?"

"I know my sister," I said indignantly.

"But I don't know your sister, and I cannot take your word for what she thought or wanted."

A horrible feeling overcame me. Had I wrongfully killed Hannipath? Is it possible he was just going to get help?

Just then my mother broke her silence and murmured, "Goliath says … true."

"Aliya, please repeat that and speak up if you can."

A little louder and more distinctly, my mother said, "What Goliath says is true."

Adamaos drummed his fingers on the table. He studied my face. "It is difficult for me to see the path of justice here. I will need to consult with King Achish and the high priest. Aliya, I will send for your daughter, Avram. You are to stay with her. If you need something from your house, tell Patibal and he will arrange for it. He will also arrange to take care of your animals. You are not to go to the house yourself."

"My daughter!"

"She will be in the mortuary. Probably there already."

'What will happen to her body?" I asked, realizing that if she were treated as a suicide she would be burned, her ashes strewn on the streets or possibly even the cesspit.

Adamaos shrugged. "That's to be determined I suppose. As for you, Goliath, you will be kept here in the palace somewhere, under guard. Again, if you need anything from your barracks, tell Patibal."

A soldier came in to lead me away. We stopped next to Patibal. "Patibal, could you please ask Antenon to look after Lost? Also, if it's possible, please have my effigy of Qetesh brought to me."

"Fine. Anything else?"

"No … wait. Would it be possible to have Antenon visit me?"

"Don't know. Don't know the conditions on your confinement. I'll ask Adamaos. Any other visitors?"

"My sister, Avram." This was an afterthought. My primary concern was to get a message to Altara and Antenon was the only one who could help me with this.

I was placed in a storeroom near the palace guards' duty room. There were a couple of mats and a chamber pot, along with a number of amphorae for holding wine and grain. There were also spare tunics, helmets, and shields. And before someone realized this might be imprudent, there were even a few swords and daggers bundled in a corner.

I passed the rest of the day alone with my thoughts, which were not happy ones. I wept for Dedra and for myself. My situation seemed hopeless. It did not matter whether I would be executed or not. Maybe that would be better I thought. Whatever happened, how would I be able to wed Altara now?

In the morning, a guard came by with some bread, water, a clean tunic and undergarment, and a slave. The slave gave me a clean chamber pot and took my old one. He was a captured Hebrew. I inferred this by the guard calling him an "accursed dog" in Hebrew—one of the few phrases I knew—and by the generous use of the lash on the slave's back.

I asked the guard whether my comrade Antenon would be coming by. "How would I know?" was his reply.

Antenon did come by a little after mid-day, bringing with him my effigy of Qetesh. He had heard what happened to Hannipath, so we spent little time talking of that. "Lost has been yowling and whimpering. He knows you're gone and since you left suddenly he suspects something has happened to you."

"Something has happened to me. Thanks for taking care of him."

"Don't mind. Just wish he wouldn't do his yowling before it's time for us to wake up."

"Friend, can I ask you to do me a favor?"

"Speak."

"I need to get a message to someone in Ashkelon."

Antenon scrunched his nose and eyebrows in puzzlement. "How am I supposed to do that?"

"There are merchants who travel between the cities. They'll take care of it. You will need to pay them. Probably two shekels. There should be five or six shekels worth of silver pieces in my leather purse in our room."

"Fine. What's the message and to whom?"

Neither Antenon nor I could write more than a few words and phrases so I had to repeat the message a few times so he could memorize it: "You may have heard. I am imprisoned in Gath for killing a man who raped my sister. Don't give up hope. I pray to the gods that I may see you again." I gave Antenon the directions to Altara's house, then her name. On hearing the name, he started to say, "Isn't she ...?" but then stopped.

After Antenon left that day, the only visitor I had for four days was the Hebrew slave. On his third trip to drop off food and pick up my slop, he looked around, pointed at me, and whispered, "Goliath?" I nodded.

"Big battle—Aphek," he said in broken Palestim, pointing at me. Again I nodded. "Me also Aphek," he said, and then he grabbed his wrists in turn pantomiming the slapping of chains on them. I inferred he was captured at the battle. I gestured to the sky, as if pointing to the gods, and then held out my left hand, turned my palm upward, and shrugged, hoping to convey to him his fate was the will of the gods. He seemed to understand.

The next day when the slave came back, he said, "You warrior, me warrior." He then knelt, folded his hands as if beseeching me to do something, stood up, pointed at me and then grabbed his neck with both hands. The message was reasonably clear. He wanted me to put him out of his misery. He was a warrior who was unlucky enough to survive the battle. I was not unsympathetic, but I tried to indicate to him that I could not do it, shaking my head and throwing my hands in the air. That's all I needed—to have more blood on my hands, and this time a palace slave. Whatever hope there was in his eyes seemed to vanish.

On the sixth day that I was imprisoned, Avram showed up. I embraced her, but whether due to my admittedly unpleasant odor (I not been given water or oil to clean myself) or for some other reason, she drew back. She did not sit.

"Mother. How is she?" I asked.

"Not well. Not well. I'm not sure she will ever recover. She's like a child now."

"How?"

Avram gave me a hard look. "It's not pleasant."

I had to ask. "Did she know... I mean about Hannipath and Dedra?"

Avram choked back her tears and said, "How could she not?"

"And what of Dedra? Her body. Have they allowed it to be buried or..."

"That's one reason I came today. There's some good news I suppose. The magistrate was going to have the body burned but she has been spared that indignity. Your friend, Ahirom, asked for the body yesterday so Dedra could be buried on his farm. Since the body would be away from the city and would not …" Here Avram broke down. Regaining her composure after a minute, she continued, "Since the body would not disgrace Gath, the magistrate agreed. Mother and I consented to this, of course. Ahirom has arranged for a clay coffin and for the transport of the body. The burial is the day after tomorrow."

My soul was in turmoil on hearing this and instinctively I reached for Avram. She let me draw her into my embrace, perhaps thinking I was expressing relief and joy. I was and I was not. My mix of emotions was like the sorcerer's brew, hot, swirling, and foul. The man who denied me what I wanted most in the world was now extending to me and my family an invaluable kindness. Yet somehow I felt more hatred than gratitude. He had real power while I never felt so impotent.

Finally, I managed to find some words. "Are you or Mother going to be able to travel … for the burial I mean."

"I'm going. Ahirom is providing a mule and escort. I don't think Mother can make it. Barekbal will stay with her."

"If you can, I would like to have something buried with Dedra."

"What?"

"My bronze helmet. Go to the barracks. Ask for my friend, Antenon. He will get it for you."

"Won't you get in trouble."

"Ha! I'm not in trouble now?"

Avram left me to my thoughts. I sat on a mat. I did not move from that spot until I fell asleep.

Over the next few days, the Hebrew slave and I taught each other some words from each other's language. We had nothing better to do. It began when I pointed to my shit in the chamber pot and said "shit" in our tongue. He repeated the word. Then, pointing to him and moving my hand like a mouth I indicated I wanted to learn the Hebrew word for shit. He complied with my request, laughing. In this way, we learned each other's words for shit, piss, fuck, ass, cock, I, you, slave and kill. Sadly, because he spent too long with me one morning, I also learned the Hebrew words for whip, blood, and scar.

About ten or eleven days into my imprisonment, Adamaos and Sardon both came to see me. Sardon asked how I was bearing up, and I replied as well as could be expected. Then Adamaos spoke. "Goliath, as I said at the outset, this is a difficult case. How we resolve this matter is largely a question of whether we decide your killing of Hannipath was justified under the circumstances."

"May I ask a question?"

He seemed displeased that I had interrupted his summary of my situation, but he said, "Go ahead."

"If I had come upon Hannipath forcing himself on my sister would I not have been justified in killing him?"

"A fair point, but that's not what happened, is it? Hannipath wasn't forcing himself on anyone when you came upon him so there was no need for immediate action. If a man comes upon another who he suspects, perhaps even knows, stole from him a couple of months ago, do we let the man kill that thief? No. The thief must be given a chance to explain his actions and the king must decide the punishment. Gath is not some remote village where the rustics stone people whenever they feel aggrieved."

I could not think of a response to that, so I said nothing.

"As I was saying, this is a difficult case, so difficult that Achish, our new king, has asked the high priest of Ekron to review your case and make a recommendation."

"Why the priest in Ekron as opposed to the priest in Gath?"

"A couple of reasons. First, the king thought it advisable to have someone from outside Gath review the case. Second, the high priest of Ekron has achieved a reputation for wisdom. Perhaps you're aware of this."

"No, I'm not. I don't … well, I don't focus on statecraft or matters of religion. I leave such things to people like you. Who is he?"

"He's Phodan. Used to live here in Gath, but for the last few years he's been in Ekron."

My heart sank on hearing Phodan's name. Phodan was to judge my case! The magistrate sensed my despair and asked, "Is something wrong?"

"I know this man."

"We're aware of that. He mentioned that himself. Said you were childhood friends, but it's been a long time since he had any contact with you, is that not correct?"

I nodded.

"Anyway, we think he can be impartial because not only was that contact with you long ago but he's also a second cousin of Hannipath, so there's some distant connection with both you and the man you killed."

The dagger was thrust in deeper. The person who was going to be my judge was not only a man who I had wronged but a relative of the man I had killed. How could I explain to the magistrate about something I failed to do as a child over a decade ago? How could I even begin the story? And what evidence did I have that Phodan held a grudge? None. I felt tongue-tied and I ended up saying nothing to Adamaos. Saying nothing regarding my saying nothing when I was a child. Seemed fitting somehow.

"Goliath?" Adamaos interrupted my reverie.

"Yes?"

"Are you all right?"

I shrugged.

"I understand you can't be happy about your confinement, especially since we have not been able to give you any news until today. I regret the delay but it was unavoidable. Do you need anything?"

"Could I have a basin, a cloth, and some water and oil to clean myself?"

"Yes, of course." He and Sardon turned to leave.

"Wait," I said. "When is Phodan coming?"

"Should be here in two to three days."

6

A couple of days later, I was taken to a back room in Gath's temple complex to be questioned by Phodan. I was calmer than when I had first heard he was to judge my case—the calm of someone who is powerless to do anything about his troubles.

I recognized him at once when he entered the room. He did not seem to have changed much. Maybe that's because the bald head he had now matched the bald head he had had as an acolyte.

He spent no time reminiscing about days gone by, an exercise of discretion for which I was grateful. Instead he asked me to recount my life history, including my relations with my family, beginning with when I became a soldier. He said he needed to know my background to reach an informed decision. He had a scribe with him to take down what I said. Took the better part of a day. After I finished, he asked me whether I had any regrets about killing Hannipath.

I thought for a moment before answering. "He deserved to die, but perhaps it would have been better to let the king pass judgment on him."

"Why is that?"

I felt like saying, "Because then I would not be here," but I suppressed that thought and said instead, "This is something we reserve to the king so when the punishment is given it can be a warning … an instruction to others."

"So you admit you did something wrong?"

"Wrong … wrong in part, right in part."

"And for that wrong that you did, a punishment from the king would be appropriate, to serve, as you put it, as an instruction to others, no?"

I suddenly had the sensation of being back in my childhood, playing Siege with Phodan. Those games were played in the portico to this temple, not thirty paces from where we were sitting. Phodan was restricting my ability to maneuver now just as he restricted my movement in that game. I was losing. Needed a different tactic.

"May I ask you a question?"

"Yes."

"What is the purpose of punishment?"

"As you said yourself, it serves as a warning to others, to try to prevent them from doing the same sort of thing."

"That's not the only purpose though, is it?"

"Go on."

"Well, when execution is the punishment, it serves to remove someone dangerous from the community."

"Yes."

"So before the punishment of death is imposed, there must be a judgment that the person is dangerous to community. Or, put another way, the punishment of death should not be imposed on someone who is not a danger to the community, and certainly not on someone who is valuable to the community."

A smile began to creep across Phodan's face. "And how, in your view, should the king determine who is dangerous? If someone kills another, that certainly suggests dangerousness, does it not?"

He had moved his piece. Now I needed to think about my move. "It would depend on what that person's motivation was. A corrupt soul is how we distinguish those who are dangerous from those who are not. Hannipath had a corrupt soul. He violated my sister, not only dishonoring her, but breaking his solemn vows to my mother."

"And you don't have a corrupt soul? From what you recounted to me today, some might say you are a violent person."

"Is the city's executioner a violent person? When I've killed, it was to serve the cause of justice and the interests of our people."

Phodan leaned back in his chair. He eyed me for a long moment. Then he stood up and called out for the guard. "When will I learn of your recommendation?" I asked.

"You will not hear of it from me. The magistrate will inform you. But I anticipate I will make my recommendation to the magistrate sometime tomorrow morning, and the judgment may be announced and the punishment carried out tomorrow as well. I believe the king and the magistrate believe this matter has been pending long enough."

As I was turning to leave, Phodan had some parting words for me. "I thought your years as a warrior might have dulled your wit, but you still play well, Goliath."

That evening I did two things. I offered what water I had to Qetesh, fervently praying that I would live to see Altara again or that, were I to be executed, she would find happiness in her life. I then broke off a piece of hardened clay from one of the amphorae. Rubbing it against the walls I fashioned a weapon as sharp as a dagger, but small enough to be hidden. My contact with the Hebrew slave had reminded me of the time the Hebrew merchants had visited the bloomery. And just as on that occasion, I had learned the Hebrews were not monsters, similarly through my daily dealings with this slave, I understood … how should I say this? Can't really express my feelings. I suppose my action speaks for itself.

When the Hebrew slave came by in the morning, he pointed to the puddle by the effigy of Qetesh and said, "Piss?" Qetesh, forgive me, but I had to laugh. We then made our usual transaction, chamber pot for bread and water, but I had something else to give him. Using my foot, I pushed the sharpened piece of clay across the floor and nodded to him. He understood. He picked it up. He buried it in my shit and left.

⇒‡ ‡⇐

7

That afternoon, three guards came for me. They asked me to stand. One of the guards used a rope to bind my hands behind my back. I was then led to the room where Adamaos had initially interviewed me. Adamaos was seated behind his table. Sardon was standing next to him.

"Prisoner, approach the table," Adamaos ordered. I did so. He picked up a papyrus scroll. "I will read to you the judgment on your case." He looked up at me. "Do not interrupt me." Reading from the scroll, Adamaos said, "King Achish, counseled by Magistrate Adamaos and the high priest of Ekron, Phodan, has decided that Goliath has wrongfully killed the man, Hannipath." Adamaos paused and fixed me a hard look. This is it, I thought. I wondered: how would I be executed? Beheaded? Or would I be bludgeoned to death?

Adamaos returned his gaze to the scroll. "However, the man Hannipath was a vile reprobate who had violated Goliath's sister. As we believe Goliath acted not out of malice but out of a desire for justice for his sister, he is to be released from custody provided he pay a fine of five mina of silver to the king and two mina of silver to Hannipath's mother, Ummishtath. In addition, because Goliath wrongfully shed blood at the entrance to his mother's house, he has forfeited all right to inherit that house or any part thereof. May Dagon's justice always prevail." Adamaos looked at me again. "Any questions?"

"No."

"You're free to go. Sardon will escort you to the barracks."

I returned to the storeroom briefly to retrieve my effigy of Qetesh. I saw the Hebrew slave one last time, as I passed him in the hallway. We exchanged knowing glances.

Sardon never was one for talking, at least to me, so the walk to the barracks passed mostly in silence. As we approached the barracks, he did say, without looking at me, "You brought dishonor on the army. Bellon thought you should be made a sub-officer. I disagreed. You proved me correct."

This scolding did not bother me much. Becoming a sub-officer was not my ambition. Sardon's words only confirmed what I suspected already, that with Bellon dead and Sardon in command, army life might not be as pleasant for me.

Word of my release had already reached the barracks by the time I arrived. Several of my comrades were on hand to receive me, including Antenon. As the greeting party broke up, Antenon said in a low voice, "I have some news. I'll tell you when you're back in our room."

Lost looked up from his slumber when I entered our room. He walked over to me and when I sat down he climbed onto my lap, rubbed me with his head, purred for a few moments, and then fell asleep again.

"Did you receive a reply to my message to Altara?"

"Yes, that's what I want to tell you. It just arrived yesterday."

"And?"

"Very short. Well, it was either very short or it's all that the boy could remember. The message was: 'I am praying for you, for us. Ahirom to say something.' That's it."

"Nothing else?"

"Nothing else. That's all."

I was consoled to learn that I had not lost Altara's affection, but the reference to Ahirom saying "something" was unclear and puzzling, and because it was unclear and puzzling, it was also worrisome. What was Ahirom going to say? And to whom?

I was still mulling over the implications of this communication at breakfast the next day. Sardon came up to me as I was finishing. "You must have been a difficult prisoner, Goliath. Or maybe you just frighten people."

"Why do you say that, sir?"

"The Hebrew slave who was attending you found a clay shard somewhere and stuck it into his throat last night. Made a mess. Do Hebrews have more blood?"

8

Clouds intermittently obscured the sun, robbing my room of light, as I sat there one evening several days after my release. The transition from light to dark and back again mirrored the state of my soul. Pleased at being alive, and again free to have desires about the future, I would begin to think about Altara, letting my memory bring forth images of her. Memory would become sweet yearning, a longing to be in her arms again. I could almost feel her embrace, could almost taste her. Then the clouds would collect and roll in, the darker aspects of my situation robbing me of Altara's sunlight. I had failed to protect my sister, and she was now dead by her own hand, my mother was a broken woman, and I had no plan—other than a sorcerer's lizard—for reuniting with Altara. I fought these despairing thoughts but was no more successful than the sun when it resists a gathering storm.

My despair became blackest when a sense of aimlessness overcame me. All I had were dreams and hopes. How to make these a reality? It was not clear to me where the path forward lay, or if there was one. What was it that I should do now?

Soon a path appeared. Although its destination was uncertain, and it was a path marked by fear rather than hope, I felt compelled to take it.

The very evening when I had been brooding over my situation, someone came galloping up to the barracks, loudly crying out he needed to be let in immediately. Too deep in self-absorption, I ignored the clamor at first, but eventually I bestirred myself and walked slowly to the staircase leading to the courtyard. My pulse quickened when I saw that many of my comrades were very excited and were beginning to yell themselves. I heard references to an attack. I moved quickly down the staircase and caught Lukioth by the arm as he was headed to the commanders' work area.

"What's going on?" I asked.

"The Hebrews have attacked in force. Apparently, they have overrun Ekron and have continued on from there. They are not far from Gath."

"How... It was not six months ago that we crushed them."

"I don't know. Anyway, I need to confer with the other sub-officers. Sardon is on his way here, and after he arrives and we have an opportunity to discuss the situation, we will make an announcement to you and the other soldiers."

I then sought out my comrades to find out what they knew. All over the barracks soldiers were huddling together in small groups, excitedly gesturing and shouting. I joined a group that included Batnoam and Antenon.

"Lukioth says the Hebrews have overrun Ekron. How is this possible?" I asked.

"They have mustered a huge army. Tens of thousands of men," Batnoam said.

"But the walls of Ekron—were they no protection?"

"I heard the messenger—a soldier from Ekron who rode here—said that they assaulted in such numbers that they were able to scale the walls even after suffering many casualties," Antenon said.

Other soldiers joined our group and some contradicted what Antenon and Batnoam had said, stating that Ekron had fended off the attack. There was much discussion back-and-forth. We could not ask the messenger to clarify matters because he was with Sardon and the sub-officers, undoubtedly being questioned at length. The only thing that appeared certain was that the Hebrews had attacked Ekron and that they had undertaken a major offensive. This was no probing attack.

After a while, the meeting in the commanders' room broke up, the sub-officers rounded up all the men for a meeting in the courtyard, and then Sardon addressed us.

"The Hebrews have crossed into our territory with a large army, perhaps as many as 10,000 men. They attacked Ekron, taking it by surprise. They have breached the city walls and taken over much of the city. You can imagine what they are doing to the people in the city. However, the citadel in Ekron remains in Palestim hands, and the king of Ekron and his family are safe within the citadel. Some of the Hebrew force has been left behind in Ekron to besiege the citadel, but the bulk of their forces have headed south. They were last reported near the junction of the road joining Ekron, Ashkelon, and Gath. I'm sending out a scouting party so we can better understand the Hebrews' plans. I'm going now to confer with King Achish. When I return, I will inform you what actions Gath will take." With that, Sardon departed for the palace.

As I had been listening to Sardon, I kept thinking about who was not there with us: Ahirom. He was on his farm, and from the messenger's report, a large Hebrew army was passing near his farm—if it had not already overrun it. Time was critical. If Ahirom learned of the danger in time, he and his family might be able to escape. I knew I had to go to his farm. I didn't weigh the reasons for and against going. I just knew I had to go. I had to do what

I could to defend this person who had been my comrade and mentor—and host. I'm glad I didn't think about the situation too much because if I had done so I might have hesitated, might have tried to consider my possible courses of action from the perspective of what was best for me.

I went to my room to collect the weapons and armor I thought I should take. I decided against the shield. Would be useful to have but would slow me down too much while running. Same for the javelin. Took the bow and a quiver of arrows instead. Not my best weapon in terms of proficiency, but less cumbersome and I wanted something that could act at a distance. Also sword, dagger. Extra goatskin of water. Yes, Ahirom had his own supply, but he and his family would have to leave immediately, without time for packing provisions.

As I was going through these preparations under the curious eye of Lost, Antenon came into our room.

"What are you doing? Going somewhere?"

"Perhaps it's better that you don't ask."

"Too late. I have asked."

I drew him close to me and said in a low voice, "You heard. The Hebrew army is somewhere near the junction of the road that connects Ashkelon, Gath, and Ekron. That junction is less than an hour's walk from Ahirom's farm. It's very likely that Hebrew patrols will run across his farm. If so … well, I don't need to tell you."

"So, you are just going to leave?"

I lowered my voice even further. "I'm going to tell Lukioth that I have Sardon's permission. Ahirom is a commander after all. Someone should check on him."

"If you get caught in that lie, lashing might be the best you can hope for."

"I'll have to take that chance. If I leave now, with any luck we could be back before mid-day tomorrow. And if Ahirom is with me, somehow I don't think I'll be disciplined."

"And if he's not? If you're too late?"

"Then I probably won't be back either, because in that case I will track down those accursed Hebrew dogs and with Dagon's help I will kill a few dozen of them before I'm taken down myself."

"I'm going with you."

"What … No. There's no need for you to do that."

"I'm saddened that you hold our friendship in such low esteem. We have fought together in several engagements, why not now?"

"Well, I was going to run as much of the distance as I could. I think with my training I could get more than halfway there before resting. You may not be able to keep up."

"I'll borrow a mule. You probably should have a mule with you anyway. What if Ahirom's family needs one?"

"You are going to take one of the army's mules?"

"If we are going to bend the truth, we might as well bend it as far as we can."

"But Lost ..."

"Oh, I think Lost can fend for himself. Probably better than we can."

I didn't have time to argue with Antenon, and, in truth, I was heartened by his willingness to accompany me. Also, if we took the mule, it could carry our shields.

Together, we went to see Lukioth. Fortune smiled on us. He was preoccupied with various matters when we approached him, and it turned out one of those matters was sending out a patrol east of our city to see if any Hebrews were approaching from that direction, so my statement that Sardon wanted Antenon and me to travel to Ahirom's farm did not strike him as particularly odd.

"Hmm, Sardon didn't mention anything to me about you two going to check on Ahirom."

"Understandable," I said. "He's had ten different things to do at once."

"So, you're going there and coming back."

"Yes, we plan to travel back and forth without stopping. As much as we would like to hunt down some Hebrews, we will save that pleasure for another occasion."

"Fine, then. May the gods be with you."

We then set out, Antenon astride the mule and me trotting alongside. It was fortunate that I had been to Ahirom's farm a few times because there was not much light from the moon, which was not much larger than a crescent, and even this wan light was occasionally blocked by the intermittent cloud cover. Pushing ourselves, we approached Ahirom's compound within a few hours. We paused at a hill about 500 paces from the farm. We did not have to look, although we forced ourselves to. After my early years in the bloomery, even at some distance I had no trouble detecting the acrid smell of a fire that had burned through wood and other materials. Ahirom's farm had been set ablaze.

My hands tore at my face and hair. Moaning, I started stomping around without direction. "We're too late, we're too late," I cried.

Antenon grabbed me roughly. "Pull yourself together. We need to see what we can do. Perhaps someone can be saved."

I then remembered the secret tunnel Ahirom had showed me. Possibly they had escaped? Could they still be hidden? Encouraged by these hopes, I regained some of my composure. I then knelt, uttered a short prayer to Dagon and Bel, and poured a token libation of our precious water. I then told Antenon about the tunnel. "You see," he said. "Don't give up hope yet."

⊫⊣⊢⊨

<h1 style="text-align:center">9</h1>

Fortified by our slim hope, we moved quickly, tethering the mule, grabbing our shields, and then approaching the compound rapidly on foot. The fire was still alive in places, but low, so it did not provide much illumination. Accordingly, we had no concern about being detected until we were just a few paces from the compound. We then advanced back to back to ensure we would be prepared for an attack from any direction. Several Hebrew bodies were clustered by the entryway, with arrows and spears protruding from their bodies. We stopped to check their condition. Their limbs were not stiff, but no blood was flowing, their bodies were cooling, and the shit and piss that some dead men give off was drying. They had been dead for at least a couple of hours, which suggested that the Hebrews had come and gone. The lack of any human voices coming from the compound confirmed this. Except for the snap and pop of some still burning timbers, all was quiet.

We passed through the entryway, whose doors had been broken down. Antenon spotted them first. He put his hand on my chest to hold me back and said, "Brace yourself, friend. The Hebrews are savages, but you knew that already."

Some ten paces within the compound were the crucified bodies of Ahirom and Elissa, their outstretched limbs affixed to X-shaped posts. They were still recognizable, as was the torture that had been inflicted on them, as the flames had singed and blackened their bodies but had not consumed them. Both had been flayed in part, principally around their chests—Elissa's breasts had been completely cut off—and disemboweled. Ahirom's neck had been broken, and his head had been turned violently so that it was almost in the opposite direction of his body. One of his eyes had been cut out.

The lizard, I thought. The lizard.

I fell to my knees weeping, pounding the earth. "Ahirom, Ahirom, what have I done!" I thank the gods that Antenon was with me or I would still be there, prostrate on the ground.

"Come, come," Antenon said as he tried to yank me up. "You said he had children. Let's look for them."

I slowly pushed myself up. "Yes, of course. Should look for the children."

There were a number of bodies strewn all around the compound, most badly burned, including seven Hebrew soldiers, who could be distinguished by their partially melted chain mail. Two of the Hebrews were by the doorway to the main house. One had his head cut off and another had a deep gash to his throat. Ahirom was responsible for those blows, I thought. He was a good soldier. I knew he would have sold his life dearly.

I paused long enough to kneel down, brush away what was left of the tunic of one of the soldiers, grab his charred genitals, slice them off with my dagger, and stuff them in the remnants of the fucking Hebe's mouth. Had the search for the children not had priority, I would have mutilated the other Hebrew bodies.

By tacit agreement, we searched the grounds first instead of going inside the house to look for the tunnel. It was as though with all the horror of the night we wanted to keep our hopes alive as long as possible. Finding no children's bodies outside, we then ventured inside the house. We had to tread carefully because part of the upper floors had collapsed and although the fire was out, some of the wooden beams were still smoldering. We glanced around, looking if we could see any bodies—or any live Hebrews. With the exception of a woman's body near the hearth, with her robe pulled up over her chest and face, there was nothing. We then went to the storeroom. My heart sank when I saw that the amphorae that had been placed before the tunnel opening to hide it lay broken on the storeroom floor and the hatch that led to the tunnel was open. If the children, or anyone else in the household, had made it to the tunnel, they were probably followed by Hebrew soldiers who could not have failed to notice the opening in the floor.

I said a short prayer and I stuck my head in the tunnel as far as it could go and called out, "Apphia, Melqath, are you in there?" Silence. I called out again. Nothing. Antenon volunteered to try to squeeze himself in. I nodded, although I was beginning to give in to despair. As Antenon squatted by the opening, however, we both heard something. A voice. A voice no louder than the rustling of the wind, but it was a voice. I stuck my head in the tunnel again and called out for Apphia and Melqath. A girl's voice responded. The words were indistinct, but it was unmistakably a girl's voice. "Apphia," I yelled. "This is Goliath. We are here to help. My friend is going to go into the tunnel. Don't be frightened."

I turned to Antenon. "While you're going in the tunnel, I'm going to go around to the opening that's on the slope outside. Try to get Apphia to head in that direction. Don't want her to come back inside and see what's happened to her parents."

I ran outside, laid aside my shield, vaulted the fence to the compound, and hurried down the slope, stumbling and falling a couple of times in my haste. In the darkness, I entered one cave by mistake before I found the correct one. I went in as far as I could and called out again. This time there was wailing. A different voice. Melqath! He was alive too. Apphia was trying to speak over him and at the same time I thought I heard Antenon's muffled voice coming from somewhere behind the children. "Apphia, Melqath," I yelled. "This is Goliath. Make your way to the cave opening. I am here. Behind you is my friend, Antenon. Don't be afraid of him."

More wailing, more attempts by Apphia and Antenon to make themselves heard, followed by more shouts of encouragement by me. This went on for some time, but finally I heard Apphia's voice come closer to me, and then shapes appeared. Apphia was in the lead, pulling a bawling Melqath with one hand and holding a bloody dagger in the other. She looked at me fiercely, ready to pounce, but then when she recognized me, her face melted, she began to cry, and she ran to embrace me.

"The Hebrew ... he came after us ... I stabbed him." Apphia's words were broken up by sobs, but I was able to make out enough of what she said to realize that a Hebrew soldier had come after them in the tunnel and that Apphia had somehow managed to kill him.

"You're a brave girl, Apphia. You're brave too, Melqath. But don't worry. You're safe now. My friend and I will … We will take you where you'll be safe." At that moment, I didn't know myself where that might be.

Antenon appeared at the top of the slope. He yelled down. "Couldn't get through the tunnel. A Hebe body was in the way. He had been stabbed somewhere and maybe also got stuck. Couldn't tell."

Apphia explained. "He came after us. He grabbed my leg, but papa had given me this dagger and told me to use it if I needed to, so I stabbed him in the arm. He let go, and then I reached and stabbed him in his face." As Apphia talked, I pictured the Hebrew in the tunnel. Probably not enough room for him to pull out a weapon and deploy it. The narrowness of the tunnel had turned the children's diminutive size into an advantage.

I put Melqath on my back, took Apphia by the hand, and we walked up the slope to Antenon. Melqath was asking about his papa and mama. I responded with evasion, telling him he needed to get ready for a long trip, he was going to be riding a mule, and so forth. When we met up with Antenon, I drew him close and whispered, "Take the children to the mule. Then, if it's safe, come back here. Don't walk fast. It will give me enough time to bury the bodies of Ahirom and Elissa. Obviously, if you spot any Hebrews, you and the children need to get away from here as fast as possible. Don't worry about me." I then turned to the children and explained they would go with Antenon to fetch our mule, while I looked for provisions. Melqath started to whine and Apphia looked frightened, but I assured them the Hebrews had gone. I hoped that was true.

Once the children were out of sight, I hastened to pull the bodies of Elissa and Ahirom down from their crosses. I then scrounged for any materials that could serve as shrouds. Stripping some pieces of unburnt fabric from the bodies of Ahirom's slaves and servants, I cobbled together enough cloth to wrap around the bodies. I then carried them outside the compound, aiming to carry them as far away from the site of the other corpses as practical. Suddenly, I remembered that Ahirom had buried Dedra somewhere on his property. But where? I had no idea and I had no time to look. I paused to say a prayer for her. It was all I could do. Then, furiously, I started digging the ground with my hands. After a few moments, I realized the work wasn't going fast enough. I ran back to where I had dropped my shield and with my shield and my dagger I was able to dig a shallow grave and place the bodies of Elissa and Ahirom therein just as I heard the children and Antenon return.

I was still on my knees when Apphia asked, "What are you doing?" "I'm praying by the grave of your parents," I said. This started another round of tears. "They are at rest now," I said, trying my best to console the children. "They fought bravely and killed many of the enemy. They fought bravely so you two could live. So, you must do everything you can to get to safety and have a long life. Otherwise you will dishonor your parents."

They were silent for a moment. Then Apphia asked, "Will we ever see mama and papa again?" Antenon and I looked at each other. "After you get old, you will go to sleep also and join the gods. That's when you will see your parents again." Children need stories sometimes.

All four of us then offered a short prayer and I dribbled a few drops of water on the ground. It was all I could spare for a libation given the precarious journey that was before us. The gods would understand.

Melqath then said we needed a stela for the grave. I puffed out my cheeks and looked at Antenon. He shrugged and said, "Well, we don't want to tarry but perhaps we can mark the grave somehow."

"Fine," I said. "I'll go down the slope and bring back some stones." I hastened to do so, and brought back enough stones to form a rough cairn. This seemed to satisfy the children.

With the children on the mule, we walked back to the hillside where we had originally tethered the animal. Antenon and I conferred. It was maybe three or four hours until daybreak. Should we continue on or rest? We decided we should rest until the morning. Yes, there was some chance another Hebrew party might come to the farm, especially as they did not usually leave their own dead unburied. One problem in reaching a firm decision was that we didn't know how many, if any, of the attacking party survived the attack. Not enough to form a burial party, clearly, but it would take only one survivor to inform the main body of the Hebrews about what happened at Ahirom's farm. Still, we decided that even so it would be some time before the main contingent dispatched a burial detachment. In addition, we all needed some rest and we did not know when we would have another opportunity.

Up at first light, we gave the children some water and bread, taking some quick swigs from the goatskin ourselves. We then set out. Antenon and I took turns as scouts, walking about fifty paces in front of the children and the mule. In terms of direction, we decided to head toward Gath as that was the closest city. The morning was uneventful. However, in the early afternoon, we began to hear some faint sounds. We halted to listen, then walked on a bit further. The sounds grew louder. Animals braying or lowing. The rhythmic trudging of many feet. The slip and crunch of wheels against pebbles. The murmuring of human voices. We stopped. Antenon was in front. Through hand signals he indicated he was going to run ahead to locate the source of the sounds. At that time we were on a rocky plateau, but we would soon be descending into valley to follow the road to Gath. Antenon ran ahead about 200 paces to the edge of the plateau and then flattened himself against the ground. We didn't have to wait long. He was up quickly, running back to us. He beckoned me to move out in front of the children so we could talk.

"Looks like it's the whole fucking rear of the Hebrew army. A couple thousand soldiers, with the baggage train, cattle. They're heading toward Gath."

"That rules out Gath as a destination. Ashkelon? It will take longer to get there, but I don't think we have a choice."

"You're right. Just hope the water holds out or we run across a spring or well."

We looked around to get our bearings. Heading south or even southwest was out of the question because even if we aimed to go well behind the Hebrew army, we would likely encounter Hebrew scouts. We decided to head due west for the rest of the day and maybe the next. This would require us to traverse some rough, hilly ground before reaching the coastal plain, but there was no alternative.

We told the children we decided to go to Ashkelon so they could be with their grandfather. "But grandpa farts," Melqath complained. That gave us the only chuckle of the day.

Our change of direction appeared to take us out of danger, as the sounds from the Hebrew host slowly faded away and the stillness of the countryside again descended on us. An hour or two passed.

A set of hills rose up to our right. There was a copse of acacia trees near where the hills met the plain. We decided to head there and stop for some shade under the trees' wide canopies. We also thought we might be able to find some seed pods that could provide us with food. Once among the trees, we tethered the mule, gave the children some water, and gathered some pods. We had just settled down to rest and eat when we heard the thudding of approaching horses' hooves.

Antenon and I sprang up and went to our weapons. A flurry of desperate activity, as I grabbed my bow, quiver, and sword, and Antenon picked up his spear, sword, and shield. We both turned toward the sound of the horses. There were five horsemen rounding the hill, maybe 100 paces away. Hebrew scouts, closing quickly. The afternoon sun was in our faces so my first arrow missed as did Antenon's spear. My second one struck home and the lead rider fell to the earth. I leapt on the riderless horse's back. The horse wasn't pleased by my bulk, and I thought I would not be able to turn it in time to meet the fast approaching Hebrews, but I yanked hard on the bridle and spun the animal around so that my sword met the next Hebrew rider's neck. Antenon, meanwhile, had his shield up and had fended off the spear thrust from the first Hebrew rider that had passed him, but the second one that came upon him plunged a spear deep into his thigh. I tried to make my way to him, catching one of the Hebrews in the back with my sword. The blade did not completely penetrate his mail, but the blow knocked him off his horse. Meanwhile, the fifth rider came up behind me. I turned in time to parry his spear, but it angled down to stick my horse's haunch, causing the horse to rear and throw me. I tumbled to the ground, losing my sword in the process. I landed near the rear of the rider who was engaged with Antenon who, despite his bad wound, was valiantly defending himself, blocking additional spear thrusts with his shield. I pulled my dagger, leapt on the back of the rider's horse, pulled the Hebrew back with my left arm and slit his throat with my right. Before I pushed him off, I took hold of his spear and hurled it at the remaining rider, who had now wheeled around for another attack. The spear caught him in the throat, passing clean through it. Somehow he managed to stay on his horse, clutching and grabbing at his neck, until he slumped over.

This left the one Hebrew who I had knocked off his horse. He was bleeding from the wound in his back, but he was still able to stagger to his feet, stumble forward to his horse and mount it. He began to ride east, toward the Hebrew army. I looked around for a spear, losing valuable seconds because none was at hand. I then made for my bow. My first arrow was in range but landed to his side. By the time I released the next one, he was too far away. Damn!

I then turned to Antenon. He had now slumped to the ground, his life blood draining from him rapidly, forming an odious raisin-dark pool in the dirt. There was no helping him; the wound in his upper thigh was mortal. I knelt next to him and lifted his head. It tilted sideways and a dark liquid fell out of his mouth. He was able to say, "Give my belongings to Dothan, my brother. Tell him where I fell so he can make a proper offering." "Yes, yes, of course," I replied, although I was already weeping, cradling my dearest friend as his spirit left his body. "We'll meet again as shades," he said with his last breath. "Yes, we'll meet again as shades." I said this as much for me as for Antenon. We all need stories sometimes.

No time to mourn. Such is the lot of the warrior. With the fury of combat now over, for the first time I realized the children were wailing and the mule was braying. Probably had been doing that throughout the fight. The children had climbed into one of the trees as far as they could go and were clinging to the branches, letting their cries join with the mule's protest to create a chorus that filled the sudden stillness. I walked over to them, took them in my arms, and tried to shush them.

"You must be brave, children. Remember, your father and mother wanted you to be brave. Antenon, who just gave his life for you, wanted you to be brave. Don't disappoint them. If the Hebrews hear you cry, they'll be back for us." Their wails diminished into whimpers and I put them on the ground. As they quieted, so did the mule. "Fine, now here is what we're going to do. The Hebrews may come looking for us again so we need to move away from here quickly. I'm going to see if I can grab one of the horses and then we will give Antenon a warrior's burial."

"What's a warrior's burial?"

"You'll see."

Two of the Hebrew horses were still in the area. Both were close together, about thirty paces away. My thought was we could travel a lot faster if the children were on the mule and I was on a horse. But in my haste, I ran up to the horses instead of walking up. This was a mistake. I spooked them and they took off running in opposite directions. One stopped about forty paces away. This time I walked up slowly, but when I came close, the horse shied away and took off running again. Fuck it. I decided I could not spend any more time trying to bring one of the horses under control, so I walked back to the children.

"You can help," I said. "We need to cover Antenon with dirt and we must do it quickly. For a warrior who has fallen in battle, you just need to put dirt on the body, you don't need a deep grave." I turned to Antenon, grabbed my shield, knelt in his blood, and began flinging dirt over his body as fast as I could. The children stayed under the tree at first, obviously reluctant to join in. But then Apphia got up, scooped up some dirt with her hands, and let it fall on Antenon's face. "Good, good," I said. "That helps." Then Melqath approached warily, tentatively dug his fingers into the dirt, and patted the dirt down on a part of Antenon's shoulder that was still exposed. "Thank you, Melqath, that's very helpful." Some of the dirt I was furiously heaving on Antenon went over the children, but they were not bothered by this. It made it more of a game for them, and they threw some dirt in my direction. Enough of it fell on Antenon that their playing helped rather than hindered.

We finished. I said a short prayer and we said goodbye to Antenon.

I stood up. I wanted to rest my aching shoulders and arms. I wanted to let my whole body rest. I knew we didn't have that luxury.

"Apphia, Melqath, we're going to be leaving in a few moments, so drink a little bit of water, pee if you have to, and eat some pods. I'm going to check the Hebrews' bodies for water or food."

I didn't find much. As one would expect, their horses had been carrying most of the provisions, but one Hebrew had a half-empty goatskin of water stuck in his belt. Perhaps he had been taking a drink right before they spotted us.

I organized what provisions we had, put most of these provisions and my shield on the mule, and placed the children on top of the mule. I was carrying my bow and quiver, a sword, a dagger, and a goatskin of water. Everything was arranged as best I could do in the short time available. I headed north, further into hill country, hoping to throw the Hebrews off our track. Although we paused as the sun set to have some bread and water, I did not stop for the night. I used the stars to navigate. It was cooler walking in the evening, so we made good progress. The children were sleepy, of course, but I secured Apphia to the mule and I placed Melqath on my back. We plowed ahead, stopping to rest a few hours before dawn.

Except for the heat, the next day was a good day. I decided it was time to risk going southwest and my hunch proved to be correct. Met no one. Almost eerily quiet. We did have to stop mid-day, sheltering in a cave, to avoid being roasted. Our water consumption was cutting deeply into our supply, and we had not run across any well or stream, so that was a source of concern, but I thought we might be able to eke out enough. "When will we get to Ashkelon?" Apphia asked. I did some calculations hoping I had some approximate sense of where we were. "Two days," I said. "Maybe three days."

My optimistic projection of two days' travel seemed warranted by our progress that afternoon and evening and the next morning. It was good progress even though I was carrying extra weight. Melqath complained that his rear hurt from riding the mule and when I checked his backside, it was red and seeping some blood, so I carried him much of the way.

As we slowly descended from the hills, scrub and the occasional tree were being displaced by more consistent greenery. I knew some water source could not be far away. And then I spotted it—a stream in the valley just a few hundred paces from where we had stopped on the bluff. Unfortunately, there were a number of men in the valley. Could they be Palestim workers or slaves? Some were by the stream gathering water, while others were in the fields, bending down, perhaps gathering pulses or millet. I stooped as low to the ground as I could and worked my way down the slope of the bluff to try to get a better look.

No, they were not Palestim. They were a Hebrew foraging party. As I scrambled back up the slope, I slipped, and on grabbing a rock to keep from falling further, I pulled the rock loose. It tumbled down the slope. I glanced over my shoulder. I had been noticed.

➤⊣⊦⊢➤

10

Back on the top of the bluff, I surveyed the situation. Fifteen to twenty Hebrews were now running up the slope toward us. Heading south and west would lead us into the valley, so those were not options. Turning around and heading back north—they would overtake us eventually. Heading east? The bluff we were on seemed to converge in the distance with the rise on the other side of the valley. Did they actually join? I could not tell, but given my choices I decided to gamble on it.

"Quick children, we're heading that way," I said as I pointed east. I put both children on the mule, told them to hold on tight, got in front of the mule and pulled on its reins, and we began to run. I was never so glad to have a mule cooperate. Our pace wasn't bad, but I knew the Hebrews running without any encumbrance would be gaining on us over time. I clung to two hopes: one, that we would reach the convergence of the bluffs ahead of the Hebrews and two, that the bluffs actually did meet or at least were close enough for me to jump across with the children. After some time, after running maybe 600 paces at top speed, I realized I was mistaken. The angle of my vision had misled me. The bluffs did converge, but at their closest point there was still a good twenty to thirty paces between them. Trapped! But then I saw that there was a footbridge between the bluffs. Hope welled up in me again—until I heard the yells of the approaching Hebrews.

We reached the footbridge. It was a rickety thing, with gaps between some of the wooden planks and the securing ropes looking far from secure. Would it bear my weight? No time to hesitate. I told the children to climb on my back and hold on tight. Of course, we left the mule behind, with my shield, much of our water and almost all our food, but short-term survival not long-term planning was our priority. I started across and the footbridge swayed worryingly. To make matters worse rocks started falling around us. There were slingers among the Hebrews. I hate slingers. Mean lowlifes. What kind of man would hurl rocks from a distance instead of using a blade like a real warrior? To prevent the children's skulls from being crushed I now had to execute a difficult maneuver. I had to stop on the bridge and move them from my back to my front. Balancing myself on this tenuous bridge swinging back and forth some hundred paces above the valley floor was difficult enough; doing so while moving two frightened children around to my chest without dropping them was a truly daunting challenge. But it had to be done and I did it just as a Hebrew rock hit my shoulder. Fucking cowardly dogs.

I started forward again as fast as I could. I was nearly at the end of the bridge when I felt the elevation of the bridge drop suddenly. I grabbed the side ropes so I wouldn't fall. The children screamed. A group of Hebrews had started across the bridge. With their extra weight, the end of the bridge was now around three cubits below the crest of the ridge, but with a heave I managed to throw Apphia on top of the ridge. "Stay there," I said. "Your brother and I will be up in a moment."

The bridge was now jolting and swaying violently, bouncing up and down in rhythm with the Hebrews' steps, while rocks and now arrows landed all around us. Suddenly the bridge gave way. I flung my arms forward to the side of the bluff and found a handhold. Melqath was still clinging to me desperately, his nails digging deep into the flesh around my neck. The rocks cut into my fingers as I struggled to maintain my grip. But I still gave thanks to the gods as about ten Hebrews hit the valley floor.

I now had to pull myself up, a task not made easier by the various missiles that were plunking around us. The Hebrews who had not been on the footbridge were still on the bluff behind us and their enmity had not abated. A rock glanced off the back of my skull. An arrow ripped through the hem of my tunic. Had to make it to the top *now*! This was a test of me against myself—my arm strength versus my size and weight. It occurred to me that if I started swinging my legs it might give me some added force and allow me to lift myself. I did so, and I pulled myself up a bit further. Once again, and again more progress. Finally, I swung my legs up above the lip of the ridge and with them as leverage I pulled myself and Melqath up the rest of the way.

"Stay low," I ordered. This instruction was not really necessary for Melqath because he was still affixed to my chest. With me stooped over and holding Apphia's hand, we hurried away from the edge of the bluff, and when I thought we had gone far enough that I could straighten up, I swung her onto my back. I then ran and ran and ran. I ran until my throat and chest burned. Until I was gasping and panting. Until my legs were leaden. And then I went further.

As darkness came, we crawled into a cave. We were all filthy. I was bruised and bleeding from multiple cuts. I felt the back of my head. My hair was matted with blood. But we were alive. I felt the goatskin I had with me. More than half-full. Gods willing, we still might make it.

Two days later, in the late afternoon, we saw the coast. We were too hungry, too thirsty, too exhausted to say anything to each other, but with our parched, cracked lips we managed some weak smiles. It was more difficult to walk in the sand along the shore than on the plateau above, but I chose the sand anyway because I wanted the comfort of knowing the sea was to my right. An hour further on we saw a settlement. Had to be Palestim for sure. It was. It was a fishing village. Despite my grime, my dried blood, my tattered clothing, my stink, and my sudden appearance out of nowhere, they knew who I was.

The children and I were given some bread, olives, and cheese, along with water. I had to counsel the children not to eat or drink too much at this first sitting so they would not get sick. The children and I slept on straw mattresses that night. A full, deep sleep. For perhaps the first time in years, I did not awake at dawn.

The next day, as we were sharing a mid-day meal with some of the villagers, there was a commotion outside the house where we were eating. We looked outside. It was a small procession. Four horsemen in military uniform and three litters, with the litters being carried by four men apiece. When the procession halted, the curtains parted on the first litter and out stepped Melqath, the children's grandfather.

⊨┼┼⊨

11

Four days later, I was in Ashkelon, in Melqath's house, having my beard cut off and my head shaved. Melqath had arranged for a barber, a slave that attended to his own hair. While he was working on me, the barber tried to persuade me to limit myself to a radical trim as opposed to complete hair removal.

"You have nice hair, nice beard," he said, in heavily accented Palestim. "Why cut it all off?"

"I have lost a sister and close friends within the last few weeks. It's a sign of mourning."

"But not everyone does this … or do they?"

"Some do, some don't. I can choose only for myself."

"The dead … Yes, very sad, but why harm yourself? You're not to blame."

I did not respond to this last comment.

Melqath had told me he would have shaved his head as well, except his hair was so thin, no one would notice.

I was to meet with Melqath the afternoon of my shave to discuss "my future" as he put it. He was not more specific than this. I had asked him to intercede on my behalf with the authorities in Gath—I was technically a deserter, after all. But that was just three days ago and I doubted he would have received word back already. Could it be about Altara? This was a subject on which both of us so far had been silent. Among other reasons, I did not know what, if anything, he knew about my relations with Altara or my discussions with Ahirom about Altara. The closest I had come to raising this topic was to say to him a couple of days before that I wanted to see someone in the city. He simply smiled and told me I needed to rest a bit longer before going on visits. My head wound was still seeping. Could he be considering offering me a reward? A position? Not out of the question.

Melqath had been very kind and gracious to me the last few days, ever since he had arrived in the fishing village north of Ashkelon to retrieve his grandchildren. Although he was devastated by the loss of his son, he had feared much worse when he learned the Hebrew army had been spotted near Ahirom's farm. The discovery that his grandchildren were alive and safe and that his bloodline would continue kept him from falling into despair if it did not entirely lift him into joy. He was effusive in his expressions of gratitude and in his praise of me.

We met in an upstairs room that had a couple of tables piled with tablets and scrolls. Melqath was still very active as a merchant. The room was large enough to accommodate two couches as well as several chairs. I had the impression that this is where he conducted much of his business.

"Come in, come in," he said, waving me in, after I had announced my presence. "Do you want to drink some wine, some water?"

"No thank you."

He studied my head and face for a moment, motioned for me to lean forward, and then stood on his tip toes to see the top of my head. "Well, my man did a thorough job. Also a fine job. I am pleased to see that he completed this task without cutting you or scratching you. Of course, that bruise and cut you received from the rock is now more visible, but I'm sure you knew that would be the case when you decided to be shaved."

"Yes, I understood. Thank you for lending me your barber's services."

"Bah," he said with a wave of his hand. "It was nothing. Please sit down," he said, motioning to one of the couches. I settled in, tentatively at first, but the couch was sturdily built and easily supported my weight. Melqath took the chair opposite me. "I have news for you from Gath."

"So soon? Your courier just left three days ago."

"He was traveling by horse and I told him to make the journey as quickly as possible. I did not want you to be anxious about your situation. Anyway, there's no reason for you to be concerned. The fact that you saved Ahirom's children makes up for your … your departure from the barracks without explicit permission. Ahirom was a commander of Gath's army and deserved protection. And as we discussed, I told the messenger to explain that there was a miscommunication, and that explanation was accepted." He leaned toward me. "It also turns out you may have played a role in disrupting the Hebrew army's plans. Our scouts have learned that they detached several hundred men from their rearguard to stay in the area where you were traveling, apparently because they feared a large Palestim force was in the area. That force was *you*." He jabbed a finger in the air toward me and grinned. Leaning back in his chair, he added, "Of course, it also helps that Gath is apparently out of immediate danger. Some malady has apparently spread through much of the Hebrew army and they never launched an attack on Gath. They're still encamped a couple of days away. Some reports say they may even be retreating."

"Dagon and Bel be praised."

'Yes, thanks be to the gods."

We were both silent for some moments, and then Melqath spoke up again. "That was one thing I wanted to tell you, but there's another." He looked away and cleared his throat. "I have learned you have great affection for Altara." He looked back at me. Our eyes met. "Oh, I knew you had spent some time with her. People tell me things. But I didn't know until maybe ten days ago, when I received a letter from Ahirom—the last letter I received from him in fact—that you had developed an affection for Altara and apparently she for you." A hoarseness in his voice developed as he said these words and he paused.

"May I ask what the letter said?"

"I will read it to you," he said as he got up from his chair. He walked over to one of his tables and picked up a piece of papyrus on which he laid an ornamented weight. His hands began to shake. "My eyes are weak. I need to walk to the window so I can have enough sunlight to read."

Once by the window, Melqath began to read from the letter. "Ahirom says 'Dear father'." Melqath stopped abruptly. His voice breaking, he said, "Well you don't need to hear that part." He moved his finger down the letter. "Here we go: 'Goliath of Gath, that city's champion and the hero of our last campaign against the Hebrews'—well, he didn't need to tell me that," Melqath said as he turned toward me. "Of course, I knew who you were already." He turned back to the letter. "So, anyway he says: 'Goliath has asked my permission to marry Altara. I have confirmed that this is also Altara's wish. After giving this matter much consideration, I've decided to grant permission. Altara has been a loyal servant to our family, and Goliath, quite apart from his heroism on behalf of all of Palestia, has also done great service to our family. I hope this decision meets with your approval. If you have any concern ...' and so forth and so on." He looked up at me from the letter. "I don't have a concern. I would have deferred to Ahirom were he still alive. I should honor his wishes now that he's dead. Plus, there's the practical matter that with Ahirom dead ... well, as you know Altara was Ahirom's concubine, to state things plainly."

He studied my face to gauge my reaction. He must have been taken aback by what he saw, because he said, with some consternation, "Are you not pleased?" "Yes, I am," I mumbled. I felt hollow inside. Knowing that Ahirom was dead, dead possibly because of the lizard's curse, and that I could no longer thank him ... it was a sick feeling.

Melqath moved back to his chair, sat down, and said, "There is one matter I want to speak to you about. Again, to speak plainly, from Ahirom's letter I'm aware that you know that I am Altara's father. She's not my only bastard, you know," he said with an apparent note of pride. "Two of my natural sons were with you, in Ashkelon's detachment, at the battle of Aphek. But Altara's connection with this family is a special one, a special sensitive one. She doesn't know of my blood connection to her and I want to keep it that way." Here he held up his hand. "Now don't think this is because I want to cut her off completely. To the contrary, I'm happy to bless your marriage and to give you twenty mina of silver as a wedding gift. You are also free to keep that house in which she is now residing. But you must pledge to me, you must give me your solemn oath, that you will never reveal to Altara that I am her father."

By his expression, I knew he wanted an answer. At that moment, I wished I were in combat somewhere, somewhere in the heat of battle. In the intensity of combat one doesn't think much. Certainly, one doesn't have to weigh choices that carry moral risk. One just kills or is killed. I was still dazed from hearing Ahirom's letter and I was now confronted with a very difficult choice. I wanted Altara. Most of my striving over the last couple of years had been motivated by my desire for her. I loved her. I wanted to marry her.

In addition, I had no desire whatsoever to quarrel with Melqath. But to pledge to keep secret from the person who would be my wife the identity of her father …? Such a pledge did not seem the best way to start a marriage.

"Well, do I have your word on this matter?" Melqath asked.

I looked at my feet. I swallowed hard. "Yes," I said.

⟞⟨⟧⟝

12

I saw Altara the next day. One of Melqath's servants had informed her I would be coming by, so she was ready for me. She opened the door herself. She was dressed in a black robe, with a black shawl around her head. Her mournful eyes widened for a moment when she saw me—presumably she was surprised by my shaved head—but then quickly narrowed. We did not speak. I stepped in. She closed the door. We embraced, both of us gently weeping.

"Gods, I have dreamed of this moment," she said. "But not like this. Too much death."

"Yes," I murmured.

How long we stood there in a mute embrace I don't know, but after some time, without saying a word to each other, we made our way up the stairs to her room. We then lay on her bed keeping on our clothes, except for my sandals and her shawl. With her face uncovered, I could see she had not applied any creams. Her eyes were bloodshot, streams of red running into the green pool at the center of her eye. We renewed our embrace, and I kissed her forehead a few times. Our hands met, then parted, going their separate ways as we ran our hands over each other's bodies, seeking reassurance that we were not phantoms of our imagining. Eventually, my mouth sought hers. Our lips touched hesitantly at first, but then we exchanged a warm, lingering kiss. Both of us knew, however, on that day we would proceed no further. The kindling for our desire had been dampened by the horror of recent events.

We talked that day. Much had happened since we last shared a bed. She told me of her fears and doubts during our separation and I told her of mine. I revealed some of what I had said to Ahirom in my efforts to persuade him to let me marry her, omitting, of course, portions of his response. I restricted myself to saying that he retained strong affection for her and was reluctant to let her go.

"I suppose I am difficult to part with," Altara said, and for the first time that day a smile crossed her face.

I did have to part from her that night, however, to return to Melqath's house. We no longer had to be concerned about embarrassing Ahirom. Now we wanted to observe our people's customs because Altara aimed to be a respectable bride. I could spend the night only after we were betrothed.

The next day, Altara was at the palace attending the queen, so my time with her was brief. It was otherwise similar to the previous day—gentle hugs, tender caresses, followed by conversation, mostly about what had happened over the last few months. She did ask me about my hair, or lack thereof.

She had placed her right hand on my cheek, stroking it, and then she looked up at me with a wry smile, focusing on the top of my head. "You do look quite different with a shaved head. How long does it take to grow back?"

"Not sure. Based on my experience when I was growing a beard, I should have substantial bristle in about a month and a full beard in less than two months. Something similar for the top of my head I suspect."

"That long?"

"Yes … I think."

A strange look appeared in her eyes, one I'd not seen before. Her mouth was partially open as if she were starting to say something and then stopped.

"I hope it doesn't bother you," I said.

"No, no," she said, "it's just so … so different."

On the third day, Altara was no longer wearing her black robe. She had on her thin white linen robe. She had also put a touch of malachite under her eyes and had applied a cream or ointment to her face. Her skin had a glow that had been absent the previous two days. Before I could say any-thing, she said, "Oh, I'll wear that black robe when I go out in public, but here in my house … why should I? Yes, I mourn the deaths of Ahirom and Elissa—and your friend and sister too, of course—but I don't need to prove that to you I suppose."

I shook my head. "No, no, you don't."

"When we lie together today, why don't you take off your tunic," she said as she stroked my shoulder. "I mean, we don't have to do anything. Maybe you're not ready for that. But I want you close to me, I want to feel you."

When we were in her room, I did as requested, retaining only my under-garment. She removed both her robe and undergarment. We kissed and hugged again and my body responded as one might expect. She noticed I was erect and, after some time, she pushed her hand into my undergarment and began to stroke me. "I need you inside me," she whispered. "It's been too long."

For the briefest moment, I was reluctant. I had not made a vow to abstain from sex for any set period of time while I was mourning, but I had not envisioned making love to Altara so soon. But my desire silenced any qualms I might have had. We made love, moving slowly, tentatively at first, as though we were afraid that the bond we were reestablishing might break if we moved too quickly. But as our passion increased, so did our tempo, and our bodies started writhing, shaking, as I moved back and forth, rose and fell with fierce intensity. My release came first, suddenly. So suddenly, I had not thought about withdrawing before spilling my seed. After my hips stopped their twitching and thrusting, I opened my eyes to look at Altara. She merely laughed and said, "Mmm, now that was something different that was nice. A warm liquid in my cunt." She must have noticed some apprehension in my face, because she said, "I don't think we have to worry about that anymore. Now keep fucking me." She punctuated this with a playful slap to my rear. I kept up my best efforts, but after some moments, I became too soft to continue. Knowing it would still be a while before I could return to the requisite firmness, I slipped off her, went to the floor, pulled her hips toward my face, and buried my mouth in her, caressing her bud with my lips and tongue, tasting the remnants of my own salty seed. Just as her thighs started to convulse, and her legs locked around my head, I grew hard again, so that while she was still in her throes I entered her, eliciting a moan that seemed to come from somewhere deep inside her. We continued to make love, oblivious of all else, as the rest the world fell away from us.

Whether it was because our lovemaking changed our perspective or broke some spell or because we were tired of speaking of the past few months, with all their sorrowful events, that evening we spoke of our future together for the first time. We started the discussion while we were still in bed.

"So … When did you want to make public our betrothal?"

She looked up at me. "When did you say you would get your hair back?"

"Is it that bad?"

"No, I'm joking … sort of. The bruise on the back of your head is still very visible. Must have hurt terribly."

"Yes, as a matter fact, it did. Look … we certainly don't have to rush. I'm going to have to go on campaign soon, as you know. Need to drive those Hebrews back to their territory and … something could happen."

"Don't say that." She sat up a bit and turned over on her back. "I don't want to think about it. It won't happen anyway. No one can kill you."

"I …"

"Don't say anything. I told you I do not want to think about this. I hate these wars. I want you to be with me." She turned back to look at me, "Don't die, right. Don't die. I would have no one."

"I don't plan to, but anyway, as I was saying, perhaps we should postpone any announcement until sometime after I return. I had only thought of doing it before the campaign began because … well … If we were betrothed, you could receive some of my money when I die. I now have a good sum. Even after paying those fines because of Hannipath, I have over thirty mina of silver."

Her face now wore a sad frown. "I *don't* want you to talk about your dying. Please."

"Fine, no more references to that possibility. But let me talk about something that is a certainty. If we don't have supper soon I might die of starvation."

Her smile returned and she pinched my cheek. "Don't worry, I know you have a big appetite, but Munika and I will take care of you. She bought more mutton today in the marketplace. Feeding you is getting expensive!"

We washed and dressed and supper was ready presently. The three of us ate in a small room downstairs that had a table and some mats as it was too cold to eat comfortably outside. Winter was coming on.

"So, Goliath," Munika asked, "when will you be leaving us? When will the campaign start?"

"Munika!" Altara said sharply. "You shouldn't be asking such a question."

"That's all right. Munika, to answer your question, I don't know for sure myself," I said. "I assume in a few days. One question that's not settled is whether I will march out with Ashkelon's contingent or with Gath's. The five cities are joining forces so eventually we will be together in the field anyway, but I'm thinking Sardon, the lead commander in Gath, is going to want me to return to Gath first."

Altara stretched her leg out until it intertwined with mine. "Don't you think you'll be able to make a transfer, or whatever you call it, to Ashkelon?

I mean being in the army is being in the army, isn't it? We have a common enemy."

"Not sure it's that simple. There's some competition among our cities."

"Melqath could help with that I'm sure. He owes you. He knows our king and I believe he knows some of the nobles in Gath."

I grimaced. "Not sure I want to ask for his help."

"Why not?"

"It would make me uncomfortable."

"Gods, why? He likes you. He likes me … I think. He sent me a message the other day saying he wants me to come over to see the children. They have been asking for me."

"Fine, I'll think about it."

"Well, if we are going to be living in Ashkelon, you'll have to work out something."

I stopped chewing and put down my drink. "Had we decided that? I do have a sister in Gath, and now a nephew."

"And I know no one in Gath. I've never known a home other than Ashkelon. We already have a house here." Altara moved her hand in a sweeping gesture.

"Something we need to think about, talk about, and decide, I suppose, once I return from the campaign." At this point, I probably should have kept quiet, but for some reason my mouth decided to continue working, speaking about something I had considered but told no one else. "The final decision may depend on which city most needs another smith."

Altara looked at me bewildered. She withdrew her leg. "Why would that be?"

"I have given some thought from time-to-time about leaving the army. I've served my five-year commitment. I'm not obliged to stay any longer."

Altara shook her head in disbelief. "Why would you do that? Why would you leave the army to become a *smith*?" She uttered this last word with evident distaste.

"Earlier today you said yourself you didn't like me going on campaigns."

"No, of course I don't. But this war is going to be over soon. We've always had intervals of peace with the Hebrews."

"Intervals of peace punctuated by bouts of single combat. I have a feeling that I will continue to be asked to be the champion not just for Gath but for other cities, until … until I lose."

"Yes, of course everyone will continue to ask you. You're the greatest warrior of our people. It's what makes you famous. People are singing songs about you."

"This is true," Munika interrupted. "I heard one in the marketplace the other day."

Altara continued, "I bet more people in Ashkelon know who you are than know the name of our king. Why… why you are as powerful as the kings themselves."

"I don't think that's true. And I'm not sure it would be a good thing if it were true, or if the kings thought it were true."

Altara shook her head. "Don't give up what makes you *you*. Being a warrior, being a champion is who you are. This is what you have achieved."

I said nothing for some moments. I was thinking about what, if anything, gave me my identity. Was there anything? Was I who people thought I was? Who they wanted me to be? I remember wishing that Ahirom was with me then. These were the type of questions he loved to consider. Finally, I spoke, having decided I did not want an acrimonious discussion with Altara. "I'm just thinking out loud. Important thing is to be with you, isn't it?"

I did not have to wait long for confirmation that Gath wanted me to return to my city as they prepared to send their contingent out on campaign. The messenger arrived two days after my not entirely pleasant evening meal with Altara. I was instructed to leave for Gath that same day. I said my goodbyes to Melqath—both the elder and the junior—and to Apphia. The older Melqath said he would sponsor sacrifices in the temple for our success, including a prize bull. He drew me aside as I was departing his home, and asked me, "Please, Goliath if you can, try to have Ahirom's farm scouted out during the campaign. See if his grave is still intact. Once the campaign is over I would like to transfer him and Elissa to our family tomb." I agreed to do so.

Then that afternoon, I said goodbye to Altara. We were both subdued. She played two tunes for me on her flute, one sorrowful, the other joyful. "The first is how I feel today," she explained. "The second is how I will feel when you return."

As I stood to embrace her, she said, "I see you are eager to leave me. You are already wearing your military belt and some of your bags."

"It's because I wanted to show you something," I said.

"Yes?"

"Remember after our first evenings together, you gave me an effigy of Qetesh and a lock of your hair."

"Yes, of course."

"Well, your hair is in this amulet," I said, as I pulled the amulet out from underneath my tunic, "and Qetesh is in this bag," I said as I pulled the effigy out.

"How did … I thought either you left it in Gath or you must have lost it when you were fleeing with the children from the Hebrews."

"It's with me always and it's the one thing I took from the mule before we abandoned it at the footbridge. Qetesh has a few nicks in her, but she survived the journey, so let's hold Qetesh together as we say goodbye. May we see each other again." We embraced.

As I turned to leave, Altara said, "It's not fair."

"What's that?"

"You have a lock of my hair with you, but" she said, as she jumped up and touched the top of my head, "you have nothing for me."

We both laughed. "It will be there when I return."

⊷⊶

13

My hair had returned by the time I was back in Ashkelon, which was about seven weeks after I left, although there really wasn't enough there to provide a lock.

The campaign against the Hebrews was over, and peace of a sort had returned, but at a bitter price.

The Hebrew army that had approached Gath had been decimated by a bloody flux, accompanied by a high fever and swollen bellies. Many of the soldiers who fell ill became motionless, unable to move before they died. As a result of the losses caused by this affliction, the Hebrew army withdrew north to Ekron, whose citadel was still besieged. We Palestim thanked the gods for this deliverance.

Unfortunately, once the Hebrews withdrew, their affliction seemed to pass. They had lost maybe 2000 men, but that still left them with a large force. To relieve Ekron and drive the Hebrews from our territory, the four other Palestim cities organized a combined force. Gath's contingent was under the command of Sardon and a new junior commander, Hanun, who was a young Gath nobleman. Sardon did not possess the strategic skill or tactical imagination of Bellon or Ahirom, and Hanun was inexperienced. These deficiencies showed. The commanders from the other cities were not much better.

When our forces reached the Hebrew host outside of Ekron, our commanders could not think of anything more imaginative than an all-out frontal assault, even though the Hebrews had dug in and there was a deep ditch surrounding their encampment. Very few of us made it past this defensive ditch, as the Hebrews massed their forces along its perimeter and a flood of javelin, spear, arrow, and rock spread destruction among us. I and a few others managed to cross to the other side, only to discover, as we looked around, that we were by ourselves. Only the grace of Bel allowed us to escape with our lives.

Perhaps the only thing that allowed us ultimately to achieve something like victory was the unfavorable site in which the Hebrews had decided to place their encampment. There were two hills that rose to the south and east of their encampment, about 300 paces away. The Hebrews had neglected to secure these hills, stationing only a few men on them, who we were able to chase away. Once on this high ground, we had a commanding view of the Hebrew encampment. More importantly, this put our archers in range of at least a portion of the Hebrew force, specifically that portion nearest their defensive ditch. Under a steady rain of arrows, the Hebrews had to withdraw any forces that were near their ditch, which meant that were we to assault their camp again, we might be able to get sufficient men across the ditch to carry us to victory. But it never came to that. Our possession of the heights also allowed us to dig a ditch near the base of the hills while remaining relatively unmolested by the Hebrews. The besiegers would become besieged.

We had just completed our encircling ditch when the Hebrew commanders made known to our commanders that they wanted to parley. Our commanders agreed. Although this caused discontent among many of our soldiers, who wanted revenge for their fallen comrades, I and some others understood the reasons for this. We had suffered significant losses. The outcome of a pitched battle was uncertain at best. Moreover, a prolonged siege would not be easy either, as we were now into winter and food supply would be difficult.

As a result of our discussions with the Hebrews, we agreed to the Hebrews' demand that they be allowed to withdraw under guarantee of safe passage to their territory. We wanted them gone from our territory—although we would have preferred dead and gone—so this was a reasonable compromise. We also agreed to the Hebrews' demand that they keep their booty. In exchange, they would release any prisoners they held. In truth, they did not hold many men, and regarding the women, most had been raped so often they probably wished they had been killed. These terms were disclosed to us while we were still massed as an army.

There was another term. Prudently, this term was not revealed until after our army had dispersed, with each contingent returning to its home city, because once it became known it infuriated many of us. The commanders, with the consent of the five Palestim kings, had agreed to return to the Hebrews what was left of their sacred chest. This demand had no purpose other than to humiliate us. The Hebrews already had another sacred chest. We saw it in the middle of their fucking encampment! How many chests did their gods need?

This demeaning demand was especially odious to me, given the role I played in capturing their chest. But there was nothing I could do about it but stomp and rage and join my comrades in expressing displeasure. One thing did mollify my fury. We had stripped all the gold off the chest already, of course, but the Hebrews wanted their two winged gods on the cover of the chest replaced. Our craftsmen were so stingy with the gold that, from what I was told, the replacement figures looked like two small winged mice, not gods. May they foul the Hebrew chest with their droppings.

Before we decamped from the fields and hills around Ekron, I asked for leave to undertake one task. Permission was granted. I wanted to go into the city to learn the fate of Phodan. I was hoping he had made it safely into the citadel, whose occupants, although so thin a strong wind would have blown them away, had survived. I learned he had managed to flee to the citadel when the Hebrews overran most of the city. However, shortly before the Hebrews requested negotiations, he had accompanied a sortie from the citadel whose objective was to bring back grain. The grain was brought back, but without Phodan. When I was told this story by some of Ekron's soldiers they expressed amazement that Phodan, the high priest, had volunteered for the mission. I wasn't surprised. Phodan had always been a fighter. Now a final silence separated us. I felt burdened by a debt that never could be repaid.

⋙╬⋘

14

Once our contingent returned to Gath, I immediately asked Sardon for two weeks' leave to travel to Ashkelon. He was displeased and seemed disinclined to grant my request until I told him it was for the purpose of getting married. I had not wanted to disclose that, in part because I knew it would lead to a swirl of rumors and gossip around Gath, but I thought this might be the only way to persuade him.

His initial reaction was one of laughter. "I … sorry … I suppose I should not be surprised, but somehow I had the impression you were not that interested in women."

"Do you mean because I don't visit the army whores?"

He leaned back, weighing his answer. "Fine. I can't refuse this request. I sometimes question your judgment, Goliath, but I cannot deny your valor. On the battlefield and in single combat, you've served us well." He then asked, "Are you going to be able to take care of everything, that is the betrothal, the wedding feast, and so forth in two weeks?"

"If you grant me three weeks, I will not refuse."

"Three weeks it is."

I did not waste this time. The first thing I did was rent a house in Gath for two months. Wherever Altara and I would finally settle, we needed to be in Gath until my situation was clarified. I then rented a mule from a merchant in the city to cut down on travel time to Ashkelon, although I did refrain from overburdening the beast by walking part of the way. I also intended to use the mule to transport Altara to Gath. In addition, I arranged for a messenger to go ahead of me to Ashkelon to let Altara know I was on the way. Finally, I arranged for supplies and went to purchase one very special item.

I went to see the goldsmith in Gath. With ample financial resources, I wanted to give Altara an exceptional wedding gift, so I had the goldsmith fashion a pair of loop earrings out of the purest gold. The earrings were fit for a queen.

When I arrived in Ashkelon, I thought about going to see Melqath first to pay my respects and stable my mule, and also perhaps to have an opportunity to wash some of the road dirt off me, but my eagerness to see Altara prevailed. Road dirt and all I needed to see her without further delay.

Fortune determined I would see her even before I reached her house. As I was turning the corner onto a street near her house, I saw two figures in the distance. Even under her modest robe, I could discern the shape of Altara's shoulders and back. Russet colored hair peeked out from under her shawl. A woman was walking next to her and I inferred this to be Munika. I picked up my pace and I yelled, "Altara!" She turned around. I was not mistaken. Impulsively, I let go of the mule's reins and ran toward her. Her eyes lit up. I'm sure mine were just as luminous. We embraced. I kissed her cheek, her forehead, her nose, her mouth. This last kiss developed into another and then another. This elicited a protest from Munika, which we ignored. Would others think our behavior improper? We didn't care. At that moment, the rest the world did not matter. We were together at last and we would be able to stay together. No more impediments.

Once we were in Altara's house, we spoke excitedly to each other about our plans. I explained I was required to return to Gath soon, so we needed to make our betrothal and marriage public within the next couple of weeks. I suggested we announce the betrothal the next day. This would serve two purposes. First, it would allow us to do at least some planning for the wedding feast. Also, I wanted to stay in Altara's house without violating our customs. She agreed. She then told me she had to show me the robe she was going to wear for our wedding feast. It was a dark red linen robe, intricately embroidered with gold thread. The pattern was of alternating fish and swans, separated by diamond shapes. It was a marvel.

"When did you … How did you …"

"I had this started as soon as you left for the campaign. Melqath asked me if I needed anything. I told him I needed this," she said as she held the robe in her hands.

"You must have been confident I'd return."

"I knew you would return. Qetesh spoke to me in a dream as clear as you're speaking to me now."

"Did Qetesh also reveal to you the gift I was going to give you?"

"No, what …"

"She must have, as it matches the thread on you robe." I then produced the gold earrings.

"Oh, gods," Altara exclaimed. "They're magnificent." She started to put them on, but I grabbed her hand. "Let me," I said. As I fastened the earrings, I nibbled and kissed at her ears, which led to more kissing, and then …

After we made love that evening, we discussed our plans for life after our wedding. I told Altara I would remain with the army as she wished. She kissed my face repeatedly upon hearing this, murmuring "my hero, my hero, my hero." I also told her I would ask the lead commander in Ashkelon if he would accept me into their company and, assuming the answer was "yes," I would then request approval from Sardon.

"You don't have to worry about that first part," Altara said.

"What do you mean?"

"I've already taken care of that," she said with a smile. "I asked Queen Tanith to speak to the king. It's all arranged."

I pushed myself up on an elbow and looked at her. "It was that easy? You didn't have to do anything but ask?"

"No. I told you you're a hero. Of course, Ashkelon wants the mightiest warrior in Palestia. The only thing the queen said was she might ask you to guard her chambers some times. That was a strange request … I mean she has nothing to fear. I suppose it's a matter of prestige for her."

"I suppose so," I said.

The announcement of our betrothal took place in Melqath's house the next day. There were but a few people in attendance, mostly Melqath's servants and some of his friends, but we didn't expect many people given the suddenness of our announcement.

The attendance at the wedding feast was more of a disappointment, at least for Altara. As the wedding feast was taking place in Ashkelon, Avram, Barekbal, and other relatives of mine could not attend nor could my comrades from Gath's barracks, but Altara was hoping the queen's attendants, with whom she worked, would be present. There were seven of them, in addition to Altara. One came. So as was the case at the announcement of the betrothal, most of the guests were acquaintances of Melqath or his servants.

Altara was pleased by a song performed by Apphia and Melqath (the younger)—performed nervously, hesitantly, with the children mumbling some of their lines, but with obvious sincerity and feeling. It was a song about two turtledoves whose love was so strong they became inseparable and any division between them "in love was slain." The children also gave me a very touching gift—a new goatskin which they said was to replace the battered, filthy, worn one that had sustained us on our journey. And the older Melqath made good on his promise of twenty mina of silver, presenting us with a papyrus certificate with his seal confirming that the metal had been deposited in Ashkelon's temple. Neither Altara nor I could read the certificate, but Melqath read it to us.

Now married to Altara, I was responsible for her safety, health, and comfort and my first test was more of a challenge than I had anticipated. We would be journeying to Gath to take up residence there at least for a while. I had the one mule, of course, and I had envisioned that Altara would ride on it. But then what of her baggage—her robes, tunics, jewelry, cosmetics, flute, mirrors, cups, and so forth? I needed to purchase another mule. Then I realized, or better said, Altara reminded me, that she was not accustomed to sleeping on the ground, not having done so since she was a child. So, I purchased a straw mattress and a tent and some cedar oil to help keep the scorpions and sand fleas away.

As we set out for Gath, I told Altara that perhaps instead of becoming a smith or remaining a soldier, I should become a merchant. I was acquiring a lot of experience in planning and making journeys.

Even with the tent and mattress, Altara was not very comfortable. She said she could not sleep because bugs kept crawling on her. She told me to get on the mattress so she could lie on top of me. "Any bugs that climb on you will tire before they reach me," she explained. Altara's draping herself over me had consequences, consequences familiar to anyone who has been young and in love. If the cedar oil did not keep the scorpions and fleas away, perhaps our noisy thrashing about did. From the weary, bedraggled look of the servant Melqath had sent along to accompany us, our nocturnal noises certainly kept him awake.

This servant, Mursilis, a freedman in Melqath's employ, was to stay with us in Gath for several days and then return to Ashkelon. It was useful having his services because the house I had rented was not really ready for habitation—another matter to which I not given sufficient thought. Among other things, we needed to purchase food supplies, fetch water, obtain straw for the stable—now that we had a mule—and so forth. I had three days left on my leave, so with Mursilis's assistance, I was able to turn the house into a home.

Avram and Uncle helped us also, with Avram bringing us bread and oil and Uncle contributing wine. These gifts were appreciated, but they also made me realize that Altara and I were lacking what many couples had, which was extensive kin connections. Altara had no one, other than Munika, who had remained behind in Ashkelon. I had Avram and Barekbal and Uncle and his family and that was about all. Uncle was focused on his work at the bloomery and Avram had her hands full with her own household in addition to taking care of her child and my mother, who had become as helpless as an infant. Oh, of course there was Lost, who I moved from his former home in the barracks, but he never had been much for helping out, outside of his narrow specialty of killing mice and bugs. I was fortunate to have the resources to hire a female servant, Arisha, the third daughter of an olive oil merchant, and, therefore, someone happy to have a paid position. Not only would Arisha undertake tasks like grinding grain, for which Altara had neither the skill nor desire, but she would provide some companionship to Altara once I had to resume my duties at the barracks.

Despite having to attend to the various tasks and chores that go with setting up a household, our first months together were a time of blissful, sensual exploration and indulgence. Uninhibited by any constraints—well, other than the occasional presence of Arisha—we kissed and touched each other at every opportunity. Our desire for each other was relentless. Anything and everything became a reason, an excuse, for lips, for hands to seek the other. Honey on Altara's fingers beckoned me, beseeched me to lick her hands. A small cut below her knee required the ministrations of my lips, as I knelt and lapped up little red drops, spreading her blood with my tongue over her thigh, and then letting my tongue glide higher. My pulling on my tunic in the morning was the occasion for her to grab the tunic's hem and, as she tugged the tunic down, to run her hands over my lower back and my rear, fondling my ass until she moved her hands around to my front to confirm the effect of her caresses. Neither of us could escape the other, nor did we want to.

One delicious pleasure was telling Altara I loved her, telling her out loud, without restraint, without embarrassment, and now without fear that this profession of love would not be returned. The words "I love you" from her lips touched me, moved me, excited me as forcefully as her kisses. These words were themselves a kiss, a kiss that could travel the distance of a room or of an eyelash with equal effect.

Being by ourselves was exhilarating, giving us a sense of complete freedom, removing any inhibitions. We wanted to know everything about each other, so we shared our bodies, and some of their functions, without shame, allowing each of us to possess the body of the other as completely as possible, while also satisfying our curiosity. Altara had me stand in the sunlight as she knelt before me and then slid under me, poking her fingers at my sack and then bouncing the sack lightly in her hand. She obliged me when I requested a similar favor, although I had to lie supine the whole time, as kneeling only brought me level with her abdomen. I asked her what she called the knob that grew harder when we made love, especially when I stimulated it with my tongue. I said no one had ever told me the name of this body part.

"That's because men don't know it exists."

"So, what's its name, I mean its proper name. Like your opening is called a vagina, or something like that, and my dick is a penis, so what's that thing?"

"I don't know. Never asked a healer priest, and they of all people probably wouldn't know either."

"Well, what do you call it?"

She laughed. "Munika and I call it 'the goddess'."

"Why 'the goddess'?"

"Because she never fails to respond if you make the proper offering," and with this she flexed her knees a bit, placed her fingers on herself, and began gently rubbing.

"I think I need to make an offering to the goddess," I said.

"Oh, really. Do you think you're worthy enough to approach the goddess?"

"I worship the goddess. I am her most devoted servant."

"Then prove you're a worthy disciple," she said, as she lowered herself, placing her lovely round rear in my hands and positioning the goddess over my mouth.

I proved I was a true believer.

In such a way we passed our days in an idyll of love—but from time-to-time two unwelcome intruders were rude enough to remind us of the demands of the outside world. First, there were my duties as a soldier, which meant being apart from Altara much of the day. Too many days, I returned from the barracks to find Altara bored and sullen. Other than Arisha and Lost—the latter never much of a talker—there was no one to spend the time with during the day. She did visit Avram a few times, but she said Avram always seemed busy, and she probably was. In addition, there was the uncertainty of when we would be returning to Ashkelon. I had made the transfer request of Sardon soon after I reported for duty after my leave, but he had put off providing me with an answer, saying he needed to give the matter careful consideration.

Finally, after being back in Gath for six weeks, I pressed Sardon for a definitive answer. He looked at me unsmiling and said, "Not sure we can do that."

"Sir, with respect, I have served my mandatory five years. My understanding of the rules when I signed up with Bellon was that I was free to leave after that. I would think I could walk out now, but I don't want to leave on bad terms."

"You're not free until I sign the release."

"Then I ask you now to sign that release."

He drummed his fingers on the table. "You'll have your answer within a few days."

Two days later before sunrise, there was loud knocking at our door. I told Altara to remain in bed. Not knowing why someone would be at the door this early, I buckled on my sword.

"Who's there?" I asked.

"Open up, Goliath, it's the king's guard."

I unbolted the door. I recognized the sub-officer as the person who was in charge of the palace's sentries.

"You are to come with us to see King Achish. Wash yourself and put on your best tunic."

15

Achish was a man in his late twenties with a neatly trimmed black beard. His black hair was styled so it fit under the fluted crown. His attire was what one would expect of a king of Gath, a purple robe with a white border embroidered with a pattern of sun and swan. Achish had a sharp, angular face, barely noticeable lips, and eyes masked by half closed lids. In combination with his dour expression, these features gave him a hard edge. His face conveyed the message: "I'm busy. Be brief and persuasive or leave." The fact that he was seated on an elevated throne did not detract from the atmosphere of condescension.

"Goliath, I understand you want to leave Gath to join Ashkelon's army. Is this correct?" Achish asked.

"Yes, Your Majesty."

"Why? Why do you want to abandon your home, the home that has nurtured you, the home to which you owe loyalty?"

"I'm recently married to a woman from Ashkelon and …"

"A woman moves where her husband tells her to move. That is the custom of our people."

"I understand, Your Majesty, but my wife, Altara, knows no one here in Gath. She has no kin here."

"How many kin does she have in Ashkelon?"

I paused. I could not say anything about Melqath or the children. "One, Your Majesty, an aunt."

"So, for the sake of your wife's one kinswoman—*one* kinswoman—you want to abandon Gath."

"Your Majesty, with respect, my understanding is that I was committed to five years of service when I joined the army. I know most men serve longer to obtain the benefits that come after twenty years of service, but I don't need those benefits. My five years have passed and I want to leave."

"Goliath, your situation is different from that of an ordinary recruit. You are the champion of Gath, which is a role you voluntarily assumed. The moment you put on the mantle of a champion, you became an essential part of our city's defenses. I have a responsibility to the whole city. I cannot permit our defenses to be weakened by allowing our champion to depart, a champion who has proven he is the most skilled warrior in all of Palestia."

"Your Majesty, even if I were in Ashkelon, would not the rulers of Ashkelon allow you to use my services?"

"Maybe, maybe not. I cannot allow the safety of my people to depend on the whims of the ruler of another city."

"Your Majesty, is there even a need for a champion anymore? The Hebrews seem more inclined to test their strength on the battlefield."

"I hope that's not the case, because it would not bode well for our people. The Hebrews are like a pestilence that will not stop spreading. I don't know if their women are having twenty children or what the explanation is, but they far outnumber us. Fortunately, they continue to have civil wars and infighting, which of course we encourage to the extent we can, but at some point they may become unified. Anyway, as part of the recent peace agreement, the Palestim and the Hebrews agreed to settle future disputes by single combat. If that agreement is honored, we may need your services very soon."

I was dispirited. I was running out of arguments. Then I thought of one. "Your Majesty, you say I'm no longer a common soldier, but the fact is I'm treated like a common soldier. My pay remains one half shekel a month and I'm expected to show up at the barracks at dawn every day except festival days."

Achish paused to consider this information. He looked to his right and signaled for one of his counselors to approach the throne. They whispered for a moment or two, and then Achish turned to face me again.

"Goliath, you will find that I am a fair, just ruler. Justice consists in giving to someone what is their due. You are correct that as you are held to a different standard than most of the soldiers, the terms of your service should also be different. Henceforth, you will be paid twenty shekels of silver a month, or four mina of silver a year. This is the pay junior commanders receive. In addition, for each single combat in which you are victorious you will receive another ten mina of silver. Five mina of silver will be paid to your widow should you lose. Finally, you need not report to the barracks except when you're explicitly ordered to report, for drills, marches, and such. This will also provide you with more time to spend with your new bride. I would think you could make her feel less lonely."

That was it. All that remained was for me to express my thanks, whether I was truly thankful or not. "Thank you, Your Majesty."

Achish stood up. The interview was over.

16

"No! No, no, no! I don't want to live in Gath. I want to live in Ashkelon." Altara was not exactly overjoyed when I told her of the king's decision.

"I understand. But we don't have a choice. The king has made it clear I must remain with Gath's army."

"It's not right," she said sobbing. "I thought we were going to live in Ashkelon. I would not have …" She stopped.

"Would not have what?" I asked.

She put her arms around me and laid her head on my chest. "I love you, but … I'm not happy here. No one to talk to."

"Well, I'm going to be here at home more often and we can ask Munika to move to Gath."

"She's taking care of the grandchildren, Apphia and Melqath."

"Something can be worked out, I'm sure."

A couple of days thereafter I went to visit Avram.

"Altara has been feeling lonely. I'm going to be spending more time with her, but I think she would also like female companionship."

Avram sighed and fixed me an exasperated look. "Goliath … Look, I'm busy. I have a young son and a husband. I need to grind grain, make bread, weave … I don't have a servant like you and Altara."

"Don't you have some female friends who might spend time with Altara?"

Avram looked away and didn't say anything for a moment. "Goliath … Altara … Some women do not want to be with her."

"What do you mean?"

Avram looked at me and then looked away quickly. "They say, they say she was a prostitute."

I drew a deep breath. "No. She was not a prostitute. She was a concubine."

Avram had a pained look in her eyes. "Goliath, why… Is that a woman you want for a wife?"

I felt the heat rising within me, but I struggled to contain it.

"I love her and that's why I want her for my wife."

"But a woman who's been with another man …"

"And what?" I said with a raised voice. "No woman refuses to marry a man who's been with another woman. If that were true, our race would disappear within a generation."

"That's different. A woman should be pure for her husband."

My voice grew louder. "So, a cunt becomes filthy when a dick is inside it, but a dick stays pure no matter how many cunts it's been in?"

"Don't talk to me like that," she yelled. Barekbal appeared in the room, having run over from his workshop. He moved his eyes back and forth between me and Avram trying to determine what was taking place. I didn't bother to explain. I left.

We were able to arrange for Munika to stay with us through the summer. She would then return to Ashkelon in the fall. Munika and Altara were happy to be reunited, although Munika being Munika, she couldn't refrain from making a complaint. "Why am I here in the summer and Ashkelon in the fall? Should be other way around. In Ashkelon, we get breeze from ocean in summer. Here nothing. Hot."

It was hot that summer. On days when I did not have to go to the barracks, Altara and I would stay in the house in the morning and early afternoon, then, after the house grew warm under the summer sun, we would go for a walk outside the city. There was a stand of fig trees on a rise above the stream that ran beside Gath. The trees were old, so they had grown large enough to provide considerable shade. We would sit or lie under the trees and talk.

"Remember when we were standing by the wall overlooking the sea, that time we went for a walk in Ashkelon?"

"Yes, of course I remember. Your hands were trembling so violently I thought they would shake the wall apart." That observation earned me a playful kick in my leg.

"Now, you, don't exaggerate. Anyway, I was just thinking about that. You said you'd like to travel on a ship. I think that would be nice too."

"It would be a different experience. I'm not sure you would like it though. Ships are pretty crowded, I've heard. Sleeping quarters especially are tight."

"You forget that when I was young I was sleeping in a room with about ten other people. I think I could manage, certainly for a trip of one or two weeks."

"Where would you like to go."

"Egypt."

"Why Egypt?"

"Well ... first of all it's about the only country I know of," she said with a laugh. "Also, well, it sounds very interesting. Ahirom's grandfather had traveled there. Apparently, they have these marvelous structures, pyramids, that are so old Egyptians themselves don't know for sure when they were built. Then there's jewels, incense, gold. Now that you're a rich man ..."

"Ha! I'm glad you think so. Egypt would be interesting. I'd also like to travel to Alashiya, if that's where our ancestors came from. I wonder what it was like. I wonder what it's like today. Ahirom and I talked about that sometimes."

A silence then hung over us for a moment, each of us thinking if the other one was thinking … Finally, I said, "Yes, it would be good to be able to talk to Ahirom. He had interesting observations about many things. Is that what you were going to say?"

Altara tilted her head away and picked at the grass. "Maybe. But you know it's not that I miss him. I mean I do, but I didn't care for him like I care for you."

"No need to explain. I'm not jealous of a dead man. I knew what your arrangement was when I met you."

"I liked Ahirom, but …" She looked at me, and put her wonderfully soft hand on my cheek. "You can't choose to be in love, I don't think. But if you're in a situation where you can't choose, like I was with Ahirom, that makes love difficult, doesn't it? No matter how kind the person may be."

I grabbed her and pulled her on top of me. "Does that mean you will still love me if I'm not kind to you?" I asked as I pinched her bottom.

She slapped my hand away. "No, that's not what I said, silly. You better be kind to me or…"

I slipped my hand under her robe. "Or what? You're going to tell Munika and have her curse me out in Thrakian?"

"No. You'll never see or speak to the goddess again."

"Oh, that would be too cruel. I better behave then."

On a couple of occasions, we brought Lost with us, placing him an improvised carrying bag and then letting him loose once we reached our stand of trees. The first time, he stayed close to us, being a bit intimidated by the unfamiliar surroundings. The next time he wandered off and then after a while brought a bird back to us, plopping it down near our heads.

"Eww," Altara said. "That poor bird. It's dead I hope."

I checked. "Yes, fortunately for the bird, Lost is still an efficient killer."

"I thought he just did mice and bugs."

"No, like other cats, he'll kill birds or anything of that size."

"Is he going to eat it?"

"Probably not. He's had enough food today I think. He just killed it because that's what cats do. They hunt."

"Well, we can't just let it stay there. We should bury it. The ants and flies are already at it."

"Fine. It fell in battle, so we'll give it a warrior's burial." I picked up some grass and dirt and threw it on the bird.

"Do you think birds have souls?" she asked. "Do they live on as shades? Are there birdsongs in the underworld?"

I looked into her eyes. "I don't know. I don't know if we live on as shades."

"Oh, I think so. I hope so, don't you?"

I shrugged. I continued picking at the grass even though the bird was now covered. "I'm not sure. If there is an underworld where we live on, the trash of all the ages will be there. All the greedy, the cruel, the liars, the hypocrites, the odious. Isn't it enough that we had to put up with them in this life?"

She looked at the horizon. "I don't know... I think there will be separate places for good and evil people." Her frown conveyed lack of conviction. "I'd like to see my mother again. Wouldn't you like to see your father again? And Dedra?"

"Mmm, yes. I suppose, but it wouldn't really be the same, would it? We could not make amends for what we failed to do in this life and yet we'd be reminded of those failures. It could be frustrating I think."

She cast me a sideways glance. "Why have I only known men who are gloomy in outlook?" Then she flashed a smile and gave me a nudge. "You know I'm teasing."

"Yeah, sure. But now that you've brought up our dead friend, Ahirom thought if our souls survive they represent the past and because they represent the past, they would be frozen in time."

Altara nestled against me. "If that's true, then make sure you hold me when I die, so I can be in your arms forever."

Thus, we passed our delicious summer of delight, exploring each other's flesh and thoughts, talking about matters profound and trivial, relentless in our desire to give and receive love.

One thing we didn't talk about in those first few months was having children. We were so much in lust for each other, we did not give much thought to the probable consequences of our lovemaking. I had no specific desire to have a child, but I knew how babies came about and I assumed eventually the seed I was placing in Altara would grow. The fact that Altara did not object to my releasing inside her indicated she had no objection to having children. Or so I thought.

⚔

17

One morning in late summer after we arose and splashed some water on our hands and faces, Altara said, "I would like to talk about something." We were in our bedroom at the time, which had only a mattress and a small table, no chairs, so I asked whether she wanted to go sit on the chairs we had on the courtyard roof. "No, Arisha and Munika might hear us, and I would not want that. We can stand while we talk."

"Fine. Tell me what you want to talk about."

"I'm pregnant."

I could feel my face erupt in a wide smile. "That's great! Are you sure?" I went to hug her. She didn't return my hug, and her arms slipped away from my hands. She moved back a bit.

"I'm sure. I have not bled in two months. I feel different. Been sick to my stomach lately and …" She seemed to be searching for the right words.

"And what?"

"I have some experience with this. I've not told you, but one time Ahirom's seed took."

"What? When?"

"About two years after I became his concubine. He didn't pull out in time."

"So … you have a child somewhere … or not?"

"No. There are ways to stop a pregnancy if you act fast enough. Munika knows of these. I had to drink this awful tasting potion. Horrible. I was sick for days but then the sprout was expelled."

"What's in that potion?"

"Don't know for sure, but it uses plants from other countries, silphium, rue, I think. Don't know if you can find them in Gath, but you can buy them in the marketplace at Ashkelon. The thing is if I'm going to take this potion, I need to do it soon, before the sprout blossoms and starts moving. Also, we

247

need to do it while Munika is still here. She knows how to make the potion; I don't. And if we need to buy the ingredients in Ashkelon, we need to send for them right away."

I was saddened and disappointed. Even though I had not thought about having a child, now I wanted one. Altara must have read my face because she said, "So … It seems you don't want me to do that. You want a child."

"I mean … I understand you didn't want one when you were not married, but now … We certainly have the means to support a child. We have the means to support many children if we wanted. But you seem reluctant …"

She bit her lip and looked down and then looked back up at me. "I'm afraid it's going to change us. These have been the happiest days of my life. I don't want them to end."

"They won't end. I'm still going to love you. I'm going to love you forever." I moved toward her and knelt. "Don't you want a child? A girl who would be as graceful and as beautiful as you? A child is a blessing that the gods do not bestow on everyone."

She looked at me. "It's painful too. That's what Munika says, and she has seen several births. She was there when I was born. She said my mother screamed."

"Yes, I know it's painful. My mother would often tell me about the agony she had to endure to bring me into the world. But she also said that after it was over she was so happy she was glowing."

I took hold of her hands and kissed them. After a moment she said, "If we can get Munika back here for the last few months, I'll carry it. I will also need a good midwife."

"I'll start making those arrangements today."

I talked to Munika about returning toward the end of winter when Altara's pregnancy would be in its last stages. She wanted to be present for the birth, so that was not an issue. I also sent a message to Melqath to make sure he had no objections.

Finding a midwife proved more difficult. I asked Avram for recommendations. She gave four names, including the woman she used. However, when I went to see them, three of them said they would be too busy in the late winter or early spring. This seemed strange. I wasn't aware of our city expecting a large number of births in the near future. I offered to pay five shekels—the standard fee was two shekels—but this failed to be persuasive.

When I reported my lack of success to Avram, she looked at me apprehensively before replying. She said, "I don't want you yelling at me."

"No, I'm not going to yell, and I'm sorry about that other day. What is it?"

"I'm telling you this not because I approve of what the midwives are doing but because you asked. You understand?"

"Yes, yes." By now, I intuited what she was going to say.

"It's because it's Altara."

I kept my promise. I didn't yell. I began cursing under my breath and then cursed out loud. "How dare these despicable bitches judge my wife. *My* wife. I who have defended the city, risked my life for the city, and now they deny services to my wife at a time of need. May Dagon and Hishara blind them and twist their hands so they become beggars."

But there was one midwife who was willing to assist—a young woman, Brisarth, who had helped with four successful births. One of the infants died after a few weeks, but that happened frequently; it didn't mean the delivery was bad. I was so grateful for her services I offered her eight shekels, even though she would have done the work for less. By the time I had reached an understanding with Brisarth, word came back from Melqath that although he needed Munika's services through much of the winter, he would allow Munika to return three weeks before the equinox, which would have her back in Gath a couple of weeks before the birth.

One final item to take care of: we did not have an effigy of Hishara, consort of Dagon and also the goddess of childbirth. I procured one from the temple that had an offering table attached. It was a fine glazed piece with deep, rich black and red designs. In addition, I purchased a jar of the best wine. Altara and I poured our first libation that very evening and we would continue this ritual throughout the pregnancy.

Summer turned into autumn and Altara's belly swelled. Her change in appearance fascinated and excited me. First thing each morning, I would insist on placing my hands and head on her belly, letting them rest there for several moments. Maybe around the fifth month I was rewarded by feeling movement.

Altara had no major difficulties during the first months of her pregnancy. The queasiness in her stomach passed. She did complain of back pains as the weight she was carrying increased and she grew tired more easily. Sometimes she would want to go to bed before the sun set. Otherwise she was healthy.

One thing that didn't change, at least not until the last couple of months of the pregnancy, was our appetite for lovemaking. If anything, my lust increased and hers did not seem to diminish. We bounced around our baby so much that we said if she was a girl, she would be a dancer, and if a boy a sailor who could navigate a ship in rough seas.

It was about the sixth month when the visitation occurred. Altara sat up on the mattress with a start and let out a yell. I awoke immediately and looked at her. She was trembling and then she turned to me weeping. "What's wrong, Altara?" I asked. "Are you hurt? Is it the baby?"

"Qetesh just appeared and spoke to me."

"Yes, yes," I said, stroking her hair. "What did Qetesh say?"

"She appeared astride two lions and then she flew up above them as the lions turned against each other and fought. She then made a prophecy. She said you would become one of the most famous warriors that ever lived. As long as the world exists, for thousands upon thousands of years, people will speak of you. People in different countries, people with many different tongues, many different colors will talk about you in awe. Your name will come to signify strength."

"Oh, alright … that doesn't sound so bad."

"No!" Altara screamed. "Then Qetesh slowly disappeared and I could only hear her voice. She said you and I would have to suffer much pain before you achieved your renown. I don't want that! I don't want to suffer!"

"There, there." I hugged her as tightly as I could. "No one wants pain, but sometimes one must endure that to achieve something great. The pain will pass." Then I put my hands around her face and looked at her. "This is actually good news. Think what this means. You and I will have a long life together. I could not become such a famous warrior unless I had your love. If I didn't have you, why would I even bother to fight?"

As the sixth month turned into the seventh and then into the eighth, Altara's belly expanded enormously. Brisarth, who was now checking with us every other day, said she had never seen such a large belly. She wondered whether our calculations might have been off, but Altara was confident about the date. Nonetheless, we made the final preparations. We purchased a birthing chair on which Altara would sit during delivery. The seat on the chair was low to the ground and the seat's back was sloped so that Altara would be squatting at an angle more than sitting. The seat was crescent-shaped, with a large open area aligning with the path of delivery. When the time arrived, Altara would be placing her feet on heated bricks, engraved with prayers to Hishara, that would elevate and warm her feet.

Into the ninth month. Munika was due to return soon, but she did not arrive. Instead, I received a message from Melqath. The message, according to the boy who delivered it, was: "Munika has taken sick, along with many others this winter. She will travel to Gath when she recovers." I told Altara, who was not present when the message was delivered, that Munika's return was delayed but she would be arriving soon. Altara was visibly distressed despite my efforts to reassure her.

I decided to ask Avram to help out. We had Brisarth, and Arisha of course, but I thought given Munika's possible absence, it would be good to have a third woman in attendance, especially one with whom Altara was comfortable. Avram agreed although she emphasized she could be there only for the delivery itself given her responsibilities to her own infant as well as my mother. I understood; I said I would send for her only after labor began.

It was before dawn one morning when Altara woke me, shaking my shoulder. "Goliath, Goliath, I think it's time. I'm having the pains and they are coming frequently. I can't sleep."

I sat up and held her hand. "Let me know when your pains come again. How are you feeling otherwise?"

"Fine. Nervous, but fine."

After some moments, Altara said she felt the pains again. They seemed close enough in time that we decided to use the time measuring device that Brisarth had given us. The midwives used a goatskin of a specific size, filled it with water, tilted it using a wooden block constructed just so, and then let the water drip into a basin. If the pains repeated before the goatskin was empty, then labor had begun. How advanced the labor was would depend on how much water was left in the goatskin. I filled the goatskin and set it on the block as we were instructed and positioned the basin. Then we waited. The pains came again before the goatskin was empty. I then went to feel the goatskin. Still maybe a quarter full.

"Yes, it has started," I said. "But we have some time. Based on what Brisarth told us it may be another half day before the baby starts out. But I will wake Arisha and then I'll go get Brisarth."

"No. Have Arisha fetch Brisarth. I want you to stay with me."

"If that's what you want."

Altara then swung her legs off the mattress and stood up.

"Where do you think you're going?" I asked.

"Not sleeping, and I don't want to sit here waiting for the next set of pains. I want to walk around. Let me get the water and bread out for breakfast."

"You're sure?"

"Yes, I'm fine. Now go wake up Arisha."

I woke Arisha who went for Brisarth. Meanwhile, Altara set out water, bread, cheese, and some dried figs on a table we had in an upstairs room. It was too cold to go outside. She didn't want to sit down, but instead walked around our upstairs rooms occasionally wincing and grabbing her back.

"Maybe you should sit."

'I'll sit and eat when the others arrive."

Arisha came back with Brisarth presently. Before we had breakfast, Brisarth wanted to do her own timing of Altara's pains, so she filled the goatskin and set it on the block. She confirmed our judgment although she said the second part of labor could begin as early as the afternoon. Then the four of us ate. Brisarth encouraged Altara to have some diluted wine to calm her nerves.

"I guess Munika is not going to be here," Altara said, with some sadness and anxiety in her voice.

"No, she will probably arrive tomorrow, having missed all the fun," I said as cheerfully as possible.

The four of us passed the time that morning telling stories, doing our best to distract Altara from her pains. Arisha sang softly at times. Altara asked me to sing.

"You sure you want that?" I asked. "The baby may think there's a monster waiting for him outside."

"Yes, I love the sound of your voice. It calms me. And what makes you think it will be a he?"

"Couldn't be happier if it's a girl."

Brisarth felt Altara's belly several times. A couple of times when she did so, she had a puzzled look on her face, so when I had a chance, I pulled her aside and asked if everything was still fine.

"Yes, the baby is very much alive. Head seems to be higher up than what I'm used to, but maybe that's because it's a large baby."

As the morning turned into afternoon, the pains came more quickly and were more intense. Altara was trying to be brave, but she did moan and scream a few times. One pain came on very sharply because she grabbed herself and yelped. She stopped walking and went to lie down. I lay next to her and put my arm around her. "This is the pain that Qetesh meant. It will be over soon, my love."

In truth, the pain went on for some time. I felt helpless. Altara was shivering and shaking. After a while, she turned her head and whispered to me, "I feel like I have to take a shit." We both laughed a little at that.

Brisarth decided it was time for Altara to sit in the birthing chair. I told Arisha to go fetch Avram, and then I warmed the bricks where Altara would place her feet. Altara said she felt better in the chair. Soon she expelled some blood and some other viscous matter.

"Do you want your husband to leave?" Brisarth asked.

"No, no," Altara said through her grunts.

Arisha returned with Avram. "How are things?" Avram asked me.

"I think good. It has been painful. For her I mean. But it's also hard for me to watch, knowing I can't do anything."

"Yes, I know how painful it can be." She went over to Altara and stroked her hair.

More fluid came out, what the women called the birth water. "It will not be long now," Brisarth said.

Altara was grunting and Brisarth was telling her to push, push the baby down. Time passed. Brisarth was positioned just below Altara. Her face grew alert as if she saw something and she extended her hand into Altara's vagina. She drew her hand back quickly. Her face exhibited worry and surprise.

"What is it?" I asked.

"It's a foot. And the cord."

I knew enough about birthing to know the baby comes out head first, or is supposed to.

"Is something wrong?" Altara asked.

"Your baby... The baby needs to shift ... or maybe we can pull it." Brisarth's voice was shakier than Altara's.

"You need to put your hands on the belly until you feel the head and then turn it," Avram offered.

"How?"

"Like this," Avram said exasperated, placing her hands on Altara.

Brisarth said, "That's not doing anything. The foot and the cord are in the same place. I need to pull the cord I think."

"No!" Avram said. "Reach in and try to turn the baby."

Brisarth stuck her hand in further and by her arm motions I could see she was trying to move the baby around in the womb, but soon she said frantically, "I can't. I can't turn it. The baby's not budging."

"Please, I don't want to lose my baby," Altara said—and this was followed by a scream of pain.

Meanwhile, Arisha had put her fists to her mouth and was moaning.

It occurred to me that childbirth was for women what battle was for men: noise, alarm, confusion, pain, screams, fluids, and blood.

The agony of this impasse continued for some time, with the baby not moving, the foot and the cord merely dangling, and Altara weeping and screaming. Finally, Brisarth decided to try to tug on the foot and the cord. "The baby's coming," she said. "I see the other foot and the legs ... No, it's stopped again." Altara moaning, "aa-aa-aa-aa."

Avram pulled me aside. "The baby is in trouble."

"I can see that," I said.

More time passed, then Brisarth yanked hard on the cord and legs. Altara screamed at the top of her lungs. Suddenly the baby emerged. A large girl. Her skull was badly compressed. Her face was blue. She was silent. She had no breath of life. Brisarth slapped her a few times, trying to force the spirit into her, but there was no point.

"My baby, my baby," Altara cried, "let me hold her." I took her out of Brisarth's hands and moved to Altara's side. Weeping, we both held our daughter. "The first-born belongs to the gods," I said. "We'll have more."

I turned and saw that a large pool of blood was forming under Altara. I looked at Brisarth. She said, "It's normal to have some bleeding after delivery. No need to get worried."

Avram looked at the bloody mass that was attached to the cord and turned to Brisarth. "It's not all there. The afterbirth still needs to come out."

"It will come out while she's bleeding."

But nothing emerged except blood. After some moments, Altara's face grew ashen. She asked to lie down. I turned to Brisarth and Avram. They nodded. Brisarth took the baby. Carefully, I lifted Altara from the chair. Blood spilled out from her, unto my arm, and then onto the floor in a harrowing dark red cascade. I carried her to the mattress and gently laid her down.

"Don't leave me," she said.

"I just want to speak with Brisarth."

"Then bring my baby back."

"Yes."

I spoke in hushed tones to Brisarth. "The bleeding. It's not stopping. It's too much. I have been on the battlefield. I know how much loss a body can have. You need to stop it."

She looked away. "I ... I don't know how.

"What do you mean you don't know how? You're a midwife."

"I've never had bleeding like this." Her eyes showed bewilderment.

I looked at Avram. Her face was a blank.

"I need to get some help then."

I took our daughter in to Altara, trying to avoid slipping on the pool of blood, and placed her in Altara's arms. Her skin felt cold, clammy.

"Lie next to me," she said in a weak voice.

"I am going to get some help. Find something, some potion perhaps to stop the bleeding."

"No, don't go. I need you here."

"My love, I'll return quickly."

"No, please don't go. I'm dying. I know it. I need you to hold me so we can be together in the underworld."

"Don't talk like that. I'll be back soon." I left to the sound of her crying.

I was in the street in a moment. It was evening. Where to now? I realized I had no plan. No point in trying those accursed midwives. Some of my comrades who treated wounds? No, they would not have any idea how to handle bleeding from a womb. The healer priests. They were my only hope.

I ran to the temple complex. A guard stopped me at the entry to the courtyard. I said, "I need help. My wife is dying," and I brushed him aside.

From having been in the complex for my interview with Phodan, I knew where the priests' residence was. I ran to the outer door of the residence and pounded on it. "Open up! I need help." I heard footsteps coming up behind me. I pounded on the door again. The door was unbolted and an acolyte opened the door. "I need to talk to one of the priests," I said. "Someone who has training as a healer. Lead me to one. Now."

The acolyte was too stunned to refuse. We went down a hallway. Voices behind me yelled, "Goliath, stop!"

The hallway led to a room with a large double door. I pushed on it. It opened. I burst into the room. Inside several priests were seated around a table eating a meal. Some dropped their meat as they looked at me, astonished.

"I need help," I said. "I need someone with medical training. My wife is bleeding to death."

One of the priests stood up. "We are eating our meal. This is a sacred rite as this meat …"

He didn't finish his sentence because I picked him up by his throat with my right hand. "I don't give a fuck for your meal. You're either going to help me or I'll smash your skull."

"Goliath!" yelled a voice from behind me. "Release the deputy high priest!"

I looked over my left shoulder to see three guards behind me, their spears pointed at me. I snatched the spear closest to me with my left hand and with the butt end I struck the guard in the face. He fell backward, sprawling onto the floor. "By the gods, I will kill you all. Makes no difference to me. Now will someone help me or not?"

After a moment, a young priest stood up. "I will help. Now please put down the deputy high priest." I did so. The priest said, "Let me go to my quarters to gather some supplies. You can tell me on the way there what the specific problem is."

We walked down some corridors, making a couple of turns. "Where is the wound?" he asked.

"She has been delivering a baby. She's bleeding from her womb."

The priest stopped short in his tracks. "I didn't realize this. I thought maybe she had cut herself or had fallen."

"Are you not going to help?"

"No, no," he replied hastily. "I will do what I can, but you must realize this is very difficult. The potion may not work and it is very difficult to apply pressure to the inside of the body, especially a womb."

We walked into his quarters. "Wait here," he said, "let me gather what I need." I looked around, not really focusing on anything, as I was in a rush to get back. I did notice the room was richly furnished, however. He emerged a moment later with a bag slung around his shoulder. "You have ample water in your house?" he asked. "And I assume you have enough kindling to start a fire quickly."

"Yes, of course. Please, let's hurry."

"Lead the way."

"May I suggest you take a donkey to ride on. I will be running back and I want you to keep up with me."

"As you wish."

He took a donkey from the temple stables, hit it with a twitch to get it going, and then I began running ahead. As I was running, I prayed. I prayed to Hishara, to Qetesh, to Dagon, to all the gods. "Please, please, let me be in time. Let Altara live."

I arrived at my house. I was upstairs in three bounds. The bedroom smelled of blood, the floor slick with it. I knelt by Altara. Her lips and nails were blue. Her eyes were vacant. Her face whiter than her whitest linen robe. "Love, love, I'm back. Stay strong my Altara." She did not respond. I noticed our daughter had slipped out of her hands. Avram and Brisarth were weeping. "Goliath, she can't hear you," Avram said. "Yes, she can!" I yelled at Avram.

The priest entered. He also knelt by Altara. He grabbed her wrist and then listened to her chest, which had begun heaving. "I will offer a prayer and make a libation. It's the best I can do. The gods will have her soon."

I lay next to Altara and brought her head next to mine. I brushed her hair and kissed her lips. I stayed there until some soldiers came to pull me away from her the next morning.

PART VI

THE FALL

1

Five years passed. Or perhaps six. It's difficult to keep track of time when one is drinking oneself into oblivion.

Not that I failed to make use of this time. I learned new skills, such as filling a wine cup to its trembling brim without spilling a drop.

And I did not lose my old skills, or at least not so much of them that it made any material difference to my fighting ability. Achish had declared me vital to the city's defenses and he took steps to ensure that my thirst for grape did not embarrass him. He had me hauled out of my house and lodged in the barracks ten days every other month, during which time I was kept under the watchful eye of Patibal and not permitted to touch any wine, except for the diluted swill served at meals. When I was at the barracks, my days were filled with endless weapon drills and runs. I did not object. The more I strained and sweated, the more I had to focus on swords and spears thrust at me, the less I was left alone with my thoughts. It was my thoughts that tormented me.

I made an effort to visit Avram and her family on some occasions when I was sober. I would say I visited with my mother, who was still living with Avram, but my mother wasn't really there. Her body was, but her soul was gone. The first time I visited Avram after Altara's death, my mother and I made a pitiful pair. My mother sat silent in a corner of the courtyard staring vacantly ahead. I sat silent on a mat by the dinner table staring vacantly ahead. The only difference between the two of us was that I managed not to soil myself.

After a couple of years, my mother's body followed her soul. She stopped eating and she refused water. Avram did not force her to drink.

More single combats came my way. I could tell for the first contest after Altara's death, there were some doubts about my reliability as I overheard discussion about Gaza's champion undertaking a journey to Gath. In the end, Achish decided to use me. Perhaps because it was a matter of honor for him. Perhaps because the stakes were relatively small—a dispute over access to a stream. Hardly something that would determine the fate of our people.

The results put any skepticism to rest. The thing is I had become indifferent to my fate, and being indifferent, I approached the combat with equanimity. No nervousness, no agitation. No concerns about what might happen. I simply let my trained body take over. My opponent, a sturdy fellow, with shoulders as broad as kraters, did not share my serenity, and this may have been his undoing. He fumbled for his shield at the start, then threw his javelin in haste, not even coming close to me. I feinted a throw of my javelin and he quickly moved up his shield to cover his head and upper body, moving it up further than he had to. I threw my javelin at his exposed knees. It doesn't take long to finish a cripple.

I had another four combats with similar results. Two combats involved mercantile disputes in Ashkelon; two combats involved disputes with the Hebrews. With respect to the combats with the Hebrews, the procedure changed in a few ways from what it had been when our peoples first instituted the practice of resolving disputes by single combat. Perhaps because of our recent sanguinary conflicts, there was even less trust between us and the Hebrews then there had been before. As a consequence, both sides marched out to the site of the encounter with considerable forces, over 300 men on our side, Gath's contingent being supplemented by soldiers from Ekron. The thinking behind this was unclear to me. There was not much opportunity for cheating in single combat, other than attacking one's opponent before the combat was supposed to start. But suspicion and mistrust have no trouble providing their own justification.

Another change was the presence of kings at the single combats. The Hebrew king surprised us by showing up for the first contest. There was much discussion about why he did so. Sardon told me there was some opposition to their king among the Hebrews—he was their first ruler to use the actual title of "king"—so perhaps he decided to be present to emphasize his position as the leader of his people. Whatever his motivation, thereafter Achish concluded he needed to be present as well. Made no difference to me other than extending our travel time to the combat site. A king's baggage train doesn't move swiftly.

Interpreters no longer accompanied the champions and their shield bearers to the field of combat. The procedure having been established, there was no need for them to be at the combat site—and they were happy to be relieved of this duty.

And I became more adept at pre-combat scowling and taunting. Had not put much effort into this before. Now in part because it made the routine of these contests more interesting, I decided to develop my skills in goading and ridicule, learning some additional words in Hebrew along the way. Did it have any effect on my opponents? No idea, really, and I really didn't care.

Another reason for indulging in this mockery: with some of the insults, such as "idiot" and "fool," I was really addressing myself. There was some comfort in this.

I was preparing for another contest not long ago—this one having to do with a Hebrew brigand who the Hebrews maintained was wrongfully accused—when I received word that my services would not be required. Surprised, I asked Sardon if I was being replaced. Had the king lost confidence in me?

"No, not as far as I know," Sardon replied. He added, with barely concealed disgust, "Achish has decided to give in to the Hebrews' demands. He's returning this brigand to them."

Stunned, I asked, "By the gods, why? If he doesn't have confidence in me, surely one of the champions from the other cities could defend our cause. Or do the Hebrews now have some frightfully formidable fighter?"

"Don't know for sure," Sardon said. "Rumor has it this brigand, David, is a friend of a member of the Hebrew king's family, which is why the Hebrews were willing to issue a challenge over him. Perhaps this is a courtesy between monarchs. I suppose you could ask Achish yourself," he added sarcastically.

That's exactly what I decided to do. Just as I had become indifferent to my fate in combat, I had little care for whatever punishment the king might impose for effrontery. I went to the palace and told the sub-officer on duty I was there to see Achish on a matter of importance. The sub-officer said he would relay the message.

"He wants to see me now," I told the sub-officer.

"I've not been notified of that. You can wait here while I transmit the message."

"I'm telling you he needs to speak with me. I'll follow you, you can announce me, and then you'll see that he wants to confer with me."

Enough doubt was introduced into the sub-officer's mind that he did not prevent me from following him. We climbed the staircase to the second level of the palace and went down a corridor. The sub-officer stopped in front of an ornate wooden door that had a copper stanchion to one side and a sentry to the other. He knocked.

"Your Majesty, my lords, Goliath is here. He says he is to confer with you on some urgent matter."

There was some inaudible discussion behind the door. I took that opportunity to correct the sub-officer. "I said 'important' not 'urgent'." I then pushed the door open before the sub-officer and sentry could react.

Achish was at the head of the table around which were seated a couple of magistrates and two other nobles. There was also a merchant. I recognized him as the trader who did the most business with the Hebrews. A scribe was seated on a mat behind Achish.

One of the magistrates said sharply, "What is the meaning of this, Goliath? You can't barge in here."

Simultaneously, the sub-officer was stammering an apology to the king. "Your Majesty, Goliath said you needed to speak with him. I didn't think he was going to …"

Achish held up his hand, signaling the sub-officer to stop speaking. Achish studied me with the caution of a cat. But I could not tell whether he considered me prey or predator. After a moment, he spoke. "Well, if I did not need to speak with Goliath before, I believe I do need to speak with him now." He gestured for the others in the room to leave. The sub-officer asked, "Your Majesty, do you want me to remain in the room, for your protection?" Achish shook his head. Looking at me directly, he said, "Goliath is a loyal servant. I have nothing to fear from him."

After the others departed, I knelt, showing the proper obeisance.

"You can stand, Goliath," Achish said. "Tell me why you need to speak with me."

I straightened up. "Your Majesty, Sardon has informed me you did not want to proceed with single combat. Instead, you are releasing the brigand. If Your Majesty has lost confidence in me then ..." Here I paused. What was I going to ask for? Had not thought about this beforehand. "Then, I respectfully suggest you find another champion."

A smile flashed across Achish's face and he said, "Goliath, if you were no longer our champion, no longer in the army, what would you do?" The question was asked in a light, cheerful tone that could not quite hide its sardonic core.

I did not have a ready answer and before I could think of one, Achish said, "Goliath, my decision to release the Hebrew brigand had nothing to do with any concern with your abilities. You are Gath's champion and will remain Gath's champion until ... until you lose. And, of course, we pray to Dagon and Bel that will never happen."

"Why then, Your Majesty, did you release him, if I may ask?"

Achish paused to gather his thoughts. Before he answered, he glanced at some papyrus scrolls on the table. He half stood, leaned over the table, and turned the scrolls over. This was an unnecessary precaution as I could not read. I did note, however, that one of the scrolls had Hebrew writing. He then turned to me and said, "My decision did have something to do with your role as champion, but not in the way you might think. How many times now have you faced a champion put forward by the Hebrews and emerged victorious? Six? Seven? Eight? We in Palestia rejoice in your success, but as you might imagine the Hebrews see things differently. Our two peoples decided to use this method of resolving disputes as an alternative to unrestrained warfare, which besides causing great misery and the death of thousands, is a very risky undertaking. For those defeated in war, the consequences can be devastating. But perhaps this risk is worth taking if the alternative is a certain loss. Do you see what I'm saying? The Hebrews think you can never be defeated, and if you can never be defeated, then why should they use the procedure of single combat to resolve disputes? We, on the other hand, like this procedure, and not simply because we have great confidence in your abilities. The fact is the Hebrews greatly outnumber us. Our army is better trained, but that advantage can take us only so far, especially now that the Hebrews are acquiring iron weapons."

I felt compelled to speak to defend the honor of the army. "Your Majesty, we can defeat the Hebrews. Let them come with their thousands and tens of thousands. Each of our soldiers is worth ten of them."

The smile remained on Achish's face, but it was now edged with impatience. "Goliath, I've great admiration for your skills as a warrior. This is the role the gods have fashioned for you and in this role you are unsurpassed. But the gods have not placed in your hands the responsibility of planning for the welfare of our people. That is my responsibility. The Hebrews have become much stronger in recent years. They showed that strength in the last war we had. Their northern and southern tribes have become united and they now have a king, their first one. It is in our interest to keep peace with the Hebrews as long as possible and to that end I want them to continue to adhere to the practice of single combat. For that to happen, I don't want them to lose that often. I don't want them to lose in a dispute that all things considered is a relatively meaningless one. Let them have this brigand, David. Who knows? Maybe this fellow will wind up causing some trouble for them."

He ended the sentence with a perplexing snigger that caused me to think he might have something specific in mind, but I could not imagine what that might be.

He was expecting some sort of reply, so I said, "Your Majesty rules by the grace of the gods. We must defer to your judgment. As for me, I will be honored to represent the people of Gath and of all of Palestia so long as the gods and Your Majesty permit me to do so."

"Excellent," Achish said as he stood up. "Exactly what I was hoping to hear. Now I think I've answered your questions, have I not?"

"Yes, Your Majesty, thank you for taking the time to meet with me."

I was backing out of the room, in accordance with protocol, when Achish asked, "Goliath, before you leave—how are things in your household? Have you found an appropriate servant, because if not, my staff can assist you, I'm sure."

I had gone through four or five different housemaids since Altara's death. They made various complaints. Some didn't like the smell of my room when I pissed myself during my binges. One woman complained that I tried to rape her. I don't recall that, which is not to say it did not happen. Besides my own messes, the last maid had complained about Lost, who was now in poor health and had difficulty walking. He used to piss and shit in a corner of the courtyard, but now with his mobility limited he tended to go in a corner of my room, unless I carried him downstairs, which I did occasionally in the predawn hours when he would not let me sleep. Don't know what the maid had to complain about. When he relieved himself in my room, Lost dependably made his deposits in a pile of dirt and ash I had in the corner. For what I was paying that maid, she should have treated his turds as silver nuggets.

Lost's lack of mobility was caused by two things, namely old age and an injury that resulted from his old age. Lost was now … what? Maybe thirteen? Anyway, with age came a decline in his speed. This lack of speed evidenced in an unpleasant encounter Lost had with a dog some months before my meeting with Achish. Lost had always managed to elude pursuing canines, keeping just one step ahead as cats are wont to do—why expend more effort than necessary?—but on this occasion the dog caught up with Lost. I awoke that night to barking, bawling, and hissing. Stumbling outside my house, I found a fast-moving swirl of dust, fur, and blood. I sent the dog on its way with a swift kick, but Lost had sustained a bad bite on one hind leg and the other leg appeared broken. It was twisted and he winced when I touched it. I considered putting an end to his suffering then and there, but he looked at me with such fierce determination that I decided to see if I could get him to mend. If the pain became too much for him, he could let me know through his yowling.

After some weeks passed, Lost was able to stand on his four legs and walk for a few moments, but his left hind leg would eventually give way and he would plop to the ground. So, he hobbled and crawled when he felt inclined to, or had a burst of energy, but for the most part he tended to limit himself to sitting in the window looking at birds that had become uncatchable. A proper companion for someone who also was captive to unrealizable desires.

But, as it turned out, at the time that Achish asked his question, I had found a new housemaid, so I thanked him for his offer, but declined his assistance. My new housemaid was a short, stocky, older woman, a widow of a villager. She had two virtues. One, coming from a farming village, she was not put off by filth or unpleasant odors. Two, she was fiercely ugly, with no neck but several chins, and years of toil had creased her face so heavily her eyes were almost hidden. No amount of drink would tempt me to force myself on her.

The evening after my meeting with Achish, I started to settle into my usual routine, which was to drink myself into numbness while carrying on one-sided conversations with Lost or the stars. After I drained my first cup, however, for some reason my soul brought forth a memory. It was of the Hebrew prisoner who had served me when I was locked up, awaiting a decision on my punishment for killing Hannipath. I recalled how he bravely ended his life rather than remain a slave. The Palestim considered the Hebrews animals, and they, assuredly, returned the compliment. Yet it was when the Hebrew slave had been reduced to the most brutal state, when it appeared all his options were foreclosed, that he had acquired a dignity. He had made a choice.

I then recalled Achish's declaration that I would remain Gath's champion until I met my death. Perversely, even though this declaration appeared to foreclose other possibilities to me, I began to wonder about other things I might have done, other paths I might have taken—or could still take? I had accumulated enough silver, even after generously sharing some of it with Avram and Barekbal, that, were it not for my obligations as a champion, I might have many options. Could I have bought a title of nobility? This had been done in Ashkelon, although to my knowledge not in Gath. But what would I do in that case other than take a prominent position in religious processions? I did not see Achish making me a magistrate or relying on me for my counsel.

There was my recurring daydream about becoming a smith. I had the means to buy out my uncle many times over if I wanted to. Would I have the patience and capacity to acquire the necessary skills, especially having been away from the bloomery for years? Would I accept the toil and sweat required to become a good, respected smith, or, knowing that I did not really have to work, would I tire of the work after its novelty had worn off?

There was actually one daydream I indulged in more frequently than the smith fantasy, and I now began to muse about this: escaping to Ashkelon and becoming a merchant or a sailor. Would the king of Ashkelon force me to return to Gath? Maybe. But perhaps not. There had to be some resentment toward Achish as a result of his forbidding me to go to Ashkelon when that city was ready to welcome me. And Queen Tanith was still on the throne, no? Perhaps she could assist me in exchange for … for whatever she wanted.

I thought about setting out on the sea, the infinite vastness of the sea, on a journey that would take years, that would take me away from the combats and conflicts and from my nightmares. When I imagined myself at sea, I could feel the undulating, entrancing movement of the waves, smell the fresh sea air, see the cloudless deep blue sky above … But so far this had remained nothing more than a fantasy, a phantom that would vanish as soon as I made any effort to reach for it. Other than on one occasion sending a message to Melqath to ask about his health and to find out if I could stay in his home were I to go to Ashkelon, I had taken no steps to make this dream a reality.

But what if I pursued this dream in earnest now? No need for my services currently; I could slip out of the city unnoticed. A thought occurred to me. Would it even be necessary to resort to secrecy? If Achish was so worried that the Hebrews would give up the practice of single combat, as they feared I could not be defeated, couldn't I use that concern to persuade him to release me from my role? I could then travel to Ashkelon without any concern and pursue my ambition to go to sea. Why hadn't I thought of this argument during my meeting with Achish? I rebuked myself silently, and resolved to raise this issue with Achish at my first opportunity.

The firmness of this resolution slowly dissipated through the second and third cups. By the fifth cup my decision to request my release was a vague recollection, indistinguishable from other, more distant memories.

So it was that I was at my home in Gath, in my cups as usual, when Patibal came to see me several weeks after my interview with the king.

⊶⊷

2

"Time to sober up," Patibal said. "A challenge has come from the Hebrews and this time Achish appears determined to accept the challenge, so get your things together to go to the barracks. The combat is in two weeks."

"What's the dispute?"

"Does it matter?"

"No, but satisfy my curiosity."

"This one seems more serious. The Hebrews claim some Palestim in a border village attacked one of their villages and took some inhabitants as prisoners."

"Did that happen?"

"Who knows? Probably. Those border villages are always getting into fights."

"If I prevail, our side keeps some Hebrews as slaves, is that it?"

"Yes, but you also prevent the Hebrews from making slaves of the Palestim villagers who supposedly carried out the attack, which is what the Hebrew king is demanding. So, either the Hebrews become the slaves of the Palestim or the other way around."

I took in a deep breath and sighed. "Fine. It won't take me long."

Once at the barracks, I went into my normal preparation routine—weapon drills, runs, no undiluted wine. However, there was one significant sharp departure from prior training routines. Unexpectedly, Achish came to the barracks one day along with the deputy high priest—the priest I had nearly throttled when Altara was dying. The king explained he wanted to observe my training. This was understandable, I suppose; perhaps he needed reassurance I could still fight. The king specifically asked to observe the exercise where I had to dodge various objects thrown my way. This was part of my training regimen that Ahirom had instituted and I still found it valuable as a way of honing my reflexes. But the priest asked me to do something entirely different, something I had never done before. He asked me to lift items of various weights, including at the end of this exercise a donkey, muzzled and with bound legs. The priest made some marks on a sheet of papyrus while he was observing me. Did they make wagers on my contests at the temple?

While lifting the donkey, my mind was visited again by the image of the Hebrew prisoner. Something moved within me, something prompting me not to yield as usual to expectations. Then Achish said, as I let the donkey slowly back down, "Magnificent, Goliath. You truly are a champion. No wonder the Hebrews fear you."

I seized the opportunity. "Your Majesty, thank you for that, for your trust in me. But your observation reminds me of our conversation not long ago when you expressed concern the Hebrews might call a halt to the practice of single champion contests because they fear they can never beat me."

Achish's eyes widened. Sardon, who was also observing the training exercises, began to yell, "Don't speak to the king unless …" Achish cut him off with a wave of the hand. "It's fine. Say what you have to say, Goliath."

"Thank you, Your Majesty. It seems to me that perhaps the best way to ensure that the Hebrews continue with the practice is to find another champion for Gath. At least this way, they would continue the practice for at least a few more occasions as they took the measure of the new champion."

Achish studied me for a moment, and then said, "You're not suggesting that we find a new champion *now* are you?"

"No, of course not, Your Majesty, but after the upcoming contest, perhaps … perhaps that would be the time to select and train someone new."

The king looked at the deputy high priest, and motioned with his head for them to withdraw a few paces to confer. Whispers, head nods. The king turned back, walked toward me. His face wore an uncanny smile. "Goliath, we could not give you an immediate release after this next combat because it's possible the Hebrews might quickly request another contest or they might even decide to attack in force out of frustration, in which case we would need your strength and skill in the field of battle. But if we can identify a new champion promptly and we have sixty days of peace in which to train him then, yes, I will grant your request to be released."

For a moment, I couldn't say anything. I suppose I had expected to be rebuffed, and the king's decision to release me after the next combat left me surprised and speechless. Words failing me, I knelt. Achish quickly said, "Oh, Goliath, please rise. No need for such a display." He then mumbled, "No need to thank me either." When I stood, he looked away from me.

Something lifted from me, some weight. A burden that I had carried for years along a rough, stony, unforgiving path had been removed. Head no longer bowed, I felt I could now stand fully erect; I could look into the distance.

Having been granted a reason to live, to prevail in the coming combat, I threw myself into training with vigor. For the first time in years, I actually felt nervous about a combat. What if I did not emerge victorious? I dismissed these thoughts as best I could, reassuring myself that I had defeated the best champions the world had thrown at me for years. Why should the next opponent be any different?

The evening before we were to set out for the valley at Elah, where the combat would take place, a boy arrived with a message from my housemaid. Apparently Lost had been upset by my departure and was yowling at night. He was also relieving himself at various locations in the house, just about everywhere other than the dirt and ash pile he was supposed to use. Not wanting to lose another housemaid, or to find a dead cat upon my return from Elah, I decided to take Lost with me.

When I stopped by the house to retrieve him, I could not find him at first. Then I saw him in a corner of an upstairs storeroom. He did not seem particularly happy to see me. In fact, when I went to pick him up, he hissed at me and bit my hand. This was highly unusual, but I attributed this to his displeasure at my leaving him alone with a new housemaid. He calmed down when I put him in the carrying bag. As my eyes adjusted to the dim light in the storeroom, I noticed that Lost had been sitting next to my effigy of Qetesh. After Altara died, I had thrown this effigy into the storeroom— why honor a deity who doesn't answer prayers? I picked it up, brushing off dust, dirt, and cobwebs, and memories of Altara started to flood my soul. Impulsively, I decided to take the effigy with me.

The journey to Elah took two nights. We arrived mid-afternoon on the third day of our travels and set up camp. As a champion, I was accustomed to having my own tent and this occasion was no different. But when the soldiers were pitching my tent, they placed it at some distance from Achish's tent, maybe fifty paces. For the two prior combats, Achish had his tent close to mine. When I asked the soldiers why this was so, I received another surprise. They said Achish wanted to ensure I had a good night's sleep as the combat would take place early in the morning. Other combats with the Hebrews had taken place at mid-day to avoid one side having any advantage from the sun. I sought out Sardon to ask about this change in procedure.

"The king thinks we should not have to worry about the Hebrews trying to gain an advantage by making you face east. The army is here to back you up in case they cheat. Plus, you can count on your shield bearer to position your shield properly."

"The fact that we have our army here at all shows that we don't think we can trust the Hebrews."

Sardon shrugged. "I suppose you can talk to Achish. I know you have no hesitation about doing that," he said with a smirk.

I walked over to the king's tent, but was stopped about ten paces away by two sentries who crossed their spears in front of me to block my path. This time there was no bluffing my way past the guards. The best I could do was to extract a commitment from one of the guards to take a message to Achish inquiring why the combat was to be held early in the morning as opposed to mid-day.

I had a couple of hours before the evening meal so I recruited some soldiers to run through some weapons exercises with me. I then strolled around our camp and then past our camp, into the valley below, stopping about twenty paces from the floor of the valley, near a grove of terebinth trees. There was a sharp contrast between the top of the hill, where we made camp, with its bleak blanket of baked dirt, pebbles, and rock, only occasionally broken up by clumps of grass, dust-stained scrubs, and a few trees, and the valley where grasses were thick and where several wildflowers were in bloom, principally the bright red of the crowfoot but also some white star flowers and chamomile daisies. I sat by the terebinth trees until the late afternoon shadows lengthened. While there I thought about my future.

The future! The last few years there had been no future. Desperately, I had filled my hours with drink and distraction so I would not have to think about the future. Now I needed a plan. I decided my first step would be to contact Melqath. It had been at least a couple of years since I last had contact with him. Didn't know whether he was still alive, but it was a reasonable place to start. Fortune seemed to be smiling on me now. Were he alive, I felt certain he would welcome me. What then? Why not ask the master merchant to train me in his trade? Still young enough to learn. I rebuked myself silently for not having pursued this possibility sooner. But now, now I would ... as soon as this combat was over. For the first time in years, I felt encouraged. With this new-found optimism, I returned to camp.

A group of soldiers was setting up tables near Achish's tent. It looked like they were preparing for a feast. This also was unexpected. I ate light before combat. The feast came later, after victory was secured. As I walked into camp, various soldiers called out to me, encouraging me or bantering with me. "Goliath," one said, "We can't wager on the outcome because we know you're going to win. So, we are trying to wager on how long the fight will last. I have you down for the time it takes to drain five goatskins, so toy with your opponent a bit will you?" I chuckled and said, "I'll see if I can get my opponent to cooperate."

Achish did send for me right before the evening meal was to commence. He was dressed informally, with a tunic and mantle instead of a robe. The deputy high priest, a couple of nobles, and Sardon were in his tent. Also in his tent was the merchant who I had seen with Achish in the palace.

"Goliath, I understand you have a question about the timing of the combat." Before I could say anything, Achish continued, "We decided to have it early in the morning so you would not be bothered by the heat of the day. That coat of mail must get awfully hot."

"Your Majesty, the heat doesn't bother me. But having the sun in my eyes might."

"There's no need to worry about that, Goliath. As you know, we are camped on the south side of the valley, the Hebrews are to the north. You're going to be walking straight into the valley from where our camp lies and your shield bearer will be placing your shield, not the Hebrews. You will not be looking into the sun."

I pursed my lips, letting my face express my concern. Achish ended the discussion by saying, "We have already made the arrangement with the Hebrews. It's too late to change it now. Even if we could, I would rather not. It would show weakness on our part."

At the dinner, a full cup of undiluted wine was placed in front of me. When I told the boy serving the wine that there was a mistake, Achish shouted down the table at me, "Drink up, Goliath. I know we have forced you to abstain these past two weeks, but I think you can relax a bit tonight." He raised his cup to me in a salute, so I had to reciprocate, but I sipped only. I was tempted to gulp it down, but renewed habits of discipline stayed my hand.

When the meal was ended, the entire company, minus some sentries, assembled. The priest then prayed to Dagon and Bel for my victory, poured libations of water and wine, and placed bread and fresh pork on the offering tables. The king then addressed us briefly, stating he had complete confidence in me. He ended with the traditional cry, "On to victory!," a cry which was echoed by our forces.

Before I retired for the evening, Achish placed his hand on my shoulder. He started to say something then caught himself. He pressed a jug of wine into my hand. "In case you need to sleep," he said. "By the way, I'm going to have sentries posted by your tent to make sure you're not disturbed." He then turned away. It might have been the glow from the flickering campfires, but his eyes seemed moist.

Once back in my tent, I did take a gulp from the jug. It was a fine wine. Another gulp. Another. Yet another. Then Lost awoke from his slumber, stumbled over to me, and looked at me reprovingly. "You're right, old friend. I should save it for after the fight." My eyes then caught the effigy of Qetesh which I placed near the head of my mattress. I had not prayed to her in years, but perhaps because of my rekindled interest in life, I used a good measure of the wine from the jug as a libation and then said, "Qetesh, you know I have not prayed to you for some time and you also know why. Forgive me. We should not question the ways of the gods. Now I beg you to show me the favor you once showed me and Altara. Let me prevail in this fight so I may go to Ashkelon." I kissed the ground in front of Qetesh and as I lifted my eyes, for an instant I imagined I saw Altara in the effigy. Without thinking, I lifted the effigy and placed a blasphemous kiss on it. The vision passed. I then amended my prayer. "If I should fall tomorrow, please let me reunite with Altara, even as a shade." I pulled a mantle over me, let Lost snuggle next to me, and fell asleep.

I awoke to Lost meowing and licking my face. I could sense it was still some time before dawn so I tried to brush him aside and go back to sleep, but he persisted. I then realized he probably wanted to relieve himself outside the tent, so I grumbled to myself, got up, picked him up, and pulled back the flap of my tent. I was expecting to have to explain to the sentries why I was up at this hour, but both were asleep. I placed Lost on the ground. "Go ahead, scoot somewhere, and do what you have to do," I said. I thought he was going to walk a few steps, sniff around, and stop. Instead he started walking and kept on walking. I followed.

The camp was dark, except for some fires around its edges, where sentries were posted. One tent, the king's tent, still had some oil lamps burning. Lost headed in that direction. "What are you doing, old man? If you're going out hunting, I'm going back to sleep," I whispered.

Lost's leg gave way and he fell to the ground. I thought he would stop then but he crawled forward a couple of paces, regained his footing, and walked some more. He stopped about fifteen paces from Achish's tent in a thicket of scrub that provided some cover. "Aha," I thought, as I squatted near him, "this must be good hunting ground." But he just rested himself as cats do, sitting on the ground with his forelegs folded under him.

As I squatted near Lost, my ears started to focus more on the murmurs I heard coming from the tent. Achish was discussing some state business with his counselors, I supposed, which for some reason could not wait until the morning. Suddenly, my ears perked up. I thought I heard my name. Then my name was clearly mentioned again. I crept forward a bit further, straining to hear. I could make out Achish's voice but not the other voices. One of the voices sounded as though the person was speaking Hebrew.

"Yes, yes, I understand your concern," Achish said. "I recognize you'll be armed only with the sling. But as we have discussed before, you need not worry. Goliath will certainly not be able to aim a javelin, and I doubt he'll have the strength …" Here Achish became inaudible.

There was mumbling from someone other than Achish. Then some long sentences in Hebrew. Additional mumbling in our own language.

"If you're as quick … won't be able to get to his shield before …"

Mumbling. Hebrew. Mumbling.

"Agreed." This was Achish again. "Now, David, how long do you think … move against Saul …"

The same pattern. Mumbling. Hebrew. Mumbling.

David. David. As I was half listening to the talking which I could not quite discern, I tried to remember where I'd heard that name before.

Then Achish was speaking again. "Yes, you have my assurance … refuge … go badly and Saul … position in our army."

Mumbling. Hebrew. Mumbling.

It occurred to me that what was happening was that someone was translating what Achish was saying to the Hebrew, the Hebrew visitor then spoke, and his words were translated for Achish.

"Glad you are confident. We need to bring peace … best way …"

Frustrated by my inability to make out more of what Achish was saying, I pushed my way through some of the scrub, holding a branch back with the left side of my face while I turned my right ear in the direction of the tent. Some bugs, probably red ants, crawled from the branch onto my nose and lips and when I brushed them away quickly I broke off the branch.

"What was that?" I heard a guard outside Achish's tent say. He looked at the other guard and then drew his sword and started walking toward the thicket.

At that moment, the pungent smell of fresh cat feces assailed my nostrils. Lost had finally—and timely—moved his bowels. I crawled back several paces, trying to get as far away from Achish's tent as I could and I then stood up. I startled the guard who was then only a few paces away.

"Goliath!"

"Shh!" I said, putting my finger to my lips. "No need to disturb anyone."

"What are you doing out here."

I forced a half-smile and a quiet laugh. "My cat had to take a shit. He can't really walk too well, so I carried him outside and then he made his way to this thicket."

The guard moved closer to me, looked around on the ground, saw Lost, smelled his shit, scrunched up his nose and said, "Fine. Just get back to your tent. Get some rest. We're counting on you, you know."

I did return to my tent, past my still dozing sentries, but the return to my tent provided no rest either for my mind or my body. I lay down on my mattress to no avail. Thoughts kept flowing and although I tried to dam them up—What had I really overheard? And what was the point of fretting about Achish's ambiguous remarks, as I had no alternative but to stay put?—rivulets of worry and wild imaginings would break loose, run together, and form a new torrent of anxiety. "Don't worry, Goliath will not be able to aim a javelin, and he won't have the strength." What could this mean? Why would Achish reassure the Hebrews about my lack of strength? And why would I lack strength? Achish also made a reference to achieving peace. Was he going to bind me in chains and give me over to the Hebrews in exchange for peace? The Hebrews undoubtedly would relish having me as a captive—a prize plaything they could parade about and then torture and kill. Or worse, perhaps I would be blinded and mutilated and forced to work as a slave.

Vainly, comforting thoughts also occurred to me. Why assume that this meeting and Achish's remarks signified some evil plan? I heard but snippets of a larger conversation. In context, the words might have a benign meaning. Achish could be clarifying the rules of the champions' combat or trying to persuade the Hebrews that it would be a fair fight.

But then why keep this meeting hidden from me?

So it went. My thoughts warred with each other for the next couple of hours until dawn approached and the camp began to stir in the half-light of daybreak. I heard shouting outside my tent. Sardon was yelling at the sentries. "You idiots, you fell asleep. I'll have you both whipped."

"Sir, we just dozed off a few moments ago. No one came in or out of Goliath's tent all night, we swear."

Sardon and another soldier then walked abruptly into my tent. The other soldier had a basin, a jug of water, and some bread and pork scraps from last night's dinner. "Goliath, get up. We have brought you your breakfast.

Eat quickly and prepare yourself for combat. When you're ready, we will report to Achish's tent."

I nodded. "Fine." Sardon did not move. "Anything else?" I asked. "You're still here."

"I'm going to stay here until you're ready," he said. I got up from my mattress, getting into a crouch and leaning forward so my head would not push against the tent. "I think you can rely on me to prepare myself with appropriate speed. I have done this before." I fixed him a hard look. After a moment he said, "We will be outside."

I splashed my face, washed off my hands in the basin, and sat down to breakfast, still trying to sort out in my mind the meaning of what I had overheard a few hours before. I munched on the bread and meat, tearing off some pieces of both for Lost. My thinking did not produce any conclusion, and as no alternative course of action presented itself to me, I made ready for combat and went to Achish's tent along with Sardon.

We entered his tent after we were announced. In a semi-circle around Achish stood two nobles, the deputy high priest, the junior commander, Hanun, and a young boy, perhaps in his early teens. The priest was holding a cup in his hands. Except for the priest and the boy, they were all bleary-eyed.

"I trust you slept well last night, Goliath."

"Reasonably well, Your Majesty."

"Good. Well, I called you in here before we assemble our forces for a couple of reasons. One, you have a new shield bearer, Ephat." He gestured in the direction of the boy. The boy and I exchanged glances and nods. "Second, our priest has prepared a drink for you which you should take now."

"Why is that, Your Majesty?"

"This drink will strengthen your muscles and provide you with additional endurance," the priest said. "It's based on a recipe that the Egyptians use."

"I've never had to drink a potion before. Don't see why I need to take one now."

"Goliath," Achish said, "of course we all recognize you are a proven champion, but along with all of us, you are aging. This potion will eliminate some of the effects of aging, bringing out your natural vigor."

I was beginning to realize what was happening. This drink would not give me strength, but rob me of my strength. This is what Achish was alluding to in his meeting a few hours before. What to do? I needed time to think.

"Your Majesty, I need to think of my honor. This is to be a contest of champions not of potions."

"Goliath, I can assure you that the Hebrew champions have always done whatever they could to gain an advantage against you. There's no doubt they drank potions, cast spells, invoked spirits, and did whatever else they could."

"But it's a point of pride for me."

With a note of exasperation in his voice, Achish said, "May I remind you that this contest is not about your pride. If you lose, a number of our people will become slaves of the Hebrews. You're not fighting for yourself but for your countrymen. Drink the potion." The priest held out the cup to me. All eyes were on me. It was while they were looking at me that suddenly a memory came to me. David. David was the name of the brigand who had been released by Achish. Was this the person Achish was talking to in the tent? I felt my stomach drop. A dry despair began creeping into my soul.

"Your Majesty, Your Majesty," I stammered. "In my rush to get here, I neglected to take care of some obligations. I have a prayer ritual that I follow. It's very important to me. I need to return to my tent."

"But the potion ..." the priest started to say.

"I will drink your damn potion when I've said my prayers," I bellowed. Sardon drew his sword. Achish exchanged anxious looks with the others. I'm sure it did not escape their attention that I was fully armed.

"Very well, Goliath," Achish replied in a subdued tone. "You may return to your tent for your prayers if you pledge to drink the potion when you come back."

I nodded.

"Fine, then. Sardon will accompany you ..."

"I need to be alone with my prayers, Your Majesty. I believe I've earned that right."

Achish put his hand to his mouth, rubbed his beard, took a deep breath, and exhaled slowly. After a long moment, he said, "Very well. But you are aware we should not be late for the single combat. The Hebrews ..."

"I will present myself on the field in a timely manner," and with that I turned and left.

A thousand confused thoughts went through my head as I walked back to my tent. What was going on? What was I to do? It was clear that Achish wanted me to lose, but why?

I walked into my tent and my few scattered possessions took on the appearance of grave goods. Amidst all my questions, there was one nearly absolute certainty: I would be dead soon. The only thing unsettled was how I would die.

I could kill Achish, but what would that accomplish? I would be killed also or, worse, I would be wounded and captured and then compelled to undergo days of torture before a slow, agonizing death. Not only that, but all my relatives would be killed. Through Avram and Barekbal I now had two nephews and a niece. They did not deserve to die.

I could refuse the potion, but then what? Given his arrangement with this fellow David, the apparent Hebrew champion, Achish would probably not let the contest go forward. He would then have me executed for treason—but not before denouncing me as a coward before my comrades. I'm sure in his telling, I would have simply refused to fight, not refused his potion.

What was going on? Now that I realized I was doomed, I wanted to know why. How could I solve this puzzle? I grabbed the effigy of Qetesh, closed my eyes, and kissed it. "Qetesh, hear my plea. Do not let me go to my death without understanding the reason." I tried to clear my mind and concentrate on recalling Achish's words from his meeting with the Hebrew, David. My death was supposed to bring peace. But how? Because the Hebrews would finally have won a contest? That might just embolden their king, this Saul. But what was it that Achish had said about Saul?

Then Qetesh revealed all to me. Suddenly, I understood everything.

David, whom Achish had freed, was acting as Achish's agent. He was to use his triumph over me to become a hero, to gain popularity among the Hebrews and then move against Saul, making himself king. With a friendly king on the Hebrew throne, Achish hoped to gain a lasting peace.

This revelation provided me with some measure of tranquility. At least my death might serve some worthwhile purpose. Peace. Peace instead of the continual conflict with the Hebrews. How many Hebrews had we killed— how many had I killed personally? And in turn how many of my people had been killed by the Hebrews? To what end? The boundaries moved a day's march here or there in exchange for thousands of lives cut short and the shedding of countless tears. The peaceful exchange of each people's goods could bring more prosperity, and much less anguish, than bitter fighting over scraps of territory.

A memory came to me of that time the Hebrew merchants first visited my father's and uncle's bloomery. Some bickering, some cursing from my uncle, and some hard trading, but no sword to the throat, no spears tearing the life out of someone. An exchange that benefited everyone. Why couldn't the Hebrews and the Palestim share the land? Was this an impossibility?

I decided. If I could be an instrument of peace, then let it be so. Perhaps my death could achieve what my triumphs in battle had not.

Achish's plan did depend a lot on this Hebrew, David. Could Achish trust this brigand? I had no way of knowing. I could only hope the gods had given Achish sound guidance.

Although I was now becoming more accepting of my impending death, there was one aspect of my fate to which I could not be reconciled, namely my death in single combat. Why should I have to fall through an ignominious defeat at the hands of this brigand? And from what Achish said, David was going to use a sling. Defeated by a lowly slinger? That potion must blind me. How else could I fail to block any rocks thrown my way with my shield? Of course—there was that new shield bearer.

I kissed the effigy of Qetesh again, and as I did so, Qetesh appeared to me in a vision and spoke. She said, "Goliath, your immortal fame depends on your death in this combat. But if you listen to me, those who come after you until the end of time will know that the Hebrew did not kill you. Fall forward before he slings his rocks. Then all who read the chronicles of your combat will know that his rocks could not have touched you." I was overwhelmed with emotion. I began to cry. I bent forward to the ground to kiss the feet of Qetesh and my lips found flesh. Familiar flesh. A scent of myrrh and sweet cane filled the air. I looked up from the feet—and saw Altara. I embraced her, kissing her madly, kissing her lips, her green eyes, her neck, and then her dewy blossom, the goddess of the goddess. But within a moment, I heard her whisper, "I go because I am but a shade." She faded away as my hands vainly grasped at the air.

Then the lions of Qetesh appeared. They leapt toward me, teeth bared, claws extended, and I fell back with a yell. They vanished. But they did remind me of one grim duty I had to perform for my lion.

I looked at Lost, who looked back at me with sad, puzzled eyes. "Come here, old friend," I said. Limping badly, he climbed onto my lap as I took out my dagger. "Old soldier, our time has come. Perhaps I'll see you on the other side." With my free hand, I stroked him, so he lay out, extending his body. He was calm, purring. My dagger hand was shaking. "Dagon, Bel, I beseech thee. Please make this the swiftest, surest cut I have ever made and turn my friend's eyes away so that he will not see the blade." Lost looked down. The blade went across his throat.

I wrapped Lost in a mantle and quickly started digging a shallow warrior's grave, using my helmet and dagger. I heard someone approach my tent. Sardon yelled, "Goliath, what's taking you so long? You've had time to pray to all our gods and the Egyptian gods besides."

"I'll be out in a moment. My cat has died. I'm burying him."

Silence. Then, "Fine, but be quick about it."

As I emerged from the tent, I shook out the dirt from my helmet near Sardon's sandals. He stepped back, anger in his eyes, but the only thing he said was, "There's blood all over your mail."

I looked down. "So there is. Better to intimidate the Hebrew."

We made our way to Achish's tent. Achish and the others were waiting. The priest held the cup out to me, but then pulled it back exclaiming, "You have blood on your hands." I grabbed the cup from him and drained it, then hurled the cup at the ground in front of him. While he was looking down, I stepped forward, grabbed his immaculate tunic, and wiped my hands on it. "You're right, my hands are bloody," I said.

"Your Majesty…" the priest said, looking to Achish for some sort of intervention. Achish merely raised his eyebrows and gave a half-shrug. What could he do?

Sardon said, "It's time."

PART VII
THE LOST SONG OF GOLIATH

I pulled my foot out of the cluster of star flowers and stood still for a moment, trying to steady myself. I looked at the other flowers on the hill. Like these flowers, we have our season in the sun and then we are gone.

What is it that could survive our deaths? As Ahirom observed, we are always changing: the baby is different from the child; the child from the young adult; the young adult from the mature adult; and the mature adult from the old man or woman. Which of these is our essence? There is no essence. We are but a stream of thoughts, feelings, and memories.

I was to fall soon, but we all fall. We begin falling from the moment we are thrown into this world.

We cannot prevent the fall, but perhaps we can influence how we fall. How we spend the short time we have. Love, like the blossom on the flower, may not last forever, but it is infinitely precious nonetheless. Perhaps more precious because its time is limited. And though we all fall, we can take responsibility for how we make use of that limited time.

Such thoughts continued to occupy me as we made our way down the slope. When we were not far from the valley floor, Ephat, who had been on my right, crossed in front of me, heading west. He continued walking at a slant once we were in the valley. Yes, I would wind up facing east. Not due east, but at enough of an angle that the sun could affect my vision. Achish wanted to leave as little as possible to chance.

The valley floor at Elah is wide, so we had some distance to cover before we reached the half-way point. We kept walking, my legs becoming progressively less steady. My arms were trembling. An ache began to take hold of my body. Before we reached the half-way point, I saw an outcropping of stones of good size. One especially stood out. It had a sharp edge pointed upwards, at just the right angle to crack open the skull of someone falling on it.

"We're stopping here," I said to Ephat, as I positioned myself on a small rise above the outcropping.

He looked at me puzzled. 'Sir, we are not at the half-way point."

"I know, but we're stopping here. Go on ahead, gesture to the Hebrew and his shield bearer, and they will come forward I'm sure."

Ephat did as I instructed. The Hebrew and his assistant stopped at first, standing in place for a few moments, but then they came forward, until we were about twenty paces apart, the prescribed distance. I noticed his shield bearer was without a shield. A nice touch. A way to embellish his legend. "David, our great champion, was so confident that he disdained any protection as he faced Goliath." It then occurred to me I should discard my helmet. Didn't need it. In fact, it could keep me alive when I fell forward and that's exactly what I did not want. I removed it with a flourish, waving it over my head and threw it at David's feet, or better said, tried to throw it. I had little strength in my arm. The helmet bounced ahead maybe four or five paces. I looked at David. He had a smirk on his face.

This was my first chance to get a close look at my opponent, this ambitious brigand. He was a young man, maybe about eighteen or nineteen, ruddy complexioned with long hair. He had a confident, arrogant air. Why shouldn't he? He knew he had nothing to fear.

"Dog," I yelled, "I know what's happening. You know and I know you don't even need your damn rocks today. You could come at me with a stick and still win." His smirk began to fade. "You win today, but by the gods if you don't keep your bargain with Achish, if you don't keep the peace, may you be accursed. May you kill your own sons and feast on their blood."

David appeared shaken. He was silent for a long moment, but then he gave his speech. A long one. I knew enough Hebrew to understand there was a reference to his gods, and how they would ensure victory over us, and so forth. Something he had memorized, clearly.

While David and I were exchanging insults, Ephat began moving away from me, with my shield. Obviously, Achish had instructed him to put it out of my reach.

"Boy," I yelled, "Take it fifteen, no, twenty paces away." Ephat looked at me unsure, confused. "This is my decision, not Achish's. Tell the people that Goliath is the one who decided to lay down his shield. If the Palestim sing of me, let them sing of me as the man who had his shield placed on the ground for peace." Hesitantly, Ephat carried the shield further away, looking at me over his shoulder while doing so. He dropped it on the ground like a thing bewitched and hurried back toward me, face down and turned away from me. Pursuant to procedure, he would leave from my side when heading out to grip the arm of David's shield-less bearer. The contest would start when they broke their grip.

I could sense Ephat's unease. "Don't feel bad," I said, "I know you're following orders." He looked up at me, frightened and puzzled. "Just tell our people what happened here today. Tell them David's rocks never touched me."

Ephat's attention was then drawn by some bird calls. He looked up in the sky. "There are many hawks circling just above us, sir."

"That's to be expected. The vultures can anticipate a feast."

"These don't look like vultures, sir. They're smaller."

I looked skyward myself. A flock of several sparrowhawks was circling very near us, no more than ten paces above our heads. I recognized the unmistakable *kee-wick* of their calls. There were several males, with their wondrous blue-gray upper body plumage, and several larger females, with dark brown upper bodies and brown-barred bellies. I stared at them for some moments and then … and then, I began to hallucinate. An effect of the potion? I imagined I saw my father's face in one of the males. Then my mother's face in one of the females. There was Ahirom. And Elissa. Antenon. A small female with Dedra's face. Then joining the flock was a sleek, beautiful female, with a melodious cry. Unlike the other females, with their yellow irises, this one had green eyes. Altara.

I brought my head down. I knew this couldn't be happening. Must be the potion. But it seemed so real. I looked up again just in time to see a fledgling join the flock. By the gods, it had cat whiskers. Lost.

I brought my head down again. Yes, this was nothing but an illusion, but the gods had granted me an epiphany. We may not have souls. We may just be a stream of memories, feelings, and thoughts connected by intentions and desires, but the stream is alive, and it can join other streams and other streams to form a river of life. In one form or another, life goes on.

It was time. I gestured to Ephat, indicating he should go forward to grip his counterpart's arm. I saw David pull a rock out of his bag and place it in the sling. The grip was broken. The contest was on.

I needed to fall. I needed to fall now. I hesitated for an instant, but then I saw David draw his sling back. I went forward, striking my head on the sharp, hard outcropping, cracking my skull. The darkness began to swirl around me.

But before the darkness overtook me completely, I heard two sounds.

One sound I heard was the hurried whisper of a rock flying well above me, landing with a loud, empty thud some twenty paces behind me. Ha!

The last sound I heard was the cry of a very large sparrowhawk, a gigantic sparrowhawk with a most unmusical cry, joining the flock above.

ACKNOWLEDGMENTS

Debra Robinson Lindsay, Karla Grossenbacher, Diane Devendorf, and Anne Lindsay read the draft manuscript for this novel and provided many helpful comments. I am indebted to them.

I have attempted in this book to provide an historically authentic account of living conditions for the Philistines in the time period of the Late Iron Age (roughly 1100-1000 BCE). In my research, I relied principally on the following books: *People of the Sea: The Search for the Philistines* by Trude Dothan and Moshe Dothan; *Life in Biblical Israel* by Philip J. King and Lawrence E. Stager; *Ancient Canaan and Israel* by Jonathan M. Golden; and *The Lives of Ordinary People in Ancient Israel* by William G. Dever. I bear sole responsibility, of course, for any inaccuracies.

AFTERWORD: A NOTE ON HISTORY AND MEANS OF EXCHANGE

Many people believe the Bible provides us with accurate accounts of events in the ancient Middle East. Most archeologists and historians disagree. This is not to say there is no kernel of truth behind some of the biblical tales, but the stories are principally reflections of the religious faith of the ancient Hebrews. Events are described in a way calculated to foster that faith. Furthermore, given that the stories relating to the Philistines, David, and Goliath were written centuries after the events, it is unreasonable to assume they are infallible accounts in every detail. Imagine trying to write in 2019 a history of Elizabeth I using only centuries-old oral traditions of the Church of England. That said, this is a novel, not a theology book, and nothing set forth herein is designed either to confirm or cast doubt on anyone's religious beliefs.

Those familiar with the biblical stories will recognize how I have incorporated elements of those accounts in my novel. In particular, aspects of the biblical account of the encounter between David and Goliath and of David's relationship to the Philistine king Achish are central to my retelling. Of course, I have given them a different interpretation, consistent with the Philistine perspective of the novel. One virtue of my retelling is that it addresses some puzzles in the biblical account: why didn't Goliath—an experienced warrior—use his shield and why did he fall forward?

Throughout the novel, I reference shekels and mina of silver, as well as pieces of copper, but I don't mention any coins. That's for a good reason. Coinage did not come into use until about 650 BCE. Precious metals based on standardized weights were used as means of exchange in the Iron Age. A shekel was about eleven grams of silver. A mina was equivalent to fifty to sixty shekels. A talent was equivalent to sixty mina. It's difficult to estimate the buying power of this metal given the vast cultural differences between the Iron Age and our contemporary world. However, ancient Mesopotamian texts indicate a common laborer earned a shekel a month; the book of Samuel states that the Philistines sold the Israelites iron plowshares for a pim, or two-thirds of a shekel (1 Sam. 13:21); and the book of Jeremiah states that one could buy a field for seventeen shekels (Jer. 32:9).

ABOUT THE AUTHOR

Ronald A. Lindsay is a philosopher (PhD, Georgetown University) and lawyer (JD, University of Virginia). Among other works, he is the author of *Future Bioethics: Overcoming Taboos, Myths, and Dogmas* (Prometheus 2008), the entry on "Euthanasia" for the *International Encyclopedia of Ethics* (Wiley Blackwell 2013), and *The Necessity of Secularism* (Pitchstone Publishing 2014). *The Lost Song of Goliath* is his first novel.

When not writing, Ron enjoys playing baseball, traveling with his wife, studying physics, and catering to his cat's whims.

www.ingramcontent.com/pod-product-compliance
Lightning Source LLC
Chambersburg PA
CBHW081206170626

46811CB00011B/3324